CU00486166

BLACKOUT

A John Milton Novel

Mark Dawson

AN UNPUTDOWNABLE book.

First published in Great Britain in 2017 by
UNPUTDOWNABLE LIMITED

Copyright © UNPUTDOWNABLE LIMITED 2017

Formatting by Polgarus Studio

The moral right of Mark Dawson to be identified as the author
of this work has been asserted by him in accordance with the
Copyright, Designs and Patents Act 1988.

All the characters in this book are fictitious, and any
resemblance to actual persons living or dead is purely
coincidental.

All rights reserved. No part of this publication may be
reproduced, stored in a retrieval system or transmitted in any
form or by any means, without the prior permission in writing
of the publisher, nor to be otherwise circulated in any form of
binding or cover other than that in which it is published without
a similar condition, including this condition, being imposed on
the subsequent purchaser.

To Mrs D, FD and SD.

PROLOGUE

JOHN MILTON tried to figure out what had woken him up.

He couldn't.

He opened his eyes and immediately wished that he hadn't. Bright light flooded in, exploding little detonations of pain in the front of his head. He squeezed his eyes shut again. The pain remained, reduced to a dull throb that pulsed behind his eyes. He felt awful. His skin was clammy. He felt sick.

Milton tried to remember.

What was it?

What had woken him?

A raised voice.

Yes, that was it. He was sure. Someone had screamed.

He opened his eyes again. He was flat on his back, lying on a bed. His head was turned to the side, and he could see the bedside table a few inches away. Beyond that was a bureau upon which was positioned an old-fashioned television. He tried to push himself upright. The pain flared and he felt an almost overwhelming urge to be sick. He fought it back, propped himself up on his elbows, and raised himself enough that he could look around the room.

It was a plain space, on the small side, and decorated in neutral colours. There were two single beds with a bedside table between them. Milton's bed was a mess: the sheets were sodden and bunched around his legs, and the pillow was on the floor. The other bed was untouched, save a scattering of banknotes that had been cast across it. Milton saw a bottle on the bedside table. The label said Grasovka Bison Grass vodka. The bottle was almost empty and lying on its side. The neck was over the edge of the table and, as Milton looked down, he saw a puddle on the tiled floor.

He started to feel uneasy.

What had happened here? He couldn't remember. He tried to recall what he had been doing the previous night, but he couldn't. It was as if his memories were obscured by a thick shroud and, despite his best efforts, he could not move it aside. He closed his eyes again and furrowed his brow, trying to remember where he was and how he had gotten here. It was hopeless.

He reached further back. He remembered arriving in Manila, checking into a hotel—this one, yes? Yes, he thought it was—and then walking to a bar. He remembered Jessica. She had been there, just as she had promised she would be. He remembered how beautiful she was and how little she had changed in the years since he had last seen her. He remembered that they had talked, but not what about.

And, after that… nothing.

Everything else was hidden behind the shroud.

His heart sank. He knew what must have happened. There was only one explanation, but the thought of it made him sick to the pit of his stomach. He had been drinking. Must have been. After days and then months and then years of sobriety, he'd thrown it all away and gone back to the bottle. He thought of the men and women that he had met in the program, the rooms around the world in which he had listened to their stories and shared some of his, and he felt ashamed.

He had let them down.

He had let himself down.

He needed to find a meeting.

He carefully swung his legs around and over the edge of the bed so that he could put them down and, careful not to step in the vodka, he gingerly pushed himself up to a sitting position. His whole body ached and he thought, again, that he was going to vomit. He steadied himself and, easing himself to a standing position, looked around the room once more. He saw another vodka bottle on the floor in the corner of the room. This one had been broken, the heavier base standing upright while the neck lay horizontally across the tile. There were two glasses near it, both shattered, tiny fragments catching the light that slanted in through a gap in the curtains.

Milton saw that the door had not been closed properly. It was on an automatic mechanism, but it needed to be pulled in order for it to close all the way. He crossed the room and opened the door fully. Heat washed into the room. It was bright and stifling outside. He peered up into the sky; the sun's position said that dawn had been three or four hours ago. There was an empty parking lot, with weeds forcing their way up between cracks in the asphalt, and beyond a row of parched palm trees loomed the swoop of an overpass. The traffic was loud, and fumes hung over the road in a vapour that Milton could taste against the back of his throat.

He closed the door and turned back into the room again.

Where was he?

How did he get here?

There was one other open door that led into the bathroom. He crossed the room and went inside.

The room was small. There was a toilet and a basin with a small cupboard beneath it.

He froze.

There was a body on the floor.

It was a woman. She was lying on her side with her torso between the cupboard and the toilet and her legs bent with her knees to her chest. Her dark hair was fanned out across the white tile. Her skin was pale, almost white, and it highlighted the obscene bruising around her exposed throat.

Her head was angled toward him and he could see half of her face.

It was Jessica.

His stomach turned and the sick churned up from his gullet in a hot, acrid rush. Milton couldn't hold it down. He stepped over the girl's body and vomited into the sink, gout after gout of it until the sink was splattered and he was left feeling hollowed out and dizzy.

"Hands up!"

Milton turned around.

The door to the bedroom was open and a woman was standing in the doorway. She was wearing a light blue shirt, a navy-blue skirt, and a navy-blue cap with a crest in the centre. Milton recognised it: Philippines National Police. The holster on her belt was empty. She had taken out a Glock 17 9mm pistol and was aiming it straight at him.

"Hands!"

Milton did as he was told.

"You speak English?"

"Yes," he said.

"Come out."

He looked at Jessica's body again and then back at the officer.

Am I responsible?

"Step into the room."

Did I do that?

Milton wanted to tell her that it wasn't what it looked like, but the words caught in his throat. He knew why: he couldn't be sure. Maybe it was *exactly* what it looked like. He couldn't remember what had happened. Was it possible? He'd killed before, dozens of times, more than a hundred and fifty ghosts who had eventually ushered him along the road to sobriety. There had been another time, years earlier, when he had woken up with blood soaking his shirt, no memory of how it had got there, and then came a communiqué from Control congratulating him on a job well done.

Is this the same?

Did I kill her while I was drunk?

He couldn't say.

He stepped out of the bathroom.

"Knees. Now!"

The police officer was young. She was holding her

weapon a little too tightly, the butt clutched deep in her palm and her index finger too rigid around the trigger. Her hand shook, making the muzzle quiver, and Milton knew that disarming her would have been a simple thing.

But he didn't want to disarm her.

He turned around, sank to his knees, and put his hands out behind his back so that the officer could cuff him.

Part One

Four Days Earlier

Chapter One

WILLIAM LOGAN stared out of the windshield, munching sunflower seeds and watching the rain streak down the glass. Russell Square might have been a desirable address once, but that time had long since passed. The grand terraces that hemmed in the square had been turned over to businesses, the houses carved up into offices. The local authority made only a passing attempt to keep the park tidy, and the benches arranged around it were as likely to be occupied by homeless drunks as by the night-shift workers who braved the rain for a cigarette beneath the shelter of the overhanging branches.

It was coming up to ten at night. A thick bank of cloud had rolled over the capital, and the stars were hidden behind it.

Logan had only just returned from Manila. His skin, usually so pale, was tanned and, if he closed his eyes, he could almost remember the warmth of the sun on his face. He had been there for two weeks, making preparations. The task he had been given was complicated and his target had a reputation that would have put doubt into the most confident operator. Logan had been responsible for similar assignments in the past, but this one was different.

This was the first that had robbed him of sleep.

He was reaching for the pack of sunflower seeds when he saw him. He was on foot, walking from the direction of the nearby tube station. There was nothing particularly impressive about him. He was a little over average height, around six feet tall. He had an athletic build, perhaps two hundred pounds. He was wearing a pair of jeans and a leather jacket. He had no umbrella, and the rain had plastered his dark hair to his scalp.

Logan watched as the man paused at the corner of the

square, waited for a taxi to roll through the puddles, and then crossed over to the single-storey structure that was set in the road next to the railings that encircled the small park. There were a handful of similar buildings all around London. Logan had seen them before and had been curious enough to investigate them online. They were shelters for taxi drivers, places where they could park their cabs and go for a cup of tea and something to eat. They had been around for years and much more numerous before competition made them less and less economic until—mostly—they were unsustainable.

The man paused at the door, ran his hand through his wet hair to sweep it out of his face, and went inside.

Logan leaned back in the seat and exhaled.

Just watching John Milton made him nervous.

Chapter Two

"I'LL BE OFF, THEN, LOVE."

The owner of the business was a bottle-blonde East Ender called Cathy. Milton took her coat from its hook and held it open so that she could put it on. It was a plastic raincoat with a leopard-skin print, the kind of gaudy style that summed her up. Milton had come to find it charming.

Milton had been back in his job for a few weeks now. Cathy had taken him back on since her son, Carl, had decided that he didn't want to follow in her footsteps and serve tea and baked beans on toast to the capital's cabbies after all.

"It'll be quiet tonight," she said.

Milton nodded his agreement. He had been working at the shelter long enough to know that she was right. The rain would empty the streets, the cabbies would have less business, and many of them would call it a night and go home. The shelter would stay open, though. It was one of the things of which Cathy was most proud: the shelter had been open three hundred and sixty-five days a year for the last sixty years. She joked that not even Hitler had been able to make them shut. When Milton had pointed out that she had previously explained that her grandfather had only opened the shelter after the war, she had laughed and told him that she never let the facts stand in the way of a good story.

There was only one driver in the shelter tonight. He finished his can of Rio and handed it to Milton.

"You still in Theydon Bois, darling?" he asked her.

She raised a hand. "You don't have to drive me, Cliff."

"Not a problem. I'm knocking it on the head. Nothing happening tonight. And I live out that way. No bother at all."

"Thank you," she said. "Save me walking to the tube in this filth."

Milton went over to clean the table. Cliff said goodbye and opened the door. Cathy told Milton that she would see him tomorrow, stepped over the threshold and followed Cliff to his cab. Milton took the dirty plate and mug to the sink and filled the basin with warm water. He watched through the small window as the lights of the cab flicked on. It set off around the square.

He washed and dried the crockery, wiped his hands on the tea towel, and then went over to switch on the digital radio. He selected the pre-set for Planet Rock and, as the new single from the Dirty Pirates began to play, he filled the urn with cold water and set it to boil.

#

THE NEW METALLICA RECORD was just winding down when Milton heard the door open.

He turned to see who it was.

"Evening."

Milton had never seen the man before. He was in his late forties or early fifties, much shorter than Milton at perhaps five seven or five eight, and slender. His hair was brown and full, held in place with enough product that Milton immediately suspected a little vanity. His face was lined, his chin bore a noticeable cleft, and his dark eyes were partially obscured behind the reflection on the lenses of his glasses.

"Are you a driver?" Milton asked.

"No," the man said. "I'm not."

"I'm sorry. There are rules here. Only cabbies can come in. If you want anything, I'll have to serve you through the hatch."

"I'm not here for refreshments."

"Then I'm going to have to ask you to leave."

"I have a message for you, Mr. Milton."

Milton stopped. He very rarely used his real surname and had never done so here. "Do we know each other?"

"No," he said. "We've never met. But I know who you are. We've worked for the same employer."

Milton found that his throat had become dry. "The government?"

The man nodded.

"I haven't worked for the government for a long time. I'm sorry to be rude, but, whatever it is, I'm not interested. I'm busy. You need to be going."

"It's a personal matter. For you, I mean. I think you'll want to hear it. It's important—I wouldn't have come if it wasn't."

Milton found that he had screwed up the tea towel.

"I don't—"

"Please, Mr. Milton," the man interrupted. "You'll thank me."

Milton looked at him. There was nothing threatening about him, but he was more concerned about the message than the messenger.

"Just five minutes. That's all I ask."

Milton relented. "Five minutes."

The man took one of the bench seats. Milton picked up a stack of dirty crockery, went through into the kitchen and put it in the sink. The water was tepid, so he turned on the hot to warm it up, watching the man in the reflection offered by the darkened windowpane ahead of him. He wondered if he had seen him before, but he couldn't place him. There were so many memories from his past that were cloaked by the fuzz of his drinking, others lost completely; he gave it a moment's thought and then abandoned the attempt. There was no point in trying. He wouldn't be able to remember.

He poured two mugs of hot tea and took them over to the table. He handed one to the man and sat down opposite him.

"What's your name?"

"Logan. William Logan."

"And what do you do?"

"I work at Manila Station. Have done for years."

Manila. That brought back memories. Milton had been to the Philippines twice, on two different assignments. The first had involved the death of an MI6 agent who had been selling secrets to the Russians and the Chinese. Milton remembered that very well: he had garrotted the man on a ferry between Manila and Cagayan de Oro and tossed the body over the side.

"We were approached a week ago by a woman who said that she knows you. You were in Manila several years ago. Operation Attila. Do you remember? There was a company shipping surface-to-air missiles to the Maoists."

"Tactical Aviation," Milton said.

"That's right. British chap at the helm."

The details came back. "Yes," Milton said. "That's right. Fitzroy de Lacey."

"You got him convicted, didn't you?" Logan said rhetorically.

Milton didn't answer.

"Been in jail ever since. Still there, as far as I know."

"What does your coming here have to do with him?"

"It doesn't," Logan said. "Not really. It's to do with you."

Milton sipped the tea. He had started to remember Attila and how much he had been drinking back then. He was nervous about what might come next.

"There was a local woman involved with Tactical. I suppose, if you were being charitable, you'd say she was employed in a hospitality role. Her name was—"

"Jessica," Milton finished for him.

"Jessica Sanchez."

"Yes," Milton said. "I remember her."

"But Miss Sanchez was working for us, too. She was on our books. She helped you get into the company."

Milton shrugged. He wasn't about to share what he could recall with a man whom he had never met before tonight.

Logan seemed content to continue. "Miss Sanchez came to the embassy two weeks ago. Wanted to see you, in fact. I told her that was impossible—we don't just arrange appointments between our agents and any Tom, Dick or Harriet who comes in off the street. But she was pushy. I told her no again, and then she said that she'd go to the local rag and spill everything about the operation to put de Lacey away. You probably don't remember this, Milton, but Tactical had people in London on the payroll. Government people. She gave me some names and they checked out. She knows all of it. And some of these people are still in post. Some of them are senior now. It would be very embarrassing if that ever got out. Very bloody embarrassing indeed." He sat back and spread his hands. "I tried to get rid of her, but she insisted. She *had* to speak to you. You and only you. And that, old boy, is why I flew halfway around the world to see you."

"How?" he said. "How did you find me?"

"Wasn't easy. I understand you had some trouble a few years ago. Went to ground for a bit?"

Milton shrugged.

"But things have calmed down since then?"

Milton thought about that. It would be a stretch to say that things had calmed down, but at least he wasn't being pursued by Control and the other crooked agents who had gone rogue with him.

"It's quieter," Milton said, "and that's how I like it. I prefer to keep a low profile."

"But you're hardly off grid. I had to dig around a bit, but I found you eventually. They have files on all of us, especially people like you."

"Patently."

"Indeed," Logan said with a smile. "Patently."

Milton found that he was gripping his mug tightly. There was no point in putting it off any more. "So," he said, "you'd better tell me. What does Miss Sanchez want?"

"That's the thing," Logan said. "Bit sensitive."

"Just tell me."

"She said that the two of you had a *thing* while you were over there. An affair. Not long. Just a couple of months."

Milton felt another twist of anxiety. He shrugged.

"Well, the thing is—and I don't suppose there's any easy way to say this without dropping a great big bloody surprise in your lap—she says that she had a child after you left. She says it's yours. You're a daddy, old man." He raised his mug ironically. "Cheers."

Chapter Three

LOGAN SAT in the back of the black cab and thought about the meeting.

Had it gone well? He thought so. There was nothing to suggest that Milton had seen through the pretence that had been arranged for his benefit.

Logan was not a foreign office functionary. He had never worked at Manila Station. He was not employed by the government, although he had worked for them as a contractor before. He was freelance and preferred it that way.

He travelled a lot. He would accept the offer of a contract and then he would go and carry it out. He was thorough and diligent, spending as much time as the diktats of the operation allowed to research his victims and the lives that they led. It was his goal that he should know them as if he were a good friend.

Milton had been much more interesting than anyone else that he had ever been sent to kill.

He had heard of him before, of course. The existence of Group Fifteen had always been a badly kept secret within the intelligence community. Milton was one of the Group's better known alumni, mostly because of the acrimonious nature of his departure and the desperate attempts of Milton's corrupt handler to locate him and bring him to heel. The extent of Control's perfidy had sounded the death knell for the Group, a fate that was underlined by the disappearance of the most recent head of the unit, Michael Pope. Group Fifteen had been mothballed, the agents dispersed, and steps taken to discreetly airbrush the whole sorry show from the annals of history.

They had deleted Milton's records, but his reputation lingered.

Milton had been Her Majesty's most dangerous assassin for many years, with more than one hundred and fifty confirmed kills to his name. He had been gone for years now, but Logan had found evidence of his handiwork in places as diverse as Ciudad Juarez, San Francisco, Michigan's Upper Peninsula and, most recently, London and Calais. It was obvious from his rather pitiful existence in London that he was trying to melt into civilian life, but a man like Milton couldn't easily do that.

Milton was a killer, and he would always be a killer.

Death would be his constant companion.

Their calling was the one thing that they had in common.

Because Logan was a killer, too.

#

LOGAN HAD a room at the Dorchester. He didn't have a permanent address. He worked all around the world, and the itinerant life suited both his profession and his temperament. Nothing about him was permanent. His name wasn't Logan, for example. It was the name of the man in his passport who bore his likeness. The picture was the same in his passports from Australia, Canada, the USA, Ireland, and Germany. Only the name changed.

He had been in the Special Boat Service for five years before he had resigned to work on his own account. British intelligence was moving away from a formalised department like Group Fifteen, preferring the greater discretion offered by a series of unconnected agents who had no formal ties to the government nor any knowledge of one another. The men and women who gave Logan government work tended to be drawn from the same small class of senior agency staff, and it was they who stood between him and his ultimate clients: a diplomatic mission with troublesome locals, perhaps a trade envoy who wanted to remove a customs official who was proving to be troublesome for British businesses, or underworld figures who were threatening vested interests. Other jobs—like this one—were passed to him after he had been recommended by previous clients.

Logan had travelled all over the world, flitting in and out of expensive hotels like this one, carrying out his orders with scrupulous care, leaving barely a ripple in his wake. He caught sight of himself in one of the lobby's big mirrors. His suit was expensive, but not so expensive as to be noticeable; his leather bag was just the same as the one toted by the man ahead of him, although Logan's held a pistol and ammunition rather than a laptop; his features were blandly unremarkable, like those of a bored provincial accountant. He worked hard to maintain that air of dour, world-weary boredom. It was a veil behind which he could conceal his true self.

Logan passed through the promenade. He watched rich Arabs and Russians being tended to by burly minders and eager women. He passed an African family dressed in garishly expensive clothes. He paused in the elevator lobby to allow an elderly couple to emerge, the cologne and perfume that drifted off them in pungent waves as redolent as the smell of money.

He put his key in the elevator and rode it to the fourth floor. He went to his room, closed the door, and took out the burner phone that he had purchased at the airport. He opened Gmail and started to type.

IT'S DONE. I MET HIM.

He saved the message as a draft and then went to run a bath.

He refreshed the browser when he returned. His draft message had been replaced by another.

WHAT DID HE SAY?

He deleted and then typed.

HE WAS SURPRISED. HE WASN'T EXPECTING TO HEAR FROM HER AND IS THINKING ABOUT VISITING. I'LL SEE HIM AGAIN TOMORROW.

He went to turn off the taps and then refreshed the browser again.

WHAT DO YOU THINK?

He typed.

GET THE GIRL READY. I THINK HE'S COMING.

Chapter Four

MILTON SLID out of bed. His bedroom was cold and he had barely slept. He went through into the tiny bathroom, stepped into the bath and ran the shower. The cold had sunk into his bones and he stood under the hot water for fifteen minutes until the warmth had driven it away.

It wasn't just the cold that had kept him awake. He had been thinking about what Logan had told him.

His memories of his second visit to Manila were patchy. He had been drinking heavily then and the alcohol had robbed him of many of his memories. He had been playing the part of an ex-soldier who was involved in close protection. One of Fitzroy de Lacey's previous men had gone missing, an occurrence engineered by Milton so that he might apply to fill the vacancy. His experience in the Regiment, together with a fabricated history as a mercenary, made him the perfect candidate for the role and he had been accepted into the organisation.

De Lacey was a suspicious man, and the effort of maintaining the facade was something that Milton had found more than usually difficult. His days had been spent gathering the evidence that would eventually be used to put de Lacey behind bars. It was stressful, a long list of untruths that Milton had to remember, and he had returned exhausted to his hotel room every night, where he would empty the minibar and fall into his bed in a stupor.

Jessica Sanchez had worked for Tactical Aviation too. Milton had lost many of his memories of his time in the city, but he had not forgotten her. She was beautiful, dark skinned and with hair the colour of midnight. Her brown eyes were large and soulful, and they sparkled with a mischievousness that was at odds with the cool demeanour that was the hallmark of her work for de Lacey. She knew that she was beautiful, and she knew that de Lacey had placed her in a role where her beauty could be deployed to his best advantage, and, despite the unpleasant men that she was paid to entertain, she maintained a professionalism that never wavered.

Milton had been attracted to her the first time that he had laid eyes on her. He had always been a terrible judge of reciprocated feelings, and he had stayed back even after he was sure that she felt the same way.

The other men in de Lacey's security detail spoke about her and the other women who were summoned up for the regular parties on his enormous yacht with no attempt to temper their lascivious thoughts. They also revealed that de Lacey occasionally shared Jessica's bed, and that, more than anything else, was the motivation that Milton needed to retreat to the hotel and the oblivion he could find at the bar.

He scrubbed the water into his face, trying to shake away the worst of the dull fugue that had settled over him.

One night stood out in his mind more than all the others. Even now, years later, even though the years had been soaked in alcohol and most of his memories had been erased by blackouts, it was the scene that had played through his mind and kept him awake. Milton had been trying to sleep, the windows open to allow a little air into the stifling room. There had come a knock at the door. Milton had not expected anyone, so he had opened it a crack with his pistol hidden behind the frame. Jessica was standing there. Her face was bloodied and bruised. He had let her in and poured her a drink from the bottle of vodka that he had very nearly finished.

She had explained: she had been with de Lacey, and he had beaten her. There had been a contract with a supplier of weapons from Armenia. The man and his entourage had flown to Manila to seal a deal, and Jessica had been in charge of ensuring that they had a trip to remember. Something had gone wrong—Milton couldn't remember what it was—and the man had left without signing the deal.

De Lacey had blamed Jessica for the failure and had exacted his punishment with his fists and his belt. Milton had seen the evidence of his displeasure as the girl stepped out of her dress: there were welts all the way down her back from the top of her spine to her waist.

Milton had been drunk. The booze, the attraction that he felt for Jessica, and the swirl of anger at what had been done to her, had all mixed into a cocktail of lust that had overwhelmed his professionalism and then his defences. In the back of his mind, despite the alcohol, he had known that it was a stupid idea, but he was unable to resist. She removed the rest of her clothes and joined him in his bed.

They had fallen asleep eventually, and Milton had stirred first. He remembered: he had been soaked through with sweat, with warm air riffling the blinds and slowly inching up the temperature in his room. His head pounded with an awful reminder of the previous night's excesses, although that was far from unusual. He had slowly levered himself upright, his hangover had ratcheted up a level, and he had turned to see the girl laid out next to him. He felt sick at the foolishness of what he had done.

Jessica, disturbed by his movement, had woken with a start, and, as she realised what had happened, she had become frantic with worry. She told Milton that de Lacey was a jealous man and that they would both be in danger if he discovered that they had slept together. They talked. They had been crazy, they agreed. It was a stupid risk. But they could rescue the situation if they kept what had happened between themselves. There was no reason why de Lacey or anyone else ever need know.

So Milton had gone to work as if nothing had happened. De Lacey was on his yacht and he had asked Milton to take him out in one of the tenders so that he could swim in the deeper water. Milton remembered being swamped with anger. De Lacey was enjoying himself, laughing and joking with him as he undressed and dived into the clear blue water. It was as if what he had done to Jessica was of trivial importance, as if it were just another administrative task that he had attended to for the good of his business. Milton had thought how easy it would be to end him there and then. The two of them were alone, a mile from land. Milton was armed. It would have been simple to shoot him, weigh the body down and let it sink to the bottom.

But he couldn't do that. He had very strict instructions. This was not a typical operation, ending with the death of the target and a clean exfil back to London and whatever came next. The aim of the operation was to have de Lacey arrested and, ultimately, incarcerated. It was more subtle than usual, more nuanced, and those strictures constrained his freedom to carry out his orders as he saw fit.

His pistol had felt red hot in his shoulder holster, but he'd left it there. Instead, he had helped de Lacey out of the water, passed him his towel, and piloted the tender back to the harbour, his multi-million-pound yacht and his breakfast.

Chapter Five

MILTON CALLED LOGAN on the number that the man had given him and arranged to meet him on the South Bank at two o'clock.

It was eleven. He had three hours before he needed to be there.

There was a meeting of the fellowship at the community centre near to Victoria Park.

He put on his coat, locked his flat, and set off.

#

IT WAS a thirty-minute walk to the meeting.

Milton followed Columbia Road up to the bustle of the weekly flower market. The narrow street was thronged with customers, clutches of them gathered around the tables as hoarse traders barked out their deals and offers, the street full of the sweet scent of lilies, roses, amaryllis, hippeastrum, shamrock, chrysanthemum, and brassicas. Milton passed by the old primary school and the old boozers that had been prettified by the relentless gentrification that had swallowed up this once rough neighbourhood. He continued to the northwest, going by Hackney City Farm and the empty BMX track at Haggerston Park; he crossed the canal and continued east until he reached the westward tip of the sprawl of Victoria Park. The meeting was in the community centre, an ugly 1960s brick building that had been put up to fill the gap caused by one of the Luftwaffe's bombs.

Milton had never been to this meeting before, and, although he recognised a few faces amid the twenty or so who were here, he didn't acknowledge anyone and took his habitual chair at the back of the room.

The secretary brought the meeting to order and opened

by reading 'How It Works' from the Big Book. Milton closed his eyes and concentrated on his breathing. He knew that he would find a small margin of peace at the meeting, and, as the speaker began to tell her story, he let her voice lull him into the meditative place where he was sometimes able to decode the buzz of noise in his head.

Was he doing the right thing? He didn't know. Common sense said that he should ignore the news that Logan had delivered, pack up his few possessions, and move away. He had finally begun to feel safe enough to live a semblance of a normal life, but now this unwelcome contact with the establishment had reinvigorated his desire to submerge beneath the surface again. The ease with which Logan had found him was disconcerting to a man whose entire adult life had been spent in the shadows. He had been thinking about returning to South America, and the idea of that— the opportunity to travel, to erase all evidence of himself in shiftless movement—was now much more attractive than it had been. There was nothing for him here. He would miss his job and the men and women who were connected to the shelter, but he didn't consider any of them to be real friends. None of them would miss him if he was gone.

No one would miss him.

Yet, even as he had persuaded himself that that was the sensible move, he knew that he wouldn't be able to do it. The news that Logan had delivered had knocked him sideways. His memories of Jessica were fresher than he had expected, and he found that he was keen to see her again.

Yet, of course, it was more than that.

She had told Logan that she had had Milton's child.

There had been women in Milton's life, both during his employment and after it. He had been promiscuous when he had been drinking, and his behaviour with women had been one of the many reasons that had eventually coalesced into an overwhelming desire to find sobriety. He had met other women during his time on the road when he had been dry. Most of them had been transitory, and that had been as obvious to them as it had been to him. There had been handful of relationships that might have grown into something else, had he allowed them the time and space to flourish. Ellie Flowers, the FBI agent that he had met in the Upper Peninsula, had been one. Mattie, the sister of a friend he had met during his time in the Regiment, had been another. There had been a connection with both women, enough for him to be confident that they would have at least tried to understand him.

But he couldn't do it.

There were things in his history that he knew he would never be able to reveal, not to anyone. Any kind of relationship needed firm foundations of truth and honesty, and Milton couldn't offer that. There would be no rock to build upon; all he could offer was a shifting sand of lies and deceit. So what was the point? It wasn't fair. He had treated women badly before, and he had forced himself to stop drinking so that he might be a better man. Encouraging a relationship when he would have to hold so much of himself back and lie about his past was beneath him now. It wasn't something that he was prepared to do.

So he had always forced himself to move on.

But a child?

Did that change things?

Milton couldn't even begin to process how he felt about that.

He felt a gentle nudge on his arm and opened his eyes. The woman to his right was holding the collection plate. Milton smiled at her, took the plate, dropped a five-pound note onto it and passed it along the row to the man on his left.

The secretary led the meeting in the Serenity Prayer and brought proceedings to a close. Milton stood up, waited until the woman had stepped into the aisle and then, with as friendly a smile as he could manage, he left the room.

Chapter Six

MILTON WALKED to Mare Street, took the 254 bus south to Whitechapel and then boarded the District Line train to the Embankment.

He was outside the Royal Festival Hall thirty minutes before the time of the rendezvous and used the extra time, as was his habit, to look for anything that might lead him to suspect that the meeting might be observed. He walked north along the promenade, passing by the under croft, with the kids on their skateboards and bikes, the walls covered with a dazzling array of graffiti'd designs. He carried on toward Waterloo Bridge and paused beneath it for five minutes with his elbows resting against the metal railing, looking out at the grey expanse of the water, the commuter taxis and pleasure boats slicing through the waves, and then at the impressive array of buildings on the opposite bank. He looked up and down the pathway, but saw nothing that gave him any reason for suspicion. He set off back to the south, the wheel of the London Eye visible above the trees. The hall was hosting the Festival of Love, with a multicoloured temporary entrance leading into the building.

Milton bought a latte from EAT and took it out to one of the covered tables.

He saw Logan at the same time as Logan saw him.

The man came down the steps from the promenade and sat at the table.

"Good morning."

Milton nodded.

"How are you?"

"I'm fine," Milton said tersely.

"What have you decided?"

Milton didn't answer.

"You have questions?"

"Why does she want to see me now?" Milton said. "I haven't seen her for years."

"I don't know."

"I can't go halfway across the world without more information, Logan."

"No," he replied. "Of course you can't. Would it help if you spoke to her first?"

"It might."

"Can you get online this afternoon?"

Milton had several hours before he needed to be at the shelter. "Yes."

"She says she'll talk to you on Skype."

Logan took a discarded freesheet from the adjacent table and scribbled on it. He tore out the page and pushed it across the table. "That's her username," he said. "They're seven hours ahead of us. She can speak after two thirty our time."

Milton looked at his watch. It was ten minutes after two.

"I think the child will be in bed," Logan suggested as a reason for the particular time.

Milton thought about that. "The child," he said, the word sticky in his mouth. "I don't even know if it's a boy or a girl."

"A boy," Logan said. "But she didn't tell me anything more than that."

Milton exhaled. "I don't know why she'd do this now."

Logan rested his arms on the table, steepled his fingers, and leaned forward. "Look, you must've thought it, so I'll just put it out there. Maybe she needs money. Maybe she's managed to bring him up without any help, but now something's changed. Or maybe she just wants to shake you down."

"She wouldn't do that."

"I don't know her. All I can do is speculate. But one thing I do know—we have to come up with something to keep her happy. Her involvement with Attila could be a problem. There are assets who worked on that job who are still in theatre. She could cause trouble, and that's not something that the FO will let happen."

"What do you mean? She'd be a threat? She'd be in danger?"

"I'm not saying that," Logan said unconvincingly. "But just because there's no more Group Fifteen doesn't mean that there aren't protocols in place for when British interests are threatened." He paused, saw Milton's glower, and added, "Look, what I'm very clumsily trying to suggest is that it would be better for all concerned if you make her feel better about things. The government will fly you out there and, if it *is* money that she wants, it'll step in and take care of that, too. You just need to find out what she wants. And… I don't know—maybe she's just reaching out now because her boy wants to meet his father. Maybe you'd like to meet him, too."

Milton looked away from the table and gazed back to the promenade, to the steady stream of joggers and the pedestrians and tourists ambling along the pavement. He looked down at his watch again. It was two twenty.

"At least speak to her," Logan said. "Find out what she wants."

Milton stood.

"You'll do it?"

"I'll call her. And then I'll think about it."

"Let me know when it's done."

Milton walked away without replying.

Chapter Seven

MILTON WALKED across the Golden Jubilee bridge, up Villiers Street and then took the Strand in the direction of Nelson's Column. There was a branch of easyInternetCafe just before Trafalgar Square. He went inside, paid for an hour, and took a seat at one of several vacant workstations. Each PC was equipped with a set of headphones and a microphone, and Milton put his on, adjusting the microphone so that it was just below his mouth. He opened Skype, logged in, and searched for the username that Logan had given him. He found it and clicked that he wanted to add the name as a contact.

He waited. Nothing happened.

And then it did.

The phone icon started to buzz and Milton heard the sound of ringing.

He accepted the call.

"Hello," she said. "Can you hear me?"

He recognised her voice at once. "I can. But I can't see you."

"Oh. Hold on."

A moment passed and then a window opened out to show the feed from the webcam at the other end of the call.

"Better?" she said.

The blank screen was replaced by the feed from her webcam. She smiled, and Milton remembered why he had fallen for her so hard. Her long black hair was tied back, revealing a slender, graceful neck. Her eyes were brown, soulful, and expressive, and, as she leaned back in her chair, she raised a hand and waved to him.

"It's been a while," he said.

"Years. I'm sorry to contact you like I did. I didn't know how else to find you."

"It's all right," he said. "I'm pleased to see you again."

"You were surprised, though?"

"I was."

"What did they say?"

"That…" He paused, finding that the words didn't come easily. "They said that you had a child."

She smiled. "A son," she said. "His name is James."

"They said that you… that you told them he was mine."

"He is." She stopped for a moment, reaching down below the line of the camera. "Would you like to see a picture?"

Milton swallowed and cleared his throat. "Yes," he said. "Of course."

She brought up a smartphone. She played with it for a moment and then turned it around and held it up so that Milton could see the screen.

"Can you see it?"

He could. The photograph was of a young boy—Milton guessed that he was nine or ten—holding up a football and beaming into the camera. He had a head of thick dark hair, tousled and untidy and falling down over his forehead. His skin was a very light brown, a shade or two lighter than Jessica's, his teeth were white and even and his eyes were a sharp blue.

"Hold on."

She flicked through additional photographs: the boy holding a PlayStation controller; riding a bicycle along a neat and tidy street; turning to the camera in a busy shopping mall, a wide smile on his face.

"He looks like you, John."

Milton swallowed once more, his throat dry. The noise of the Internet café faded out, and his focus narrowed on the screen and the pictures of the boy. There was a resemblance.

"John? Can you still hear me?"

"Yes," he said. "Sorry, I… He's a handsome lad."

She smiled. "He's started asking about his father. There's only so much that I can tell him. I just say that his father didn't know about him."

"I didn't," Milton said.

"Of course. I'm not blaming you for anything, John. It was my choice. I didn't think it would be a good idea. But I wonder, now that he is older, whether I made a mistake."

"I wouldn't have been a very good father," Milton said. "And it would have been complicated. My work—"

"I know. I don't want you to feel I'm resentful. And I don't want any money from you. We are comfortable. He has a good school and he works hard for the things that he has."

"They didn't tell me—"

She cut him off. "James wanted to know whether you would come here to meet him. I said that it might not be as easy as that—that you have an important job, that you—"

"I don't," he corrected her with a wry smile. "A lot of things have changed since the last time you saw me."

"You don't work for the government?"

"Not for a long time," he said. "But that's a long story."

"Perhaps you could come here and tell me about it?"

He looked at the screen and, within it, the window from which Jessica was smiling hopefully at him. He had been reluctant to speak to her, to risk opening up old feelings and long-buried memories, but now, with her familiar face in front of him, listening to her warm, reassuring voice, he found himself responding.

"When?" he said.

"You'll come?"

He nodded. "When are you thinking?"

"I don't have any plans."

Neither do I, he thought. *Nothing at all.*

There was no point in waiting.

"How about tomorrow?" he said.

Chapter Eight

MILTON PUSHED up the blind and gazed out of the porthole window at London laid out below them. It was dark, and the lights of the city glittered around the dark snake of the Thames as it wound its way out to the sea. The pilot banked and continued their climb to cruising altitude. The flight was scheduled to take thirteen hours and forty-five minutes. Milton hoped to be able to sleep through most of it.

There had been no reason to delay once he had made his decision. He went into the shelter after he had spoken to Jessica and told Cathy that he needed time off for personal reasons. She was understanding, didn't ask questions, and said that his job would be waiting for him when he came back. As she reached up for him and gave him a warm hug, Milton wondered, again, whether he was doing the right thing. He had a life here, or at least a semblance of one. The job was the anchor around which he could arrange everything else. It was a point of normality, a steadiness in an existence that had, for so long, been a vortex of uncertainty and confusion.

But then he thought of Jessica and he knew that he had no choice.

There were other things he had grown used to. He had his flat. He had a series of meetings that he had come to rely upon, the emotional bulwark that helped him deal with the burden of his guilt. The longer he went without meetings, the heavier that guilt would become and the more likely he was to resort to his old method of coping.

He resolved to find a meeting in Manila as soon as he landed.

Logan had offered to pay for his flight, but Milton did not want any more contact with him and the government than was absolutely necessary. The fact that they had found him was disturbing enough; it was a wake-up call that he had relaxed a little too much, and he would take steps to change that from now on. He would guard his privacy. He had a little money salted away, so he used it to purchase a non-stop Philippine Airlines flight from Heathrow to Manila.

Milton looked at his cheap Timex watch. It was just after ten. They would arrive mid-morning. The plane levelled out and the captain switched off the fasten seatbelts sign. The cabin crew busied themselves with the dinner service. Milton put on his sleeping mask and then slid his headphones over his ears. The steward was approaching with the drinks trolley. Milton could do without being asked if he wanted a drink or the temptation of the jangling bottles.

#

THE WOMAN sat three rows behind Milton on the other side of the aisle. She couldn't have asked for a better spot: she was able to watch him without the need to move, able to observe him with the discretion that would be necessary for a mark like him. Another member of the team had followed him from the café that afternoon. They did not know what to expect, but he hadn't been particularly careful; they had three of them on standby should he attempt any counter-surveillance techniques, but he had not. Rather, he had gone to the tube station, travelled across London to Paddington, and then taken the Heathrow Express to the airport. The woman had picked him up as he had arrived at the departures hall. Logan had taken the precaution of booking seats on all of the direct flights to the Philippines, and it had been a simple enough matter for her to check in at the same time as he did and then follow him down to the gate.

She watched as he reclined his seat and put the eye mask

over his face. This part of the operation was simple. They just wanted to know where he was and, particularly, that he was doing what he had promised to do.

The difficulty would come later.

Chapter Nine

THE APPROACH had been spectacular. Milton had looked out of the window as they passed over the islands that made up the Philippines, many of them marked by tall volcanoes and others garlanded with sandy crescents of beach that were as white as bone against the deep blue of the ocean. There were acres of paddy fields, vast rectangles that were separated into hundreds of uniform terraces.

They touched down on schedule and taxied to Terminal NAIA-1. Milton watched the baggage handlers fussing with the luggage as it was unloaded from the hold, and then followed the shuffling queue of passengers as they made their way down the aisle to the air bridge. He felt the warmth and humidity as he left the plane and crossed over to the terminal. The captain had announced that the temperature was already eighty degrees, and that the forecast was for ninety by the time the day was done. Milton had packed a T-shirt in his case and he stopped in the first bathroom to change into it, splashing his face with lukewarm water in an attempt to scour away the rheum of sleep. He followed the windowed alleys to the luggage reclaim and went straight through since he had only brought his carry-on with him. He passed through health control and stood before the infrared camera as a glum-looking official checked the temperatures of the arriving passengers and asked a few cursory questions about SARS and bird flu. Milton carried on, queued for immigration and finally shuffled forward to hand over his passport and arrivals card. He bought some Philippine pesos at the exchange desk and, finally, pushed through the doors into the muggy soup outside the terminal.

He waited there for a moment, watching the other travellers as they emerged onto the concourse.

He spotted a woman dressed for business, with a sheen of sweat on her skin, and went over to her.

"Hello," he said.

She looked at him with an expression that mixed surprise with resignation.

"Tell Logan that I don't need to be followed," he said. "I'm here like he wanted. But if I see anyone else following me, that'll be the end of things. I'll just disappear. All right?"

"I-I—"

"The same goes for your friend on the train," he said. "He was just as sloppy as you. Now—piss off and enjoy the weather."

He took one of the yellow airport taxis and asked to be taken to the city. The driver pulled away and Milton watched through the rear window as the woman fumbled in her purse for her phone.

The driver made no effort to engage Milton in conversation, turning on the radio and resting his forearm out of the open window as they set off. Milton was fine about that. He was happy to look out of the window, remembering the occasional buildings and landmarks from his previous visits to the city.

It was a twenty-five-minute drive from the airport to the city. Milton took out his phone, waited for it to connect to the local network, and then called for an Uber to meet him at Raffles. They arrived in Makati and Milton leaned forward and told the driver to drop him off. He paid the fare, not commenting on the fact that he had grossly overcharged him, and got into the waiting black BMW.

"Makabat Guesthouse?" the driver said, consulting the booking information on his own phone.

"That's right," Milton said. "In Malate."

The Uber driver was chattier, telling Milton that he used to be a driver for KFC, delivering chickens and supplies to local restaurants. He complained that he had been making five hundred pesos per day but now he made fifteen thousand a week. Milton congratulated him on his new job, but then settled back to watch out of the windows to check that he wasn't still being followed. The driver was happy to fill the silence and all Milton had to do was make encouraging noises every now and again. In the end, the driver turned up the radio and they continued along the route in companionable silence.

#

HE HAD found the place on TripAdvisor before he left London and had booked a room for three nights. It was mid-range, and the reviews suggested that the rooms were clean with reliable air conditioning. It was just as advertised: small, tidy rooms, and a pleasant respite from the heat of the morning outside. Milton put his carry-on suitcase on the bed. He wrote down the address of the two o'clock meeting and ordered another Uber.

It took twenty minutes to drive to the Church of the Holy Trinity. It was a busy meeting and Milton was five minutes late. He made his way to the back of the room and sat down on a metal folding chair.

The proceedings were being conducted in Filipino, and, since Milton didn't speak a word of the language, they were incomprehensible. The structure of the meeting was identical to what he would have expected at home, however, and, as the secretary handed over to the evening's speaker, Milton was able to close his eyes and tried to relax.

He realised that he was nervous. It wasn't something that he was used to feeling. Milton planned everything that he did with exacting precision, and, as much as he could, he minimised the effects of chance. Excellent preparation reduced the scope for surprises and that, in turn, gave him confidence. But the future was impossible to plan for. He had no idea what Jessica would say to him and no idea how he would feel. It made him uneasy. She had suggested that they meet in a bar, too, and that made him even more nervous. There was an old AA adage that he had always found particularly apt: if you go into a hairdresser's, eventually you'll get a haircut.

Milton knew himself too well: he would be tempted to drink. He would be unable to make a plan that would insulate him, and the conversation that he would have with Jessica tonight had the potential to change his life.

He concentrated on his breathing, maintaining an even rhythm, in and out, and tried to tune out the thoughts racing through his mind. He listened to the speaker, the clatter of the unfamiliar language, and tried to find his usual quiet space of calm.

Chapter Ten

LOGAN FOUND the bar. It was called the Lazy Lizard, and it was in Poblacion in Makati. It was hot outside, the heat pressing down on the busy streets like a dead weight. The temperature seemingly incited the drivers, who thronged the roads impatiently, and he ignored a cacophony of horns as he reversed his rental into an empty bay a hundred feet down the road from the bar. One of the drivers who had been forced to wait until the conclusion of his manoeuver opened his window and gave him the finger. Logan ignored it and walked back to the bar.

Logan had been in the city for twelve hours. Milton had flown in after him. He had been irritated, although not especially surprised, that Milton had made the tails who had been following him. Logan didn't like to feel bested, but he didn't allow it to bother him. It was temporary, and, of course, Milton had no idea what he was walking into. He would let him have his small victory.

The bar was a cheap dive that catered to tourists. It lacked any semblance of glamour, the decor resembling a hut rather than the sleek futurism of the glass and chrome establishments that were popping up elsewhere. Those places were not suitable for what Logan had in mind. He needed somewhere quieter, somewhere he could exert influence over the staff. The Lazy Lizard was perfect.

He went up to the bar. The owner was the only member of staff here today, as Logan had expected. The man was not much older than thirty-five. He had a sleeve of tattoos all the way down his right arm and long, lank, black hair. Logan sat on the stool and smiled at him until he came over to serve him.

"Hello, Rodrigo," Logan said. He used English; he knew that the owner spoke it well.

"How do you know my name?"

"That doesn't really matter."

"Who are you?"

"You can call me Logan."

Rodrigo looked flustered. "What do you want?"

"A drink would be a good start."

"Sure. I—"

"What beers do you recommend?"

"We have Cerveza Negra," he said. "Or Colt 45. It's stronger."

"Cerveza will be fine. In a cold glass, please."

Rodrigo took a bottle from the fridge, popped the top, and poured it into a chilled glass. He set a napkin on the bar top and rested the glass on it. He rang up the purchase and laid the ticket next to the glass.

"Thank you," Logan said. He raised the glass in salute and then drank a little.

The bar was quiet. Logan could tell that Rodrigo would have liked to leave him be, but there was no one else to serve. He made do with taking a cloth and wiping up a puddle of spilled beer. Logan watched. He could tell that he made the man uncomfortable.

"Do you need anything else?"

Logan picked up the napkin, folded it in half and then meticulously wiped his lips. He laid the napkin down again and rested the glass atop it.

"Can I speak frankly with you, Rodrigo?"

"What do you want to talk about?"

"Your financial situation."

"I'm sorry," Rodrigo said. "I don't know who you are or what you want. You've got your beer. I have work to do."

"Can I tell you what I know?" He loosened his top button and went on before the barman could react. "You've been open here for six months. You took a large loan from the bank to get started, but now that money is nearly all gone. How am I doing?"

Rodrigo didn't respond; he looked confused.

Logan went on. "The rent was late last month and your landlord threatened to throw you out unless you paid. Your bank manager isn't flexible, and you knew there was no point in asking for any more money. So you had to be creative. One of your regulars has an under-the-counter loan business and, when no other options presented themselves, you approached him. This lender—Espinosa, I think his name is—was happy to front you the cash. He encouraged you to let it ride for a month or two, but then, when you had the money and were ready to pay it off, the interest had doubled the amount that you owed."

"This is none of your business."

"I'm afraid it is my business," Logan said. "Mr. Espinosa sold me your debt. I paid him a little less than he was owed. Men like him will always tell you that the full amount must be repaid, but, in my experience, they are businessmen. I'm sure he looked at you and saw that you would never be able to do that, especially with the interest that was accruing. My offer was generous, so we were able to do business."

"I don't understand. I—"

"It's simple, Rodrigo. It means that you don't owe him anything any longer. You owe me instead. I suppose you could say that I own this bar. So you can see what I mean when I say that your financial dealings are very much my business."

"Why would you do that?"

"Because I have a use for you."

"You're wasting your time. I couldn't afford to pay him. I can't afford to pay you."

"There are different ways to meet your debts. Money is one way. You have another option. There's something that you can do for me."

Rodrigo watched as Logan reached into his jacket pocket and took out a small clear plastic bag. It contained a dirty white powder. Logan left it on the bar.

"Drugs? I don't do drugs. Have you seen what happens

to drug dealers under Duterte?"

"Relax," Logan said. "This wouldn't upset the president. It's not drugs."

"So what is it?"

Logan ignored the question. "Two people are going to come into the bar this evening. A man and a woman." He reached into his pocket again and took out a piece of folded paper. He unfolded it and laid it on the bar next to the bag. "Look, please."

Rodrigo looked down at the paper. It was a printed photograph of Milton. The photograph had been taken at a police station in Texas; Milton was holding up a board with a number, a name—SMITH, JOHN—and measurements that recorded his height as six feet and his weight as two hundred pounds.

"His name is John," Logan said. "And John is going to be meeting this woman."

He took out a second piece of paper. It was a photograph of a woman. She was good-looking, with long dark hair and soulful eyes. "Her name is Jessica."

"So?"

"I want you to put half of that powder into his drink and half into hers."

Rodrigo pushed the pieces of paper back across the bar. "Are you mad? No!"

"Then pay me my money."

"Drug them?"

"It's not dangerous."

"So do it yourself."

Logan pushed the photographs back across the bar. "It's up to you, Rodrigo. You owe me sixty thousand pesos. I know I look different to Espinosa, but just because I wear a suit and tie shouldn't blind you to the fact that I am more dangerous to you than he would ever have been." Logan reached back his left hand and pulled back his jacket. He was wearing a shoulder holster with a pistol beneath his arm. "You have a choice. Put that powder into their drinks and have your debt written off. Or pay me back. But if you want to do that, I'm going to need all the money—plus another thirty thousand for my inconvenience—tonight. So it's up to you."

Rodrigo swallowed down on a dry throat. He pointed down to the bag of powder on the bar. "So what is that?"

"A tranquiliser. It'll just loosen them up a little."

"And I put it in their drinks?"

"That's right. It'll dissolve. You wait until it's invisible and then you give it to them. And that will be that. You won't owe me or Espinosa anything."

"All right," he said.

Logan stood. He straightened his jacket so that the pistol was hidden once again. "Very good."

"The money?"

"You do that for me, and everything goes away. You'll be a free man."

Logan took out a note to cover his beer and laid it on the bar. He took a final swig, replaced the half-finished glass, nodded his farewell, and made his exit.

Chapter Eleven

MILTON DISTRACTED himself by spending the rest of the afternoon looking around the city.

He had forgotten how much he liked it. It was a dizzying confection of influences: the cosmopolitan nature of Paris, the glitz of America and the naïve capitalism of China. Apart from Filipino, Milton saw signs in English, Spanish and Arabic. The traffic was relentless, the heat brutal, the poverty everywhere and the growth rampant and seemingly out of control. One street would be chaotic, the sidewalks crammed with pedestrians and the roads choked with cars and trucks, yet, just a turn or two away, he found peaceful alleys that led to souks and courtyards that were like oases amid the sound and fury. He visited the citadel at Intramuros and had a savoury brioche of *ensaymada* for his lunch. He walked to the Marikina shoe museum and shook his head at Imelda Marcos's vast collection. He went to Binondo, the colourful four-hundred-year-old Chinatown, and had a *halo halo*—a concoction of shaved ice and evaporated milk jumbled with candied fruit, *nata de coco*, and crème caramel—to cool him down when the heat became too oppressive.

He returned to his room at five, stood under a cold shower until his skin prickled, and then shaved in front of the bathroom mirror. He knew he looked different from when Jessica had seen him last. He was older, and the weight of the passing years and the worries that they had brought with them had been written in the fresh lines on his face and the grey in his hair. He looked at his tattoos, each of them testament to some event in his life. The biggest—the angel wings across his shoulders and back—was from his drinking days; he couldn't remember having it done. The newest—the IX across his heart—was a reminder of his constant need to make amends, and a testament to the example set by Eddie Fabian.

He took out the ironing board and ironed his only other clean shirt. He dressed, checked himself in the mirror one final time, and went out into the night heat to meet his Uber.

#

JESSICA HAD emailed Milton to say that she would meet him at the Lazy Lizard in Poblacion. Milton sat quietly in the back as the driver took him to Makati. The bar looked unappealing from the outside, but Milton had eschewed places like this for long enough to know that he was far from an expert as to what was passing for chic these days.

He went inside. It was quiet, with just a few other drinkers. Jessica was already waiting for him. She sat at the bar, looking down at her phone, and didn't see him as he came inside. He stood and watched her for a moment. Skype had not done her justice. The years had only touched her lightly. She was as beautiful as he remembered, her long black hair reaching down her back and a single silver bangle shining against the brown of her skin. She was perched on a stool, her slender legs crossed elegantly and offset by an olive dress and a pair of black heels.

Milton felt the burn of the tension in his stomach. He was frozen to the spot and had started to entertain thoughts of leaving when she pushed the phone away and turned in his direction.

She saw him and smiled.

Milton was committed now. He couldn't turn back.

He didn't want to.

He crossed the room.

"John!"

Jessica stood and, smiling again, put her hands on his shoulders and reached up to kiss him on the cheek. Her perfume was of apples; Milton was dizzied, the smell immediately casting him back to the last time they had met.

"You look great," he said.

"You too."

Milton allowed himself a smile. "I look old and tired."

"Tired, maybe. How was your flight?"

"Long."

"And your hotel? Where are you staying?"

"Malate. It's fine. Clean and tidy. That's all I need." He pulled up a stool. "I didn't think I'd ever see you again."

"That would have been your fault. It was your choice to leave."

"Not really. I couldn't stay, could I?"

"No. I suppose not."

"And you could have come with me. I offered."

"To England?" She shook her head. "The Philippines have many problems, but cold weather is not one of them."

She sat, and Milton did the same.

"Do you want a drink?" she said, nodding down to the empty glass before her on the bar.

"I'll get them," he said.

"No, let me. What would you like?"

"I'll have orange juice."

She looked at him quizzically. "Sorry?"

"I don't drink."

"Really? You used to drink all the time."

He flinched with discomfort. "I told you lots of things have changed since the last time."

She had seen him at his worst. She probably remembered the foolish things that he had done and said even as the alcohol had wiped them from his own memory. The realisation made him cringe with shame.

"What happened to make you stop?" she asked.

"I was drinking too much," he said. "It took me a long time to realise, but, when I did, I knew I couldn't do it anymore. I've been in recovery for a few years."

Her face fell. "Recovery?"

"It's nothing that big," he said, trying to minimise it. "I go to meetings. We sit around and drink coffee and talk about how we ended up there. They've made all the difference."

"Is this okay?" she said, gesturing around at the bar. "We could go somewhere else."

He shook his head. "It's fine. I've been dry long enough that I can come into a bar and not get a drink."

#

LOGAN PARKED his car down the road, not so close to the bar that Milton might spot him, but close enough to attend to things when the time was right. The windows of the rental were tinted. Milton wouldn't be able to see him.

Logan had received a text to confirm that both the woman and Milton had arrived and that they were talking at the bar. Jessica had instructions to keep him there long enough for his drink to be spiked. She had impressed him with her ability to dissemble. She and Milton had a lot of reacquainting to do, he supposed. He didn't think that Milton would be leaving any time soon.

He had stopped at a 7-Eleven on Juan Luna Street on the way to the bar and purchased the things that he would need for his work this evening: two bottles of vodka and two six-packs of strong beer. He had moved on and bought a box of powdered green nitrile gloves in the pharmacy next door. The items were in a plastic bag on the seat next to him.

He had almost everything he needed.

Now he just needed Milton.

#

JESSICA ATTRACTED the attention of the bartender—a man with a sleeve of tattoos down his right arm and a head of greasy black hair—and ordered another gin for herself and an orange juice for Milton. The man turned away and busied himself with the drinks. Jessica put her hand to her mouth and cleared her throat. She seemed reluctant to address the thing that had brought Milton halfway around the world to meet her. Milton found that he didn't mind the delay. He realised he was anxious about what he might hear.

"You said you didn't work for the government anymore," she said.

"No. I left. About the same time I stopped drinking."

"So what are you doing now?"

"I'm a cook."

She stared at him.

"I'm serious. I work in a little café in London. It's nice."

"I don't believe you. After what you did before?"

"I know," he conceded. "It's not what you might have expected. Like I said, my life's taken a few unusual turns since I was here last."

"You're full of surprises."

The bartender brought their drinks. Milton reached into his pocket, took out two three hundred-peso notes, and laid them on the table. The man put his hand over the notes and swept them away.

"What about you?" Milton asked. "What are you doing?"

"I work with my father. We have a bakery in Lucena."

"I don't know where that is."

"Two hours south. We make *pandesal*. Sweet breads. You should come. I remember you have a sweet tooth."

There was a moment of silence. Milton glanced up at the mirror behind the bar and used it to look back into the room. One of the tables that had been occupied when he arrived was empty now. There was hardly anyone else here.

"I'm surprised you stayed here," he said. "I thought you might leave."

She shook her head. "No. This is my home. And I didn't think it was necessary. You were thorough. Fitz went to jail. And…" She paused. "And there had been a change in my circumstances."

She smiled a little weakly at him, but then continued before he could speak.

"My parents were here. I was young, and I didn't know

if I wanted to be a mother. It wasn't planned."

Milton put his elbows on the bar and steepled his fingers. This was the moment. The question he knew he would have to ask.

He turned and looked directly at her. "And you're sure?"

"That I'm a mother?" She smiled at him. "Pretty sure."

"That James is my son?"

Jessica reached down into her bag and took out a small leather-bound book. "Here."

She laid it on the table and pushed it across to Milton. It was a scrapbook. He opened the pages, the protective plastic sheaths sticking together until he peeled them apart. A series of photographs had been affixed to the adhesive surfaces of the pages and further secured in place with the sheeting.

He looked at the photographs.

The first page contained pictures of a baby. It was a boy, with fat cheeks and a shock of messy black hair. His skin was smooth and coloured the lightest of browns. His eyes were blue, piercing, as he looked into the camera.

He turned the page.

The baby was older now. A toddler. The hair was more blond than brown, but his plump cheeks were a little less fat. His eyes were no less blue.

He turned the page.

The toddler was a small boy, and then, as he flipped through, a bigger boy. Milton was terrible at guessing the ages of children, but even he could see the passage of time. Five years. Ten years.

He felt choked. He felt a stickiness in the back of his throat and a tightness in his chest.

"He's…" he began. "He's…"

"Yes," she said. "He's yours."

"There wasn't—"

"Anyone else?" she finished when he could not. "There was de Lacey, like you know, but… he doesn't look like him, does he? He looks like you."

Milton thought that he had processed the information, but, as he sat at the bar with Jessica, he found that he had not. He felt blindsided.

"Would you like to meet him?"

"I… I…"

"It's Independence Day here the day after tomorrow. There's a parade and fireworks. James wants to go. Maybe you could come, too?"

Milton emptied the rest of his drink in one swallow. "I need a cigarette," he said. "You want one?"

"Are you okay?"

"Just need a breath of fresh air," he said.

"I know it's a lot to take in," she said, laying her hand on his arm. "Can I get you another drink?"

He got up. "Yes, please. The same again."

Chapter Twelve

LOGAN SAW the door to the bar open and watched as a man walked outside.

There was a brief flare of red and then a steady glow as the man lit and drew down on a cigarette.

Milton.

Logan held his breath. Milton looked up and down the road, but it was apparent that he was distracted. He took a couple of puffs and flicked the unfinished cigarette into one of the large plant pots that flanked the entrance to the bar. He paused for a moment—Logan was concerned that he was going to leave—but then turned on his heel and went back inside.

#

RODRIGO WATCHED the man buy a pack of cigarettes from the machine and leave the bar. The woman was still sat on the stool.

"Could I get the same again, please?" she asked.

"Another orange juice and a gin?"

"Yes."

"Of course."

She got up, collected her phone from the bar and went back to the bathrooms.

Rodrigo swallowed hard. He was nervous. He had been thinking about what Logan had told him and, the way he figured it, he didn't really have a choice. He was deep in the hole, there was no way he could find the money to pay him back, and, worse, there was something about the way Logan had looked at him that made him even more fearful than he had been with Espinosa. The loan shark was a typical thug, covered in tattoos and with a mouth full of gold caps. Logan was neat and tidy, well dressed, not the kind of man who would come and hang out in a dive like this, but there was something icy about his manner. He had looked at Rodrigo with disdain, as if he was nothing, and, when he had showed him his pistol and made his polite threat, Rodrigo had believed him.

He quickly filled both glasses with ice, added gin and tonic and a slice of lime to one and poured orange juice into the other. He had the bag that Logan had given him in his pocket. He reached down, found it amid the loose change and lint, and brought it out. He unsealed the mouth of the bag and tipped half of the dirty white powder inside it into the gin and then the other half into the orange juice. He took a stirrer and whisked it around in both drinks until the powder had dissolved.

The woman returned and, a moment later, the man came back in through the door.

Rodrigo dropped the plastic bag on the floor, picked up both glasses and set them on the bar. His hands were shaking.

"Thank you," the woman said, taking out three hundred-peso notes from her purse and handing them to him.

He took the money and put it in the till. When he returned to them with their change, they had both taken sips of their drinks. He put the change on the bar and had to clasp his hands together to stop them from shaking. He expected them to comment on an unusual taste and then to ask him what he had done with their drinks, but they didn't seem to notice the powder. Perhaps it was tasteless, as Logan had suggested.

Another customer signalled that he wanted to order drinks. The distraction was a relief. Rodrigo left them as they took another sip of the drinks, and went to take the new order.

#

LOGAN LOOKED at his watch.

Fifteen minutes had passed. He had no idea whether he

had frightened the barman enough to have him go through with what he needed him to do. That unpredictability was the only weakness in Logan's plan. If he didn't, Milton would gain a reprieve. Logan's instructions were very precise. It would have been easy to take Milton out now, just as it would have been in London or at the hotel earlier. But that was not what he had been ordered to do. His task was more complicated, and it relied upon the behaviour of others that was impossible to guarantee.

His phone buzzed. He took it out of his pocket and opened the messaging app. He read the message, deleted it, and put the phone back into his pocket again. He instinctively reached up to check the holstered pistol beneath his armpit and, reassured, opened the door and stepped outside into the muggy night.

#

RODRIGO DIDN'T know what to do.

Thirty minutes had passed. The man and the woman were both still at the bar, but they were incapacitated. It was as if they had gone from being sober to utterly drunk without having to take another drink. The man, Smith, was slumped forward, seemingly unaware that his elbows were resting in a pool of spilt beer. He wore a look of confusion on his face, his eyes closed and his brow wrinkled from frowning. His friend, Jessica, was faring no better. She had slipped from her stool and now she was standing next to Smith, her hand clutching his elbow as her knees buckled.

Rodrigo looked at the other customers. This was the kind of place where people came to get wasted, but it was early, and no one else was nearly as drunk as they appeared to be. They stood out. He felt bad for what he had done to them. Logan had promised him that they wouldn't be harmed, but now he worried that he had been lying. He wondered whether he should call someone for help. Perhaps he should call for an ambulance.

He opened the hatch and had just stepped out from behind the bar when he saw a man and a woman sitting in a booth at the back. It was dark, and they had positioned themselves there so that they could watch what was happening in the room via the mirror that Rodrigo had installed to make the dance floor look bigger than it really was. They stood now and stepped into the chequers of light that swirled down from the disco ball above the dance floor.

And then Rodrigo saw Logan, too. He was wearing the same neat suit, the glitter of the lights sparkling off the lenses of his glasses.

The other man and the woman headed toward the bar. The man was dressed similar to Logan, although his suit was not as well fitted. He was bigger, too, his jacket a little too tight around muscular shoulders. The woman was compact but plainly fit and strong, with a hardened look to her face that suggested it would be foolish to annoy her.

Logan came up to him.

"Well done," he said.

The man and the woman arrived behind him.

"Who are they?" Rodrigo said to Logan, gesturing to the other two.

"They're here to help me."

"To do what?"

"We're going to take them with us."

"You didn't say—"

"I'm not asking for your approval. I'm telling you what's going to happen."

"You said they wouldn't be hurt."

"And they won't."

The second man ducked down and looped Smith's arm over his shoulders. He put his arm around Smith's waist, straightened up, and then carefully helped him slide off the stool. Smith had no strength in his legs, and he almost collapsed. The man was strong, though, and he was able to hold him upright. He pretended to say something to Smith, laughing as if they were old friends and he had made a joke about the condition that he had found him in. Smith tried to speak, but the effort was too much for him, his mouth curling around the words as if he had forgotten how to speak.

Logan stood aside as the man helped Smith to the exit. "If anyone asks, you don't know who they are."

"I *don't* know who they are."

The woman put her arm around the woman's torso and half-carried her in the same direction.

"They got drunk, their friends arrived, they left. That's it."

"I don't know about this," Rodrigo said before he could think to be silent.

"Do you want your debt to be paid, or do I have to look at collecting it another way?"

"No. It's fine. Just go."

Logan nodded, and, without another word, he turned and followed the others out the door and into the street beyond.

Chapter Thirteen

MILTON HAD a key in his pocket. It was attached to a fob inscribed with a notice that requested that if the key was lost, it should be returned to the Makabat Guesthouse in Leveriza Street, Malate. Logan put the address into his satnav, pocketed the key, and drove there. It was a cheap place, down at heel, the sort of dive where you could pay by the hour if that was what you wanted. Logan let the engine idle as he glanced around. There were other cars in the lot, but there was no one else here.

Milton and Sanchez were in the back of the car. They were awake, but neither of them was aware where they were. Sanchez was whimpering, her words unintelligible. Milton was breathing deeply, almost asleep. The man and the woman from the surveillance detail were in the car, too. Their names were du Plessis and Faraday, and they had been loaned to him by the British government. The man, du Plessis, sat between Milton and the door, and Faraday was in the passenger seat next to Logan.

Logan reversed into the space nearest the door to Milton's room. He stepped out, crossed the narrow veranda, and examined his surroundings carefully. He saw two small cameras fixed to the underside of the veranda roof.

"Wait here," he said into the car.

He followed the cables that led from the cameras along the ceiling of the veranda. They reached the end of the building before crossing the gap to a freestanding building five metres away. Logan approached it. There was a sign reading OFFICE next to the door.

He stood by the door for a moment and listened carefully. Nothing. He reached into his pocket and took out the box of powdered green nitrile gloves that he had purchased earlier that afternoon. He pulled out a pair and put them on, the elasticated openings snapping against the skin of his wrists. He tried the door handle. It was unlocked. He opened the door slowly and stepped into a small office. Logan saw a PC, an old-fashioned screensaver sending colourful pipes around the screen in isometric patterns. There was a cash box, a row of shelves with lever arch and box files, and piles of paper.

It didn't take him long to find what he was looking for. He looked up at the ceiling and saw the point where the cables that led to the cameras—clipped together now in a thick bundle with additional cables—entered the room. They descended along the join between two walls into a cupboard next to the door. Logan opened the cupboard. There was an old-fashioned D-Link digital video recorder on a shelf. Logan pulled it out, yanked the cables from the back, and, after satisfying himself that there was no one who might see him outside, he took it back to the car and dropped it in the trunk.

Logan crossed back beneath the now-defunct cameras, unlocked the door to Milton's room and pushed it open.

He checked: the room beyond was empty.

He signalled to du Plessis and Faraday. They opened their doors and stepped outside. Milton was first, Faraday on one side of him and du Plessis on the other as they dragged him across the lot. Milton's toes caught on the edge of the veranda and then scraped along the wood as they brought him inside. They hauled him to the bed, turned him around and then let him fall back onto the mattress. Milton groaned, then started to mumble something that Logan couldn't understand. It didn't matter. He was too far gone to go anywhere or do anything.

Logan followed du Plessis and Faraday back to the car. Sanchez was asleep, her head turned to face the door, snoring gently. They reached down and eased her out. There was no point in trying to help her to walk, so du Plessis scooped her up in his arms and crossed the short distance back to the veranda and the room.

He laid her in a chair.

Faraday paused at the door. "What do you want us to do now?"

"You're done," Logan said. "You can go."

They didn't question him, nor ask what the rest of his plan would entail. They would be able to join the dots if they read the news tomorrow, but Logan was unconcerned. They were paid well and loyal to the government. They had no idea who either of the people on the bed were, nor the reasons for Logan's attention to them. For all they were concerned, they might be enemies of the state, deserving of whatever might come next.

Logan waited for them to go and then went back outside to the car. He opened the door and took out the plastic bag with the items that he had purchased earlier that afternoon. He took the bag inside, closed the door, turned the key and fitted the safety chain. He did not want to be disturbed.

Milton hadn't moved. Logan crossed the room to the bed and looked down at him: he was breathing easily, in and out, his eyes closed. It looked as if he was asleep. The roofies contained flunitrazepam and were ten times more powerful than the diazepam found in Valium. It relaxed the muscles, reduced anxiety, and had a strong sedative effect. It also produced a strong amnesia, which was one of the reasons Logan had chosen it over the alternatives.

Logan addressed the room.

He had things to do.

He took off his jacket, hung it on the edge of a chair, and swept his hand down it, straightening out the creases. He went over to the suitcase and opened it, carefully rifling through the clothes that Milton had brought with him. A spare pair of trousers, a crumpled T-shirt, underwear; he was travelling light. There was a book inside the suitcase. Logan took it out. It was dog-eared and bore the signs of being well thumbed. It had a deep blue cover, with the words *Alcoholics Anonymous* written across it in bold white type. Logan flipped through the pages. There were words written in the margins and passages that had been picked out in faded yellow highlighter. He glanced over at Milton and thought of his pitiful existence in London, his minimum-wage job and the meetings with other drunks, where they would open their hearts and wallow in self-pity.

He still couldn't connect the reality of what John Milton had become to the details of the exploits that he had read in his file. Why had he been so nervous? Milton was a husk of a man. Hollowed out. Weak. Pathetic. Perhaps Logan was what Milton had been ten years ago. One thing was sure: he was more than his match now, and he had proven it.

Logan took the bottles and cans from the bag and stood them all out on the table.

Twelve cans of Red Horse.

Two bottles of Grasovka Bison Grass vodka.

He took one of the six-packs into the bathroom, pulled the ring pull on each of them and poured the contents down the sink. He took the empties into the bedroom and dumped them in and around the bin.

He collected one of the bottles of vodka, cranked off the lid and poured it out over the bed. He tipped a little over Milton's chest and then rested the bottle on the edge of the bed, allowing it to glug out onto the floor until it was half empty.

Milton did not stir.

He took the other bottle and dropped it on the tile, the liquid splashing everywhere, rivulets that ran around the shards of freshly razored glass.

One more thing to do.

He turned to Sanchez. She was still asleep. Her head had fallen back, exposing her long and shapely neck. He crossed the room until he was standing over her. She had been useful to him. Her desperation for money and her previous closeness to Milton had combined in a fortunate intersection, but her utility was coming to an end. She had done well, but she had one last role to play. It was unfortunate for her, but necessary. Bad luck. Logan didn't care.

A strand of hair had fallen over her face. Logan reached down and gently pushed it away with one gloved finger.

He leaned down and eased the girl onto the floor. She stirred a little, snuffling in her sleep, but she did not wake. Logan knelt down on either side of her body, her loose arms pinned to her sides by his knees. He reached for her throat with both hands, his fingers on either side and his thumbs meeting over her larynx.

And then he squeezed.

Her eyes opened, bulging with panic, but there was nothing that she could do. He was too strong and her body was deadened by the sedative.

Logan pressed down hard until the muscles in his arms locked.

It didn't take long. Her weakness meant that he could be precise, placing his thumbs to ensure that he cut off the flow of blood to her brain.

Ten seconds.

She stopped her gentle struggling and lay still.

Logan kept pressing down for another ten seconds and then he relaxed his grip.

He stood.

He took the girl by the wrists and dragged her body across the room. He left her in the tiny bathroom. He inspected her throat: red shadows from his fingers were already evident, darkening as the bruises slowly started to form.

Milton had not stirred. He was snoring more loudly now. Logan looked at him and thought how easy it would be to kill him now. He was as helpless as a baby. Logan's profession usually required the death of his target, but Logan had not been paid to kill Milton.

Quite the opposite.

He checked the room one final time and, satisfied with

his work, he opened the door and stepped out onto the veranda. He pulled the door to, not quite closing it, and then crossed the lot to his waiting car.

Part Two

Chapter Fourteen

POLICE OFFICER Josie Hernandez watched as the suspect was loaded into the back of the squad car. Her partner, Manuel Dalisay, shut the door and went around to the front. Ideally, she would have gone back to the station with the suspect, but manpower within the department was a serious issue and she knew that she would have to take care of the crime scene until the lab technicians arrived.

"Put him in the cells until I get back," she called out to Dalisay.

"No problem."

It was a hot morning, already up in the high nineties with stifling humidity. It had been hot last night, too, and Josie's two-year-old son had been unable to sleep. Josie had lain on the floor next to his crib until the boy finally drifted away, but she had found it difficult to sleep herself after that and had eventually given up, taking a shower and getting into the department two hours earlier than usual.

Her career had taken a turn for the better over the course of the last month. She had been promoted from Police Officer 1 to Police Officer 2. She was a good cop, but she knew that the promotion was as much about expediency as about her talent. The streets of the capital had been swamped with vigilantes tempted by the promise of bounties if they prosecuted the president's war on drugs, murdering the men and women who had been put on semi-official kill lists for their alleged involvement in the drug trade. Those slayings all needed investigating, even if they were almost always signed off without the killers being brought to justice. Duterte had vowed to clean the streets with the same brand of outlaw justice that he had unleashed in the twenty-two years he had served as the mayor of Davao. They said that his death squads were responsible for nearly fifteen hundred killings in the once-lawless southern city, and his hard-line attitude had been responsible for his election. They called him 'Duterte Harry,' and it was an appropriate sobriquet. He could back it up.

She took out her handkerchief and mopped the sweat from her face. The door to the hotel room was still open and she went back inside. The room stank of alcohol. She saw the bottle on the table and the broken bottle on the floor, and, as she made her way farther inside, her boots squelched through the sticky residue on the floor. There must have been some party here last night.

There was a small suitcase parked at the side of the room. She took a pair of latex gloves from her pocket, pulled them on, and went over to it. The lid was unzipped, and she opened it. There were clothes inside: a pair of jeans, a pair of shorts, two plain T-shirts and a plain black shirt. She left them as they were.

There was a thick blue book titled *Alcoholics Anonymous* with a subtitle that announced "This is the Third Edition of the *Big Book, New and Revised*. The Basic Text for Alcoholics Anonymous." Josie riffled the pages, noticing that the corners of several had been folded back and that inked annotations had been made in the margins.

Whoever owned that book had fallen off the wagon in a big way.

She turned to the bed. There was a pack of cigarettes on the bedside table and a vintage black cigarette lighter that looked expensive. There was a scattering of banknotes and a cigarette that was floating in a finger of vodka.

There was little to go on. There was nothing to identify the man who had been arrested. He would be searched when he reached the station; he was a westerner, and the suitcase suggested that he was here for a visit, so they ought to find a passport at the very least.

She stood and went over to the bathroom.

She guessed that the victim was in her early thirties. She had been beautiful, but her beauty had been marred by the obscene red welts around her throat.

Josie wasn't in the habit of leaping to conclusions, but it was difficult to look past the obvious explanation for what had happened in the room last night. There had been drink, too much drink, and an argument had become physical, and then, eventually, deadly. She looked down at the body again and then turned to gaze out the door as Dalisay put the car into gear and set off.

No, Josie thought. This wasn't going to be difficult. The only thing to do would be to find out the names of the killer and his victim.

Chapter Fifteen

JOSIE STEPPED back outside into the heat. The crime scene technicians had arrived and, after a quick explanation of what they would find, she surrendered the room to them and walked the short distance to the hotel office. It was a small hut on the other side of the parking lot, and by the time she had reached it she was sweating again.

There were three people in the office. The manager had met Josie when she had arrived. He was a nervous man, forever kneading his hands together and picking at the loose edge of a fingernail. A murder on his property was cause for concern; perhaps he was worrying about the effect it might have on his business. There was a woman next to him and, from the way she fussed and fluttered around him, Josie guessed that it was his wife. The third person was dressed in a maid's uniform: a light brown jacket and loose trousers with flip-flops on her feet.

"I'm Officer Hernandez," she said. She indicated the two women. "Could you tell me who you both are?"

"I am Mrs. Santos."

"My wife," the manager added redundantly.

"And I am Vilma Cruz," the maid said.

Josie turned to the maid. "You discovered the body?"

The woman nodded.

Josie nodded back toward the room. "There must have been some party there last night. Two bottles of vodka."

"I don't know," the manager said.

"Did anyone complain?"

"No," he said.

"There was no noise?"

"No one has said anything."

"Were the rooms on either side occupied?"

"Yes. The hotel is full. The holiday."

Josie nodded. Tomorrow was Independence Day, the public holiday that marked the national Declaration of Independence. People descended on Rizal Park from all around the country so that they could join in the festivities. All of the hotels would be full.

She turned to the maid. "Tell me what happened."

"I came to clean the room," she said. "The door was open a little. I knocked and there was no reply, so I went inside. The man was on the bed. I saw him. Asleep. I was about to leave when I saw the woman…" She stopped, her lip trembling.

"And next?" Josie said. "What did you do after that?"

"I think I screamed. The shock. I…" She paused, swallowing as she tried to compose herself. "I have seen many strange things in rooms like these, madam, all across the city, but I have never seen a dead body before."

"You ran?"

"As fast as I could. I went to the office and told Mr. Santos what I had seen. He called the police."

"Did you go into the room, Mr. Santos?"

"No," the man said. "Just to the open door. We went back and waited in the office. We could see the room from there. No one came in or out."

Josie looked through the window to the row of rooms. She saw a camera flash through the open door. The investigators were collecting their evidence.

"When did he check in?"

"Yesterday," the manager said. "In the afternoon."

"What was he like?"

"Friendly."

"You spoke to him much?"

"A little. He mentioned the weather. It was very hot last night."

"Do you know his name?"

"He registered under the name of Smith. He's English, I think."

Chapter Sixteen

JOSIE PUT her notebook away and went back to the room where the body had been found. The dead woman had been zipped into a body bag and placed onto a gurney. Josie stepped aside as the gurney was wheeled out of the room, into the parking lot and toward the open doors of the waiting mortuary wagon.

The crime scene investigator was a middle-aged woman who was always disturbingly cheerful—strange, given the number of crime scenes and dead bodies that she was responsible for examining every week. She was supervising a young colleague, who was dusting the bathroom for fingerprints.

"Good morning," the woman said as she noticed Josie standing in the doorway.

"What did you find?"

"Not too much to say about this one, really. We've got plenty of prints, but most of them will belong to people who were staying here before. It'd be a nightmare to try to track them all down."

"You think that would be necessary?"

She smiled and shook her head. "Not really. Pretty obvious what's happened. The two of them come back here with a couple of bottles of vodka, they get drunk, they fight, it gets out of hand and…" She let the sentence drift off and spread her hands expressively.

"Will they do an autopsy?"

"I doubt they'll bother. The morgue's backed up, and they're only looking at ones that are important or where something's unclear. That's not the case here. This one is obvious. She was strangled."

"You've taken your pictures?"

She nodded. "Of course. We've got everything we need.

We'll finish up on these prints and then we'll hand the scene back to the hotel. The manager's been waiting for us to finish. He says he can't afford for the room to be left empty." She laughed. "Can you believe that? He's going to try to let it out again tonight."

"Holiday tomorrow," Josie said. "He says he's full."

The woman's assistant shone a black light around the bathroom, satisfied himself that he had taken the relevant prints, and started to pack away his brushes and powders.

"I'll have a report for you in a couple of days," the woman said. "It'll be short."

"Thanks."

Josie watched them as they loaded their equipment into their car. She noticed a small camera fixed to the underside of the ceiling of the veranda. She looked more carefully and saw that there were two of them, each pointing in opposite directions. She stood back and considered the arc that they would be able to cover. One of them was pointing almost directly at the door to the room. This case was so obvious that she didn't need a break to solve it, but the footage would be useful for the purposes of confirming what she already knew.

The manager and his wife were watching at the edge of the crowd of ghouls who had gathered to observe the scene.

She went over to them.

"It is finished?"

"Finished," Josie said with a nod.

"Is there anything else?"

"You said his name was Smith?"

"John Smith. He said he was from London."

"How did he pay?"

"He booked online and paid cash."

"Do you have his address?"

"No."

"Anything else, Officer?" the wife said. "We are very busy. We'd like to get back to work."

Josie pointed over to the cameras that she had seen.

"Do those work?"

"Yes," Mr. Santos said. "We have had problems in the past. There were—"

"There were *problems*," Mrs. Santos cut him off, presumably uncomfortable with discussing the prostitutes and pushers that Josie suspected were the reasons for the difficulties and the installation of the cameras.

"I'd like to have a look at the footage."

Mrs. Santos sighed. "Is that necessary? I thought it was obvious what had happened."

"I think it is, but I like to be thorough."

"Can you do it?" Mrs. Santos said to her husband, her tone clipped and impatient.

"I'll have to set it up for you," the man replied. "Can you come back tomorrow?"

Josie had to come by the hotel on her way back to her mother's house in Alabang.

"Get it ready for tonight," she said. "I'll be here at eight."

#

LOGAN WATCHED. He had been listening to the police radio and had heard the report of the murder as it was called in. He had arrived at about the same time as the responding officer. She was a woman and, he noted to his satisfaction, she looked young and inexperienced. That was good.

A small group of onlookers had gathered to gawp as Milton was hauled out of the room, taken to the police car and driven away. Logan had parked his rental at the other end of the lot. The sedan had tinted windows, and he knew that he would not be visible from the outside. He waited there for another hour, watching as the police officer went back and forth between the office and Milton's room. The girl was wheeled out of the room on a gurney and loaded onto the back of the mortuary wagon. Logan waited. The man and woman who owned the guesthouse came out of the office and hovered at the fringe of the onlookers.

Logan was happy. Everything was as he wanted it to be. He put the car into drive and slowly drove away.

#

JOSIE GOT into her car and set off for the station. She waited until she had merged into the heavy traffic and made a hands-free call to her mother.

"Hello? Josie?"

"Hello, Mama. How is Angelo?"

"He is good."

"What time did he wake?"

"An hour after you left. He was asking for you."

She drummed her fingers on the wheel. She knew that her mother meant well, that she was trying to say that Angelo missed her, but every reminder of the fact that she couldn't be there for her son was a fresh wound.

She and her husband had decided that she would stay at home to look after the child for the first few years of his life, putting her own career on hold until he was old enough to start school. It was a sacrifice, but she wanted to be there and it was one that she was prepared to make. It was a fine plan, but life had taken a different turn. Her husband had run off just after Angelo had been born. He had told her that he wasn't cut out to be a father, that he had too much life to live and wasn't prepared to accept the changes that his son's arrival would require. Josie wasn't one for sentiment and had written him out of their lives as soon as he had moved out. She had guessed that he was cheating on her and, once he had confirmed it, her trust had died. She didn't try to change his mind. Instead, she cancelled the rent on their tiny flat in Taguig and moved in with her mother in Alabang.

Her husband had been arrested shortly afterward on suspicion of drug offences. There had been insufficient evidence to charge him and he had been released. His body had been found in Pasay one week later. He had been killed by one of the execution squads; a note on his body said: "I am a pusher. Don't follow."

Her promotion had come shortly afterwards. It led to a small increase in Josie's salary, but the extra money had not, so far, made up for the increase in her workload. She left her mother's place at six in the morning, before Angelo was awake, and returned at eight or nine at night, long after he had gone to sleep. She would eat her dinner in his room, staring at him inside his crib as she ate the meal that her mother had prepared for her.

"What time will you be home tonight?"

"Late, I think."

"Josie—"

"It can't be helped, Mama. There's been a murder—"

"There's always a murder—"

"And I have to interview the suspect."

"Don't you think you should see your son?"

"I want to," she said, her fingers tightening on the wheel as she tried to keep her tone civil. "But he needs me to make a living."

"He hasn't seen you for—"

"Look, it might not take long. It should be an easy one. This man was asleep in the same room as the victim. It looks like they'd both been drinking. I'll speak to him. I doubt we'll be looking for anyone else. Maybe I can be home in time to put him to bed."

"Try, *anak*. He misses you."

"I miss him, too."

She ended the call and swallowed down on a dry throat. It upset her to think of Angelo. She wanted to be with him, but she had to find the money to raise him, too.

It was a fifteen-minute drive from the guesthouse in Pasay to Police Station 4 in Pio Del Pilar. The traffic was thick on Bautista Street, and Josie cranked the malfunctioning fan all the way to the max in an attempt to get some cool air into the cabin. She had a lot to do, and she just wanted to get started.

Chapter Seventeen

POLICE STATION 4 was next to the crossroads where Vicente Cruz Street crossed Tuazon. Railway lines crossed the road to the left of the building and there was a hissing and popping lattice of electrical cables and telephone wires overhead. The building itself was small, a white-painted two-storey construction with the window frames and the balcony on the first floor all painted blue. It was surrounded by a low blue wall with taller white railings attached to it, and the entrance was shielded from the sun by a white awning with the words SERBISYONG MAKATOTOHANAN advertising the government radio initiative that was designed to teach the public how to prevent crime. Josie went under the awning and had the same thought that she always had: it was difficult to expect the public to take such measures seriously when there was so much municipal crime and corruption all around them.

She waved good morning to Gloria, the woman behind the desk who almost single-handedly ensured that the station ran efficiently, and went through into the back.

Bruno Mendoza was in his office.

She picked up her pace as she approached the open door, hoping that he might not see her.

"Josie," he called out, "could you come in for a moment?"

Mendoza was Josie's commanding officer. He was an inspector and had clawed his way up to that rank after a twenty-year career distinguished only by a tenacious desire to advance himself, and in spite of rumours of graft that had never been adequately proven. Everyone knew that he was also involved in the semi-sanctioned police death squads. No one would talk about it openly, but it was an open secret in the locker room. Josie could guess at the membership of the team and knew that they met in the back room of Mendoza's favourite brothel to discuss their hits. The fact that he was so jolly made the fact of his involvement in something so bloody even more jarring. Mendoza was married, but he had a thing for her, an unfortunate attraction he regularly demonstrated with offers of dinner that she found increasingly difficult to turn down with grace.

She stepped into the office. "What's up, Bruno?"

"You picked up a murder this morning?"

She nodded.

"Bad luck."

"This isn't going to be a difficult one."

"Go on."

"Maid goes into a room, sees a man asleep on the bed and a dead body in the bathroom. There's booze everywhere. Pretty obvious what happened."

"Drunken fight?"

She nodded.

"He's English?"

"Yes, sir. How do you know that?"

"I was in the yard when they brought him in."

"I'm going to interview him now. Is there anything else?"

"How's Angelo?"

"He's fine," she said, suppressing the usual shudder as he fumbled an attempt at intimacy.

"Are you taking him to the park tomorrow? They're saying the parade is going to be something special."

"I don't know," she said. "I haven't worked out what I'm doing yet."

"If you need to leave early, that would be okay." He shuffled papers. "I'm going to be there. I'd love to meet him."

"Let me think about it," she said, her skin prickling with discomfort.

"Fine," Mendoza said, grinning at her. "You do that."

"I'd better get in there."

"Let me know how it goes."

Josie said that she would, left the office and—grateful to be away from him—went to her desk to collect her notes and her voice recorder.

Manuel Dalisay was waiting for her.

"How was he?" she asked.

"Didn't say a word the whole time."

Dalisay had a paper bag of jellybeans and he offered one to Josie.

She took it and put it into her mouth. "What do you make of him?"

"Cold," he said. "I saw him looking at me in the mirror. Dead eyes. Freaked me out."

"I'm going to interview him now."

"Good luck with that."

She started away from the desk and then turned back. "I forgot to ask," she said. "How was the party?"

Dalisay and his wife had been struggling to have a child for years, and, in something of a miracle given that Dalisay's wife was in her early forties, a little girl had finally been born a year ago. They called her Mariel. Yesterday was her first birthday party.

He smiled. "It was good. I got there late, which didn't go down well. You remember that shabu lab near Arayat?"

Josie remembered it well: two trailers off the road to Magalang, east of Route 8, in the middle of nowhere. They had busted it six months earlier.

"What about it?"

"We went back yesterday morning. They were using it again. Can you believe it?"

"The Chinese?"

He nodded. "The same crew. Eight of 'em this time. We only found out when they blew one of the labs up and the smoke was reported." He reached down for a jellybean. "Anyway, by the time we'd wrapped that up and got back down to the city I was twenty minutes late. I thought Mary Grace was going to kill me, but the party was so good she forgot all about it. Lucky me, right?"

"I'm pleased it went well," Josie said. She reached into the open bag, snagged another candy and popped it into her mouth. She tapped the recorder with her finger and headed to the station's solitary interrogation room.

Chapter Eighteen

JOSIE LOOKED through the peephole. The room beyond was sparsely furnished, with just a table and two chairs and a bench seat against the far wall. There was a single barred window, and a naked lightbulb above the table flooded the space in harsh white light. The man was sitting at the table. His wrists were cuffed and the chain was attached to a bracket on the table. Josie would have been nervous at the prospect of a solo interrogation when she first started, but she had done so many by now that it had become commonplace. And, in a case like this, it wasn't as if she would have to be inventive in order to secure a confession. That wasn't necessary. This interview would be almost entirely administrative.

She unlocked the door and went inside.

The man looked up.

"Hello, sir," she said.

He gave a shallow nod. She looked at him: he had dark hair, a single comma of which uncurled over his forehead. She guessed he was in his mid-forties, with the usual lines and marks at the corners of his eyes, the edges of his mouth and nose. It was his eyes, though, that caught her attention: they were blue, icily cold and dispassionate. Dalisay was right. He was cold. He looked up at her and she had to swallow down a twist of apprehension.

"You're English?"

"Yes."

"Do you speak Filipino?"

"No."

"I can speak English a little. Tell me if you don't understand me."

"I understand you."

She took out her recorder and laid it on the table. "I'm going to use this," she said.

He shrugged.

"What is your name?"

"John Smith."

"I'm Officer Hernandez. I'm in charge of the investigation into what happened at the hotel."

Smith nodded, but said nothing.

"Have you been offered a lawyer?"

"I don't want one."

"Are you sure?"

He nodded.

"Suspect confirms with a nod that he is not requesting a lawyer," she said for the benefit of the recording.

"What do you do, Mr. Smith?"

"I'm a cook."

"And what are you doing in Manila? Holiday?"

"Something like that."

"I think you should talk to me about what happened."

The man looked straight at her but didn't speak.

"Mr. Smith?"

There was an expression of disconsolation on his face. She had interviewed many suspects over the course of her career, and their reactions could be easily categorised: anger from those who knew that they had been caught, slyness from those who thought that they were clever enough to talk their way free, confusion and despair from those who often turned out to be innocent. Smith's reaction was more akin to confusion, but there was more to it than that.

"Mr. Smith?"

"I can't remember what happened."

"What do you mean?"

"You can ask me whatever you like. I'll answer honestly as best I can."

"But…?"

"There are long stretches of yesterday evening that I can't remember."

"So tell me what you do remember. Let's start with that. Who was the girl?"

Smith sighed, splayed his fingers on the table and looked down at them. "Her name is Jessica Sanchez."

"How do you know her?"

"We were in a relationship. A long time ago. Years."

"So why were you with her last night?"

"She said that she wanted to speak to me. She said it was important."

"About?"

"I'd rather not say."

"You're not in a position to be selective with the questions you answer, Mr. Smith."

He paused and then decided to speak. "She said that she had a child and that the child was mine."

"And what did she want? Money?"

"I don't know," he said.

"You didn't talk about it?"

"I don't remember what we talked about."

She felt frustration. Smith's attitude was honest and confronting, all at once. He wasn't doing himself any favours. "What *do* you remember?"

"I remember getting to the hotel, checking in, going to my room. I went to Intramuros and Binondo and then I went back to the hotel. I'd been out all day, so I was hot. I took a shower, listened to music for a little while and then got changed and went out. I was hungry, so I bought *kwek kwek* from a street vendor and then I went to the bar."

"Which bar?"

"The Lazy Lizard."

"In Poblacion?"

He nodded. "Jessica was there when I got there."

"What time was this?"

"Eight."

"And then?"

"We spoke."

"About?"

"Small talk. Nothing in particular. We hadn't seen each other for a long time and there was a lot to catch up on."

"But not the child?"

"I don't remember."

"So you had a drink?"

"I don't know."

"But you got drunk."

"I don't remember ordering anything other than orange juice."

"There were two empty bottles of vodka in your room, Mr. Smith. Cans of beer, too."

"I know. I saw them. I don't remember buying them."

"Are you an alcoholic, Mr. Smith?"

He stared at her. "Did you find my book?"

"Answer the question, please."

"Yes, I am. I haven't had a drink for several years."

"Until last night."

"I can't remember."

"You keep saying that, Mr. Smith. It's not helping you. Unless you tell me what happened so I can investigate it, I'll have to fill in the blanks from the evidence. If I do that, you're going to be charged with murder."

Smith paused; Josie could see that he was considering what to say next.

"When I was drinking," he said, "I used to have blackouts. They don't affect everyone who drinks, and those who are affected get them in different ways. I used to get them very badly. I'd wake up in places with no idea how I'd got there. I'd wake up with women and I didn't know their names. It was embarrassing, and, in the end, it got to be frightening. It was one of the reasons that I stopped drinking."

"You think the reason you can't remember what happened is because you blacked out?"

"I can't think of another reason."

"I'll be honest with you. At some point between you meeting Miss Sanchez at eight and the cleaner coming into your room this morning, she was killed. At the moment, Mr. Smith, it looks very bad for you. Unless you can give me another reason why she was found dead in the bathroom while you were asleep, I'm not going to have any choice other than to charge you. Can you do that?"

"I can't," he said. "I don't know what to say. I can't remember."

"Fine."

Josie stood.

He looked up at her. "What will happen next?"

"You'll be moved to a detention facility."

"And then?"

"If you're charged, you'll go to trial. For a case like this, you won't have long to wait. A month, maybe. You'll need to find a lawyer."

"Do I get a phone call?"

"Who would you like to call?"

"A friend. I need to tell him what's happened."

"Yes," she said. "Of course. I'll speak to someone for you."

She slid the chair back beneath the table. The interview had been disconcerting. The man's attitude confused her: he was open about his memory problems when most would never have admitted to them; he answered her questions with seeming honesty; and, above all, he was fatalistic.

Josie found that unsettling.

"I'll arrange your call," she said.

She opened the door, stepped outside, and locked it again.

Yes, she thought. It was the fatalism that had perturbed her. It was, she realised, as if Smith couldn't remember what had happened but that he was refusing to give himself the benefit of the doubt. It was almost as if a murder was something that he could consider himself doing.

Chapter Nineteen

MILTON WAS taken from the interview room to a smaller room, where he was photographed and had his fingerprints taken. The officer asked him to undress, and then he was photographed again. They took swabs from his mouth, scraped out the material from beneath his nails and then took blood.

Milton cooperated without complaint, but it was an intensely uncomfortable experience for a man who had been so used to sliding beneath the surface of things; the last time he had been arrested, the Russian secret service had located him and sent an agent to the Texan jail where he was being held in order to bail him out. There were people who would have given a lot to know where he was now, especially when he was so compromised. He was travelling under false papers, but that was no guarantee that his anonymity would be maintained. His legal predicament was bad enough, but, beyond that, he was vulnerable in so many other ways.

They went through his possessions. They took his fake passport, his wallet, the Ronson lighter that his father had given him, his cigarettes and the handful of loose change that he had collected in his pockets.

He did not protest and, once the formalities of his booking were completed, he was led down into the basement of the building to a holding cell. It was a twenty-by-twenty space with a set of substantial iron bars that divided the room into two. Two cameras had been fixed to the ceiling, their motors buzzing as they panned left and right to take in all of the room. Milton looked through the bars at the collection of men staring back at him. The cage was full to overflowing, with the bench seats around the sides all taken and another ten or so milling around in the centre. The occupants glared with baleful malevolence as his cuffs were removed.

There were just two officers down here: the man who had brought him down from the custody suite and the officer who was in the basement to watch the detainees. Both men were armed, but neither moved with the caution that would have been prudent; they would have been much more careful if they had an inkling of Milton's past and the things of which he was capable.

The custody officer unlocked and opened the cage door.

Milton saw the butt of his pistol jutting out from his holster and knew how easy it would be to relieve him of the weapon. He felt the prickle of adrenaline, the itch in his palms, but he drew in a breath and allowed the moment to pass.

This was not the time to make an attempt at leaving. Even if he was able to disarm the two officers, there was a good chance his actions would bring unwelcome attention. The men in the cell would likely make a noise, and then there was the matter of the two cameras overhead. He was in the basement of a police building. If he was compromised, he would have to fight his way out, through the ground floor and then out onto the street.

He might make it, but he didn't like the odds. And he would have to kill.

He wasn't prepared to do that.

Chapter Twenty

MILTON TRIED to gauge the time as best he could, but it was dark in the basement and there was no window where he could assess the passage of time. Police officers came and went, delivering new suspects to be detained and taking others away again, but no one came for him. He waited for the chance to make his phone call, deciding that he would contact Hicks, but it seemed as if he had been forgotten. When he tried to speak to one of the guards to remind him that he was still waiting, the man shrugged and pretended that he didn't understand English.

There was no point in pushing it. Milton sat down to wait it out.

#

MILTON GUESSED it was another two hours before they came for him.

"Hey," the guard said, "English. Come here."

Milton stood and came to the door of the cell. "Phone call," he said, extending his thumb and little finger and putting them to his mouth and ear.

"Hands."

The guard opened the slot at waist height and told Milton to slide his hands through so that he could cuff him. Milton did as he was told and didn't react as the cuffs bit into the skin around his wrists. He withdrew his hands and stepped back as the door was pushed back.

"Out."

Milton stepped out of the cell.

"Phone call," Milton said.

"No phone call," the man grunted.

"Where am I going?"

"Transfer," he said with an unpleasant smirk.

"To where?"

"Bilibid."

"What's that?"

"Prison."

"In Manila?"

"Move."

The guard took out his baton and used it to prod Milton in the back. He walked on, the guard jabbing him between the shoulders to ensure that he kept going.

They passed through two heavy doors and then out of the building through an exit into a yard. There was a Toyota HiAce parked alongside the building. It was painted white, with the livery of the national police added in blue and red. The rear doors were open, offering access into a compartment that was kept separate from the driver and his passenger by a wire mesh cage. The guard prodded Milton in the back once again and, still biting his tongue, he reached for the door frame with his cuffed hands and pulled himself inside.

The doors were slammed shut. The vehicle was not air-conditioned and the rear wasn't ventilated. The temperature inside the cage must have been more than a hundred degrees.

There were bench seats on either side of the vehicle and Milton lowered himself onto one of them and waited for the driver and another guard to get into the front. The driver started the engine and, with a creak from its suspension, the HiAce pulled out of the jail compound and onto the road outside.

#

THE BENCH seat was uncomfortable. It was directly over the wheel arch and it vibrated unpleasantly every time the van bounced over uneven stretches of road. The two men in the front of the van spoke in Filipino. Milton was unable to understand their discussion and quickly tuned it out.

He tried to assess his situation. He located west by looking for the sun. It was in the afternoon, and he was able to judge that they were headed in a generally southerly direction. They passed signs for Makati and Taguig and ignored the turn-off that was marked for the airport. He estimated that they had been travelling for around ninety minutes at a speed of around sixty miles an hour. Milton did not know the geography of the island, but, based on his assumptions, he suspected that they were around ninety miles to the south of the capital.

They turned off the main road at Alabang. They continued, the road becoming smaller and narrower as it passed through a series of villages and hamlets. Vegetation thronged on either side and, as Milton turned his head to glance at a clutch of children watching them go by, he caught sight of a road sign. It was in English and read INSULAR PRISON ROAD. They continued for another five minutes, eventually slowing and pulling onto a driveway that terminated at a large iron gate. There was a checkpoint next to the gate and the driver wound down his window so that he could speak with the guard. The guard stepped out of the hut, put his hands to the window, and looked in at Milton. He went back to the driver, exchanged a curt word, and then opened the gate.

The van drove through.

Milton looked ahead through the windshield. They were approaching a large white building with two towers on either side. The parapet atop the walls had been crenelated and a vinyl banner had been strung up above the entrance. The banner contained a mixture of English and Filipino, but Milton was able to see WELCOME! and, beneath that, NEW BILIBID PRISON.

They drove into the main prison compound. Milton looked out and saw tall brick walls that were topped with razor wire with elevated guard posts every hundred feet or so. He saw armed guards in the posts and powerful-looking spotlights. Vast palm trees swayed outside the walls, their fronds sixty and seventy feet above the ground. The buildings were simple, whitewashed and substantial. The van followed the road around to an admissions area and, as they slowed, Milton was able to catch a glance through another gate into a courtyard, where he saw hundreds of men. They milled about in groups; some sat on the ground, while others ran or worked out. Milton saw a man in a pair of bright blue shorts lying on an improvised weight bench; he was lifting an iron bar that had been fitted to two cylinders of concrete.

The van stopped by an open entrance. Two armed guards opened the doors of the van and indicated that Milton should step down. Harsh, bright light streamed into the back of the HiAce and Milton blinked into it as he descended. One of the guards held a pair of leg irons, and he bent and closed the shackles around Milton's ankles. They were attached to a chain with just enough play to allow Milton to take a step. A second chain was attached to his handcuffs and, with Milton now duly trussed up, the guard indicated that Milton should go through the archway and into the darkened space beyond.

Chapter Twenty-One

MILTON PAID close attention as he shuffled through the arch and into a building beyond it. They were still outside the main prison compound, close enough to the courtyard that he had seen earlier to hear the sound of a basketball bouncing against the ground and the clamour of dozens of voices. Every forward step took him farther away from his liberty, but he was already beyond the point where he could have done anything to go back.

He was shackled and the guards were armed; what was he going to do?

The new building was evidently dedicated to the processing of new inmates. Papers were handed over to a man sitting behind a desk. He looked up to regard Milton, and, with a disdainful flick of his hand, he indicated that Milton should continue into the gloomy room beyond.

Milton was shoved in the back and nearly tripped, the chain clanking as it went taut and then loose once more. The guards followed close behind him as he emerged into a wide space. There was a long table with a stack of prison uniforms wrapped in plastic sheaths. In the middle of the room was a pile of shoes, each pair tied together by the laces. There was a mirror on the wall and, opposite it, a coiled fire hose with a dripping nozzle.

He was delivered into the custody of two guards. They were also armed, with pistols holstered on their belts. One of the guards stepped around and unlocked the cuffs that secured Milton's arms and legs. The man removed them, the chains ringing against each other, and Milton took the opportunity to massage his wrists.

The nearest guard looked at him with unmasked contempt. "Take off clothes."

Milton knew that he had little choice other than to

comply. He undid the buttons of his shirt and took it off. He took off his trousers and underwear and stood his ground as he was searched. The guard paused, noting the tattoos that covered Milton's body and, perhaps, unnerved by his poise and lack of fear. He told Milton to spread his legs and then bend over and, moving with practised ease, satisfied himself that he was not transporting contraband.

Milton had seen the dripping hose and knew what was coming next.

The guard pointed. "Against wall."

Milton crossed the room. The floor was sodden and the paint had been scoured off the wall. The guard took the hose, aimed it squarely at him, and cranked the tap. A torrent of freezing cold water rushed out. It pummelled Milton in the chest, driving the air from his lungs and shocking him with the sudden drop in temperature. Milton clenched his jaw, unwilling to give the guards the pleasure of seeing his discomfort. They laughed anyway, the guard with the hose training it down at his genitals and then up to his face. Milton closed his eyes and turned away so that the jet thrashed against the side of his head.

The tap was turned and the flow stopped. Milton stood where he was as the water sluiced off his body. His skin tingled.

The guard assessed Milton's size, selected a uniform from the pile, and tossed it down onto the floor in front of him.

"Dress."

The uniform was orange. Milton tore the pack open and took out the two items inside: a pair of trousers and a short-sleeved shirt. They were made from rough denim and they scratched his damp skin as he put them on. The guard looked at Milton's boots, shared a joke with his comrades, and put them to one side. Milton guessed that he wouldn't see them again. The guard took a pair of sneakers from the pile and tossed them over. They were old, with a hole in the upper and cracks in the tread. Milton put them on. They were a little small, but not unbearably so; he decided that he would make do rather than invite them to give him a pair that was even more uncomfortable.

There were other items on the table, and Milton was instructed to take one of each: he collected a cotton blanket, a threadbare sleeping mat of woven *pandan*, and a plate and mug made out of cheap, pliable tin.

The guard grabbed him by the shoulder and shoved. "This way."

Chapter Twenty-Two

THE GUARDS led Milton deeper into the prison.

They passed through the outer door of the administration building and followed a dim corridor that cut directly down the centre of the building beyond. There were barred partitions at regular intervals; the guards were able to open these with the keys on their belts. Milton looked left and right; everything he saw reminded him that his liberty had been removed: the cage doors through which they progressed; the barred doors on either side, secured with thick sliding bolts; the guards in their khaki uniforms and caps, with holstered pistols and billy clubs that hung on fabric loops from their belts.

They reached a third barrier and, rather than unlock it, this time the guards were required to speak into an intercom. Milton glanced up and saw a camera, its unblinking black eye staring down at him. There was a short conversation, unintelligible to him apart from the mention of the name 'Smith,' and then an electronic buzz as the gate was unlocked. The guard opened it, stepped to the side and indicated that Milton should make his way through.

This new room looked to be the final one before the start of the main compound. A guard wearing the same uniform was positioned behind a lectern that bore a clipboard replete with papers. Milton was put in mind of a maître d' standing station outside a restaurant, although the comparison was grotesque in the circumstances.

The man collected the transfer papers from the guard and assumed custody of Milton. He looked at the papers and typed details into the computer terminal that was on a small desk next to the lectern. Once he was finished, he gestured that the guards should bring Milton around to him. He took Milton's right hand, pressing his fingerprints against an ink pad, and then recorded the impressions on a slip of card that would accompany his details in a filing cabinet somewhere within the prison's bureaucracy.

He was moved to the wall and given a black strip of card that he held up to his chest. It bore a series of numbers and a letter: 13653-S.

"That is your name. Not Smith. You are 13653. Understand?"

"I understand," he said.

The guard nodded behind him to a small gate that had been opened from the inside.

Milton went through.

#

A GUARD was waiting for Milton on the other side of the gate. He was obese, his belly straining against the buttons of his khaki shirt. His skin was slick with sweat; there were damp crescents beneath his armpits, a sheen on his face, and droplets caught in the hairs of his moustache.

"Welcome to New Bilibid, 13653." The man laughed at that, as if he considered it to be a particularly choice joke. "Where are you from?"

"London."

"And you are a murderer."

It wasn't a question; it was a statement. Milton did not respond.

"You murdered a woman. Better hope that stays secret."

The corridor was dark and it took Milton a moment for his eyes to adjust. There were other men here: a guard, his hand on the butt of his pistol, guided an orange-clad teenager into an adjoining room; another inmate pushed a trolley that carried a bucket and mop and other cleaning implements; another prisoner was on his knees, bent close to the floor so that he could scrub it with soapy water and a brush. The man—Milton saw that he was little more than a boy—sprang to his feet and stood ramrod straight as Milton and the guard approached.

"You are used to nice things in London? Clean clothes? A comfortable bed? Good food and drink? Yes?"

Milton kept walking.

The man turned his head and spat at the wall. "You have nothing like that here. It is dirty, it smells, and the men you will be kept with will kill you if you let them."

They passed a group of four inmates soon after and, at a gesture from the guard, they dropped to their haunches and pressed themselves with their backs against the wall and their heads bent in a token of their servility.

"You will have a trial soon. And then, when you have been convicted, you will be returned here for your sentence. If you are lucky, you will go to the room where we have the injections. You should pray for that sentence. Life here, if that is what you get, will be bad in comparison."

They reached the door at the end of the corridor. The guard rapped his knuckles against it and then stepped back as it was unlocked and opened. Milton blinked as he was assailed by bright light. He had expected that his cell would be in the main building, but it was not. Instead, the corridor opened onto a wide plaza with a network of wire mesh fencing that split it into separate sections. The ground underfoot was bare, the earth cooked in the sun until it was as hard as asphalt.

The guard led Milton to a building marked with a notice as Building No. 1. It was a long building, several storeys tall and oblong in shape. The entrance was halfway down the long flank and, as they walked between two wire mesh fences to reach it, Milton counted twenty windows. Each was small and dingy, bars bisecting the dark apertures and a further screen of mesh increasing the security and, Milton guessed, reducing the light that was allowed to filter inside.

He heard a loud metallic rattle and the noise of barked orders, and, as he turned back into the yard, he saw a group of fifty or sixty inmates being herded deeper into the compound. They were shackled together, each man fitted with leg irons and then chained to the men in front and behind. They wore faded orange shorts and were shirtless, their bodies exposed to the scouring sun. Their heads were shaved and their skin was slick with sweat. The formation was shepherded by a team of guards, their batons drawn so that they could be flicked out to encourage stragglers to greater effort and dissuade those who might consider the possibility of dissent.

"You see them?" the guard said. "They are *castigados*. They have broken prison rules. Perhaps they have smuggled contraband, or they have gambled, tried to escape, or committed sodomy. They are punished."

"What kind of punishment?"

"Hard labour. They break rocks. They work in the sun until they collapse and then they are returned to isolation. They do it again until they agree that the rules must be obeyed. Understand?"

"I do," Milton said.

The guards brought the phalanx to a halt and circulated among the men, inspecting them. One of the prisoners refused to respond to a comment from the guard standing before him. The guard pulled his baton from his belt and struck the man on the shins with a downward backhand slash. The prisoner looked up and spat at the guard's feet. The guard called out, and two of his colleagues hurried to his side, their own clubs drawn. The three men struck the prisoner again and again, their blows landing on his legs and torso and against his shoulders and arms as he tried to protect his head. The man fell to his knees, but his weakness seemed only to provoke his attackers to greater effort, and they continued the beating until he was face down in the dust, blood running freely from a deep cut to his scalp.

"Inside," the guard said to Milton.

The entrance to Building No. 1 was a broad opening in the wall. There were two doors, barriers that could be slid back on runners that were fitted into the concrete. The first door was made of two pieces of solid steel and the second comprised two rows of iron bars. They had both been pushed halfway open to allow access. There was a guard slumped in a plastic chair in front of the doors. He glared sullenly at Milton as he was pushed inside.

The entrance led into a hexagonal space from which a number of corridors trailed away. There was a flight of stairs that led up to the first floor and, running directly to the left and right, was a corridor that Milton assumed must have been the main means of accessing the cells. It was blocked in both directions by iron doors that were secured with padlocks. There was a table just inside the gloom, at which sat two guards. They were engaged in a board game that Milton did not recognise, and neither paid him any heed as the guard nudged him toward the door on his right.

It was unlocked and Milton was led inside.

The corridor was constructed from bare concrete blocks. It opened out into a wide lobby that had been arranged around a flight of stairs. Milton looked up: the building was open, and the stairs ascended to the fourth floor high above. Each floor had a landing, and each landing offered access to cells. Milton looked at the cells on the ground floor: there were doors on either side of him, each made from solid metal bars that were also covered in wire mesh.

There was an open antechamber, where another group of guards was waiting. There was a brief conversation and one of the men got up from his plastic picnic chair and took a large bunch of keys from a hook on the wall. He led the way to the stairs and then climbed them to the second floor. Milton was shoved along the landing until he reached a cell on the right-hand side. The guard unlocked the door and pulled it open.

The man stepped aside. Milton didn't resist. He felt a hard shove in his back and stumbled into the darkness beyond.

Chapter Twenty-Three

MILTON'S CELL was tiny.

It was two metres deep and a metre and a half wide and was empty except for a toilet bowl that was fixed to the wall in the far right-hand corner, shielded from view by a waist-high wall made of cement blocks. Water was provided from a tap to the left of the toilet; it dripped, and a slimy puddle had formed beneath it. There was no furniture within the cell. There was just the cement floor, the cement ceiling, and the cement block walls.

There was a single window. It was high in the wall, with a sill at shoulder height. Milton went over to it. It was bisected with a lattice of sturdy bars with the same mesh screwed down over it on the outside wall. Milton looked out through the mesh. He could see a row of whitewashed buildings, with guards gathering between them. The wall of the compound was visible beyond the buildings and, looming above everything, there was a guard tower with a searchlight and a machine gun pointing over the parapet. The sun was sinking and, as it moved by degrees to the west, the angle opened so that the brightness could seep inside.

Milton realised that he was carrying his bed beneath his arm. He spread out the bedroll on the floor next to the wall. It was thin and stained, and, as he lowered himself down onto it, he knew that he was going to have a difficult time sleeping.

The light was better now, and he could make out more detail. The walls had been whitewashed at some point in the distant past and, since then, they had grown dirty and smeared. Some of the stains were from bedbugs and cockroaches that had been crushed against the abrasive surface. There were inscriptions where names and messages had been scratched into the brick.

Bayani.

Rodel.

Sayen.

Milton couldn't read the messages, but he could guess at the sentiment. There were downward scratches in groups of six, the seventh mark slashing diagonally across them to commemorate the passing of another week. Other marks were different. There were religious inscriptions. Someone had scratched an image of a woman. There was a patch of wall above Milton's head where a reddish stain had been left. There was a rough circular patch and then four vertical stripes; Milton reached up his hand and laid it over the stain, realising as he did that it was a bloody palm print.

Milton thought of the man he had seen outside and the beating that he had taken.

He was uneasy. He was different from all the other prisoners that he had seen, and he knew that would mark him out for special attention from them and from the guards. And he was accused of murdering a woman. That, too, would play badly for him.

Milton lay flat. His left shoulder was against the wall and he was able to reach out with his right hand and touch the opposite wall. It was a tiny room, but at least it was just him, at least for now. He closed his eyes and tried to remember back to his training in the Regiment. They had put him in smaller spaces than this, kept him there for hours as they tried to approximate what might happen if he was ever captured by the enemy. That had been unpleasant, but it was very different. He had known, even if he didn't know how long it would take, that the door to his cell would eventually be opened and he would be allowed to leave. He would be able to get into his car and drive into Hereford and have a drink with the other men in the Regiment.

This was different.

He knew that he was going to have to keep a low profile if he wanted to stay alive.

Chapter Twenty-Four

JOSIE BUSIED herself with her usual duties for the rest of the day. She had a backlog of three murders that had been solved, but still needed to have the paperwork completed. She checked the evidence that had been prepared for a forthcoming trial—another murder—and called the pathology unit to check whether they were going to autopsy the woman from this morning. They said that it wasn't planned. Josie thought about that and, on a whim, asked them to conduct one anyway. The clerk grumbled that they were busy but that it would be ready in the next couple of days. She told him she wanted it done faster than that, and then she rang off.

The clock ticked around to six and she decided that she had had enough for the day. She was tired and she wanted to see Angelo before he went to bed.

Her phone rang as she was getting ready to leave. She thought about answering it, but decided to let it go to voicemail. She closed down her computer, put the evidence for the trial in her bag, and, careful to avoid Mendoza, left the station. She went around to the back, slid into her car and cranked the air conditioning all the way to the maximum. She put the car into gear and set off.

#

ON IMPULSE, she decided to make a quick stop on the way home. Instead of going south to Alabang, she turned to the east and drove to Poblacion. The Lizard Lounge was a nasty-looking dive fitted with a series of crude neon signs designed to lure tourists inside. Josie parked her car beneath a yellow pint pot with BEER in electric blue and white froth that blinked on and off.

She got out, passed through the doors and went inside. She went to the bar and attracted the attention of the barman.

He came over to her. He was in his mid-thirties, with a head of long greasy hair and a sleeve of bad tattoos on his arm. "What do you want?"

She laid her badge on the bar. "I'm Officer Hernandez."

The man shifted nervously. "What do you want?" he said again.

"The owner."

"That's me," he said.

She regarded him dubiously. "Really?"

"This is my place," he said again. "What do you want?"

"Last night," she said, "were you working?"

"Yes. I work every night."

"There was an Englishman in here. Do you remember?"

"Don't know," he said, with a shrug. "We had a few in last night. The holiday tomorrow—going to be busy all week."

Josie took out the mugshot of Smith that had been taken at the station. She laid it on the bar. "This is him. Have a look. He was here. Try to remember."

The man made the pretence of examining the mugshot. "I don't know. Like I say, there were a lot of people here last night. I can't remember everyone."

"He met a woman here. It would have been around eight. Have a look again, please, sir."

The man did as he was told, screwing up his face in an approximation of concentration. He shook his head and slid the photograph back over the bar. "No," he said. "I don't remember him."

Josie watched him. People reacted in different ways when they were spoken to by the police, and nervousness was not unusual. Working in a bar meant that he probably had secrets that he would much rather stayed secret; perhaps he had arrangements with local pimps, or he was paying protection money to underworld enforcers, or he knew that drug pushers operated from his premises and he worried that that might make him a target for the president's crackdown. Whatever it was, he was anxious.

"That's fine," she said. "Thanks for looking."

The man shrugged. "Anything else?"

"Yes, actually, there is." She pointed up at the glossy lens of the CCTV camera on the wall above the till. "I'd like to have a look at the footage from last night."

The request flustered the man. "Really?"

"Is that a problem?"

"There's no problem," he said, trying to recover. "It's fine. I just need to make sure it was running."

"Could I have a look now?"

He shuffled. "No," he said. "I mean, yes, you could, but the video is in the storeroom and I just need to make sure it's okay to go in. We've just had a delivery."

He was stalling. Josie was sure now that he was hiding something. "I'm sure I'll be fine," she said. The bar was hinged at the end so that a section could be raised to gain access. She reached for it and started to push it up.

"Josie?"

She stopped, returned the hatch to its lowered position and turned.

Bruno Mendoza was behind her. He was smiling warmly.

"Hello, sir," she said.

"What are you doing?"

"Following up on the murder this morning," she said.

"Come over here, would you?"

He put a hand on her shoulder and guided her toward one of the empty tables. He pulled back one of the chairs and held it for her. She sat, clenching her jaw as he trailed his finger across her shoulder. He took the other chair and sat down opposite her.

"Why are you wasting your time, Josie?"

"What do you mean, sir?"

"The case is finished. The Englishman did it. It's done."

"I'd rather be thorough."

"It isn't necessary. The prosecutor called. There's enough to bring a case. Smith will be charged tomorrow. We don't need anything else to convict him. He did it and now he'll get what he deserves."

She bit her lip.

"What?"

"There's something about him."

Mendoza shook his head. "Come on, Josie."

"What if he didn't do it?"

Mendoza stared at her with something approaching disbelief. "What's the matter with you? He was found in the same room with the girl. He can't explain what happened. What more do you want?"

She felt unbalanced by Bruno's certainty and instinctively knew that she should be cautious. "You're probably right. I just like to make sure everything lines up."

"And that's one of the reasons you're such a good officer." He reached across the table and patted her hand. He nodded his head toward the barman. "What did he tell you?"

"He doesn't remember Smith."

"You showed him a picture?"

"Yes. Nothing."

"Anything else?"

"I asked if I could see the video from last night. They have a security camera over the bar. He didn't seem all that keen on me seeing it."

"Good idea," Mendoza conceded. "Leave it to me. I wanted to speak to him anyway."

"What for?"

"There was a killing outside this afternoon," he said. "Drugs. The usual—they found his body in an alley, tape around his head."

"What does that have to do with you?" She spoke abruptly, and, at his cocked eyebrow, she added, "I didn't think you got involved in investigation anymore."

"You know how we're stretched. There's no one else. All hands to the pump." He stood. "Go home, Josie. It's late. See your son. I'll take care of the video. We can talk about it tomorrow."

Josie said goodbye and went outside to her car. An old man had wheeled a banana-que stall to the roadside and was starting to cook. She got into the car and started the engine. Something about this case was wrong. She didn't know what it was, but there was something that was prickling at her, an itch she couldn't scratch.

She shook her head and tried to put it out of her mind. She was too tired to think about it tonight.

She wondered if Angelo might be awake when she got home. She hoped so. There was nothing that she wanted more right then than to have a long, cool shower and then to hold her boy in her arms.

Chapter Twenty-Five

A KLAXON sounded.

Milton opened his eyes and, for a moment, he didn't know where he was.

He was on his back, lying on a thin mattress that did nothing to cushion his back from the hard floor beneath it. He saw the marked walls, the single light bulb, and, as he turned his head, the bars that blocked him inside the tiny cell.

He felt groggy. It had taken him several hours to fall asleep. He had tried again and again to pierce the veil that had descended over his memory of the evening with Jessica, but, despite his best efforts, it was hopeless. He was unable to fill in the blanks between the moment that he had met her in the bar and his sudden awakening the following day.

He heard footsteps approaching and barked commands in Filipino that he didn't understand.

The guard reached his cell and drew his billy club back and forth across the bars. "Get up," the man said in English. "Bring your plate and mug. Breakfast."

#

THE CELL door opened and Milton followed the rest of the inmates as they shuffled along the landing to the stairs. They gathered there, covered by a guard with a shotgun in a glass-fronted booth above them. There was a shouted command and the men at the front of the queue started to make their way down. Milton followed, very aware that he was the only westerner in the throng.

He followed the crowd along the corridor that led away from the lobby at the foot of the stairs. He had come into the building in the opposite direction last night, so he paid close attention to his surroundings in an attempt to assemble a more complete understanding of where he was being kept. He saw an open archway that led to a large communal shower room, another that opened into a large bathroom, and then another row of barred doors that guarded cells from which the prisoners were not being released.

The corridor bent around to the right before they reached a set of double doors that had been wedged open. Beyond the doors was a large mess hall. There were four rows of tables separated by a passage that led to a serving area, with metal cabinets and a hatch where the inmates who worked in the kitchen doled out the food that had been prepared. The tables were busy with men who had already been served. There were guards around the perimeter of the room. It was noisy and raucous.

Milton joined the queue of men waiting for food. The meal was tapsilog, pieces of cheap beef marinated in soy sauce and served with eggs and rice. Milton proffered his plate to the server. The man doled out a meagre amount. Milton waited, expecting another ladleful, but the server scowled and then Milton was nudged firmly in the back by the inmate waiting behind him.

He took the plate and looked for a place to sit. The tables were busy, but he noticed one with empty spaces at one end and set off toward it.

He sat. The others around the table looked at him with undisguised hostility but, when they saw that their aggression did not faze him, they returned their attention to their food and ignored him.

Milton ate. The food was unpleasant, but he hadn't been given anything to eat since his arrest and he was famished. The men were not trusted with cutlery, so he fed himself with his fingers, the stringy meat leaving greasy stains on his skin.

He was shovelling the soggy rice into his mouth when he realised that he was being watched by the men at the next table. He looked over at them and held their gazes until they returned their attention to their food.

Milton knew that he was about to face his first test.

He finished his water, put the plastic cup on the table with his plate, and, taking a breath, he stood.

The men who had been watching him stood, too.

There were four of them. None of them was large—none of them taller or heavier than Milton—but they had the tough, wiry build of men who had nothing better to do than work out for hours every day. They were tattooed, with every inch of flesh covered in ink, and, as they got up from the table, he could see that he was in trouble. They fanned out around him, demonstrating enough knowledge of basic tactics to come at him from different directions at the same time.

He decided not to wait.

If he was going to take a beating, he would hand some out himself.

There were two ahead of him. Milton feinted in the direction of the man to his left and, as the man stepped back, he pivoted and threw a left-handed punch at the man to his right. The man was caught by surprise, and, as Milton's knuckles crunched into his jaw, he dropped to his knees.

The other men in the canteen stopped what they were doing and turned to watch. There was a moment of quiet and then exclamations of glee at the promise of free entertainment.

The other man ahead of Milton took a step back, but Milton surged forward and hammered him with a left to the ribs. The man gasped, and Milton followed up with a jab that landed flush in the middle of his face, collapsing the bones of his nose.

The inmates responded with whoops of bloodthirsty appreciation.

Milton saw the guards on the perimeter of the room. None of them looked interested in intervening.

The third man leapt onto Milton's back, looping his arms around his neck and squeezing. Milton bent forward sharply, throwing the man so that he flipped through the air and crashed down onto the table. He jack-knifed, sliding backwards and landing on the floor. Milton crouched down, jabbing his straightened fingers into the man's throat. The strike caused a spasm in his trachea, making it difficult for him to breathe.

Milton was about to stand when he saw a flash of motion to his left. It was too late to evade and he felt a crash as a chair broke across his shoulders. It shattered, wooden fragments falling all around him.

He propped himself against the table and turned to see that the first man was back on his feet again.

The man with the broken nose was also standing.

Milton glanced down at the next table and saw a plastic cup that was filled to the brim with hot tea. He swiped it and, in the same motion, threw the hot liquid into the face of the first man. He squealed in pain, clawing at his face.

Many of the other inmates had closed in now, forming a tight semicircle that pinned Milton and the two men between them and the wall. Milton glanced at the faces of the orange-shirted inmates all around him: their eyes bulged and their mouths hung open as they screamed their encouragement.

There was a tray on the table. Milton grabbed it and backhanded the man with the broken nose in the face. He went down for a second time.

Milton took a step away, looking for the fourth man, but, before he could retreat—if that was even possible—he felt a sudden blow to the side of his head. Pain flashed out and he felt blood in his eye.

He danced back. The man was at his side, opening and closing his fist.

Milton put his fingers to his brow and, when he looked down at them, he saw that they were daubed with his blood.

He felt the usual surge of adrenaline and rode it.

Perhaps the inmate noticed the steel in Milton's eyes. He took a step back, away from him, but the wall of orange-shirted men watching the display did not part, and the man was shoved hard in the back. He stumbled forward, right at Milton, and Milton put him down with an elbow to the side of his head.

That was the four of them.

Milton looked left and right, staring into the avid faces of the spectators, daring any of them to step up.

None of them did.

Milton sat down, waiting for the guards to tell him and the others what to do. He felt the throb of the blow he had taken to the side of his head, but he didn't acknowledge it. He knew that the others were watching him, and he was not about to undermine the display he had just given them by showing any signs of weakness.

Chapter Twenty-Six

IT WAS six in the morning when Josie awoke and checked her watch. She had been back in time to put Angelo to bed, but she wouldn't see him this morning. She showered and dressed, pulling on the uniform that her mother had ironed for her. She collected her gun belt, strapped it around her waist, and left the room. She stopped in Angelo's bedroom on the way out of the house. He was asleep, clutching his teddy, with his bare arms and legs sticking out of the light blanket that she had covered him with last night.

She took a slug of orange juice from a carton in the refrigerator and went outside. It was already warm; the forecast on her phone suggested that it was going to be another burning hot day.

She got into her car and set off. It was thirty kilometres from Alabang to Manila, a trip that would normally have taken her an hour. But it was Independence Day, and the traffic on the Metro Manila Skyway was already dense. She was stuck in a slow-moving snarl of vehicles five kilometres from the city as the sun rose over the grasping fingers of the downtown buildings. The temperature inside the cabin almost immediately started to increase and, as she cranked the dial of the aircon to try to compensate, she found that it was barely working at all. She slammed her fist against the console and was rewarded with a pitiful puff of air and then nothing.

She groaned and wound down the windows, prepared to breathe in the smog in exchange for a little air to circulate.

#

MENDOZA WAS in his office.

"Morning, sir."

106

He looked up and smiled at her. "Good morning, Josie. How's Angelo?"

"He's fine," she said.

"And ready for today? Did you think about what I said? I'd love to take you both to the fireworks."

"He's too young," she said. "Thank you for the offer, though."

"Another time, perhaps?"

"That would be nice," she said. She found his small talk excruciating and moved the conversation along. "Did you get it?"

"Did I get what?"

"The video. From the bar."

She saw a flash of irritation before he shook his head. "Wasn't working," he said. "The owner said it hasn't worked for weeks. There's nothing there."

"He didn't say that to me," she said. "He said—"

"I went and looked myself," Mendoza interrupted her. "He showed me the unit in the back. It's just there for show. But it doesn't matter, does it? What would it have shown us? Smith said he met the girl there and we know what happened next. I don't know why you're so interested in it. The case is closed, Josie. It's finished. Why are you pressing?"

"Because I don't think it's as straightforward as it looks."

"I disagree."

"Bruno—"

"No. Drop it. I don't want to hear *anything* else about it. File the evidence for his trial and move on. You're too busy to waste time on cases you've already solved."

She stood in the doorway, her cheeks burning and her fists clenched, but she managed to stop herself from retorting. "Yes, sir," she said. "I'm sorry. You're right."

She excused herself, pulling the door closed behind her. She clenched and unclenched her fists. Mendoza was wrong. It wasn't as simple as he thought it was. She looked right, down the corridor to her desk, but decided against it.

She turned left and started toward the way out.

She wanted to see for herself.

Chapter Twenty-Seven

SHE GOT back in the car, pulled out and headed through Ortigas toward Poblacion. She passed the jail in Quezon, so full to overflowing that it was becoming a national embarrassment. It was where Smith would be spending his time until he was tried. She navigated the traffic, plotting a series of shortcuts until she arrived outside the Lazy Lizard. The doors were closed and, as Josie drew closer, she saw that they had been fastened with a heavy chain.

She got out of her car and approached. It was obvious that something was wrong. She put her face to the window and looked inside. The room was dark, just partially lit by the glow from the neon sign for Czech beer that was fixed to the wall above the bar. The chairs had been stacked upside down on the tables. There was no sign of anyone inside.

"Not opening today."

Josie turned. The vendor who owned the banana-que stall in the street next to the bar was looking at her.

"What happened?"

"The owner."

"What about him?"

"Dead. They said he was selling drugs. Shot him as he came out last night and left him in the street right where you're standing."

Josie felt sick. "Did you see it?"

"It was a man. Shot him after he locked up and then shot him when he was on the ground. Three or four shots. Then he left. No one tried to stop him."

"Did you see his face?"

"He had pale skin. Not from around here, I think."

"Thank you," she said.

"You want to thank me, why not buy one of my bananas?"

"No," she said. "I'm not hungry."

#

THE TRAFFIC was dreadful, and it took two hours to cross the city to the Makabat Guesthouse. Josie parked in the lot, facing the room where the body had been found, stepped out and crossed to the office.

The door was ajar; she pushed it open and went inside. The manager, Santos, was standing in the middle of the room, his back facing her.

"Good morning," she said.

Santos turned at the sound of her voice. "Oh," he said. "I was about to call you again."

She frowned. "I'm sorry? Call me again?"

"I left you a message last night."

"I haven't had a chance to check my messages. What is it?"

"We were burgled." He stood and pointed to an open cabinet. There was a shelf with loose cables trailing down from it. "They took the hard drive for the cameras."

Josie went over to the cabinet and looked down at the empty space where the drive had been. "It was in here?"

"Yes," he said. "It was a cheap one. All the cables from the cameras fed into it."

Josie turned. "The door looks okay, though. Not forced."

"It was open," the man said shamefully. "With everything that was going on, I forgot to lock it."

"They take anything else?"

"We had some money to pay the staff," he said. "That's gone. And maybe some documents. I can't be sure. I haven't had a chance to check everything yet."

"When did this happen?"

"I only noticed when I sat down to go through the video for you. Could have been yesterday or last night."

Josie stood back. There wasn't much that she could say. There was no obvious reason for the man to lie to her.

"Thank you," she said.

He swept an arm around him to indicate the office.

"What about this? What do I do? I need to tell the insurance company something."

"Call the station again and ask for someone to come over," she said.

"But you're here," he said.

"They'll look after it for you."

"Can't you—"

"Call the station, sir. Goodbye."

She opened the door and stepped out into the sticky heat. Traffic rushed over the flyover, a constant hum that lodged in her brain. She heard the sound of horns as angry drivers confronted one another and then, almost as pervasive, the up and down yowling of a siren.

Josie slid back into the car, flinching from where the cooked leather touched her skin. She laid her hands on the wheel and tried to think. Something was wrong. Very, very wrong. She had long since learned to trust her instincts, that it was always worth digging a little deeper when the equations didn't add up. And this investigation, while it had been so obvious yesterday, was now starting to peel and fray at the edges. It might very well have been a coincidence that the owner of the bar had been killed just a few hours after she had visited him. It was possible that he was involved in drugs— many people were—and, heaven knew that was a dangerous occupation to be involved in these days. Mendoza had told her that there had been another killing outside the bar the same day. So, yes, it could be one of those things.

But what if it wasn't?

So much about what she had discovered was peculiar.

The way Smith had behaved during the interrogation.

The murder of the owner of the bar.

And now the missing hard drive.

Josie swung the wheel and saw Santos watching her from the doorway of the office.

She wasn't ready to go to the station yet. She merged onto Visayas Avenue and retraced her path, heading back to Quezon City.

The prison was there.
Smith was there.
She wanted to speak to him.

Chapter Twenty-Eight

JOSIE KNEW that there would be nowhere to park on the street near the jail, so she drove around the block and parked in the lot of Police Station 10. She walked across Bernardo Park, made her way to the entrance of the facility and went inside. The reception area was overcrowded as relatives of the men held inside the jail waited in line for opening hours to begin. Josie went to the front of the line, showed her badge, and thanked the attendant who opened the door to let her go inside.

She went to the office and waited in line to speak to the harassed clerk, who was trying to juggle telephone enquiries with the questions of the people waiting before her desk.

Josie waited for her to put the phone down.

"Yes?" the woman said, shooting her a withering look.

"You've got a prisoner I need to speak to. John Smith. He's English."

The woman turned to her monitor and tapped out Smith's name on her keyboard.

"He's not here anymore."

"What does that mean?"

"He's been transferred."

"When?"

"Yesterday afternoon."

"He'd only just got here!"

"I'm just telling you what happened."

"Where to?"

"New Bilibid."

Josie shook her head. "But he hasn't been convicted."

The woman shrugged. "I know."

"But that's not how it works, is it?"

"No, Officer, it's not. I did the transfer. I thought it was strange, but everything else was in order. It's not my place to argue."

"Can I see the papers?"

The clerk shrugged with a mixture of irritation and disinterest. "Hold on."

The clerk tapped another key and a printer whirred to life beneath the desk.

Josie was confused. Suspected men were always kept in Quezon City until their trial. Smith hadn't been tried. He hadn't even been charged. New Bilibid was the facility where men were sent to serve their sentences. Josie had never heard of another instance where a man had been sent there at this stage.

The woman reached down, collected the printout, and handed it to Josie.

"There. Anything else?"

"Thank you."

There was an empty chair at the other end of the room. Josie sat down and scanned through the transfer papers. She recognised the handwriting and knew who had filled it out before she reached the familiar signature at the bottom.

Bruno Mendoza.

She stared at his signature. Why would he arrange for Smith to be transferred? There was no reason for it.

Josie looked at her watch. It was half past twelve.

Smith might have been moved, but she still needed to speak to him.

Chapter Twenty-Nine

IT WAS a two-hour drive to get to New Bilibid. Traffic was fair, although the long queues as drivers tried to get into the city for the Independence Day celebrations did not augur well for her return trip. She reached down to the radio and turned the dial until she found Jam 88.3, a station that played the alternative and indie music that she liked. Green Day was playing, and she distracted herself with it as she left the city limits and settled down for the trip.

The song ended and, as 'High and Low' by Empire of the Sun started in its place, Josie's phone buzzed. She had dropped it into the cup holder and, as she reached down for it and held it up to see who was calling, she recognised Mendoza's number. She held the phone for a moment, her finger hovering over the button to accept the call.

She decided against it. She put it into her pocket and left it until it rang out.

Josie didn't want to speak to Mendoza right now.

He could wait until after she had spoken to Smith.

#

JOSIE HAD never been to New Bilibid. There was no reason why she would need to come. Her work was in assembling the evidence so that crimes were solved, the by-product of which was the fact that men she helped convict were brought out of the capital and transferred to this facility.

She pulled into the parking lot, switched off the engine and waited in the car for a moment. She knew that she was taking a chance by coming. Smith's unorthodox and unexplained transfer, and the role that Mendoza had played in that, made her more certain than ever that something was wrong.

But she was here now.

No going back. She needed to know what she was involved in.

She was opening the door when her phone rang again. She didn't even bother to take it out of her pocket. It would be Mendoza calling again, frustrated, no doubt, that he had been unable to get through to her. She let it ring out and then, thirty seconds later, felt the buzz against her hip that signified that a message had been left. She would deal with it later.

She got out of the car and set off toward the entrance to the facility.

#

JOSIE SAT down on the hard wooden chair. She rested her hands on the table, but couldn't stop her fingers from fidgeting. She must have looked nervous. Surely it was obvious to anyone who looked at her. She laced her fingers together so that she couldn't fret with them.

The visiting room was plain and sparse. She had hoped that she would be given a room with a little privacy, but that had been wishful thinking. Instead, the guard had led her through the complex to the communal meeting room, where those prisoners fortunate enough to be able to entertain visitors were allowed to meet them.

The room was busy. Josie was grateful for that. She had used her police credentials to gain entry to the compound and then to request the meeting with Smith. There was nothing unusual in that save that Smith shouldn't have been in this facility and that she had travelled from the capital to visit him. At least their meeting would be hidden among the others that were taking place that morning.

That assumed, of course, that Smith would see her.

There were two ways into the room. One—guarded by two armed men—offered visitors a way in and out of the room. The other was a pair of double doors that led into a holding area, where inmates were searched before and after their meetings.

She was wondering whether Smith would turn her down when she heard the squeak of the double doors as they caught against the vinyl floor.

A man was standing in the doorway with a guard next to him. The side of his face was blackened with an ugly bruise and it took Josie a moment before she recognised him. It was Smith. The guard pointed across the room to her table and he started toward her with an awkward gait that suggested that it was a painful effort to walk.

"Mr. Smith," she said.

"Hello, Officer."

"What happened to your face?"

"I met some of the other inmates."

"Have you—" She was going to ask whether he had reported it to the guards, but stopped herself when she realised that wouldn't have got him very far.

"Don't worry," he said. "I can look after myself." He rearranged himself on the seat, the effort triggering a wince of pain. "Why are you here, Officer? I thought you said the case was closed."

"It is."

"And you're still here."

"There are some things I'm not happy with. I'd like to talk to you about them."

He grimaced; it took her a moment to realise that he was smiling. "I'm not going anywhere. You can talk about whatever you want."

"I was looking through the evidence again. There are some things that don't make sense."

"Like?"

She glanced around the room. She knew that she was taking a risk coming here. The guards were watching, and if any of them recognised her, it might provoke questions for her that would prove awkward to answer.

She said, "Is there anything you haven't told me?"

He paused. "I don't think so. I've tried to remember what happened, but I can't."

She paused, unsure whether she should continue. Discussing her concerns about the investigation with the man who was likely to be charged was the kind of foolishness that could kill a career. Yet, she reminded herself, she had already ignored a direct order from her commanding officer and then driven all the way down here to speak to Smith. It was too late for qualms now.

"All right," she said. "I went back to the bar where you met Miss Sanchez. I spoke to the man who served you."

"Mid-thirties? Long hair?"

"And tattoos. That was the owner. He said he didn't remember you or her. So I asked for the video from the security camera."

"And?"

"And my senior officer turned up and said that he'd handle it for me. But when I checked the evidence, there was no tape. So I went back. I was going to speak to the owner again, but I can't."

"Why not?"

"Because he's dead. He was shot the night I spoke to him. It looks like a drug killing."

"But you don't think it was?"

She lowered her voice. "I don't know."

"Did you mention any of this to your boss?"

"No. Because—" She stopped.

"Because you think he might have done it," Smith finished for her.

"I don't know," she said, unable to hide her confusion. "He's been telling me I need to stop looking into your case. And then I went to Quezon City to find you. That's where you should be—everyone awaiting trial goes there. But you weren't at Quezon. They brought you here. They showed me the transfer papers. He signed them."

"You have any idea why he'd do that?"

"I don't. You haven't even been charged yet. It doesn't make sense."

Smith was quiet for a moment; the silence made her uncomfortable.

"I don't know why I came here," she said. "I was hoping you might have remembered something."

"I'm sorry," he said. "I've tried, but I can't remember anything. Everything after I got to the bar is gone."

Smith looked as if he was about to say something, but then changed his mind and looked down at his hands.

"This is ridiculous," Josie said, overcome with frustration. She stood. "Look around, Mr. Smith. You're in prison. The way it stands now, you won't be getting out of here for a very long time, and that's if you're lucky. You've got to give me more than this. I can't help you if you won't talk to me."

"There is something you could do," he said, "to help me."

"What?"

"Make a phone call."

"Not until you tell me everything."

He gave a gentle shake of his head. "I'm sorry. I've told you all I can."

"Then I can't help," she said.

She pushed the chair back beneath the table and signalled to the guard that she was ready to leave.

"Can I make a suggestion?" Smith said.

"Sure."

"Be careful."

Chapter Thirty

MILTON WAS returned to his cell after his meeting with the policewoman. He had only been there for a few minutes when he heard the sound of a guard's footsteps echoing on the metal catwalk.

The man stopped outside his cell. "You have visitor."

"Who?"

"Come," the guard snapped.

Milton thought of the policewoman again. Had she had second thoughts and come back?

The guard unlocked the door and stepped back, his hand on the handle of his billy club.

"You come now," he said.

#

MILTON CONCLUDED that he wasn't being summoned to see a visitor.

The guard was behind him, and, with sharp jabs from the tip of his club, he prompted him in the opposite direction to the visiting room, taking him instead back toward the canteen. A second guard joined them as they continued on their way. They continued until they reached an open archway. And then the guard told him to stop.

Milton had been past the room this morning and he remembered it. It was a shower room. He looked inside: it was filthy. A row of shower heads had been arranged along the left-hand side of the wall. They dripped, leaking a stream of dirty water onto a sloped floor that deposited the run-off in a gulley that, in turn, led to a clogged drain. The showers faced a series of chipped china sinks and there was an open archway in one corner of the room through which emanated the unmistakable stink of an open latrine.

The guard jabbed him in the back again and Milton stepped inside.

He turned. The guards had stayed in the corridor, and, as he stepped back, they stepped up to block the way out.

Milton clenched his fists. "What do you want?" he said.

The men stepped back and then stood aside.

A big Filipino came between them.

Milton's stomach dropped.

The man filled the doorway. Milton guessed that he gave up at least a hundred pounds to him. The big man was much taller than he was, too, with an advantage of at least four inches. The top of his head was only an inch or two from the top of the doorway. His shoulders were broad, his arms were thick with muscle and his body, while fat, was dense and solid. He looked like a pro wrestler or an NFL lineman.

Milton backed away and looked around the room. The windows were barred and there were no other exits. The only way out was through the door he had used to come inside, and now that way was blocked.

If he was going to get out, he was going to have to fight.

The big man rolled his shoulders, laced his fingers together and then cracked his knuckles. He grinned, revealing a mouth full of vulgar gold caps. He didn't speak, but, instead, he stepped all the way inside the room.

Milton took another step back. He glanced around for a weapon, but there was nothing that he could see.

The big man took another step into the room.

The guards in the corridor watched intently, their eyes gleaming with the promise of violence.

Milton launched himself straight ahead.

He fired out a right cross, putting all of his forward momentum into it and aiming for a point six inches behind the man's face. His fist drilled him and, for a moment, Milton thought that he was going to fall. He staggered to the side and was forced to reach out an arm to prop himself up against the wall.

The guards reached for their batons, worried, perhaps, that they might be next.

The big man shook his head and spat out a mouthful of blood.

Milton shook out the sting from his fist and started forward.

The big Filipino loomed up to his full height and grinned; the gold caps were stained red.

Milton charged. The man caught his fist in his big hand and squeezed. Milton's progress was arrested and, as he tried to free his hand, he was unable to defend himself against a left hand that clobbered into his ribs.

He buckled, arching to his right and dropping his free arm to cover the sudden blaze of pain.

The man yanked on Milton's arm to draw him into range and then butted him flush in the face.

Milton staggered, dazed. The man still had his hand around his fist and he yanked again, drawing Milton forward and then pounding him with a right-handed jab.

Milton saw stars and, the next thing he knew, he was flat on his back on the wet floor.

The light from the window was blocked out as the man lowered himself, his knees on either side of Milton's body. Milton saw the first blow coming, managing to cover up as a meaty right hand crashed against his forearm, deflecting its momentum so that the man's knuckles cut into the top of his scalp. The left fist followed, cracking into the side of Milton's temple, and then, his defences scrambled, another right and then another left.

Each fresh blow detonated a starburst of pain, flashes of bright white light that cascaded behind Milton's closed eyes. He tried to cover his face, but the man had taken a moment to pin Milton's right arm beneath his knee, his bulk holding it in place. Another blow—Milton had lost count of the number now—and then he felt his left arm similarly restrained.

He was helpless.

His head pounded with so much pain that each fresh impact was just an echo of the last. His ears rang, but, as the darkness became blacker and more complete, even that started to fade. The strength drained from his body and he felt his neck go limp, just dimly aware that his head was swinging left and right with every new blow.

And then even that awareness drained away, too.

Chapter Thirty-One

THE GUARDS picked Milton up and dragged him down the corridor. They took him beneath the shoulders and he allowed himself to hang limply as they left the main block and went outside. He blinked, but his vision was too fuzzy for him to make out anything beyond a blurred penumbra. He caught sight of flashes of blue as other guards went on with their business, none of them stopping to intervene.

The men took him across the main yard, through a gate in a mesh fence and into a quieter part of the compound. He raised his head a little, not enough for them to know that he was conscious but enough for him to be able to see where they were taking him. There were palm trees here and far fewer men than there were on the other side of the fence. Milton looked ahead and saw several wooden buildings. They looked like small houses: two storeys, shingled roofs, two windows on each floor and verandas with outdoor seating. If it wasn't for the fences and the machine-gun nests in the watchtowers, they might have been able to pass for large holiday chalets.

The guards changed course and aimed for one of the buildings. Milton was dragged along the ground, his toes scoring gouges through the sand. His head hung limply between his shoulders and, as he gazed down, his vision swam in and out of focus. He felt the blood running from his nose and saw the spots that fell onto the muck. His torso and shoulders ached from where he had absorbed the punches and kicks, but he didn't feel as if anything had been broken. He had been fortunate. He had been badly beaten, and there would have been nothing he could have done had the big man wanted to inflict more damage on him.

The guards climbed the two steps to the veranda and passed through the open door into a cool interior beyond.

Milton heard the whir of a ceiling fan and felt the air on his skin. He heard the sound of classical music and, in another room, the sound of muffled conversation.

The guards dumped Milton on the floor. He lay still. The men exchanged words in Filipino and one of them walked away, his feet rattling against the wooden boards. A door was opened and the sound from the next room grew clearer: the music became brighter and, beneath it, he thought he could hear English being spoken. The door was closed and the sound was muffled once again.

Milton opened his eyes. He could see the feet and lower legs of the remaining guard. He wondered whether he might be able to overpower him, but quickly disabused himself of the notion. He would still be imprisoned. There would be no way for him to get out of the compound. Struggling now would more likely make things worse for him in the short term. Far better for him to lie in wait and work out what had happened to him.

And there was no point in pretending otherwise: he wanted to know who had arranged this welcome for him.

Chapter Thirty-Two

HE DIDN'T have long to wait.

The conversation in the other room stopped and the door opened. It was left open this time, and Milton was able to identify the music as Mozart. He heard the sound of several pairs of feet as they came through into the room.

He opened his eyes and looked. There were three men in the room with him now. The guard who had helped to drag him across the compound was nearest to him. At the edge of the room, next to the open door to the room in which the music was playing, was the big man who had beaten him.

The third man was walking toward him. Milton's vision was blurred. He couldn't focus.

"Jesus, Tiny," the man said to the big man. "You didn't pull your punches."

"You told me to—"

"I know what I said," the man said. "I said soften him up. I didn't say half kill him."

"I'm sorry, Mr.—"

"Never mind. Wake him up."

The man spoke in an English accent.

Milton recognised his voice.

The big man strode across the room. Milton felt strong hands beneath his arms. He was hauled upright and dragged over to a sink. The tap squeaked as it was turned and Milton's head was jammed down into the bowl. Water splashed onto his skin and across his scalp. It brought him around and, as he blinked his eyes, he saw that the water ran red with the blood from his wounds.

The man spoke again. "Sit him down."

Milton was dragged back across the room to a wooden chair. He was dropped onto it; powerful hands locked onto his shoulders to stop him from sliding off it.

"You want a drink, John?"

Milton looked up.

His eyes wouldn't focus beyond the cup that was held in front of his face. He smelled alcohol and instinctively turned his head away.

"It's true, then? You don't drink?"

The cup was taken away and Milton straightened his head again. His head throbbed with the start of what he knew would be a brutal migraine, but his vision cleared enough for him to look at the room more carefully. It was large. The walls were concrete, although an attempt had been made to soften them with framed pictures and drapes. The floor was composed of wooden boards. Comfortable furniture had been arranged around the space: a chaise longue, a large corner sofa, a coffee table with a bottle of vodka and two glasses, a bookcase filled with books and, on the wall, a large LCD screen. This was not a cell. It was more like a villa.

A second wooden chair was drawn up opposite his and the man who had been speaking lowered himself onto it.

"Come on, John. I was expecting a warmer welcome. I haven't seen you for years."

Milton glanced up. The man was sitting, but he could tell that he would have been taller than six feet when he stood. He had a leonine build that was showing the spread of a lazy middle age. He wasn't wearing the prison uniform. Instead, he wore a pair of khaki shorts and a linen shirt. His clothes looked fresh, almost as if they had just been ironed. He might have been going on safari. His hair was neatly trimmed and he was tanned.

Milton knew him.

His name was Fitzroy de Lacey.

"Hello, Fitz," he said.

"I'm glad you remember me."

"Was all this necessary?" Milton managed to croak. "You could just have asked me to come and visit."

The man allowed himself a chuckle. "You haven't lost your sense of humour, John. That's good to see. How are you?"

"I'll be honest—I've been better."

"I'm sorry about Tiny," de Lacey said, indicating the big man behind him. "He's heard a lot about you, and then you put on a little show in the canteen this morning. Your reputation goes before you—not that it'll mean too much in here. You can fuck off now," he said to the guard, waving him away with a flip of his hand. "Wait outside. You can take John back to his cell when we've had our chat."

The man bowed his head and backed out of the room.

"You did all this?"

"Did all *what*, John?"

"*This*. Setting me up."

"That's one way to describe it."

"Why go to all this trouble? You found me… if you wanted to—"

"If I wanted to have you shot?" He laughed again. "God, no, John. That would be much too easy. It wouldn't do, letting you off the hook as easily as that. No. That wouldn't do at all."

Milton reached up and pressed his fingers to his temple. He felt dizzy.

"Look around, John," de Lacey said. "Look where you put me."

"What do you mean? This looks comfortable. You should see my cell."

"Yes, of course. I still have money and influence. You can buy comfort in a place like this if you have enough of either. Books, a television, better food, clean clothes—all of those things are commodities that can be purchased. Loyalty is the same. Men like Tiny. The guards. All the same. Of course, I can also buy the opposite for you. A cramped cell. Dreadful food. Men who will compete to make your life as unpleasant as possible and, when the time comes—and it won't come for months yet, John, not for months—men who will clamber over each other to kill you in the most painfully creative way."

"This is just to make me suffer?"

"Of course. I've been thinking about that ever since you put me in here. I want you to suffer and I want you to know *why* you are suffering. Killing you was never going to be enough. I want you to have the same experience that you gave to me."

"Logan works for you?"

"That's right," de Lacey said. "I've never actually met him. He was recommended to me. Is he very good? Must be, to have fooled you like this."

Milton ignored that. "And Jessica?"

"Surely that's obvious now, John? I needed a reason for you to travel here and then a reason for your conviction."

"I haven't had my trial yet."

"'Innocent until proven guilty'? You're not that naïve, John. You know that's a foregone conclusion. Your sentence is the only thing left to be determined. That's something else that I can purchase. I'm going to arrange for it to be life. Well," he corrected with a chuckle, "life for as long as I deem it. You'll die when I say so."

De Lacey gestured and Milton was hoisted out of the chair.

"You're going to get another beating tonight, John. It'll be the same tomorrow, and the next day, and the day after that. Every day, John, over and over and over until you can't tell where you end and the pain begins. I want you to think about me and what you did. Every time they leave you in a heap on the floor, I want you to see my face. Because I'm going to be outside, living my life. And you're finished. The only way you'll ever leave here is in a box."

De Lacey nodded and Tiny held Milton upright. He had no strength in his legs, but the man was strong enough to suspend him.

De Lacey took a pair of knuckledusters from the table. He slid his fingers inside, closed his fist, and struck Milton in the side of the face. The metal cut into his cheek and clashed against the bone. His mouth filled with blood.

"You stole ten years from me, John," de Lacey said. "You've got ten years of pain to catch up with."

Chapter Thirty-Three

MILTON WAS taken out into a yard at the back of the villa and tossed to the ground. The big man, Tiny, took off his shirt and worked him over once more. Milton covered up, protecting himself as best he could. It was mercifully brief this time, although each blow heaped pain upon pain until his body felt like one single throbbing bruise.

He was picked up and hauled back through the prison to his cell. The door was opened and he was dumped inside.

"Are you okay?"

Milton groaned.

"Hey. Wake up."

Milton put his palms flat on the floor and raised himself up. He tried to open his eyes and found that his right was already swollen shut. He opened his left eye. A man was kneeling down in front of him. He was thin, with spindly limbs and elbows and knees that jutted out from the sleeves of his orange prison-issue shirt and the legs of his shorts. His face was deeply tanned and lined with age.

Milton struggled to raise himself. The man reached down and helped him into a sitting position with his back against the wall of the cell.

He tried to speak, but his mouth felt as if it were clogged with dust.

"Here," the man said, handing Milton a plastic bottle of water. He put it to his lips and poured the water in, swirling it around and then spitting it out onto the floor at his side.

"Drink," the man urged.

Milton did, slugging the tepid water down until his thirst was slaked.

He gave the bottle back to the man. "Who are you?"

"My name is Francisco," he said. "Everyone calls me Isko. You are John, yes?"

"How do you know that?"

"I have been in Bilibid for many years. Some of the guards are friendly to me. They talk. They tell me about you. You are John. You are English. They say you murdered a Filipino girl."

The sky through the window was dark. The only illumination was from the bulb overhead.

Milton took the opportunity to look at the man more closely. He was more than just thin; he was emaciated to the point of malnutrition.

"I didn't," he muttered.

"They all say that, John."

"How did you get in here?" Milton asked him.

"This is my cell, too. They moved me here this afternoon. We will share it."

Isko gestured to the side and Milton saw a second bedroll that had been arranged on the floor. There was barely enough room for it next to his.

"You think this is cramped?"

"A little," Milton admitted.

"We are lucky. There are sixteen thousand men in Bilibid. It was built for a quarter of that. Many cells like this have six or seven men inside."

"I don't think I'm the sort of person you'd want to be around."

The old man waved that away. "You need a friend, I think. Someone to help you."

"Why would you do that?"

"Because you need it. I have done bad things in my life, John. I seek to make amends for them. I try to help when I can. And I think you need help. You have made a powerful enemy."

Milton closed his eyes and saw de Lacey's face again, the bloodlust in his eyes as he had watched Tiny laying into him.

"Tell me about him," he said.

"Mr. Fitz is a very important person in Bilibid. He cannot leave, but he lives like a king."

"I saw his place," Milton said.

"His villa? Yes, I have seen it from the outside. There are several just like it where the men with money live. His neighbours are the drug lords. They say he has parties there. The guards bring women and alcohol and drugs. He has money and power. He does not mix with the rest of us. Why should he? He has his own cook, who prepares his meals for him. And he has men he pays to protect him and to make sure that others do as he wants."

"I met one of them," Milton said, wincing as he arranged himself into a slightly more comfortable position. "Big guy. Gold teeth."

"Tiny," Isko said with a nod. "He is a dangerous man. He has killed many other men for Mr. Fitz."

Isko reached forward with the bottle and put it to Milton's lips again. "Why did Fitz do this to you?"

Milton had no interest in revealing too much to a man he had only just met. "We have history. It goes back a long way."

"Why are you in here?"

"I'm still trying to work that out."

"But you didn't kill the girl like they say you did?"

"No," he said. "I think they drugged me. Fitz set me up." Milton swallowed a mouthful of water, tasting his own blood as it went down.

"You must be careful here," Isko said. "The other men notice you because you are English. Maybe they find out what they say you did. Men who kill women do not last long in a place like this. Or maybe they find out that Mr. Fitz is your enemy, and they want to make him their friend. You understand?"

"I don't think I need to worry about that," Milton said. "Fitz wants to keep me around for a while yet. I'm going to be punished before he gets rid of me."

"I just say be careful. This is not a safe place, especially not for you."

"You should be careful, too," Milton said. "If he finds

out you're helping me, it might not go down well."

Isko smiled, revealing a mouth full of snaggled and tar-blackened teeth. "I am an old man, John. I have been here most of my life. I will never leave. What are they going to do to me?"

Milton raised a hand to his face and prodded at it. Each press and poke was rewarded with a shot of pain. "How do I look?"

"Like you have been hit by a truck. Have you eaten?"

"No," Milton said. "Not since breakfast."

"Here."

Isko handed Milton a package wrapped in paper. He opened it and looked down at a handful of dried sardines.

"It is dried in the sun and then dipped in vinegar."

He took a mouthful. His jaw ached every time he tried to chew and the food was cold and unpleasant. But he was hungry, and he knew that he would need to maintain his strength if he was going to survive. He finished the fish, screwed up the paper and put it down on the floor.

"Thank you."

Isko held up his hands. "You are welcome. Now, you should sleep. I show you around properly tomorrow."

Chapter Thirty-Four

IT TOOK Josie two hours to finalise the paperwork that set out the case against John Smith. The procedure was straightforward enough: Smith would be brought to the courthouse and given the opportunity to plead guilty or not guilty to the murder charge that would be laid against him. In the event that he pleaded not guilty, he would have a minimum of fifteen days to prepare for trial and then the trial would begin thirty days after he received the pre-trial order. The president had made it a campaign pledge to improve the efficiencies of the legal process. One way was to reduce the number of suspects who ever made it as far as trial, the trail of bodies in the streets a testament to how diligently that course of action had been pursued. The other way was to ensure that the courts ran smoothly, dispensing verdicts and shuttling the guilty into custody without delay.

Josie's evidence made it obvious that this was a simple case and that Smith's culpability was clear. She had no doubt that the case would be brought against him and that he would be found guilty and sentenced to life behind bars before the end of the month.

Yet as she studied the photographs that had been emailed to her by the crime scene techs, she couldn't dispel the doubts that had been nagging her ever since she had started investigating the events of the previous day.

The death of the bar owner.

The burglary at the guesthouse.

And the unexplained transfer of Smith from Quezon City to Bilibid.

Josie spread the photographs out on her desk. The evidence was strong. Smith had no answers to rebut the case against him. She knew, though, that he had been holding something back during their conversation. That was his choice, but it left her with no alternative but to make the case against him.

She collected the photographs, slid them into their plastic sheath and clipped them into the ring binder that she would send to the prosecutor's office tomorrow.

Josie looked at her watch. It was eight. Damn. She had completely forgotten that she had promised her mother that she would be home in time to put Angelo to bed. She would need to call her so that she could tell her that she was going to be late again.

She took her phone out of her pocket and saw that she had voicemail. She remembered: the two calls that she had ignored on her way down to Bilibid.

The phone was very nearly out of juice. There was just one message. She played it.

"Hello. This is a message for Officer Hernandez. This is Mr. Santos from the guesthouse in Malate. I forgot—we have a Wi-Fi backup for all of our data. It's in the other room. The murder, the burglary, it's made such a mess of things it completely slipped my mind. My wife insisted on it… I feel foolish for not telling you. I checked it today and it's all there. The footage you wanted. I think you need to see it. I'm no expert, but it looks like it's important. So… I don't know, call me back, please? I'll call the station. Maybe you're there. Goodbye."

Chapter Thirty-Five

SHE SAW the plume of smoke from miles away.

At first she thought it must have been because of the celebrations. The sky was regularly lit up with colour as fireworks rocketed up from the park, detonating high above the city. But, as she drew nearer to it, she saw that it was something else. The smoke stretched up into the sky, a darkening pall against the dusk. She thought nothing of it until she drew closer to Malate and she realised, with a sense of growing unease, that it was coming from the direction of the hotel.

The traffic snarled up where Leveriza Street passed to the east of the Zoological and Botanical Gardens. Pedestrians milled around, spilling into the road as they made their way to bars and restaurants and to the municipal celebrations in the park. Josie had no option but to stare impatiently as the finger of smoke slowly faded into the darkness of night.

The traffic started to flow. She pulled off the street and into the parking lot and saw that the manager's office was engulfed by flames.

Oh, shit.

A tender from the fire department was already on the scene. Firemen were arranged around the building, two of them attending to a hose that was directing a deluge of water over the flames. A crowd of men and women had gathered at the other end of the lot, kept away from the fire by the crew from the tender.

Josie parked her car at the fringe of the crowd and stepped out. The heat from the blaze was intense, even at that distance.

"What happened?" she called to one of the onlookers.

"I don't know," the man said, shouting to make himself

heard above the angry crackle of the fire. "I'm staying over there." The man pointed back at one of the rooms. "I saw smoke and then the flames. I called the fire department."

"Where are the owners?"

"I haven't seen anyone."

Fireworks boomed as they exploded overhead. Trailers of bright light fired out in all directions and rockets whistled as they arched into the night sky. The smoke piled upwards, a column that reached for hundreds of feet. There was a call from one of the men aiming the hose and then a hand signal directed back to the tender; the water pressure weakened and then stopped.

Josie walked closer to the wrecked building. The fire looked like it was out, but the heat still radiated across the lot in thick, woozy waves. The windows had been shattered and the tiles on the roof had collapsed into the building, the blackened joists naked to the sky.

She caught the attention of one of the firemen. "You got it under control?"

The man's face was covered in soot. He nodded. "It's out."

"I'm Officer Hernandez," she said.

"Andrada," the man replied, wiping the sweat and grime out of his eyes. "I'm the senior fire officer."

"What station?"

"Malate volunteers."

"What happened?"

"One of the guests called it in. By the time we got here, it was out of control."

"Any idea what caused it?"

The man shook his head. "Not yet. We'll have a look when the heat dies down."

She took out her phone, ready to call it in, and noticed that she had ten missed calls.

They were all from her mother.

A huge rocket detonated, the echo of its explosion fading into the hiss and fizzle as it scattered red and blue sparkles over the city.

Josie felt a sudden weakness in her knees.

She tapped, trying to return the call, but nothing happened. She held it up again; the screen was black.

She had run out of battery.

She turned and ran back to her car.

Chapter Thirty-Six

JOSIE DROVE south as fast as she could. Her mother lived on Summitville, in a three-storey building that had been converted into six compact apartments. It was not an expensive area of town. The street was home to a number of vendors who hawked food and drink from carts that they parked on the sidewalk, and there were always groups of customers—usually male—who gathered around them to eat and talk. The buildings were rickety, often in need of restoration, and the bright paints that had been used to decorate them had been bleached by the sun. Electricity cables buzzed and fizzed, and lines weighted down by wet washing crossed overhead.

She parked and ran to the front door. She unlocked it and climbed the stairs. She unlocked the door to the apartment and tried to push it open. She couldn't. The security chain had been fastened.

"Mama," she called, "it's me."

She heard her mother's footsteps as she shuffled down the hall. The chain was disengaged and the door opened.

"What's the matter, Mama?"

Her mother looked frantic. She reached for her and drew her into an embrace. Josie looked over her shoulder and saw that one of the knives from the kitchen had been left on the table next to the telephone and the mail.

"Mama?"

"Where have you been?" she said as she released her.

"Where is Angelo?"

"Asleep."

"Where have you *been*? I left messages for you."

"I'm sorry," Josie replied. "I've been at work and then my phone died. What's the matter?"

Her mother went into the living room. Josie followed

her to the coffee table. There was a plain envelope there. She handed it to Josie. The envelope had been opened, and, as she upended it, a single bullet dropped into the palm of her hand. There was something else in the envelope, too. She slid her fingers inside and pulled out a photograph. She recognised the building in the shot: it was Angelo's school. There was a group of children coming out of the gates and, her stomach plummeting, she saw her son staring across the road and into the lens.

"Angelo?" she said, hurrying for the bedroom door.

"He is fine—"

Josie didn't stop. She carefully opened the door, pushing it open enough to look inside. Her son was in his bed, hugging his favourite teddy to his chest, the glow of his night light falling onto his upturned face.

Josie exhaled; she felt a wave of relief so sudden and dizzying that she had to put out a hand to steady herself against the frame of the door.

"He is fine," her mother repeated, drawing her back and pulling the door closed once more.

Josie held up the envelope. "Where did you find this?"

"Underneath the door," her mother said. "Two hours ago."

"Did you see who it was?"

"No."

Josie went to the door, locked it and then attached the security chain.

"There's something else," the old woman said, taking her daughter's elbow and taking her to the window. The blinds were drawn. "Outside," she said. "The car across the street."

Josie parted the slats and looked out. It was dark, the illumination provided by the lights in the windows of the opposite building. There was a stall selling banana *lumpias* on the other side of the road, a line of empty tuk-tuk style tricycles parked alongside it with their drivers waiting to be served or bunched in groups together to talk.

"You see it? There, there!"

Josie followed her mother's pointing finger and looked farther up the street. There were seven tricycles. Behind the last one, parked up tight against it, was a black BMW with tinted windows. It was close enough to their building for whoever was inside to keep it under easy observation.

"It's been there for two hours," her mother said. "There's a man inside it. I saw him go and get food from Gregorio."

"Did you see what he looked like?"

"It's too far."

"Anything, Mama?"

"Dark hair, I think. He was wearing a white jacket."

"Stay here," Josie said, heading for the door.

"What are you doing?"

"Stay here. Keep the door locked."

She slid the security bolt, unlocked the door and opened it. She was aware that her mother was at the door, but she ignored her and started down the stairs to the entrance. She undid the retaining clip of her holster and rested the heel of her right hand on the butt of her Glock. She stepped into the damp muggy warmth of the night. The smell of the deep-fried banana and jackfruit was pungent, and the rowdy chatter of the tricycle drivers merged with the sound of the traffic on the busy road beyond the street to make a steady hum of noise. Gregorio looked up from his cart as Josie passed, but she did not stop.

A fresh volley of fireworks erupted from the direction of San Guillermo Street down by the bay. Josie closed her hand around the butt of the Glock and pulled, starting to free it from the holster.

The BMW was ten metres away. The tinted windows together with the glare of the overhead streetlamp that reflected off the glass meant that she couldn't see inside. She was five metres away when she heard the engine growl into life. The headlamps sparked on and she blinked into the sudden illumination. She took out the Glock with her right hand and held up her left, calling out for the driver to stop the car. The BMW did not stop; instead, it pulled out into the street and sped in her direction, passing her with the squeal of rubber and the roar of high revs.

Josie turned and watched as the car slowed for the junction, the taillights glowing for a moment before the driver released the brakes and stepped on the gas once more. The engine hummed and the car turned sharply to the right, quickly passing out of sight behind the corner.

She glanced up and saw her mother's face looking down from the window of the apartment. She gripped the Glock a little tighter. Her palm was slick against the polymer butt, and she could feel the perspiration running down her back. She wasn't sweating because of the heat. It was a cold sweat.

Mendoza?

He had black hair and he wore a linen jacket.

Josie was frightened.

She took the stairs two at a time and went back into the apartment.

Her mother was waiting. She stared down at the Glock in Josie's hand.

"Pack a case," Josie said.

"Why? What is it? What's the matter?"

"We have to leave."

Chapter Thirty-Seven

MILTON LAY DOWN and closed his eyes, but sleep did not come.

His mind was restless, a flashing of emotions through the static of pain.

There was relief. He had wondered whether he might have killed Jessica. At least he knew that he had not.

And there was fear.

Fitzroy de Lacey.

He remembered.

#

MILTON HAD been given a file on de Lacey while he was serving in Group Fifteen. He didn't remember exactly when it was, but it had been during the start of his descent into alcoholism. Those months and years had congealed into a vague mess, and it was difficult to peel them apart. He remembered receiving the file and being briefed by Control. De Lacey had come to the attention of the spymasters in the River House, and Milton was to be the agent responsible for bringing him down.

The intelligence had been excellent and the report was voluminous. There had been a man—a member of de Lacey's inner circle—who had fled after his son had been murdered by another colleague. MI6 had been able to flip the man, promising him retribution for his son's death in exchange for his returning to the fold and providing his new paymasters with the information that they needed to bring de Lacey to justice.

There had been a detailed portrait. De Lacey was around the same age as Milton, but the similarities ended there. He had enjoyed a privileged upbringing, the scion of an ancient family. He had been educated at Bryanston and then read law at Cambridge. He became Earl of Montgomery following the death of his father, Percy de Lacey, the nineteenth Earl of Montgomery.

De Lacey began in the aviation industry in the mid-1990s. He had moved to the United Arab Emirates to pursue his legal career and was seconded to the local offices of an air freight company that operated out of Dubai's international airport. He saw how much money the company was making despite the fact that the management—which he despised—had no obvious business acumen. He quit his job and, leveraging some of the connections that he had made while working at the airport, he recruited a pilot and rented a Russian cargo plane.

Tactical Aviation was an immediate success and, within six months, he had been able to recruit additional pilots and crew and had put together a small rented fleet of planes. He did business all around the world, with a focus on Africa. He transported agricultural equipment, domestic appliances, textiles and furniture from his base in Dubai to Benin, Botswana, Namibia, Rwanda, Senegal and the Congo. He developed contacts in Afghanistan, initially transporting Afghani textiles from Kabul but quickly increasing the variety of goods that would ship.

It was reported that he became close to elements within the government in Kabul. The Taliban was making advances from its redoubt in the south of the country, and the government was interested in resupplying its army with new weapons. De Lacey was approached by a source close to the Afghani president and asked whether he would be able to source and deliver a large amount of weapons. The profile had marked him down as a gambler and someone who was adept at thinking on the spot. He had no way to fulfil such an order, but he told the Afghanis that he could.

He then set about finding a source who could provide the goods. He had previously done business with a businessman in Latvia. The man—Mariss Gulbis—was comfortable operating in the grey area between legal and illegal trade. De Lacey flew to Riga to present him with a proposal: if Gulbis could source the weapons, he would transport them. They would share the profit equally.

The Latvian black market was swamped with weapons from the former Soviet Union, and Gulbis put together a cargo that matched the Afghan request. The continued rise of the Taliban meant that the initial contract was renewed and then renewed again. The quantities doubled and then tripled. De Lacey stopped his business in legitimate freight and moved exclusively into running guns and other weapons.

After six months, with business continuing to grow, Mariss Gulbis was shot in the street outside his apartment in Riga. Local police had no leads and, after a cursory investigation, the case was closed. It was never proven, but off-the-record sources said that de Lacey had paid a corrupt police inspector to murder his associate and then shut down the investigation.

Tactical ran into regulatory problems with the authorities in Dubai, and de Lacey transferred his business to South Africa. He found an airstrip that was suitable for his large Ilyushin IL-76 cargo planes in Polokwane, a city two hundred miles to the northeast of Johannesburg. He set up an array of companies all around the world, many of them fronts through which he could funnel his burgeoning profits so as to minimise taxes and the ability of the authorities to investigate his activities.

He had contracts with the Rwandan government to supply arms during the genocide. At the same time, another contract transported UN peacekeepers into the country. The soldiers who had travelled on his planes were attacked with the weapons that he had sold.

He did deals with the corrupt regime in Liberia.

He sold surface-to-air missiles to Hezbollah.

He sold tank rounds to the Libyan regime.

He supplied machine guns to the rebels in the Sierra Leone civil war.

The Igla missiles he supplied to rebels in Kenya were used to attack an Israeli airliner as it took off from Nairobi in 2002.

He met with Hezbollah officials in Lebanon in the run-up to the 2006 war, and documents found in the wreckage of Muammar Gaddafi's former intelligence headquarters proved that de Lacey had a commercial presence in Libya and aimed to increase his dealings there.

He was ruthless and amoral.

A fresh contract supplied the Tutsi militias in Congo. Millions of civilians were massacred. If his complicity in their deaths preyed upon his conscience, it was not apparent. De Lacey bought a palatial retreat in the south of France. He filled the garage with supercars, commissioned his first yacht, and purchased a Gulfstream to take him to and from his business meetings. Tactical Aviation grew, employing several hundred people and leasing nearly fifty planes.

But his success brought him to the attention of the authorities. MI6 took an interest and, when he was described in the House of Commons as a "merchant of death" following the discovery of a shipment of arms to the Tutsi militants, it was decided that something needed to be done. Discussions were undertaken in conference rooms in the Vauxhall Cross headquarters of MI6. Intelligence mandarins considered the benefits and disbenefits of de Lacey's continued activity. Chief among the latter was the fact that he was a British citizen and that he was working against British policy in some of the most flammable areas of the world. A decision was made and a file was created. It was sent to the shabby building nearby that was the base for Group Fifteen. The file was passed to Milton. Usually, those files spelled the imminent death of the men and women whose lives were laid out within those pages, but, when it came to de Lacey, a different course of action was proposed. He would be taken out of circulation another way.

Milton had found that curious, but it wasn't his place to ask questions.

He was responsible for putting the plan into effect.

De Lacey was to be set up and put in prison.

\#

MILTON COULD hear the sound of Isko's light snoring as he slept. The man was close; Milton could have reached out and touched him without stretching his arm. He shifted, trying to find a position that didn't press up against the tender spots all over his body. It was impossible; the mattress was too thin and he had bruises everywhere. He rolled over onto his back, folded his arms across his chest and looked up at the ceiling. The light in the cell was off, but the illumination from the lights outside meant that it wasn't close to being dark. He heard the sound of conversation from the nearby cells and, higher up, the sudden shrieking of a man in pain.

Milton closed his eyes. He tried to think. He would need to be smart if he wanted to stay alive. He would need all of his experience.

His thoughts slowed, and, eventually, his mind became fogged with sleep. He saw Fitzroy de Lacey swimming in the sea as Milton watched from his yacht. Jessica was there, too, lying on the deck in a bikini with a cocktail close at hand. She looked up at Milton and smiled.

He allowed his breathing to deepen and, finally, he slept.

Chapter Thirty-Eight

JOSIE DIDN'T get much sleep.

She woke from a light doze and fumbled for her watch on the nightstand next to her bed: it was six thirty. She blinked her eyes, slowly bringing them into focus, and saw her pistol on the nightstand, too.

It all came back to her.

She wasn't in her own bed.

She wasn't in her mother's apartment or even in Alabang.

Last night had been awful. Her mother was stubborn and cantankerous, but she didn't demur when Josie told her that they had to leave. It was a family joke that Josie was slow to panic, and she must have seen her alarm and heard the urgency in her words. Both women had packed small cases and then they had packed a third case with Angelo's things.

Josie had woken her son, scrubbing the fright from her face as she told him that he needed to get dressed for an adventure that she and his *lola* were going to take him on. He was too lost in sleep to protest and had fallen asleep on her mother's lap as Josie went outside to bring the car closer to the door of the apartment building. She had loaded the cases into the trunk and then she had waited for her mother to scoop Angelo into her arms. Josie led the way down the stairs with her Glock in her hand. She went outside first and waited anxiously while her mother carried her boy to the car and strapped him into his seat.

They had driven north, continuing for thirty minutes until they reached Taguig. Josie pulled over outside the city and, using her mother's phone, found a suitable place to stay, calling ahead to ensure that they had a vacancy and that they would be able to check in after hours. The place was on Labao Street, and Josie had entered the address into her phone and followed the directions. It was called the Napindan Castle. It was a budget B&B, clean and tidy, and she had enough money in the bank to afford two rooms for a month or two.

She scrubbed her eyes and turned over. Angelo was still asleep beside her, his breathing slow and even. The boy had been confused by the night's activities, but, once they had settled into the room, he had very quickly burrowed against her and drifted back off into a carefree sleep.

Josie wished that she might have done the same thing herself, but she couldn't; she remembered the fire at the hotel, the bullet with the picture of her boy, and the black car in the street outside the house.

She had been given a message, and its meaning was clear.

Her continued investigation into the death of the girl at the hotel had been noticed.

She was being warned off.

She lay back and closed her eyes, trying to maintain her composure. She needed to be rational.

She had spent hours last night trying to work out who might have been responsible for the threats that she'd received, and, as much as she tried to steer her thoughts in another direction, ultimately she could not.

It had to be Bruno Mendoza.

There was no question that he was involved.

He had transferred Smith to Bilibid.

The owner of the bar had died the night after meeting him.

Josie knew too much about him. She knew that he ran a death squad out of the station, a group of officers who prosecuted the president's war on drugs with a spree of extrajudicial executions. Killing the owner of the bar would have been a simple matter for him. He could have sent any one of his flunkies. The same could be said for the fire at the hotel.

She doubted that he would have any compunction in doing away with her, too, if he decided that her investigation was dangerous to him.

And he knew everything about her: that she had a son and where she lived.

She had done the right thing in leaving and coming here.

But now they were here, what next?

She had given thought to calling in sick and staying off work, but she decided that that would not help her. She was never sick, and to be away from the station now would signal to Mendoza—and anyone else involved in the conspiracy—that she was frightened. And that might suggest that she had something to hide.

No, she concluded once again. If she stayed away, she would be telling them that she had a reason to be fearful. She couldn't afford to do that.

She needed to go to work.

Chapter Thirty-Nine

ISKO WAS already up when Milton awoke the next day. He heard the sounds of exertion and, as he opened his eyes and looked over at the old man's bedroll, he saw that he was working through a set of push-ups. He had taken off his shirt and Milton could see his ribs, a corrugated pattern visible through his parchment-thin skin.

Isko noticed that Milton was awake. "Good morning," he said between push-ups. He performed another three to complete the set, dipping down so low that his chest touched the bedroll and then pushing up again. "How did you sleep?"

"Not bad," Milton said.

"The noise did not wake you?"

"What noise?"

"There was a fight last night. Two men in the cell along from this one. I saw through the door—one of them was hurt. They took him out on a stretcher."

"Does that happen much?"

"It is not unusual," Isko said with a shrug that suggested it was mundane.

The old man rose to his feet and put on his shirt.

"What time is it?" Milton asked.

"A little after six. We will have breakfast soon. How do you feel?"

Milton assessed the damage. He had been hurt, but it was superficial. His bones appeared to be intact. His face was tender and his body was sore from the kicks and punches that Tiny had delivered, but that was the extent of it.

"Better than last night," he said.

"You look worse," the old man said with a grin that exposed his disastrous teeth.

Milton managed to get his feet beneath him and pressed himself upright. He winced from the effort as he slowly straightened his back.

He heard a sudden clattering from the corridor.

"*Rancho!*" came a shouted call.

"What's going on?"

Isko stood. "Breakfast."

Milton heard the squeak of unoiled castors as the breakfast cart was wheeled down the corridor and the rattle of chains as the prisoners who were still restrained started to rouse themselves. The cart was attended to by a prisoner who, under the lazily watchful eye of a guard, deposited a bar of soap and a metal billycan of food for each inmate. There was a small opening at the bottom of the bars, and a second inmate slid the cans inside with dexterous flicks of his feet.

"We're not going to the mess?"

"Not today. Sometimes they prefer to keep us in the cells. Not a bad thing for you, perhaps."

"I'm not complaining," Milton said.

#

THEY SLID THE BREAKFAST CANS back out of the cell so that the inmates could collect them and stack them on the trolley as they made their way back along the corridor in the direction that they had arrived.

Milton took a moment to close his eyes and think about the Steps. He wished that he still had his copy of the Big Book. It had been left behind in the hotel room when he had been arrested. The book had accompanied him around the world. It was well thumbed, the pages turning to particularly familiar passages when he let it fall open. The margins were decorated with his annotations, and the text was garlanded with underlining and highlighted passages. He doubted whether he would ever see the book again.

One of the guards walked down the corridor, shouting

out a word that Milton did not understand.

"What is he saying?"

"Exercise," Isko translated for him. "We have an hour in the sunshine."

Chapter Forty

THE CELL doors were unlocked and opened and the men were allowed out into the corridor. They did not dawdle, immediately turning in the same direction and setting off. Isko waited for Milton to join him outside and then led the way.

"You know anything about Bilibid?"

"Nothing."

"They built it eighty years ago," the old man explained as they descended the stairs to the ground-floor lobby. "It was made for two thousand men. In twenty years they had eight thousand. There was trouble—riots, murders—so they tore it down and built again. It made no difference. There are still many more men here than there should be. You will see."

The wall of the corridor was replaced by a wire screen that allowed them to look at a row of eight cells, each sealed by iron bars. There were men inside the cells; there was no indication that their doors were to be unlocked.

"What have they done?"

"They are the *bitay*," Isko explained. "They have been convicted of crimes serious enough for them to be killed. They are kept here until it is time for their sentence to be served."

"Death row?"

"Yes. They will be taken to the room where they have the machine that will kill them." Isko put his index and middle fingers together and mimed an injection, his thumb serving as the plunger.

They reached an antechamber similar to the one that Milton had been brought through on his way to the cell. Bright sunlight streamed inside, revealing a guard lounging back on a picnic chair with his billy club in his lap. He glared at them as they went outside.

Milton felt the warmth of the sun on his face and immediately felt a little better. He looked up into the purest of blue skies, an infinite vault that was clear and cloudless for as far as he could see. The prisoners were corralled by a tall wire fence within a wide space. Guards with rifles patrolled outside the fence and the two watchtowers that looked down on the yard were staffed by guards who stood at attention, unlike some of their colleagues.

There would be no opportunity to escape today. Milton put the thought to the back of his mind. He would be watchful and take the chance to consider how the security functioned, but he would concentrate on enjoying the sun and the opportunity to stretch his legs.

Men were circulating around the perimeter. Isko joined the flow and Milton followed.

The old man turned and pointed back at the building. "The cell house is like a prison within the prison," he explained. "We have three types of prisoner: the *castigados*, those who have been convicted of serious crime and who await death, and political prisoners, like me."

"What did you do?"

"I am a member of the Communist Party. I was convicted fifteen years ago. I have been here ever since."

"How long is your sentence?"

"For as long as they wish to keep me," he said. "Nothing has changed. My organisation is still forbidden. They still see us as a threat to the country."

"Do you have anyone on the outside?"

He shook his head sadly. "I had a wife. She was put in prison at the same time as me. She died five years ago. The last time I saw her was at our trial."

"You couldn't appeal?"

"This is not like your England. Things are different here. You can appeal, but it would be a waste of time. A judge does not go against the regime. He would not be a judge for very long if he did." The old man put a withered hand on Milton's arm. "It is all right. I have grown accustomed to my life here. I don't know what I would do if I was ever released. Time has moved on. I have been forgotten. There are people I know here. I have friends. Perhaps you will be another."

Milton was taken by Isko's sense of calm. He had seen it before in the meetings, the serenity that he, too, had sometimes found when he had accepted that he was helpless over his disease and there was no sense in pretending otherwise.

They continued around the yard.

"You said that Mr. Fitz set you up."

"I think so," Milton said. "I think he had a friend tell me a story that would make me come here, arranged for me to be drugged and then made it look like I was guilty of murder."

"What will you do?"

Milton glanced left and right. There were no other inmates or guards within earshot. "I need to get out."

Isko shook his head. "That will not be easy."

"Has it happened before?"

"Yes, many times. But they don't last long. The government rebuilt this prison to be a symbol of law and order. It has a reputation that they wish to maintain. There was a man, a year ago, he managed to climb over the wall. There was a weakness at the back of Building No. 3, a blind spot where the guards couldn't see you from the tower. He climbed the wall with a rope and got away."

"And then?"

"And then they hunted him down. They told us what happened to him. They had guards with dogs. They found him hiding in a ditch. They let the dogs have their way with him, and then they shot him. They showed us pictures. It was a warning. They were telling us that the same thing would happen to us if we tried to escape."

"This blind spot—"

"It has been fixed," Isko interrupted. "And, John, please. You must think carefully. You are not a Filipino, and this is not Manila. There is jungle around the compound, and then there are villages where the locals would never have seen a man like you. You would stand out. They would call the police. They know that the regime would punish them if they did not."

Milton knew that Isko's concerns were well founded. It would be difficult to escape on his own. He would need help.

"I need to deliver a message to a friend," he said.

Isko shook his head. "I'm afraid that won't be easy, either. You are new. If you're lucky, maybe they'll let you send letters when you have been here a few months. But they will open the letters and read them."

"What about my lawyer?"

"Perhaps. But you will be fortunate if you can find one who will break prison rules for you. If they are found out, they would be punished. Perhaps they would join us here."

Milton frowned and looked down at the sandy surface of the exercise yard. It was baking, waves of lambent heat quivering as they rose into the air. He felt stymied. He knew that he couldn't stay here, but, at the same time, it wasn't obvious how he could leave.

"Your trial, perhaps," Isko suggested. "That will be held in public. Perhaps that would be an opportunity for you to say something. Perhaps they will let you speak to your embassy."

Milton glanced over and saw a guard coming toward them.

"You," the man said, pointing his truncheon at Milton. "English."

Isko and Milton both stopped.

"What's the matter?"

"Come here."

"Do whatever they say," the old man said. "I will see you later."

Milton walked the short distance across the yard to the guard.

"Come with me."

Chapter Forty-One

MILTON WAS taken back to the latrines.

He was thrown inside. The guards waited at the doorway, blocking his way out. It didn't matter. Where would he go?

He heard the sound of feet approaching along the corridor. The guards parted and Tiny made his way inside.

"You again," Milton said, backing away to put a little space between them. "You didn't get enough last time?"

The big man grinned at Milton's bravado.

Milton closed in and led with a right jab. His fist found its mark, glancing off the corner of Tiny's jaw, but it had a limited effect. Tiny tried to grapple him, but Milton was able to dance away to the right, ducking beneath the clumsy attempted bear hug and swinging a big left hook that terminated in the side of Tiny's temple.

The punch hurt him. Tiny fell away to the side, his right hand reflexively going up to protect the point of impact and leaving his ribs exposed. Milton swung another left, putting all of his power into it, and his fist sank into the rolls of flab that protected the bigger man's ribs.

Milton was caught up in the moment. He forgot that his future would not be best served by embarrassing Tiny, that he was guaranteeing a worse beating with every punch that he landed, and that they would take pleasure in ripping away every last shred of resistance. He surrendered to instinct and hammered a right-hander that detonated against the left side of Tiny's head. The big man staggered back, turning away from the open doorway and retreating to the other side of the room. Milton followed him, closing in quickly and drilling him with a right-left-right combination to the head, ribs and head once again.

Tiny ran out of room. He backed against the wall, both

hands raised to protect the sides of his head with a wide gap left open between his chubby forearms. Milton drew back his right fist until it was all the way back behind his head, felt the tension and power surge into his shoulder, and then released it, pummelling Tiny square in the face.

The big man slumped back against the wall, his hands covering his face.

Milton kicked him, left and right, the side of his foot landing against his ribs and shoulders. Tiny began to slide down the wall, and Milton's kicks landed against his forearms. He heard an animal sound, an angry growling and panting, and realised that it was him.

Tiny was down on his haunches, low enough for Milton to step in closer so that he could start to use his knees and shins.

He cracked his right knee into the side of Tiny's head, then stepped back to switch legs when—

—his vision went black and his head was filled by a single high-pitched tone.

He lost consciousness and, when he came around again, he found he was flat on his face on the floor. The concrete was cold and damp and it smelled foul. He caught a quick glimpse to his side and saw one of the guards, his billy club raised above his head, and realised that he had been cold-cocked. The guard slammed the baton down, the wooden end cracking against his crown. The other guards came into the room, their own clubs raised. They rained blows down onto Milton, the ends of their clubs finding their marks as the men fell upon him. Milton tried to cover up, but they just switched their targets, hammering his trunk and then, as he rolled up, his kidneys. Milton curled into a ball, bringing his knees up to his chin, painfully aware that his back and ribs were vulnerable. He closed his eyes and gritted his teeth as the blows rained down on him again and again and again.

Chapter Forty-Two

MILTON BECAME aware of hands on either side of his body. He was being gripped beneath his shoulders. He opened his eyes and looked straight down at the floor. It was moving beneath him: he looked down at pebbles and rocks, patches of sand, and then an uninterrupted run of rough paving slabs. His head hung limply and his face felt like one huge, throbbing bruise. His mouth was open, and streamers of saliva stretched down. He dabbed at the inside of his mouth with his tongue and tasted blood. He felt for his teeth; he thought that they were still there. A small mercy.

He looked left and right and saw the legs of the men who were hauling him onwards. They were shod in shining leather boots. The guards. He allowed his head to dangle enough so that he could try to look behind him, but the effort made his head pound so that he felt like retching.

He closed his eyes again.

When he opened them again, he was back inside. He recognised the floor of the cell block, and his feet bounced off the stairs as he was carried upward. His cell door was open and he was thrown inside. He landed on the floor between the two bedrolls.

"Hello again, John."

He looked up: Fitzroy de Lacey was standing before him.

Milton didn't move. His body pulsed with pain.

"You still with us?"

"Hello, Fitz," he mumbled.

De Lacey laughed. Milton concentrated on what he could feel without having to open his eyes. His arms were splayed out, and, as he moved his fingers, he felt the imperfections in the concrete floor. He concentrated his attention on the multitude of individual aches and throbs that he could feel. His face was the worst; he was lying against something sharp, and it provided a pinprick of intensity that was just perceptible as a peak amid the general swelling. He allowed his attention to travel down his body. His ribs throbbed, as did several distinct areas on his back and legs.

"How are you feeling?"

Milton could feel the blood on his head, the warmth of it ebbing away as it started to clot. "Not feeling so great," he said. "Sorry if I don't get up."

"They told me you took the fight to Tiny this time. How'd that work out for you?"

"I think I broke his nose," he said.

De Lacey chuckled again. "You should have just taken your medicine. He wants to kill you now. I told him no. Don't want you checking out, old boy, not yet. He's going to be in charge of your morning exercise. I managed to placate him with that. He's looking forward to it."

Milton tried to roll over, but the effort was too much. He lay still.

"I had a cell like this when they first put me in here," de Lacey said. "Bloody awful. Can't really say anything good about it, can you? You've got a window, I suppose, but that just makes it worse, doesn't it? Seeing the sky. Knowing you'll never see it as a free man."

Milton heard de Lacey's footsteps as he moved around the room, and then felt the toe of his boot against his tender ribs.

"You look pathetic, John. Pathetic. It's not how I remember you. You were something when we met before. You had a confidence about you. A *swagger*. I've been thinking about that. I always thought I was a good judge of character, but you put one over on me. Made me doubt myself. I keep coming back to it, how you were so confident. Arrogant. You knew I was dangerous and you acted like it didn't bother you. As if you belonged with us.

I believed every word of it. I'll be honest, old boy: it took me a while to get over how stupid you made me feel. But you don't look so confident now, John. All that cockiness is gone. You look weak."

Milton took a deep breath and felt a stabbing pain in his chest. He crawled ahead a few feet, pain flashing with the effort, and managed to fall onto his bedroll. He brought his knees up beneath his body and pressed up with his hands, raising himself enough so that he could turn and sit, his back up against the wall of the cell.

He opened his eyes and looked over to where de Lacey was standing. He was wearing a pair of expensive-looking jeans, a white poplin shirt and a pair of new desert boots.

"Going somewhere, Fitz?"

"Funny you should say that." De Lacey undid his cuffs and rolled up his shirtsleeves. Milton saw a heavy and ostentatiously expensive watch on his wrist. "As a matter of fact, I am. Leaving tomorrow. They've changed how they see me in London. The new regime here has been fortunate for me, too. I've been negotiating with them for years, obviously. The previous lot let me move into the villa and they let me run Tactical, but they wouldn't release me—they didn't want to upset the Americans, apparently. But Duterte doesn't care about that. Wants the world to see him as a strong man. Doesn't want anyone to think the Americans can push him around. He's been much more receptive to what we've offered. The rest of my sentence is being commuted."

Milton closed his eyes. "What did you have to put up for that?"

"What do you think? Think of the favours I'll be able to do once I'm in circulation again. You put me in here, John, but people haven't forgotten about me. Far from it. My old clients are very excited about the business we'll be able to do together. And I have new clients, too. It's going to be a good year." He paused, chiding himself with a theatrical tut. "I'm sorry, that was insensitive. It's going to be a good year for me. Not such a good one for you."

De Lacey took a step toward the open cell door.

"Fitz," Milton managed.

De Lacey stopped. "Yes?"

"You said this would be the last time you saw me."

"It will be."

"No," Milton said. "It won't. I—"

De Lacey interrupted him with a chuckle. "Oh, come *on*, John," he said. "Do you know how ridiculous that sounds?" He turned and took the step necessary to bring himself directly in front of Milton. He crouched down and put a hand on Milton's shoulder. "Look at you. You're done, old boy. You're finished. Threats only work when they have substance. You can't threaten me. You're in here. I'll be out there. But when I say that you're going to be beaten every day, you should take that seriously. It's not an empty threat. And when I say you're going to die, you should believe that, too."

Fitz stood and backed out of the cell.

Tiny stepped up and took his place.

The big man had a dressing across his nose. He laced his fingers and pushed, cracking his knuckles.

"More?" Milton said.

Fitz smiled through the bars. "Lots more. Have fun, John. Goodbye."

Chapter Forty-Three

"ARE YOU all right?"

Milton coughed. He felt bubbles of hot blood in his mouth. His nose was clogged up with plugs of solid blood. He had to breathe through his mouth, and, as he did, he felt stabs of pain from the back of his mouth. He probed with his tongue and felt the sharp sliver of enamel that had once been his back molar.

"John?"

He managed to groan. It was the best he could do.

He felt Isko's hands as they slid beneath him, then heard him grunt as he tried to roll him onto the bedroll. Milton was in too much pain to help. His body throbbed, as if every last square inch had been pummelled repeatedly with a hammer. The pain swamped over him in waves.

The old man persevered and managed to push him into a half roll that ended on the mattress. Milton lay still, face up, his eyes closed. There was more blood in his mouth, and, lying like this, it started to trickle back into his throat. He managed to turn his head so that his mouth was pointing down and then tried to push the blood out with his tongue.

He felt a dampness on his skin and then the sensation of something moving up and down in a gentle pattern. He opened his eyes. Isko was crouched next to him. He had poured the water from his mug onto Milton's forehead, and now he was very carefully brushing it across his face with the tips of his fingers. The water was tepid, but his skin was burning hot and it felt good. The old man washed it over the cuts and bruises, gently brushing away the dried blood.

"It was Mr. Fitz again?"

Milton managed a moan. "And the big guy."

"You were unconscious when I got here. He beat you worse than last time."

Milton wanted to tell Isko that he had embarrassed Tiny and that he didn't think it had gone down very well, but the sentence was too long and he didn't have the strength for it.

"We need to do something," the old man said. "You can't go through this every day."

Milton tried to speak, but all he could manage was an uncontrollable cough.

"What?"

Milton waited until it subsided. "Got any ideas?"

"Not really."

Milton managed to raise himself to a sitting position. "Fitz," he said. "He said he was getting out."

"You think that will make things better?"

Milton shook his head, but the movement was dizzying and it made him feel sick.

"No," Isko said, finishing for him. "I don't suppose it would."

"Message," he said.

"What?"

"Need to get message out."

"To who?"

"Manila," he said. "Can you help?"

"Perhaps. I might be able to find an inmate who has a visitor. I am friendly with some. Perhaps they could arrange it. Who do you need to speak to?"

"Police," Milton said.

Chapter Forty-Four

JOSIE'S MOTHER didn't want her to go to work.

She had to reassure her that it was the right thing to do, but the effort meant that she was half an hour late getting out the door. She had never driven in from Taguig before, and the traffic was terrible. It meant that she was forty minutes late in getting to the station.

She tried to hurry along the corridor to the desk, but she hadn't managed to get more than a handful of paces beyond Mendoza's open door when he called out to her.

"Where have you been?" he asked her.

"Angelo is sick."

He feigned concern. "What's the matter?"

"A temperature."

"I'm sorry. Poor boy. Are they at your mother's place?"

He fixed her with an inquisitive look as he put the question, and Josie knew, for sure, that he knew very well that they had moved and that he was probing to see what she would say.

She was prepared to call his bluff. "They are," she said.

Mendoza nodded solicitously. "I hope he feels better soon. If you need to leave early tonight, that's fine."

"Thank you," she said.

She turned to go.

"Wait," he said. "Shut the door."

She found that her throat was dry. She did as he asked.

"You were at the hotel last night."

It wasn't a question. It was a statement. "Yes," she said carefully.

"You saw the fire."

"Yes. How do you know that, sir?"

"The fire department report mentioned your name. What were you doing there?"

167

She remembered what he had told her about not pursuing the investigation. "I was driving home," she said. "I saw the smoke."

"Really? It was just a coincidence?"

"Yes, sir."

"But that doesn't make sense. It's not on your way home. You go south on the Skyway. The guesthouse is north. So don't lie to me—why were you there?"

She thought on her feet, finding the expression of concern that would be expected of someone who had just been accused of dishonesty by their boss. "I was seeing an informant," she said.

"Really?"

"I met her in Intramuros."

Mendoza let the answer hang in the air and then smiled, almost as if he hadn't just accused her of dishonesty. "Just a coincidence, then?"

"Yes. I was passing."

"That's good. Because we talked about that case and how there was no point wasting time on it."

"We did. And I understand."

"Excellent. You've been working long hours, Josie. Don't stay late tonight. Go home to your boy."

The mention of Angelo made her flinch. "Thank you, sir. I will."

"He needs his mother. You should spend more time with him. I appreciate your dedication, but you're working too hard. And Manila is a dangerous place."

She knew exactly what that was: a threat.

"Thank you."

She was barely halfway out the door when Mendoza said, "One more thing. Your informant."

"Yes, sir?"

"Who is it?"

She prayed that she could maintain her composure. "Her name is Fleur."

"Get her details for me, please. Leave them on my desk

before you go home."

"What for?"

"I want to speak to her."

"Yes, sir."

She felt dizzy as she left the office. The bathroom was beyond her desk, and that was fortunate. She tried to look as nonchalant as she could as she headed to the door, but, as soon as she was inside and she was sure that she was alone, she locked herself in a cubicle, leaned over the toilet, and vomited.

Chapter Forty-Five

JOSIE WASHED her face with cold water and then went back to her desk. She sat down and stared at her blank screen for five minutes. She needed to think, but it was as if her thoughts had been coated with Vaseline. She couldn't focus on anything for more than a few seconds. She kept thinking about Angelo, the car outside the house and the bullet that had been slipped beneath the door.

She knew that she should ignore the murder of Jessica Sanchez. She had been warned, explicitly, what would happen to her and her family if she kept putting her nose back into it. She thought again of the bullet and the photograph of Angelo, and what Mendoza had said to her this morning. She thought of the owner of the bar and how his death was so obviously linked to whatever had happened to Smith.

She thought of the fire.

And, even though she knew it was folly and that she would be putting herself and her family in danger if her disobedience was found out, she couldn't do as she was told.

She picked up her phone and called the forensics department. She asked whether the autopsy had taken place on the body of Jessica Sanchez. She was connected to the pathologist.

"I took a look at her last night," he reported. "Cause of death was strangulation. Extensive bruising around the neck, as you would have seen. In addition to that, there was clear evidence of asphyxiation: pinpoint haemorrhages in the skin and the conjunctiva of the eyes."

"What else?"

"There isn't too much to report. It was very straightforward."

"Toxicology?"

"Nothing. What were you expecting?"

Josie made a leap. "Had she been drinking?"

She heard the man tap on a keyboard. "Eight milligrams of alcohol per hundred millilitres of blood."

"That's hardly anything."

"A single shot of spirit. Half a glass of wine."

She made a second jump. "I sent in a specimen that we took from a suspect," she said. "John Smith. Could you check if that's been tested?"

"This isn't convenient, officer. I've got two autopsies to do this afternoon."

"Please? It would be very helpful."

The man sighed. "Hold on."

There was a pause. Josie grabbed her car keys and left the building through the door that led out to the yard.

She was in the parking lot when the man spoke again.

"We tested his blood this morning," he said.

"And?"

"It was clean."

"No alcohol?"

"No," he said. "Not a drop."

#

THE HEADQUARTERS of Malate Fire Volunteer and Rescue was on Mabini Street. The squad's two tenders were parked at the kerb and their operations were managed from two huts on opposite sides of the street. Josie parked in a space between the two bright red fire trucks and approached the nearest building. It was painted white, blue and orange, and there was a portrait of President Duterte stuck to the pane of glass in the door. Josie pushed it open and stepped inside.

"I'm looking for Andrada," she said.

"He's in the back. Who are you?"

"Officer Hernandez. I met him last night."

"Stay there."

Josie waited while the officer went back into a room at the rear of the building. When he returned, the officer that Josie had spoken to last night was with him.

"Hello, Officer," he said.

"You remember me, Chief?"

"Sure I do. You were at the Makabat fire last night. How can I help?"

"You got anything else on it?"

"On what caused it?"

She nodded.

"We do. Come with me."

He took her through a door that led into a yard at the back of the building. There was a wooden lean-to built against the office. He collected a large jerry can inside a clear plastic evidence sack and put it on the ground at her feet.

"We found that around the back of the office. It had gasoline inside it. Pretty obvious what happened. Someone poured it out as an accelerant and then torched the place."

He put the can back where he had found it and headed over to a vending machine next to the office door. "You want anything?"

"I'm fine," she said.

He reached into his pocket for change and dropped some coins into the slot.

"Are you investigating it?" he said as he collected a can of Coke.

"No," she said. "Arson's not really my scene."

"Not because of the arson," he said. "Because of the bodies."

"What bodies?"

"You don't know?"

She shook her head.

He popped the top of the can and took a long swig. "Okay," he said. "Maybe the report hasn't been processed yet."

"What bodies?" she pressed.

"The door to the office was locked when we tried it, so

we broke it down. There were two bodies inside."

Josie swallowed hard. "Male and female?"

He nodded. "We had forensics come over right away. A man and a woman, like you say. We couldn't tell shit, they were so badly burned up, but they were able to ID them from their teeth."

"Oscar and Imelda Santos?"

"That's right, Officer. The manager and his wife. They took them away and autopsied them. They'd both been shot in the head. So we're thinking it's obvious what happened. Someone kills them, locks the door and sets the office on fire to burn the bodies."

"Thank you, Chief," she said.

"You need anything else?"

"No," she said. "That's it."

#

JOSIE DROVE back to the station and went back inside through the rear door. There was no sign of Mendoza, and, as she glanced up the corridor, she saw that his door was closed.

"Where's the boss?" she asked Dalisay.

"Went out an hour ago," the officer said.

Josie's desk phone rang. She picked it up.

"Hernandez?"

It was Gloria, out in the reception. "Yes?"

"You got a visitor."

Josie hurried along the corridor and into the reception area. Gloria pointed to the old man waiting there for her. He was pacing back and forth.

"Hello, sir," Josie said. "I'm Officer Hernandez. You wanted to see me?"

"I have a message for you."

"I'm sorry—I don't know you, do I?"

"You don't. But you want the message or not?"

The man was clearly uncomfortable in a police station.

"What is it?"

"My son, Hector, he is in Bilibid. And Hector knows another man there. Isko. And Isko says that he has a message for you from a prisoner he knows. This man is English. His name is Smith."

Josie turned. The only person she could see was Gloria. But she wasn't prepared to take chances.

"Come outside, please," she said.

If the man found her suggestion odd, he did not say so. Instead, he followed her out into the broiling heat.

"What's your name, sir?" she asked.

He shook his head. "Doesn't matter," he said. "You know Smith or you don't? Isko said you'd know who he was."

"I know who he is. Go on."

"Isko says Smith wants to see you. He says he has information you need. He says you need to go there as soon as you can."

"When did he say this?"

"I don't know, lady. Hector called me this morning, said I had to say it was urgent. I'm just delivering the message."

"Is there anything else?"

The man shook his head and then flinched as two officers ambled by them on their way into the station.

"Thank you," Josie said.

The man shrugged and, without another word, turned and retreated quickly down the street.

Chapter Forty-Six

MENDOZA HAD told Josie to think about Angelo, so she took him up on the suggestion. She called the station and said that his sickness was worse and that she was going to take the rest of the day off so that she could stay with him. Without allowing herself the luxury of second-guessing herself, she got into her car and drove out of the city, heading south toward Bilibid once again.

#

SMITH WAS waiting for her in the visiting room, but it took her a moment to recognise him. His face was bruised much worse than it had been the first time she had been here to see him. His right eye was swollen almost completely shut. There were abrasions beneath both eyes and around his nose, and his top lip had been split. The right side of his jaw was inflamed as if he had lost teeth.

She sat down opposite him.

He gestured up to his face before she had a chance to speak. "I know," he said, the words mumbled around a swollen tongue. "I've made some excellent new friends."

"You look terrible."

"Felt better."

She looked around the room. It wasn't private. The guards at the door were eyeing the prisoners and their guests with sour watchfulness. Josie felt vulnerable. Mendoza was a powerful man with extensive connections, and she had no doubt that his reach extended from Manila all the way down to the prison. There was no guarantee that he wouldn't come to hear of her visit. She was taking a risk, yet she hadn't been able to resist it.

She tried to put that out of her mind.

"You wanted to talk to me?"

"Yes," Smith said. "Thank you for coming."

"What is it?"

"I know what happened to me. The murder—I can explain it now. I know what happened."

She thought of the additional information that she had accumulated since she had seen Smith, the questions that she needed to have answered. She would wait, though, and see what he had to say. "Go on."

"There was an inmate here. His name is Fitzroy de Lacey. He's English. Very rich and very powerful. He made his money running guns. He was released yesterday."

"What does he have to do with you?"

"There are some things I haven't told you. About me. I said I was on holiday."

"And you're not?"

"No. And my name isn't Smith."

"So what is it?"

"Milton. John Milton."

"Why would you lie about that?"

"Because I don't travel under my own name. I made enemies during my career. People like de Lacey."

"Fine," she said. "I've driven two hours to get here, so I might as well indulge you. What did you used to do?"

"I was involved in the intelligence service."

"Like a spy?"

"That would be one way to describe it."

"You told me you were a cook."

"Would you have believed me if I said I was a spy?"

"I don't suppose I would."

He spread his hands.

"And you were involved with de Lacey?"

"In a fashion. He had a big organisation. He did deals all around the world. I got into the business and found the evidence to shut him down. He was working on a deal with the communists in Manila."

Milton—Josie was about to think of him as Smith, but

caught herself—shifted in his chair and looked at her, as if gauging her reaction.

"Let's say I buy all that," she said. "What does de Lacey have to do with you being here?"

"He blames me for what happened to him. He framed me. He orchestrated everything, and I fell for it. He knew that I knew Jessica. I don't know how he did it, but he arranged for her to contact me. I told you what she told me: she had a child, and she thought it was mine. I believed her, she told me to come out here, and I did. The night we met, de Lacey had her killed and he made it look like I did it. I don't think I was drinking. It wouldn't have been like me, but I just couldn't remember."

"You weren't drinking," she said.

"How do you know that?"

"We tested your blood. There was no trace of alcohol in yours."

"And Jessica?"

"She had had one or two drinks."

Milton's relief was evident, but it was quickly supressed. "The bottles in the hotel were left there to make it look like we'd been drinking."

"That's a possibility."

He shook his head. "It's more than that. That's exactly what happened. Whoever de Lacey got to do this made sure it looked that way. First they drugged us—my money would be on flunitrazepam because of the memory loss—and then they killed her and set me up. You said the owner of the bar was shot."

"The same night I saw him."

"Maybe that's why. Maybe he had the drugs. Maybe he was a loose end. Maybe you frightened him when you went to investigate. Or maybe your going to see him frightened someone else. It's too much of a coincidence otherwise."

One of the guards cleared his throat. She looked over at him anxiously, but he was looking the other way.

"There's something else," she said, leaning closer to him.

"I only found out this morning. The owners of the hotel where you were staying were killed last night. I went to see them and the security footage was gone. Someone broke in and took the drive. And then I went back again and the place was on fire. They were inside. They'd been shot."

"Someone's cleaning up behind themselves."

"Everything about this is wrong. The bar. The hotel. And you being moved here—that shouldn't have happened."

"You said your boss did that."

"He did."

"Then he's involved."

"You think I don't know that?" she hissed. "I've been threatened, too. There was a car outside my mother's apartment. They took a photo of my son coming out of school, put it in an envelope with a bullet and pushed it under the door."

"It was him?"

"He told me I needed to be careful. He's not subtle. I'm sure it's him."

"I wouldn't be surprised if de Lacey has him on his payroll. You need to be careful."

She let her head hang. "This is getting out of control."

"What are you going to do?"

"I have no idea."

"I could help."

"How are you going to do that, Milton?" she hissed. "You're in fucking *prison*."

"Then get me out."

"Yeah, sure. I'll just go and get the rope out of my car and throw it over the wall." She clenched her fists and fought to control herself. "I don't know. Maybe I can dig into it. Maybe… maybe I could give you something to go to the court with. You got a lawyer?"

He shrugged. "A public defender."

"Who is it?"

Milton frowned as he tried to remember the name he had been given. "García."

She groaned. "Great."

"Not good?"

"Eddie García is a drunk," she said, before remembering that Milton was an alcoholic. "Sorry, I—"

"Forget it," he said, waving her embarrassment away.

"And he's corrupt. That's worse. I could give him evidence that says there's no way you were responsible and it'd make no difference. If this is a conspiracy, he'd just bury it."

"So we have to think of another way."

"Got any great ideas?"

He placed both hands on the table and looked straight at her. "There is something."

"What?"

"If I can get out of here, I'll be able to make progress that you can't make."

"What does that mean?"

"The people we're dealing with—they don't play by the rules. That means we can't play by the rules either."

"You say 'we'—this isn't a team, Milton."

"Dress it up however you like. But we share the same goal. I want to fix this. And when I do, I'll fix it for you, too."

"It doesn't matter what you say you can do. *I can't get you out of here.*"

"Not officially. But you can still help." He looked around. "I told you before. I need to get a message to a friend. He'd be able to help, but they won't give me a phone call. He doesn't know that I'm here. No one does."

"You want me to contact him?"

"If you want to help me, that'll be the best way."

"And assuming I did… What could he do?"

"Could you get him in here to see me?"

"Maybe." She shrugged. "Probably. But what difference would it make? You'd still be here."

"I was a soldier," Milton said. "My friend was, too. We have the same history. The same skills."

"You're going to try to break out?"

"Unless you can do it another way?"

"What's the man's name?"

"Alex Hicks. Do you have a pen and paper?"

"No," she said. "But I have a good memory."

Milton recited a telephone number. "It's an English number," he said. "Call him. Tell him we've spoken. Tell him he needs to fly out here as soon as he can."

"And he'll do that? Just like that?"

"Hicks owes me. And he's a good man. He'll come."

"And then?"

"Bring him in here to see me so we can talk."

The clock ticked over to the hour and a buzzer sounded. "Time up," one of the guards shouted. "All guests out— now."

Josie tried to assert some order over the chaotic parade of thoughts that flashed through her mind. It was a mad flurry: the threats against her and Angelo; the murders at the hotel and the bar; Mendoza's complicity; Milton's untruths, and whether she could trust someone like him. She had always worked to lay down solid foundations upon which she could build for the future and now, for the first time since her husband had left her and Angelo, it felt as if those foundations were unstable. Her options seemed limited. Milton had lied to her, but, despite that, she couldn't get away from the conclusion that he was as invested in solving this mess as she was.

It wasn't saying much, but he was the best that she had.

"Josie?" Milton said.

She stood. "I'll do it."

Chapter Forty-Seven

MILTON WAS taken back to the cell. He walked on, conscious of the guard behind him, and wondered whether Hernandez would follow through. He realised that he was relying on her. If she didn't deliver the message, there would be very little that he would be able to do. He knew that he stood no chance of winning his freedom at trial; she had made it very clear that the deck was stacked against him. He couldn't even say with certainty that he would make it as far as the trial. The beatings were taking it out of him. He was at Tiny's mercy.

He would have to try to fashion his own escape, but, despite subjecting the security arrangements to as detailed an assessment as his limited opportunities allowed, he had not discovered any serious weaknesses that he would be able to exploit on his own. He would have to ask Isko to tell him about the weakness that had been fortified, or push him to consider other weak spots that would be worthy of investigation. If worst came to worst, he would find a way to get over the wall, but, as Isko had made clear, even if he managed to get away, he would be an obvious target in an unfamiliar and hostile landscape.

He would try, but the odds would be long.

He needed help.

First, though, he needed time.

Isko was waiting for him. He was brushing his teeth with a toothbrush he kept in a cloth washbag with a cake of old soap.

"She came?"

"She did," he said. "Thank you."

"They came for you again," he said. "The four of them who work for de Lacey."

"I'm sure they'll be back."

"You can't carry on like this."

"No," he said. He looked at the toothbrush and had an idea. "Could I borrow that?"

Wordlessly, Isko handed it over.

Milton took it and held it in his hand, the brush in his palm. It was just long enough.

"Can I borrow your lighter, too?"

Milton rolled over so that he was facing the wall and, with Isko keeping watch, he took the lighter and thumbed flame. He used the fire to soften the plastic, waiting until it was blackened and soft. Once he was happy with it, he started to rub the edges back and forward against the abrasive surface of the concrete wall. He worked at it for an hour, turning the brush halfway through so that he could concentrate on the opposite side. He scrubbed, peeling away the plastic and then heating it again so that it stayed soft. By the time he was done, he had rubbed away enough of the plastic so that the shaft ended in a point. Milton touched the end. It was sharp. It was a poor substitute for a metal shank, but it was the best he could do on short notice. The plastic was easy to grip; he would have liked some duct tape to roll around it so that he had something more substantial to grip onto, but he doubted that would be possible.

He would make do with what he had.

Chapter Forty-Eight

THE GUARDS unlocked the cell doors in the afternoon so that the inmates could have their exercise. Milton took the sharpened toothbrush and slid it inside his trousers, the point prodding his thigh as he followed Isko down the stairs and out into the yard.

"Be careful," the old man said as they started to stroll around the same circuit as before.

"Stay away from me," Milton warned. "You don't want to get caught up in this."

"I know what you're doing. It's dangerous."

"I have to do something. You said so yourself."

"They might beat you in solitary, too."

"They might. But Tiny is definitely going to keep working me over if I stay where I am. It's worth trying. What do I have to lose?"

Milton tensed as he saw a group of four inmates walking out to intercept them. He reached down and plucked out the toothbrush, sliding it up his arm so that the handle was pressed against the inside of his wrist and the sharp point rested against his cupped fingers. The men wouldn't be able to see it until he wanted them to and, by then, it would be too late for them.

"Go on," Milton said. "Keep walking."

"Good luck, Smith."

Isko continued on.

Milton stopped. The men were closing in. He recognised them: two of them had been in the group that had attacked him the first day in the canteen, and the remaining pair had been part of the group who had beaten him in his cell before delivering him to de Lacey. Beyond them, Milton saw a pair of guards with shotguns waiting by the entrance to the exercise yard. There were another ten guards scattered around the periphery of the space, and two watchtowers loomed at either end.

"You," the nearest man said. "You come with us."

"Again?"

"Come."

"Not today, lads. Tell Tiny I'll see him tomorrow."

"We don't ask," the man said. He took a pace ahead, stepping in front of Milton, less than an arm's length away. "We tell you. You come—"

Milton dropped the shank into his hand and slashed out with it. He backhanded him with an upward diagonal, the point slicing through the man's cheek and continuing up across his eye and up his forehead. He shrieked with pain, his hands automatically flying up to his face.

He wasn't a threat any longer; Milton ignored him and turned to the next man. Milton's arm was still raised from the first swipe, and he brought it back down and across in a forehand hack that found the side of the man's jaw and then tracked down across the soft flesh of his throat.

It was a deep incision, and bright red arterial blood frothed out.

The man fell to his knees as Milton pivoted. The third and fourth men were frozen to the spot, agog at the sudden detonation of brutal violence.

Milton closed the distance to the nearest inmate with two quick steps and flashed the blade across his face. The man managed to raise his hands, and the point of the shank sliced across both outward-facing palms.

The fourth man backed away.

There came the unmistakable boom as a shotgun was discharged.

He heard the sound of a raised voice. He couldn't translate the Filipino, but the meaning was clear.

He glanced to his right. One of the guards at the gate had fired into the air, and his partner was coming forward with his own shotgun aimed squarely at Milton.

He dropped to his knees and raised his hands.

"Lie down!" they bellowed.

He did, covering his head with his arms.

He heard the sound of the guards' boots in the sand as they ran across to him. He tensed, anticipating that he was going to take another beating, and they didn't disappoint him. They jammed the butts of their shotguns down onto his torso, working up his shoulders to his folded arms. He couldn't protect all of his head, and they jabbed down with the shotguns and struck him with kicks and punches, so many of them that he dimly assumed that others had come over to join in.

He felt consciousness retreating and, once more, the familiar curtain of blackness twitched at the edges of his vision. The blackness grew pregnant and swollen and rushed over him, sweeping him away again.

Chapter Forty-Nine

ALEX HICKS was having dinner with his family when his telephone rang.

They were celebrating. The results of Rachel's last PET scan had been delivered that morning and, after another round of chemotherapy, the cancer was officially in remission. They had gone out to the Pizza Hut in the centre of Cambridge, and Hicks had somehow been cajoled by his boys to eat the hottest pizza on the menu. They had conspired with the waiter to add extra chili to the topping and, loath as he was to admit it, he was struggling. He grimaced as he started on the penultimate slice, aware that a light sheen of sweat had formed on his forehead. His sons found his discomfort hilarious, and Rachel smiled to see them so happy. It made Hicks happy, too. It wasn't so long ago that the diagnosis had seemed like a death sentence.

His phone was in the pocket of his jeans and he felt it buzz for fifteen seconds before it stopped. There was a pause and then the phone buzzed again to indicate that a voicemail had been left. Not many people besides his family had his number, and it rarely rang. He finished the slice, exaggerating the heat of the chili for another cheap laugh, and then said he was going to the bathroom to run the cold tap directly into his mouth.

He took an empty cubicle, shut the door, took out his phone and navigated to his missed calls. He didn't recognise the number. It wasn't that it was unfamiliar to him, although that was true; he didn't even recognise the country code.

He went to voicemail, set it to play the last message and put it to his ear.

"*Hello.*" Hicks didn't recognise the voice. It was a woman, with an accent that he couldn't place. "*This is a message for Mr. Hicks. Mr. Alex Hicks. My name is Josie Hernandez and I am calling from the Philippines on behalf of John Milton. He is in trouble and he asked me to contact you. It is urgent. Please call me back."*

The woman's English was halting, the accent heavy and difficult to decipher. She recited the same phone number that Hicks's phone had recorded and then ended the call.

He stared at the screen for a moment as he absently wondered what to do.

It didn't take long.

He tapped the number and waited for the call to connect.

"Hello?"

"You left a message for me."

"Mr. Hicks?"

"Yes."

"Thank you for returning my call."

"You know Milton?"

"A little."

"You said he was in trouble?"

"He has been arrested for murder. He is in prison, waiting for his trial."

"And what does that have to do with you?"

"I am a police officer in Manila. I arrested him, but now I do not believe he did what it is said that he did."

Hicks lowered the lid of the toilet and sat down. It was only thanks to the money that Milton had provided that he and Rachel had been able to fly to America for the experimental treatment that had saved her life. He had helped him with a small matter since then, but it did not extinguish the debt that he owed. Milton would not have called if it wasn't necessary. Hicks believed the woman: the fact that she had his number was evidence that Milton was involved and proof that he was in trouble.

"I can't talk now," he said. "Can I call you in an hour?"

"Yes. I will wait to speak to you. Please, do not forget. It is urgent."

He ended the call and went back out to finish dinner. The kids had been waiting to see the new Avengers movie for a week, and he and Rachel had promised to take them. The boys were playing with their action figures in anticipation of the film.

"Is everything all right?" Rachel asked him quietly.

"I had a phone call," he said.

"Alex," she said with a sigh, "not now. We're having dinner."

"It was about Milton. I think he's in trouble."

Rachel knew that Milton had provided the money that had funded the treatment. Her exasperation evaporated. "What kind of trouble?"

The children were distracted, but Hicks kept his voice low. "He's in the Philippines. He's been arrested. For murder. The call was from a policewoman. She said that Milton needs my help."

"How?"

"I don't know. I said I'd call back this evening."

"The Philippines? Are you going to have to go there?"

"I don't know. Maybe."

Rachel was patient, and she knew that they owed Milton everything. "If you have to, you have to. Are you going to miss the film?"

"I've got to call her back."

She nodded to their children. "They'll be disappointed."

"I know. She said it was urgent."

"Don't worry—I'll take them. Just promise you'll keep me in the loop."

"Of course," he said.

He kissed her on the cheek, told his boys that he would take them to see the film for a second time, and then went to find a taxi to take him home.

Chapter Fifty

MILTON AWOKE. It felt as if he had been drugged. He could hear the sound of voices, but they were a distance away from him and he was too groggy to understand them. He waited until he came around a little more. The voices were speaking in Filipino. Raucous laughter punctuated the conversations. He couldn't understand a word of what was being said.

He was lying on a hard surface. No bedroll this time. His body ached and his head throbbed. He opened his eyes and wished that he hadn't. It seemed to trigger a fresh wave of pain, a surge that pulsed from his head and all the way up and down his body. He felt nauseous and weak.

He was in a cell. It wasn't the one that he had shared with Isko. There was no natural light and, as he tilted his head as far as he could without intensifying the pounding in his skull, he confirmed that there were no windows. The walls, floor and ceiling were all fashioned from slabs of bare concrete. The only way in and out of the cell was a metal door with a blocked-off slit at head height. The light was from a single fixture overhead. Milton would have preferred it to be dark, but it was not; the light was bright and merciless.

He was in solitary confinement. That, at least, was what he had banked upon. He remembered de Lacey's four stooges ready to haul him out of the prison yard so that Tiny could beat him again. He knew that he had hurt three of them; it was possible that he might even have killed the man he had slashed across the throat. The guards had subdued him, beaten him until he was unconscious and then brought him here.

That was good. It was what he had wanted. He had been battered yet again, but he hoped that it would be more difficult for de Lacey to reach him here.

He tried to work out what time it was, but that was impossible. He usually had an instinctive feel for day or night, but not now. He would make it a priority to find out the time. He had been kept in solitary before, and having a rough idea of the time was a crucial part of hanging onto sanity. The passing of hours and days was a constant around which he could balance out the loss of his liberty.

He heard the sound of footsteps. He gingerly rolled over and tried to sit. His muscles had locked up, and the effort of raising himself up was excruciating. He pushed himself to a sitting position as the slot in the door scraped open.

"You are awake," a man's voice said.

"What time is it?"

"That is unimportant. You will stay here now."

"Where am I?"

The man didn't answer. "You killed another inmate. Killed one and badly hurt two others. You will be kept here for your own safety until you can be tried. After that…" The man let the words peter out. "Well," he began again, "after that, you will return to the main prison and I doubt you will last very long. But we must keep you safe until your sentence is passed."

"Water," Milton said. "I need a drink."

"Later."

The slide scraped back again and Milton heard the footsteps retreating.

It was progress, he told himself. It was what he had wanted.

So why didn't he feel any more optimistic?

Part Three

Chapter Fifty-One

HICKS PUSHED up the blind and looked out of the porthole window. The 747 was on its final approach and he could see the lush green canopy of trees as they descended over a forest and then the sprawl of metropolitan Manila ahead.

He had purchased a ticket to the Philippines last night. He knew that Rachel was not pleased to see him go, but he explained that he couldn't ignore Milton and she had told him that she understood. He had been a soldier for many years, and during that time there had been months that he had been forced to spend away from his family. They had hoped that those days were behind them, but this was something that could not be ignored.

Hicks told her that he expected that this would be only a brief absence. She told him to hurry home.

He had driven to Heathrow and caught the overnight Philippine Airlines flight. It was scheduled to take just under fourteen hours, and he had watched a film with his dinner and then slept.

He watched through the window as the jet descended. There was a seemingly long moment as the jumbo slowly navigated the final few feet to the ground, the hangars rushing by in a blur, and then the wheels bumped and the rubber squealed and the reverse thrusters roared to slow the plane down.

Hicks looked out at the terminal bathed in a brilliant bright afternoon sunlight that promised a hot day and found himself wondering what his stay would bring.

#

HICKS MADE his way through immigration into the arrivals hall. He had arranged to meet the woman here, but, as he looked into the sea of expectant faces, he realised that he had no idea what she looked like. He had her cellphone number and was about to call it when he noticed a young woman working her way to the barrier. She was holding a piece of paper with his name scrawled across it.

He raised his hand and, as she acknowledged him, they both set off to meet at the end of the barrier.

"Mr. Hicks?" the woman said.

She was wearing a police uniform: a dark blue skirt with a lighter blue shirt. The shirt was decorated with the badge of the Manila Metropolitan Police, there was rank insignia on the shoulder, a ribbon above her right breast that noted her citations and a nameplate that identified her as Officer Hernandez. She wore a pistol belt with a holstered Glock.

"That's me," he said.

"I'm Hernandez," she said.

"Nice to meet you."

"How was your flight?"

"Long."

She led the way out of the terminal building. The early afternoon heat washed over him.

"Hot, yes?"

"You could say that."

"It'll get hotter. I'm afraid the air conditioning in my car doesn't work very well, either. And we have a long drive ahead of us."

She led the way across the road to a multi-storey parking lot.

"Where are we going?" Hicks asked her.

"To prison," she said. "We need to see your friend."

Chapter Fifty-Two

HERNANDEZ DROVE them to the south. Her car was a bit of a wreck; the transmission sounded as if it was on its last legs and the air conditioning was shot. The foot well was littered with trash: empty cans and paper coffee cups, newspapers, empty sandwich wrappers and fast-food packaging, a plastic carrier bag. Hicks swept it aside with his foot.

"Sorry about that," she said, nodding down at the detritus.

"How long have you been in the police?" he asked.

"Long enough."

"How is it?"

She shrugged. "It was better before."

"Before what?"

"The president. There's a lot of violence now that wasn't here before. A lot of mess for us to clear up."

They had spoken on the telephone for fifteen minutes yesterday, but now she took the opportunity to take him through everything that had happened to Milton since he had arrived in Manila. She explained what she had found at the hotel room on the morning before Independence Day, and the process by which she had peeled away the layers of lies and deceit until she was convinced that Milton had been framed.

"You didn't say why he agreed to come out here," Hicks said.

"The woman said that he was the father of her son."

Hicks had never heard Milton speak of children before. "And is he?"

"I don't know."

They cleared the city and she was able to pick up speed.

"How do you know him?" she asked.

"What has he told you?"

"That he worked in intelligence. And that he was a soldier before then. And that you have a similar background."

To a point, Hicks thought. Milton was the reason that he had *not* gone into intelligence; he had refused his transfer to Group Fifteen because he saw something that he believed made him unsuitable for the role. It turned out that Milton had been right about that.

"Well?" she asked.

"I was a soldier," Hicks said. "For a long time. I got out and I found myself in trouble. Milton helped me."

"That's why you came? You owe him?"

"Yes," Hicks said. "I do."

#

IT TOOK two hours to drive to Bilibid. Hicks looked through the windshield at the building ahead of them. It was oddly ostentatious for a prison, with a facade that looked like a castle with two towers and crenelations across the top of the structure that looked like battlements. A tall flagpole, easily a hundred feet high, held aloft a Filipino flag that draped limply in the feeble breeze. A sprinkler chugged rhythmically back and forth across the wide patch of lawn between the parking lot and the entrance.

"That's a strange building," he said.

"That part is old. The prison is behind it. It's new. They built it a few years ago."

"It's secure?"

"Yes," she said.

"So what do we do now? How are you going to get me inside?"

"I'll come in with you. I'll say you're from the British embassy and that you need to speak to him."

"Why would I come to the local police to do that? Wouldn't I just come down on my own?"

"They won't ask questions. The guards are lazy."

Iron gates rolled shut behind them, restricting their access to the road by which they had arrived.

"If they do?" Hicks asked.

"They won't. Trust me."

#

HICKS GOT out of the car.

Josie followed him. "I'll go first," she said. "And let me do the talking."

"Understood."

They crossed the lawn and followed a neat path that led to the main entrance. There were two guards at the open doors, leaning against the wall with cigarettes in their mouths. They glanced up at Josie and then Hicks and then resumed their conversation.

Hicks followed Josie inside. It was cooler here, the shelter of the thick stone walls providing pleasant relief from the strength of the sun outside the door. Hicks saw an office with a Plexiglas window dividing it from the lobby. There was a short corridor ahead of them and then another lobby that was equipped with two X-ray machines and an airport-style metal-detecting archway.

The guards might be lazy, he thought, but it wasn't going to be easy to bring anything into the facility.

Josie made her way to the Plexiglas window and spoke through a grille to the clerk behind it. Hicks waited a few paces behind her. He watched the comings and goings in the lobby: uniformed guards passed through on their way to or from the interior of the facility, all of them armed with pistols that they wore holstered on their belts; clerks and officials crossed the space, using the doors on either side to, Hicks guessed, make their way to their offices. He saw a blaze of bright light from the second lobby with the security equipment, a pair of double doors had been opened, and he caught a quick glimpse of the courtyard beyond.

"This way, please," Josie said to him.

"Is everything all right?"

He saw satisfaction in her eyes. "Yes, sir," she said. "Mr. Smith is going to be brought to the visitors' room. We'll see him there."

Chapter Fifty-Three

THE VISITING room was functional. It was the communal space where the inmates were brought to meet with their visitors. Hicks would have preferred somewhere private, but they would have to make do with what they had been given. He was grateful that he had been able to make it this far without his cover story being questioned. Officer Hernandez had accompanied him to the room and then taken a chair in the waiting area. Hicks said that he would collect her when he had finished with Milton and then they would leave together.

He glanced around the room at the other inmates: they were male, tough and bore the bleakness of their situations across dead-eyed and expressionless faces. Many of them had prison ink on their exposed skin, their arms, legs, and faces decorated with crude tattoos. The inmates were distinguished by their orange shirts. Their visitors, for the most part, were dressed poorly, their tired and mismatched clothing suggesting that they, and the men that they had come to visit, originated from the poorest strata of Filipino society. Hicks remembered the gleaming new airport and the skyscrapers of upscale Manila that he had seen as he and Hernandez had driven south, and knew that a place like this would have collected the dregs.

Hicks looked at his watch. He had been here for ten minutes. He turned to the door, wondering whether he should go and speak to Josie, when the main set of double doors on the north wall opened and a man was brought inside. He was marked out as an inmate by the same uniform as the others, and Hicks almost disregarded him. His face was bruised and marked by cuts that had been clotted with dried blood. One eye had been forced shut by a socket that was swollen and blackened. He walked with a limp, hunched over with an arm pressed to his side as if to protect damaged ribs.

Hicks looked away, and then, as he noticed that the newcomer was coming across to his table, he looked again.

He hadn't recognised him. It was Milton.

"Jesus," he said.

Milton nodded and lowered himself gingerly down onto the hard wooden seat. "Thanks for coming," he said.

"Can we speak safely?"

"They don't listen in," Milton said. "We're lucky. If this was a room to ourselves, they'd bug it. I don't think they care here so much." He stretched out his shoulders, exhaling painfully from the effort. "How do I look?"

"Terrible."

"I've felt better. I've been roughed up every day since I've been here. You got my message, then?"

"She called me last night."

"And you came right away?"

Hicks nodded. "I flew overnight."

"I bet your wife was pleased about that."

"We owe you, Milton. She knows."

"You don't owe me anything."

Hicks waved that away. "We'll have to agree to disagree on that."

"Well, thank you. I appreciate it."

"What's happened to you?"

"You mean how did I end up here?"

Hicks nodded.

"I was tricked."

He told Hicks his version of the story: how he had been approached in London, how he had been told that he was a father and that the mother of his child wanted to see him. He explained how he had been framed so that he could be brought here to be tortured by a man from his past with a grudge to bear.

"They're clever," Milton said when he was finished. "They knew me. They knew exactly which buttons to press.

I've been alone for a long while. And that's fine—I don't want sympathy; it's my choice. But when someone says that you have kin… a son…" He paused. "I let it blind me. I should have been more careful and now, because I wasn't…." He paused again. "She's dead and here I am."

"This man—who is he?"

"Fitzroy de Lacey. He's an arms dealer. I was responsible for him being convicted. He was here for ten years."

"*Was* here?"

"He got out two days ago. I don't know how. The regime changed. Maybe it's more friendly to him. Maybe he's offered to work with them. But he's had help from the police. I should be in a holding facility in Manila, not down here. Hernandez said that her boss arranged the transfer. And then she was threatened and thinks it was him. So I think we can assume that he's involved."

Milton glanced meaningfully at Hicks. He waited until the guard who had approached their table from behind had continued upon his way.

"You're not going to be able to take many more beatings like that," Hicks said.

"I know," Milton said. "But I think I've bought myself a little time. I put some of de Lacey's goons in the infirmary when they came for me yesterday. They said I killed one of them. They've put me in solitary until they can work out what to do with me."

"And when they put you back in circulation again?"

"I'm hoping you might have been able to get me out by then."

Hicks sucked his teeth. "That won't be easy," he said. "The guards aren't anything special, but the building looks secure."

"I agree. You're going to need help."

"You got any ideas?"

"Actually, I do. I have someone in mind: a man I worked with when I was in the Group."

"*One* man? This isn't a two-man job, Milton."

"I know, but he's brilliant." He hesitated. "Well, he's eccentric, but he's also brilliant."

"At what?"

"Computers. I think this will be right up his street."

"What's his name?"

"Ziggy Penn."

"Never heard of him," Hicks said.

"No reason why you would. He's a bit of a hermit."

"It's your funeral. Where do I find him?"

"The last I heard he was in Korea, but he'll have moved on now. He doesn't stay in one place long. Tends to wear out his welcome. The last time we worked together I had to bail him out of trouble with Yakuza in Tokyo."

"So? How do I get to him?"

"There's a UseNet group. It goes way back, before forums. It's run by fans of The Smiths."

"Right," Hicks said. "The Smiths."

"The site's legitimate, but Ziggy monitors it. He has software installed. It pings him if a certain message is posted."

"What do I post?"

"You'll need to remember it: 'The last night of the fair, by the big wheel generator.' Make an account, open a new message, and post that."

Hicks screwed up his face as he tried to remember. "What is that? 'Rusholme Ruffians'?"

"I didn't know you liked The Smiths, Hicks."

Hicks smiled and shrugged. "I lived in Manchester when I was younger. I prefer the Mondays, but I can live with Morrissey. I'll do it as soon as I'm out. What'll happen next?"

"He'll reply and tell you how to contact him off the board. He's a bit unusual, like I said. Cut him some slack. We're going to need him. Tell him what's happened and that he needs to get here as soon as he can."

"If he says no?"

"He won't. He owes me a favour or two."

"I see a theme developing here."

Milton grimaced; Hicks realised it was actually a thin smile.

"You need anything else?"

Milton's expression was wry once again. "A helicopter in the yard?"

"I'll see what I can do."

Milton reached across the table and took Hicks by the hand.

"Hey!" a guard shouted.

Milton squeezed Hicks's hand. "Thanks. I won't forget this."

"Hey! No touch!"

Milton let go.

"Try to stay in one piece," Hicks said.

"Get Ziggy and then work out how to get me out of here. I can look after myself until then."

#

JOSIE LED the way out of the prison. She was silent until they got back into her beaten-up old car.

"Well?" she said. "What are you going to do?"

"You don't need to worry about—"

"You're going to try to get him out?"

"He shouldn't be in there," he said. "You know that. He's been set up."

"I know he has," she said.

"And we can't wait for him to go to trial."

"It wouldn't matter," she said. "It wouldn't be fair. It'll be fixed."

"There you go."

"So you're going to get him out?" she said again.

He didn't reply.

"You know you're going to need help, don't you? I don't care who you are or what you and he used to do. You're out of your depth here."

"You don't know that," he said.

203

"No," she said, shaking her head. "I do. And you are. You need help."

"You've done enough. Milton wanted me to say thanks. He's grateful. But that's it. He doesn't want you to get involved."

"I haven't got a choice," she said, laying her hands against the wheel. "I *am* involved. Do you have any children, Mr. Hicks?"

"I do. I have two."

"So you'll understand. I have a little boy. Someone pushed a picture of him outside his school under the door to my mother's apartment. There was a bullet with the picture."

"Milton told me. And that's more than enough reason to get as far away from us as you can."

"And go where? And do what? If you try to get him out, what do you think is going to happen to me and my boy? They'll find us." She shook her head. "My boss is involved. I don't know how, just that he is. If I help you get Milton out, you can help me. Right?"

"Help?"

"Help me find answers. And make it how it was before."

Hicks looked at her. Her face was set hard, but he could see the twitch of a muscle in her cheek. She was trying to play it tough, but she was frightened. That wasn't unreasonable. Hicks knew what the climate was like in Manila these days. Murder was common currency. The police acted with impunity. Milton had already been caught up in the maelstrom of corruption and violence that had been unleashed here. Josie and her son were on the edge of the vortex, trying to strike away from it, but she was compromised and the pull of the current was relentless.

Hicks would have been frightened, too.

"Okay," he said.

Chapter Fifty-Four

HICKS WAS at the airport at midday. He found a space by the rail in the arrivals hall and held up a piece of blank paper upon which he had written the name ANDY ROURKE.

Both his time of arrival and the name of the passenger he was ostensibly there to meet had been agreed upon over the course of a series of emails that had taken place the previous evening. He had visited the UseNet forum that Milton had identified and had left the message as he had been instructed.

What happened next was still a matter of some confusion for him: a forum reply had appeared beneath his comment that comprised just a single, nonsensical hyperlink. He had clicked the link and a chat box had appeared. The conversation had been very one-sided, with his interlocutor—Hicks had presumed that it was Ziggy Penn—firing off a series of curt questions.

Hicks had initially been reluctant to reply freely and had said as much; the reply was instant and indignant. The chat was secure, Ziggy said, and protected with military-class encryption. And unless Hicks answered each of the questions to Ziggy's satisfaction, the conversation would be terminated and there would be no second chances.

Hicks had little choice but to trust that Ziggy was as Milton had described him, so he had answered the questions thoroughly. He explained that Milton was in trouble and that he had requested that he contact Ziggy so that he might come and help.

That had been twelve hours ago.

And now Hicks was here to wait for him.

He looked up as the next group of new arrivals emerged into the hall. There was the usual mixture of men and women on business, backpackers, tourists and locals returning home. One of the passengers stood out: he was of middling height, a little overweight, wearing a New York Jets ball cap and a pair of dark glasses. He was carrying a laptop bag over his shoulder and he walked with a pronounced limp.

He glanced at the signs that were being held up by the waiting taxi drivers and paused as he saw the one that Hicks was holding up.

"Mr. Hicks," he said.

"That's right. Ziggy Penn?"

He didn't answer the question. "I recognise you," he said instead.

"I doubt it. You've never seen my—"

"Of course I have," the man said peremptorily. "Your Facebook profile took ten seconds to find. You're not very good at keeping out of the limelight." Hicks started to protest, but Ziggy cut him off. "Don't worry, neither is Milton. He thinks he's off grid, but he doesn't know what that means these days. Not really. Right, then—where's your car?"

"Outside," Hicks said, pointing in the direction of the short-stay parking lot.

"Let's get going."

#

HICKS OFFERED to put the bag in the trunk, but Ziggy declined, clutching it tightly to his chest like a toddler with a cherished toy. Hicks went around to the driver's side of the car, opened the door, and got in.

"Where are we going?"

"We're going to meet someone who might be able to help us."

He turned out of the parking lot and headed east. The rental had an integral satnav unit and Hicks had entered the address in Taguig that Josie Hernandez had given him. It was a short drive to the east on Andrews Avenue. The satnav suggested that they would be there in thirty minutes.

He glanced over at Ziggy. He had taken out a large cellphone and was flicking his finger down the screen, scrolling through pages of text that Hicks did not immediately recognise.

"What are you doing?"

"Nothing that you need worry about."

He killed the screen and put the phone back into his backpack.

Hicks turned left at the Colonel Jesús Villamor Air Base and merged onto the southbound Metro Manila Skyway.

"I know plenty about you already," Ziggy said, apropos of nothing.

"Really?"

"There's not much I don't know. Alex Hicks. Two kids, wife, you live near Cambridge, you're ex-military."

Hicks got the sense that the man was showing off and that he wanted Hicks to be curious to know how he had found that out about him. He was tempted not to indulge him, but he couldn't resist. "Okay," he said. "How did you get all that?"

"You logged into the forum through your Google account, which is stupid, by the way. And your password was embarrassingly easy to crack. Your wife's name and your birthday. *Really?* It took me ten minutes while I was waiting at the airport. I did it on my phone—that's how easy it was."

Ziggy spoke quickly, punctuating his words with little jabs with his fingers. He was animated, too, as if Hicks's failure to secure his data, or the question of how Ziggy might have discovered so much about him, was a personal affront. He was not a physically impressive man, but the routine way with which he dissected Hicks's life was unsettling.

"You bank at Santander. You have six thousand pounds in a savings account and a little under two thousand in your current account. Your mortgage is with Lloyds. You bought your house five years ago, and the repayments stretch you a little."

"So you hacked me," Hicks said with a tight little smile. "Well done."

"I wouldn't be so grand as that. It wasn't difficult enough to call it a hack."

Hicks had always believed that he was an easy man to get along with. He was relaxed and laid-back, and it took a lot to rile him up. He could see, though, that Ziggy Penn was going to challenge his patience.

The satnav indicated that he would need to come off the Skyway at the next junction. He indicated and turned off when he saw the signs for Taguig.

"How do you know Milton?" Ziggy asked.

"So you couldn't find *everything* out?"

"Not everything."

"We've worked together."

"But not in the Group? I would've known that."

"No. Milton was Number One when I was put forward. He turned me down."

"That's awkward," he said.

"Not really. I wasn't cut out for it. He could see that. I wouldn't have been very good at what he did. He did me a favour."

"So?"

"Our paths crossed again a few months ago. I was in a sticky situation and he helped me get out of it. And then he helped my family."

"Your wife?"

Hicks realised that Penn was referring to the cancer. The same glib way he dispensed that most personal piece of information was very irritating. "We won't be talking about that," he warned.

Penn frowned, as if struggling to understand the sudden flare of anger, before he gave a little shake of his head and said, "I'm sorry. That's personal. I don't mean to pry. Force of habit. I'm a careful person. I don't fly halfway around the world to meet someone I don't know without doing my research. But I don't mean to cause offence."

"Forget it," Hicks said. "He did help with her illness. He helped us find the money for the treatment that she needed."

Hicks decided not to go into too much more detail about that. The money that they had used to save his wife's life had come from the illicit deals arranged by an ex-Regiment man with whom Hicks had been working. Hicks had been desperate and had made a terrible decision; Milton had intervened and had extricated him, most likely saving his own life as well as Rachel's.

"That's one thing we have in common," Hicks said.

"What?"

"We both owe Milton."

Ziggy shuffled a little uncomfortably. "He told you about me?"

"He told me you worked together when he was in the Group. There was a time in New Orleans, during Katrina?"

"I was badly hurt," he said. "Hence the limp. Milton got me out."

"And then you got into a mess in Tokyo?"

Ziggy waved a hand in the air. "I've made a few mistakes."

Hicks could see that the conversation was causing a little discomfort and, much as he found that he enjoyed putting the shoe on the other foot, he decided to relent. "Don't worry," he said. "I only know a little. Much less than you know about me."

Finally, Ziggy smiled. "You don't know the half of it."

#

THE ADDRESS that Josie had given Hicks was on Labao Street. It was a budget B&B with a sign outside that declared it as the Napindan Castle. It was painted a garish orange, and the crude crenelations atop the wall were a clumsy stab at giving the building a feature to befit its name.

Hicks pulled up on the street outside and, as they had arranged, he took out his phone and called Josie's number.

She came out of the hotel and checked the street left and right. Hicks flashed the lights and watched as Josie hurried across to the car. She opened the rear door and lowered herself onto the seat.

"Is everything okay?" Hicks said as he put the car into drive and set off.

"I don't know," she said. "I didn't go to work again today. I said my son was still ill."

"Your boss?"

"I didn't speak to him. But he must know something is wrong now."

"This is the man I told you about," he said, inclining his head at the front-seat passenger.

Hicks watched in the mirror as Josie looked forward at Ziggy.

"What's your name?

"Ziggy."

"I'm Josie Hernandez."

Hicks had hoped that Ziggy would show a little less attitude, and was pleased when he turned to look back at her to return her greeting.

"Are you going to help?" she asked.

"That's the plan. Can we go to the prison now? Hicks says we need to hurry."

"I won't be able to get you inside," she said.

"I don't need to go inside."

Hicks saw Josie give a little shrug. "It's fine." She looked at her watch. "If the traffic is okay, we can be there by seven."

Chapter Fifty-Five

THE IRON gates had been rolled across the entrance to the prison compound and Josie said that there would be no way for them to get any closer to the buildings without arousing suspicion. Hicks pulled over to the side of the road. It was a little after seven, and the light was beginning to fade.

Ziggy pushed the sunshade up and looked out at the buildings beyond the gate. "Have you scouted it?" he said to Hicks.

"I went inside when I saw Milton," he said. "I couldn't see anything that looked like a weakness, but I didn't get to see all of it."

"There won't be an easy way out," Josie said. "The jail this one replaced was very bad. Men escaped all the time. This is more secure."

"What's the technology like inside the prison?"

"How do you mean?"

"What about the network? Is it low tech or high tech?"

"I have no idea."

"Do they have Wi-Fi?"

"I've never needed to find out."

"Well, we'll need to know. Here." He handed her a phone from his bag.

She took it, looking down at it dubiously. "I already have one."

"Not like this," he said. "This one is special. You need to take it into the building."

She handed it back to him. "Not unless you tell me what it's going to do."

"The phone and my laptop are linked. I can control it from here. I need you to take it inside so that I can analyse the network. I need to know where the vulnerabilities are."

"Will the guards be able to tell what it's doing?"

"No. It'll look and act just like a normal phone." He offered it again and Josie took it. "What happens when you go inside?"

"What you'd expect," she said. "They put your stuff through an X-ray machine. You go through a metal detector and if it goes off, they pat you down."

"The phone? Do you have to leave it there?"

"They have locked drawers. You put the phone in a drawer. They note down which one it's in and give you a receipt."

"But you can leave them switched on?"

"Yes."

"That ought to be okay. I should be able to get what I need from the network connections in the guardhouse."

"How long will you need?"

"I can't say. Not long."

She looked anxious. "What is it?" Hicks asked.

"There's no reason for me to be seeing him. I've already been in two times, and then I came back with you. If it gets back to Mendoza—"

"Who's that?" Ziggy asked.

"My commanding officer. If it gets back to him, he's going to be more suspicious than he already is."

"Is there another way?" Hicks asked.

"Someone has to take that phone into the guardhouse," Ziggy said. "I can't do it. I doubt you can."

"You can't," she agreed. "It has to be me. When?"

"I can't do anything until I know what the network is like," he said.

"So we do it now." She swallowed. "Tell me what I need to do."

#

JOSIE WALKED to the gate and showed her credentials to the guard. The man was armed with a rifle, but he carried it with the lackadaisical air of a man who had no real idea of how to use it, nor any expectation that he would have to. He glanced at her badge, gave a surly nod, and opened the smaller gate that was reserved for pedestrians. Josie thanked him and walked through.

She could feel the shape of the phone in her pocket. It was larger than her own, and she suddenly felt certain that it was going to give her away and betray her purpose. She reached across her body with her right hand and tapped her fingers against it. She tried to find her balance again. It was a phone. It looked just as it should. There was no reason why it should arouse suspicion.

She crossed the lawn and entered the main building. The late hour meant that there were far fewer members of staff in the lobby than had been the case during any of her three earlier visits. There was a clerk behind the Plexiglas screen, and she went over to stand before him.

"Hello," she said into the grille.

"It's late, Officer. What do you want?"

She smiled through the man's bad temper. "You have a suspect here. A man involved in a case I'm investigating."

The clerk was distracted by a TV that was out of sight.

Josie knocked on the glass. "Excuse me?"

The man scowled as he looked back at her. "What?"

"I want to see one of the inmates."

"Too late for that."

"I'm sure an exception can be made. Do I need to speak to the governor?"

The man cursed under his breath. "Who is it?"

"He's English. John Smith."

"Smith," the man said, tapping at his keyboard. "What about him?"

"He's been moved into solitary."

The man looked at the screen. "That's right. Two days ago."

"Why?"

"He attacked other prisoners. Slashed them with a

shank. He killed one and put two of the others into the infirmary."

"I wasn't told—"

"No reason why you would be told, Officer. Smith is our responsibility now. He isn't under police jurisdiction."

"He also hasn't been tried."

"You're based in the city, aren't you?"

"Yes."

"So you should have called before you drove down here. You've wasted your time and now you're wasting mine."

"I'm sorry. I need to see him."

"Not tonight."

"Tomorrow, then. First thing. Can you arrange that?"

"What for?"

"Police business." She found the right amount of annoyance. "I've had enough with your attitude. I'm serious. I'll speak to the governor if I have to. What's your name?"

The clerk made no secret of his own exasperation, rolling his eyes theatrically. "Fine. What's your cell number?"

The mention of her phone gave Josie a flash of alarm that she was afraid she wasn't able to mask in time. Her heart skittered and she felt the clamminess of cold sweat on her palms. She looked up at the clerk, but, if he had noticed her reaction, it wasn't obvious. He was scrabbling around his desk for a piece of paper.

Josie recited her number and waited as he finished jotting it down.

"Fine," he said. "I'll speak to the warden. Someone will call you tomorrow."

Chapter Fifty-Six

JOSIE WAITED for the gate to be opened. It was all she could do not to run back to the car as soon as she was beyond it.

She saw a faint green wash across the interior as she drew closer and, as she opened the rear door and slid back onto the seat, she saw that Ziggy had opened his laptop and was scrolling through a page of incomprehensible data.

He didn't look away from the screen as she closed the door behind her.

"Did it work?"

He didn't answer.

"Did it work?"

"*Ziggy*," Hicks said when he didn't reply.

He rested the laptop on the dashboard. "Sorry," he said. "Yes. It worked. You did well." He paused. "But that doesn't mean this is going to be easy."

Hicks frowned. "Meaning?"

"I thought that the network security would be basic. It's not. I used the phone to sniff the Wi-Fi. They're using WPA2 encryption. That's the standard level, and it's very secure."

"You can't hack it?"

"I could, but getting a handshake could take weeks. And it doesn't sound as if we have weeks."

"We don't," Hicks agreed. "He's bought himself time in solitary. As soon as they take him out, he's going to be beaten again."

"So we have to get in another way," Ziggy said.

Hicks encouraged him to go on. "And you've thought of that?"

Ziggy grinned. "I have. As Officer Hernandez waited in the security building, the phone picked up another signal. A

Bluetooth connection. It's for a keyboard or a mouse—probably a keyboard. Every Bluetooth device has a unique hardware identification number. If I can learn the number for the keyboard, I can spoof it to my own keyboard dongle. Then I can transmit from my device to the computer in the security building. If I do it right, the computer will think the keystrokes are coming from the keyboard it's been paired with, only they're not. They're coming from me. And chances are that the computer is networked into the prison's system with a static, always-on connection. Which all means that if I can get into the laptop by spoofing the keyboard, I can get into the prison network. If I can do that, I might be able to start causing trouble. You know, opening doors, setting off fire alarms, that kind of thing."

"I've said I'll go back tomorrow."

"Can you get it ready in time?" Hicks asked.

"It's not easy," Ziggy said. "I'll have to rig up just the right kind of payload. But…" He shrugged. "If I work overnight, it should be possible."

"You're sure it'll work?"

"I can't say for sure until I'm inside. I'm assuming that the control network for the internal prison security—the doors, the CCTV, their alarms, that kind of stuff—is on the same network as the standard systems."

"Is that likely?"

"Maybe. If we were in America, there would probably be separation with air gaps, firewalls or VLANs. But even there, I've seen cases where everything is on a flat network, completely open. Shit like this goes down all the time. And those kinds of places are given decent systems funding. The network guys here aren't going to be playing in the same sandbox. I'm guessing they didn't have the time or the funds to set up anything funky."

Hicks waved his hand impatiently. "What do I need to do? Practically."

"It's not you," Ziggy said. "I think it has to be Officer Hernandez."

"Go on," she said.

"You need to get close enough to the computer in the security building so that I can access the Bluetooth."

"How?"

"The phone. Same again. This time, it'll connect with the computer and make it think it's the keyboard. And then I'll be in."

"As simple as that?"

"You need to stay close enough so that I can access the connection."

Josie shook her head. "If I go through security, they'll take the phone and put it in the storage cupboard."

"That might not work. Is it near the keyboard?"

"No."

"And you need to be close to it."

"For how long?"

"Hard to say. A minute. Maybe a couple of minutes."

"So you want me to small-talk the guards?"

"Whatever you need to do."

"It's going to look weird if I have to stay there for long. They get people in and out as quickly as they can."

"I'll be as fast as I can."

Josie took a breath. "Fuck," she said.

"You did good just now," Hicks said. "And this is similar. Right, Ziggy?"

"Exactly the same."

Josie was thinking about what would happen if the plan they were seemingly concocting on the fly went wrong.

She let that thought play out a little more: what would happen if it all went *right*?

"I need to get home," she said. "I want to see my son."

Chapter Fifty-Seven

JOSIE SLEPT in Angelo's bed, clutching her son close to her. Her rest had been fitful and when she woke she had bleary eyes and a fatigued ache in her bones. Her mother noticed that something was bothering her, and Josie dismissed her concern with a brusqueness that she was unable to avoid, but one that she had immediately regretted.

"What are you doing today?"

"Work, Mother," she lied.

"When will we be able to go back home?"

Her mother's concern was entirely appropriate, but Josie did not want to get into a prolonged discussion about why a bullet had been pushed underneath the door and why they had had to leave. To do so would have forced her to confront the threat and then to explain what she was doing to make it go away. Her mother would have been even more frightened than she already was, and, more than that, Josie knew that if she thought for too long about the plan that she had allowed herself to be drawn into, her doubts would get the better of her.

What am I doing to keep my family safe? Well, Mama, I'm colluding with two men I don't know to spring a man accused of murder from the most secure prison in the country.

She insisted that she would get Angelo up herself, and read two of his favourite books with him before she glanced at her watch and saw that it was seven. She looked out through the window and saw Hicks and Ziggy in the car on the street, waiting for her as they had arranged the previous night.

Her mother watched her as she strapped on her gun belt.

"Be careful," she said.

"I will. I'll be back later."

She kissed her son and her mother and made her way out to the car.

#

HICKS HAD rolled down his window.

"Morning," he said as she approached.

"Good morning."

Ziggy was in the back of the car today, so she went around to the passenger side and got in next to Hicks.

"You get some sleep?" he asked her.

"Some," she said.

"You ready for this?"

"I think so."

"You don't have too much to do," Hicks reminded her. "Just get the phone near to the computer."

"I know," she said. "I remember."

Josie turned around and looked into the back of the car. Ziggy was in the middle of the bench seat, with an open laptop on either side of him. The phone that she had taken from him yesterday was hooked up to one of the laptops. He was wearing a pair of headphones through which she could hear the thump-thump-thump of bass. He didn't look up.

"Don't expect anything from him until we get there," Hicks apologised. "He's been working on this all night."

"But he's ready?"

"He says he will be."

"Best we get going, then."

Josie turned around and looked up at the window of their hotel room. She saw Angelo's face between the curtains as Hicks put the car into drive and pulled away.

Chapter Fifty-Eight

JOSIE WALKED through the open gate and made her way across the lawn and into the faux castle that, in turn, led into the main prison building. She walked with as much confidence as she could muster, doing her best to mask the fear that was churning in her gut.

Ziggy had worked on whatever it was that he was doing for the duration of the drive south, and his regular curses of irritation, rendered louder than they might have been by the fact that he was listening to music and couldn't hear himself speaking, did nothing for her confidence. He had had all night to finish whatever it was he was working on, and he was still finalising it. The clatter of his fingers on the keyboard became faster and faster the nearer they got to Bilibid, and he only handed the phone over to her as Hicks pulled up in the same place that he had parked yesterday, outside the prison complex. Ziggy's summation of his work as he folded up one of the laptops was that he had done the best that he could do; his dissatisfaction didn't do much for her confidence.

She went through the main door and made her way through the lobby. It was busier again, with the same bustle of staff and visitors as she had seen during previous daytime visits. There was a queue of men and women waiting to pass through the scanner in the security lodge and, as she made her way across the hall to the Plexiglas window, she noticed that there were two people already waiting ahead of her.

That, at least, was good. It would grant her a little added time for Ziggy to do whatever it was that he was proposing to do.

But her good luck did not hold. A second clerk sat down behind the counter and beckoned her to step up.

"How can I help you?" the man said. It was the same

clerk as last night. He looked up and recognised her, adding, "You again."

"Yes," she said. "Smith. Has a visit been arranged? I wasn't called."

"Hold on."

The man turned to his computer and scrolled through the information on the screen. Josie reached into her pocket and took out the cellphone that Ziggy had given her. She looked down at the screen, pretending to use it. There was no indication that the phone was anything other than normal, no tell-tale information on the display that might betray the alchemy that Ziggy had promised.

There was a narrow sill on her side of the window, and she placed the phone on it, sliding it so that it was obscured by the computer on the other side of the glass and, she hoped, out of the clerk's sight.

"Go through to the visiting block. They'll bring him out when you get there."

"Thank you," she said.

She turned away and started for the security lodge.

"Excuse me!"

She stopped and turned back.

"Your phone."

The woman who had been standing behind her in the queue was proffering the cellphone that she had left behind.

Josie managed a bashful smile, thanked her, and took the device. Her stomach dropped. She had only been at the desk for a minute. Ziggy had said that it might take him longer than that. Had she given him the time that he needed? There was no way of knowing and now she was committed. She had to follow through with the rest of the plan.

She felt sick as she put the phone back into her pocket and made her way to the lodge and the line of people waiting to be searched.

#

JOSIE WASN'T taken to the communal visiting room.

Instead, the guard led her farther down the corridor to a private room. She waited for the door to be opened and then followed the guard inside. There was a table and two chairs, one of which was positioned over an iron bracket that had been fitted directly into the concrete floor.

"Take a seat," the guard said. "He's on his way."

Josie did as she was told, sitting down and lacing her fingers together on the table. They had taken her gun and the hacked phone when she passed through the security lodge. She had felt uneasy handing it over, relying on Ziggy's assurance that his homebrew alterations were undetectable and the assumption that it would just be dropped into a box until she returned to collect it, but still fearful that it would give her away. She felt exposed and vulnerable.

The door opened and she heard the jangle of metal. A guard came through first, stepping aside so that Milton and a second guard could follow him inside. Milton's wrists were shackled together; the metal chain rattled as he moved. The guard pulled back the chair for him so that he could sit, and then knelt down and attached a tether to his chain and fastened that to the bracket.

The guard turned to Josie. "Ten minutes," he said. "Then he goes back again."

"Thank you."

The guards retreated to the edge of the room, but made no move to leave.

"Alone, please," she said sternly.

The guards paused.

She nodded down to the loop of chain that connected the cuffs around Milton's wrists. "What's he going to do? If I need you, I'll shout."

The guards exchanged a glance. The first guard shrugged, repeated that she had ten minutes, and led the second one outside. The door was closed. She could see the silhouette of one of them through the smoked glass.

"Talk quietly," Milton said in a low voice.

"Bugged?" she mouthed silently.

"Probably," Milton said.

She shifted in her seat. She was aware of a prickling sensation between her shoulder blades, as if someone was behind her, watching.

"I've met your friend," she said.

"He came?"

She nodded. "Is he usually so strange?"

"He has a way about him," Milton said.

"They said you killed someone."

"One of the inmates who was working for the man responsible for this. I wouldn't waste any sleep over him."

You sound just like the president, she thought. She started to allow herself to think about the moral equivalence between the two of them, both prepared to be the arbiter of whether someone should live or die. She quickly stopped herself. She didn't want thoughts like that in her head. She had committed herself to Milton and his friends. They were the only way she could see to untangle herself from the problems that, paradoxically, had been caused by her refusal to ignore the obvious injustice of Milton's plight. The last thing she needed now was to start second-guessing herself, and him.

She lowered her voice again. "They wanted me to tell you that you'll need to be ready."

"What did they say?"

"Ziggy says you'll know when it happens."

"Nothing more specific?"

"He says he's working it out. I think he's the sort of man who favours big gestures."

"About as vague as I'd expect," Milton said with a grimace.

"He gave me a phone number. He said when it all starts, you should get to a phone and call it. He'll guide you out. He said you need to remember it."

"Go on."

She recited the number. Milton closed his eyes, made her repeat it, and then nodded.

"You've got it?"

"Yes."

She looked up at the door; she could see the silhouette of the second man now, too. They were both close to the door.

"Thank you, Josie. I know you've taken a risk to help me."

"You'll help me? Once you get out? Me and my boy?"

"You have my word."

"Good luck."

She got up and looked down at him. He had been battered, his face marked with bruises that ran through blues and purples and blacks, but there was a certainty of purpose about him that was impossible to mistake. He reminded her of her father. He had been a promising catchweight fighter before an accident at work had ripped up his knee. He had died when she was a teenager, but she still remembered the fights that her mother had taken them to watch, and the iron determination in his eyes as he stepped through the ropes to face opponents who were often bigger than he was.

Milton had the same dauntless certitude.

They exchanged a glance.

The door opened.

She walked out on him without turning back.

Chapter Fifty-Nine

THE GUARD unclipped the tether from the bracket and told Milton to get up. He did as he was told. The cuffs were tight, cutting into the flesh on his wrists, but he didn't give them the satisfaction of seeing that he was sore. That was just the latest of his inconveniences: his muscles were still tender from the beatings that he had taken, one of his teeth had worked its way loose, and his neck and shoulders ached from being forced to sleep on the cold stone floor.

The guards took their places again, one in front and the other behind. "Move," the guard behind him said, jabbing him in the back with the point of his baton.

They escorted him out of the visitors' block and back toward the main building. He recognised the entrance to the isolation wing, but they passed by it.

"Where are we going?"

The guard jabbed him in the kidneys. "Quiet. Walk."

They made their way to Building No. 1 and went inside through the main door. They followed the corridor until they reached the stairs, then climbed up to the second floor.

The door to Milton's old cell was open.

Two guards emerged from the cell. They were bearing a stretcher between them. There was a body on the stretcher. Milton looked down at it as the guards negotiated their way around him.

Isko.

The man's eyes were closed and one arm hung limply over the edge of the stretcher.

He was dead.

The guard behind Milton put his hand on his shoulder and pushed.

Milton took another step. He turned and looked into the cell.

There was a man inside. He was big—much bigger than Milton—and wearing an evil grin.

Tiny.

#

HICKS LOOKED at his watch.

It was ten. Josie had been inside the building for an hour. He had a good view of the prison forecourt from their spot outside the gates. He could see the parking lot and the lawn and, finally, the ostentatious building with its vinyl banner and grand entrance. He had watched her disappear inside, but she had not yet come out.

He turned and looked into the back of the car. "Well?"

Ziggy had taken out a USB dongle and inserted it into the port of one of his laptops. He ran his finger down the screen, chewing on his bottom lip. "Here," he said, finally. "TUUSAN 21. That's the Bluetooth connection I saw from before."

"What are you doing?"

"Running a Linux script. Getting the unique ID of the keyboard." He paused, dragged his finger across the laptop's trackpad, and stabbed his finger on the return key. "There," he said.

"Done?"

"I've spoofed it to this laptop and paired with the computer."

"You're in?"

"Nearly."

Ziggy's fingers flashed across the keyboard.

"How much longer?"

"Nearly there."

"She can't stay there."

"Shut up, Hicks. It'll take longer if you keep distracting me."

He typed in commands and then sat back, leaning against the seat, his hands held up. He turned the laptop around so that Hicks could see the screen. There was a download bar slowly filling with green from left to right.

"What's that?"

"I'm connected to the FTP server that has the exploit I wrote last night. I'm uploading it to the computer in the security building."

The bar crawled. "It's taking ages," Hicks complained.

"Download speed here is prehistoric," Ziggy said with a shrug. "Not much I can do about that."

The bar was halfway full.

#

"INSIDE."

"Again?"

"*Inside.*"

He jangled the cuffs. "At least take these off. Give me a fighting chance."

"Move," the guard said curtly, putting his hands on Milton's shoulders and shoving him.

Milton staggered into the cell. Isko's bedroll had been shoved to one side; Milton could see splashes of blood on it. He held up his hands. "Come on," he said. "You just killed an old man. You want to try with someone who can fight back?"

Tiny dominated the space. His head was just an inch or two beneath the ceiling, and there was barely enough room to pass on either side of him. Milton was close to the door. The guard put his foot against his lower back and pushed, causing him to stumble another two steps inside.

The door scraped across its runners and then clattered as it crashed into the other side of the doorway, the lock fastening with a loud click.

Tiny was almost within touching distance.

"Take these off," Milton said.

The big Filipino maintained his hungry grin.

"You scared?" Milton said.

"You die now," Tiny said, his English awkward and halting. He raised his hand up and drew his finger across his throat. "Like your friend."

Milton heard excited voices behind him and, when he risked a quick turn of his head, he saw that the guards were still there. They had been joined by three others.

Front-row seats. The guards were going to watch him take his beating.

Milton laced his fingers together. He knew that he was outmatched. Tiny was bigger and stronger than he was, and, despite the rest that he had managed to get without being beaten every day, his body was still bruised and sore. In addition to all of that, his hands were cuffed.

Tiny took a step forward.

Milton swung both hands at him. It was impossible not to telegraph it, and Tiny leaned away from the clubbing blow, raising one arm and deflecting it with his wrist. Milton lost his balance and stumbled closer in. Tiny crashed his right fist into Milton's face. It was a quick jab, without too much momentum behind it, but it was still stiff enough to jerk Milton's head back against his shoulders. He staggered away until his back was up against the bars of the cell door.

He heard laughter from the watching guards.

He felt the taste of his own blood in his mouth and spat a gobbet on the floor.

Tiny smirked.

Milton laced his fingers together again.

Chapter Sixty

JOSIE CAME through the security lodge and waited in line to collect her gun and the phone.

"Josie?"

She stopped.

"Wait."

She turned. Bruno Mendoza was hurrying in her direction.

"What are you doing here?" he said.

Her breath was clenched deep in her gut. "I came to see Smith," she managed.

"Why?"

"I had some questions for him."

"*More* questions?"

"Loose ends."

"I don't understand," Mendoza said. "I told you this was finished. I said you were wasting your time. Why did you do what I told you not to do?"

"I was being thorough. I had to speak to him again."

Mendoza reached out and grasped her firmly around the elbow.

"What are you doing?" she protested.

"I want to talk to you."

He led her into the lobby. She tried to jerk her elbow free, but he just tightened his grip and yanked her after him.

"You're hurting me."

Mendoza pulled her over to the left, toward the doors that led into the administrative wing of the building. There was a guard sitting at a desk next to the door.

"Open it," Mendoza said.

The man was looking down at his computer. He pressed the return key half a dozen times, each one harder than the last.

"I'm sorry, sir. My computer is down."

Mendoza looked from the guard and then back to Josie. She flinched; there was no way that he could possibly have guessed what Ziggy was trying to do, yet she felt as if he was able to look past the lies and obfuscations and see the truth.

"Open the door," Mendoza said.

The man got up from the desk and opened the door.

Mendoza yanked on Josie's elbow, and she followed him inside.

#

MILTON THUDDED against the wall and then crashed down against the floor.

Tiny had grabbed him beneath the arms and flung him across the cell. He had managed to twist in mid-air so that he might take the jolt against his back rather than crash into it headlong, but now he was winded. The back of his head had bounced off the stone and, when he looked up, he had to blink away the darkness that was leeching around the edges of his vision.

The big Filipino flexed his shoulders, his muscles bulging.

Milton scrabbled to his feet.

Tiny lunged for him.

Milton was able to duck beneath his grasping hands, crouching low enough so that he could swivel and slide through the narrow gap the big man had left between himself and the wall.

He stumbled back until he was up against the bars once again.

He took a deep breath, filling his lungs with as much air as he could.

He felt a sudden prod against his back. One of the guards had taken out his billy club and was jabbing him with it.

Milton knew it was hopeless. He was buying time, but he wouldn't be able to do that forever.

#

ZIGGY'S FINGERS flashed across the keys.

He had downloaded the exploit to the computer. Now he needed to push it into the jail's wider network. The security was as lax as he had hoped it would be. The network was flat, with no obvious firewalls or air gaps. He could see that he would have control of everything.

"Where is she?" Hicks said.

Ziggy ignored him.

"This shouldn't have taken so long."

The upload bar seemed to hang, the last portion stubbornly refusing to fill up.

"Ziggy—come on."

"The network is slow."

"Make it go faster."

"I can't do that."

The computer bleeped its satisfaction.

Ziggy looked down: the download bar was solid blue. "I'm in. Stand by."

He knew that he would have to move fast. He typed commands, his fingers a blur.

He hit return.

"Here we go," he said.

Nothing.

He looked down at the laptop.

"Well?" Hicks said.

The cursor blinked at him.

"I don't—"

He heard the sound of sirens.

"Is that you?"

"I told the system that there's a fire," Ziggy said. "The doors are programmed to open if that happens."

"The cell doors?"

"*All* the doors."

Chapter Sixty-One

A LOUD siren blared out.

Tiny stopped.

The lights faded out.

There came a series of clicks and thunks as the locks on all of the doors along the corridor were released.

The lights flicked back on again.

The doors juddered and rattled, all of them sliding back.

One of the guards outside the cell cursed.

Milton spun around.

Two of the guards were close. He leapt at the nearest one. The man had his baton in his hand, holding it loosely with his fingers outside the leather strap. Milton lowered his shoulder and tackled him backwards, all the way across the walkway to the metal balustrade that guarded against the drop to the floor below. The guard was lighter than Milton and he was at a disadvantage. Milton reached for the baton, his left hand closing around the wooden shaft. The balustrade served as a fulcrum, the guard's body arching over it before he overbalanced, the weight of his torso dragging him over the side. He slipped over the edge, crashing down against the concrete floor of the concourse below.

One down.

Milton spun around. The guard to his right had managed to take his Taser out of its holster. He was raising his arm to aim it as Milton backhanded him with the baton. The end of the shaft struck him on the side of the head. It was a stunning blow, and the guard dropped to his knees.

Two down.

The guard dropped the Taser.

Milton dropped to one knee and took it.

He sensed movement from the cell. He swivelled his hips, aimed blindly and fired.

Tiny was too big to miss. The prongs deployed, one striking the big man in the fat of his belly and the other in his chest. The Taser discharged, fifty thousand volts unloading along the cable for a full five seconds. Tiny started to reach for the darts, but he was overwhelmed by the sudden and uncontrollable contraction of his muscles. His spine straightened before he toppled back like a felled tree, his legs and arms twitching spastically.

Three down.

Milton swivelled back. He pushed back up to a standing position and brought the Taser around in a forehand uppercut that cracked into the chin of one of the three remaining guards.

The man went down, unconscious before his head bounced off the metal walkway.

Orange-shirted inmates started to emerge from the cells.

Milton ejected the spent cartridge from the Taser.

The two guards who were still standing knew that they were in trouble.

One of them had managed to fumble his baton out of its retaining strap. He swung it at Milton's head, but the wild swipe was simple enough to duck beneath. Milton swept the man's legs and, as he landed against the walkway with a heavy thud, he pressed the Taser into the man's chest and pulled the trigger to stun him.

More inmates appeared.

The last guard started to panic.

He turned away from Milton, but froze. The way ahead was blocked by a clutch of prisoners.

The man was caught between them and Milton.

There came an angry shout.

Milton looked up.

He saw the elevated booth above them on the other side of the building. It was manned by a guard whose job it was to open the cell doors remotely. The booth was encased in glass, like a bubble, with the glass reinforced by security bars. It offered excellent visibility all along the walkway. The guard had opened the window and was pointing a 12-gauge shotgun through the bars and down at them.

Milton flung himself into the cell.

The shotgun boomed.

Tiny pellets chimed as they rang off the metal. It was birdshot, the same ammunition that sport shooters used to blow up clay pigeons and hunters used to kill birds and rabbits.

The noise in the walkway changed from jubilation to anger.

Tiny was still on the floor. The contractions had eased, and his fingers were crawling across his stomach like bloated spiders as he felt for the two darts. Milton looked down at him. Tiny found the darts and plucked them out. He pushed himself into a sitting position.

Milton thought of the beatings that Tiny had meted out. He didn't care so much about himself. He thought about the other men whom de Lacey must have thrown to his house thug.

He thought about Isko.

Milton slipped behind the big man and looped his cuffed hands over his neck. He clasped both hands together and then pulled until the chain that connected the cuffs was tight against Tiny's throat.

The big man knew that he was in trouble.

He started to struggle, but Milton had the advantage now. He pulled back as hard as he could.

Tiny was strong. He jerked forward. He managed to get his right foot on the ground and pushed up, hoisting Milton with him.

Milton's toes brushed the floor of the cell as Tiny reversed, driving Milton back into the wall.

The impact was powerful, driving the air from his lungs, but he was tenacious. He held on.

Tiny tried again.

Milton tightened his grip and held on.

He looped his legs around the big man's waist and

leaned back, pulling with everything he had.

The choke was depressing the carotid artery, starving the brain of oxygen. Most people would have lost consciousness within ten seconds, but Milton knew that the thick muscle in Tiny's neck would buy him a little extra time.

Didn't matter.

Milton yanked again, his biceps bulging, and, finally, Tiny overbalanced.

They both hit the ground. Milton gasped from the impact, pinned beneath Tiny's weight, but he maintained the hold.

He locked his legs tighter.

He pulled back harder still.

Four seconds.

Eight seconds.

Tiny's body went limp.

Milton pulled.

Fifteen seconds.

He leaned forward, raised his arms and removed the chain from Tiny's neck. He slid out from beneath the big man's body.

There was no time to check, but it wouldn't have been necessary.

He was dead.

Chapter Sixty-Two

"GET OFF ME."

Mendoza tugged her deeper into the building.

"You want to tell me how you knew I was here?" she said.

"Shut up, Josie."

"I'm serious. How did you know? I didn't tell anyone."

"I got a phone call about an officer nosing around in business that didn't concern her. I tried to tell you."

"How deep are you into all this?"

"All this?"

"The conspiracy against Milton."

"Who?"

"Smith," she corrected herself. "Who's paying you?"

He ignored her. "I *warned* you to let it go, but you didn't listen. You kept pressing and pressing and *pressing* and now look."

"Oh shit," Josie said, as she made a connection. "Santos said he was going to call the station. Did he call you?"

Mendoza dragged her onward. He yanked her to the left, through an open doorway and then down a flight of stairs.

Josie tried to free herself, but he was too strong. "He called you, didn't he? He left me a message and said that he would. What did he tell you? He told me they had a backup of the security video and that I needed to see it. Were you on the video?"

"No," Mendoza said. They reached the bottom of the stairs. They were in the basement. There was no one else there with them.

"But you went there, didn't you? You saw the tape. Did you kill them because of it?"

He stopped short and wheeled around to face her.

"Admit it, Bruno."

His lip curled into a snarl. "I didn't want to do this, but you haven't given me a choice."

"You didn't want to do…"

The sentence trailed off.

His hand twitched in the direction of his holstered gun.

Josie went for it, but he blocked her. He brought up his elbow and struck her in the face.

She fell away from him.

His hand slid into his jacket.

And then they heard the siren.

Mendoza was distracted for a moment, and Josie took her chance.

She swung her elbow up into his face. The bony point caught him on the side of the temple. He was taller than she was, and it was difficult to put any power into the blow, but it caught him by surprise. He tripped and fell to the floor. Josie followed with a kick, driving the point of her boot between his open legs and into his crotch.

Mendoza yelped in pain.

Something fell out of his jacket pocket onto the floor.

His cellphone.

She scooped it up.

"Josie!"

She kicked him again, turned away and ran back up the stairs.

#

THE NOISE grew louder.

Milton edged to the open doorway and glanced out.

The walkway swarmed with inmates. They were spilling out of the cells.

He looked up. He could see through the metal slats of the walkway above him that the doors had been opened on that floor, too. More men were coming out, their curiosity quickly changing into something more urgent and desperate.

The prison was full of dangerous men. Under normal

conditions, it exchanged the loss of liberty for order and security. It was a menacing place, but, if you played by the rules, it was possible to serve out a sentence and leave in one piece.

This was different.

It was chaos now, and, for as long as chaos suppressed order, the prison was almost unimaginably perilous.

Without order, grudges could be settled.

Vendettas followed.

Blood spilled.

Milton didn't care for the quarrels of his fellow inmates, but he needed to get around them so that he could start to make his way out of the building. One of the unconscious guards was just outside the open door. He reached and grabbed the man's ankle, yanking him inside. He frisked him quickly. He had a bunch of keys attached to his belt, and Milton flipped through them until he found the one that would open his cuffs. He bent his right wrist back so that he could work the key into the lock, twisted it, and popped the mechanism. The cuffs sprang open and Milton shook them off.

One orange-shirted prisoner ran by the open door and tackled another to the ground. The first man pinned the second to the metal and pounded at his head and face, a flurry of lefts and rights that splashed blood and saliva and mucus over the metal surface. The man kept punching, even as his victim lay still, his fists rendering his face unrecognisable.

He was about to leave the cell when he heard another boom from the shotgun. The inmate's body was suddenly riddled with shot. The pellets shredded his clothes and the flesh beneath. He fell forward, his blood commingling with his victim's.

Milton risked a look up at the booth. The guard was reloading.

He had to move.

The inmates were spilling down the stairs to the

communal area at the bottom of the building. Milton took the billy club with him and stepped out of the cell, following the flow along the walkway. The atmosphere was charged with a frantic energy, and exultant whoops bounced back from the walls. The breakout was gathering momentum. Soon it would be difficult to stop.

There was going to be a full-scale riot.

Milton was borne down the stairs by the surging crowd. He reached the bottom and caught a glimpse into the first cell as he was jostled ahead: two men were holding a third man down as a fourth watched. Another pair of inmates was scuffling, toppling back against the table tennis table and bumping the two sections apart.

Milton heard a scream and looked up. The elevated booth had been breached, and the guard with the shotgun was struggling with the prisoners who had surged inside. The man was dragged out onto the platform and, as the men paused to watch, he was thrown over the balustrade. His body fell through the vaulted space and bounced horribly as it slammed into the concrete floor just yards from where Milton stood.

Chapter Sixty-Three

JOSIE RAN back in the direction that Mendoza had brought her.

The building was chaotic. Staff were running freely along the corridors, hurrying to the exit.

She bumped flush into a guard.

"What is it?" she asked him.

"The cells. The doors. They're open."

Ziggy, she thought. *It worked.*

The man looked at her, panic in his eyes. "The inmates! They're getting out. There's going to be a riot. You have to leave. We all have to leave."

"Which way is it?"

"I'll take you."

The guard set off and Josie ran behind him. He took a left and then another left. The corridors all looked the same and she hadn't been paying attention to where Mendoza had been taking her. She was quickly lost.

They turned a corner and she saw two orange-shirted inmates coming straight toward them.

The guard crashed into both of them. The first inmate drew back his fist and stabbed it into the guard's chest. Josie saw a flash of something metallic as he withdrew his arm and then the droplets of red blood on the bare concrete floor.

The inmates spotted her, smiled, and stalked ahead.

Josie was next to a door. She turned the handle. The door was unlocked. She pushed it open and darted inside.

The room was dark. Josie glimpsed the shapes of a table, two chairs, and a sofa. It was some sort of waiting area. There were no windows.

She shut the door and looked for a key. She couldn't see one.

The handle rattled as it was turned and the door opened an inch.

"Come on," a voice called out.

She slammed it shut again and put her back to it.

"Come on, baby. Open up."

There came an angry hammering at the door.

"It's just me and my little shank. Come on. Open the door."

Shit.

The pounding stopped. Josie waited with her back to the door, hardly daring to move. She waited another fifteen seconds and then, knowing that she had to do *something*, she went to the sofa, grabbed it with both hands and pulled. It was heavy, but she was able to muscle it across the room, the legs scoring marks across the wooden floor. She hauled it in front of the door and pushed it until it was flush with the wall.

It was just in time. The handle turned again as someone tried to force the door open; the sofa jerked forward an inch or two until she pushed it back and held it in place.

Now what?

She was stuck here.

She looked around the room. It was practically empty. She wished that she still had her pistol.

That reminded her.

She reached into her pocket and took out the cellphone that Mendoza had dropped.

It was unlocked. She tapped in the number that she had just given Milton.

The phone rang three times.

"Milton?"

"No. Hernandez."

"Where are you?" It was Ziggy.

"I'm inside the building. The inmates are out. There's a riot. I can't leave."

"Hold the line."

There was a moment of silence and then Hicks came on the line.

"Are you safe?" he said.

"I've barricaded myself in a room."

"Where?"

"I don't know. Somewhere in the administrative building. The door's not locked, though. I don't know how long it'll stand up."

There was another crash as the men outside hurled themselves against the door again.

"Josie?"

"You need to hurry. I can't hold them out for ever."

"I hear you. Stay on the line. Ziggy wants to speak to you."

There was another moment of silence as the phone changed hands.

"I need you to send me your location," Ziggy said. "Put the call on speaker and do as I say."

She did. Ziggy told her to launch the messages app and then start a text conversation with him on the number she had memorised. She tapped on the details icon and then told the phone to send her current location.

"Got you," Ziggy said. "I know where you are. I'll call the police and tell them that you're trapped."

There was another heavy thud against the door.

"I don't have time for that," she said. "It's a *riot*. The police will wait for the army, but that won't be for hours. The inmates know I'm in here. They'll break the door down."

She couldn't hear a reply. She pressed the phone to her ear.

"Ziggy!"

"Stay where you are. I'm working on it."

"Please hurry."

Chapter Sixty-Four

MILTON FRISKED the body of the guard who had fallen to his death.

He was unarmed, but, in his back pocket, Milton found a small Nokia cellphone.

He took it and dialled the number that Josie had given him.

The call connected.

"It's Milton."

He heard Hicks. "Where are you?"

"There's a full-scale riot. I need a way out."

"You can come out the front. The guards in the watchtower have cleared out."

"Anything else?"

"We've got a problem. Hernandez is trapped inside."

Milton gripped the phone a little tighter.

"Where is she?"

#

JOSIE SAT down with her back to the sofa, planted the soles of her feet flat on the floor and braced her legs. There came another thump as whoever it was outside in the corridor tried to force the door. The sofa jerked a little bit farther into the room and the door opened a crack.

"Open the door!" the man cackled through the gap.

"I'm a police officer," Josie shouted back. "And I'm armed."

"Sure you are, baby," the man said.

"I'll shoot anyone who tries to get in here."

"Yeah? I say you're bluffing."

Josie heard a gale of laughter and then a stream of salacious suggestions about what the men outside would do to her once they got through the door.

She wished that she *was* armed. That might have given her a chance. But she wasn't. Her gun was still inside the security lodge. If the inmates were logical enough and thought about it, they would be able to loot the office and arm themselves. That the situation could get worse was obvious, but it was also an irrelevance as far as Josie was concerned.

It was already bad enough.

There was no way out. No windows. No other doors. She was trapped, a female police officer lost inside the swirling chaos of rioting prisoners, many of whom had no hope of being released and no hope of ever being with a woman again. They had nothing to lose. The fact that they could take out their anger and frustration on a police officer at the same time would be just another bonus for them.

There came another almighty thud as something was slammed against the door. It was weightier and harder than before, more solid than the shoulder charges that she had been able to fend off.

A heavy object.

There came a second crash.

And then a third.

Josie heard a splintering and, as she looked up above the back of the sofa, she saw that the door was splitting down the middle.

#

MENDOZA SHOULDERED through the door that led into the main lobby.

He stopped, his feet slipping on the floor.

There were two orange-shirted prisoners blocking the way ahead.

Mendoza didn't pause. He reached into his jacket, yanked his Glock out of its holster, and shot both of them. The men went down, one of them dead before he hit the floor and the other trying to staunch the sudden rush of blood from his abdomen.

Mendoza gripped the pistol tightly and ran for the door.

Josie was still in there for all he knew, but he didn't care about that.

She was the reason he had come down here. Her interference and disobedience had put them both in danger.

Maybe the riot would put an end to that once and for all.

It would save him the job.

Two more prisoners emerged from the security lobby.

Mendoza turned and fired. Both rounds missed, but the prisoners got the message. They dived into cover.

He had seven rounds in the magazine and another in the chamber. He had to get out.

He backed away, the pistol aimed at where the men had hidden, and then he turned and ran.

#

JOSIE PUSHED back until her thighs burned.

She wasn't going to give up.

She closed her eyes and thought of Angelo.

She would hold out for as long as she could.

There came another crash and then another rending creak as the door panel continued to split down the middle.

There was a fresh cackle of laughter, an exhortation to redouble efforts, and then…

The sound of something heavy falling to the floor.

Josie sat up.

She heard a scream interrupted by a yelp of pain and then the unmistakable sound of something hard colliding with flesh and bone. There was another impact as something dropped to the floor. She heard a cry of angry indignation that was choked off before it could be finished and then the slap of running feet that quickly faded out.

"Josie!"

She pushed harder, her muscles burning. "Who is it?"

"It's Milton."

She stayed where she was.

"Open the door."

Josie found that she was trembling, her muscles quivering uncontrollably. Was it Milton? He had found her? She was too scared to allow herself to believe that she might have a way out. Maybe it was a trap. But how would anyone else know to pretend to be him? There was no logic to suggest that it was anyone other than Milton, but panic was obscuring her logic.

"Josie," Milton said through the crack in the door, "they'll be back. We need to move. Please. Open the door."

She got up and heaved the sofa aside. The door had splintered down the middle and wouldn't have stood too much more punishment. She opened it: Milton was standing outside. He was holding a prison officer's billy club in his fist. Three orange-shirted inmates sprawled on the floor, unmoving; one of them was bleeding freely from a wound to his scalp, the blood pooling around his head. Milton's own orange shirt was flecked with red, and there was sweat on his face. There were fresh marks, too, and darkening patches that promised fresh bruises.

"Ready?" Milton said.

She nodded.

"Come on."

He started to jog. Josie followed, matching his easy pace. He reached into his pocket for a cellphone and put it to his ear, speaking as he loped along.

"Is it still clear?"

Josie couldn't hear the reply.

"It's Hicks," he explained as he put the phone back into his pocket. "They're out the front. They'll pick us up."

"What about the police?"

"There's no one there yet."

"They'll be coming. The army, too."

"That's why we've got to hurry."

Milton led the way to the main entrance hall. A fire had been set in one of the adjoining rooms, and smoke was pouring out of broken windows and an open doorway. They saw other prisoners choking as they emerged into the dimness of the main room. The security lobby had been overrun, with inmates passing through the defunct scanner and making their way to the doors and the clean, open air beyond. They were fixated on the prospect of their freedom, and none of them stopped to give Josie any heed. The one man who did divert his direction to intercept them, making a lewd comment as he approached, was briskly persuaded to see the foolhardiness of his ways. Milton swung the baton at him in a diagonal downward swipe that caught him on the bony knuckle of his knee. He yelped in pain, rolling to the ground and clutching his leg.

The main doors had been forced open, and now they swung impotently on broken hinges. Milton shouldered them apart and, reaching back to take Josie's hand, led the way outside.

She looked up at the watchtowers and remembered seeing the rifles of the guards stationed there. But the guards were not there now. More smoke piled out of smashed windows and formed vast pillars that were already several hundred feet tall. She saw the hungry yellow and orange of flames through other windows and heard the sounds of screams, whoops and breaking glass.

"Run," Milton said. "Don't stop for anyone."

Milton set off to the main gate. Some inmates were gathered just outside, as if unsure what to do now that they had their freedom. She saw flashes of orange as others, perhaps wise to the inevitable arrival of enforcements, hurried across the neighbouring fields and into the dense vegetation that fringed them.

The gates had been forced, too, and now they hung limply, creaking in the breeze.

A car was approaching them at speed. It flashed its lights.

"There," Milton said, changing direction.

The car raced up to them, skidding to a sudden stop. The rear door opened and Josie slid in, bumping up against Ziggy Penn. His laptops were still open. Hicks was in the front, and he reached over to open the passenger door. Milton slid across the hood, opened the door all the way and dropped into the seat.

"Go!"

Hicks did not need to be asked twice. He stomped down on the gas and the wheels squealed as the rubber bit into the rough asphalt. The car jerked forward and then swung around as Hicks turned the wheel to full lock, the rear end fishtailing and smoke pouring out of the wheel arches. Hicks straightened up and, stamping down on the gas again, they raced away.

Chapter Sixty-Five

MILTON REACHED over and clapped his hand on Hicks's shoulder.

"Well done," he said.

"It wasn't me. It was all Josie and Ziggy."

Milton turned. Ziggy was looking at him with a self-satisfied smirk on his face.

"Good to see you again," he said.

"That was fun," Ziggy said. "Impressed?"

"You've never failed to impress me."

Milton knew Ziggy well enough to know that he responded best when his ego was massaged. He could certainly be irritating, but the fact of it was that he was able to back up his hubris with ability. Ziggy had helped Milton hack the headquarters of the Mossad. What he had done today was just the latest in a long line of increasingly impressive demonstrations.

He turned to Josie. "Are you okay?"

"I'm fine. Thanks for coming for me. You could've—"

"No," he interrupted. "Thank you. I'd still be in there without your help."

"I don't have anyone else to turn to."

"I meant what I said."

"You'll help?"

"You need to help me first. Tell me everything."

Josie had explained her suspicions to Milton before, it was useful to have her rehash them. Milton and Hicks listened intently as she went back over the details of Milton's arrest and how she had come to be so certain that he had been framed. She recounted the death of the bar owner and the role that her commanding officer had played in moving Milton from Manila down to New Bilibid so that he could fall completely under de Lacey's control. She reminded him of the threats that she had received and her conviction that the same man was responsible for them.

"He was there today," she said. "It's why I couldn't get out. He grabbed me."

"Where is he now?"

"I kicked him between the legs and ran. I don't know what happened to him."

"What's his name?" Milton said.

"Bruno Mendoza."

"Ziggy?"

"I'm already on it."

Milton watched as Ziggy's fingers flashed across the keyboard. He had tethered his laptop to his phone and, now that they were north of the prison and he had a reliable signal, he was typing in a string of commands.

"What are you doing?" Josie asked.

"I'm going to find out where he lives."

"How?"

"Hack the police database."

"This might be easier," she said, holding up the phone she had taken from Mendoza.

"That's his?"

She nodded.

"Give," he said.

Josie handed it over. Ziggy plugged it into one of the laptops and started to examine it.

"If he can find the address—"

"Found it," Ziggy interrupted. "He has a place in Makati City."

"Fine," she said. "We know where he lives. What do we do now?"

"Pay him a visit," Milton said.

She bit her lip.

Milton could see that she was reluctant. "What's up?"

"Am I doing the right thing? I don't know—maybe I should go and see the chief inspector. I mean, I could tell him what I know."

"You don't know how far the corruption goes up the chain," Hicks offered.

"He's right," Milton said. "You know you can't do that. It could be dangerous. It'll also be slow. And we need to move today. When he finds out what's happened and that I'm out, maybe he runs. He certainly makes it more difficult to get to him. You won't be safe if that happens."

"And then? When we find him?"

"We ask him who else is involved."

"You think he killed your friend?"

"I don't think so. I think I know who that was. But maybe Mendoza can help me find him."

"And then?"

Milton knew what she was asking: how would he make her safe?

"There are two ways we can play this—"

"I don't… I don't want him dead," she interrupted.

"Then you'll need to get the evidence to build a case."

It was clear to Milton that Josie could see the scale of her quandary now. It was obvious. She could find evidence and build a case, but she wouldn't be able to do it alone. She would need help from senior officers that she could trust. And, from the look on her face, Milton could see that she was already struggling to think of anyone of sufficient rank that she could confide in. Maybe she didn't know anyone well enough beyond Mendoza to be confident that they would not be involved and that they would take the side of a junior officer against her more senior colleague. Milton already knew that Josie was moral—she had worked to get him out despite the risk to herself—but now she would face a test of her convictions. Milton would be true to his word and would do whatever he could to make her safe. He didn't have the same qualms as she did, though, and his way would be safer than any alternative. Following the law would bring greater risk. But she would have to choose. Milton would do whatever she asked.

He looked at her. She was biting her lip and gazing out of the window.

"Where are we headed?" Hicks asked.

Ziggy recited an address in Makati City.

"It's an apartment," he said.

"Where?"

Hicks waited for the satnav to calculate the route. "Not far," he said, once the green line had overlaid the map. "We can be there in an hour."

Chapter Sixty-Six

THEY PARKED the car in the underground lot beneath the apartment block.

"Both of us?" Hicks said to Milton.

"It won't hurt."

"I'm coming," Josie said.

"You don't need to do that," Milton said.

Josie shook her head. She wasn't about to take a step back now. She felt as if she were in a maze, stumbling for an exit that she couldn't yet find, but she knew that she had to be involved.

"I'm coming. This is a police investigation. I'm not backing off now."

Milton shrugged. "Fine by me."

"I'll stay," Ziggy said. "I'll see what else I can get off his phone."

Josie stepped out. Hicks and Milton followed, and they took the elevator to the ground floor.

Josie went up to the desk. She took out her badge and held it up for the porter to see.

"How can I help you, Officer?"

"I need the key to the penthouse."

"Can I ask why?"

"Police business."

"But—"

"Inspector Mendoza lives there," she finished for him. "I know."

"I don't understand. He just left."

"When?"

The man looked at his watch. "Fifteen minutes ago."

"How was he?"

"He looked like he was in a hurry. What is this, Officer?"

"Give me the key, sir."

"Do you have a warrant?"

"You really want to go through all that?"

"Then I should call him. I can't just let you inside."

"Last chance. I'll arrest you if I have to, sir. What'll it be?"

The man blanched. He stood up, took a blank key card and programmed it in a machine on the desk. He handed it to Josie.

"Here," he said. "Top floor. The lifts are over there."

#

THEY TOOK the lift in silence.

It ascended quickly, fast enough for it to add to the empty feeling in Josie's stomach.

She closed her eyes and thought of her son. What was the point of doing her job if she allowed herself to ignore what Mendoza was doing? She wanted to bring Angelo up to know right from wrong, and she would be worse than a hypocrite if she allowed her fear to take control.

The lift arrived at the twenty-ninth floor and the doors opened.

Milton stepped out first. They were in a lobby. The floor was thickly carpeted and the walls were decorated with tasteful pieces of art. It was gloomy, with dim lights set into sconces. There were two doors: one for the emergency stairs and the other for the penthouse.

"Just because he's not here doesn't mean the flat is empty," Milton said in a low voice. "We need to be careful."

Josie nodded.

She slid the key card into the reader.

The lock buzzed and the door clicked open.

Milton touched the door with his fingertips and gently pushed it all the way open.

Josie automatically reached down for her pistol. Her fingers touched up against the empty holster. The pistol wasn't there. She had left it in the prison's security lodge.

"Shit."

She wished that she had it.

The room inside was dark. She paused, allowing her eyes to adjust to the gloom. The door opened into the living room. It was open plan, with a dining area and, beyond that, a kitchen. There were curtained windows to her right and she went over to open them. There was a balcony outside and she could see the tops of the neighbouring buildings poking up into the bright midday sky.

Milton and Hicks walked inside and turned to the left. Josie followed.

Milton opened the door to the master bedroom. It was empty.

She crossed the apartment to the kitchen. There were two other doors: one led to a bathroom and the other to the second bedroom. Both of those were empty, too. She went into the bedroom. Clothes were strewn across the bed, and the wardrobes stood open. She ran her finger along a rack of empty clothes hangers.

She turned. Milton was in the doorway. He had taken off the orange T-shirt. His torso was lean and muscular, and his skin was decorated with a number of tattoos. She could see the IX inscribed over his heart and, as he angled his body to look down at the dresser, she saw a large tattoo of an angel's wings across his back.

"You want something to wear?"

He realised that he was half naked. "Sorry. I needed to change out of the prison gear."

She took a shirt from the rail and tossed it over to him. Mendoza was around the same size and, when Milton put it on, it was a decent fit. He looked in the full-length mirror that was fixed to the back of the wardrobe door. "What do you think?"

The shirt was garish: mainly black, but decorated with a series of yellow sparkles and splashes. Josie allowed herself a smile. "Suits you," she said.

He took an empty bag from the bed and stuffed the

nside. "You found anything?"

side and indicated the clothes that had been

e wardrobe. "Look."

er was right," Milton said. "He did leave in a

same in the other bedroom."

"But ... re did he go?"

Milton had an envelope in his hand. He handed it to her. It was stamped with a logo that featured a stylised mountain peak with a smudge of red that she guessed was intended to denote the sun. The name beneath the logo read Mount Malarayat Golf & Country Club. The envelope was open. She reached inside, took out the letter and read it. It was from a woman with the title of residential manager and congratulated Mr. Mendoza on the purchase of his luxury villa.

"How far away is that?"

Mount Malarayat was near Lipa City. "Two hours to the south. You think he's gone there?"

"Unless Ziggy has a better idea, I think that's our best shot."

Chapter Sixty-Seven

THEY DROPPED Ziggy off at the airport. They had no clear idea where Mendoza had gone, but a flight out of the country was an option that they could not discount. Ziggy agreed to watch the terminal and contact them if he saw anything. He would also be able to hook into the Wi-Fi network and provide backup as they needed it.

Hicks drove them. Lipa City was in the Batangas region, seventy miles south of metropolitan Manila. They followed Route 3 as it ran down the shore of Laguna de Bay, through Cabuyao and Calamba and, finally, into Lipa. The drive took two hours and it was three in the afternoon by the time they arrived at the address they had found in the apartment.

The property was located inside a gated community. The way into the complex was blocked by a barrier that was raised and lowered by a guard, who sheltered from the sun in a neat little hut. They could see the villas nearest to the gate from their position on the road. They were obviously luxurious, even from the outside: each looked spacious and was constructed with a natural stone facade that reminded Milton of similar villas that he had seen in Japan. A notice fixed to the wall of the compound announced that further construction was under way and that the compound would soon be equipped with a clubhouse, sports complex and retail outlets. Prices were noted to start at one million dollars.

"Nice," Hicks said. "The police are better paid here than they are at home."

Josie snorted. "Don't be crazy. They pay us next to nothing. I live with my mother—there's no way I could ever afford a place like this. He shouldn't be able to, either."

"Our friend Mendoza is on the take," Milton said. "And he probably has been for years."

"How do you want to do it?" Hicks asked.

"I'm going to take a closer look," he said.

"I'm coming," Josie said.

"No. Stay here with Hicks. It'll be easier for me to go in alone."

"If he's there?"

"I'll call you. Keep your phone on. And call me if you see anything."

#

MILTON GOT out of the car. It was swelteringly hot. He had found a pair of dark glasses in the glove compartment and he put them on, shielding his eyes from the glare as sunlight reflected from the windows and the pools of the apartments next to the road. The complex was secure, encircled by a six-foot-tall stone wall. Milton walked the perimeter until he found a quiet spot that was not overlooked. He heaved himself up, wincing from the flash of pain caused by the sudden effort, and dropped down onto the other side. The compound had been planted with a fringe of bamboo and dwarf fruit trees just inside the wall, and Milton was able to find a spot where he could observe without fear of being seen.

A gardener had clambered up a coconut tree and was leaning back in a harness, a *bolo* in his hand; he lopped down with the blade, removing coconuts from the tree before they might fall on those passing below. He chopped down the leaves, too, and a mate collected both and stacked them in the back of a small motorised trolley.

Milton moved around, staying within the cover afforded by the bamboo. Mendoza's villa was near the entrance to the development, although not visible from where the car was parked. Milton found a spot where he could observe it. He watched as maids pushed trolleys loaded with fresh laundry and bottles of water. Expensive sedans and SUVs rumbled by. There were delivery trucks. Milton concentrated on the property. There was no sign that it was occupied.

He waited until there was no one else around, and then he left cover and crossed the lawn. He moved confidently, as if he belonged there. The property was delineated by a low fence that reached up to Milton's chest. He glanced over it into the garden: the pool was the centrepiece, with two recliners arranged at one end.

Milton reached the villa. They had all been built around the same design, all of them featuring generous windows to let in as much light as possible. Most of the windows were obscured by closed blinds, but Milton was able to look in on two of the bedrooms. There was no sign that anyone was here or that anyone had been here for some time.

There was no one in sight. He clambered over the fence and made his way to the door to the garage. It was wooden and not particularly thick. He would have preferred to pick the lock, but he didn't have anything that he could use.

Instead, he looked back over the fence again and, satisfied that he was still unobserved and that no one was in easy earshot, he approached. There was an art to kicking in a door, and Milton had done it many times before. He aimed his heel at the point just below where the bolt would protrude into the strike plate and then the frame. He kept his balance by driving the heel of his standing foot into the ground at the same time and avoided the lock itself for fear of injury. The door was made of soft wood and was hollow; it started to give way. The deadlock bolt extended only an inch into the frame and gave almost no resistance.

The first kick loosened the lock, but the second broke it apart.

The door opened.

Milton went inside.

There was a car in the garage and, next to that, a pair of bicycles hung from a bracket that was fitted to the wall. He paused once he was beyond the door so that his eyes could adjust to the gloom. He made out a set of shelves beyond the bikes and, opposite him, a tall American-style refrigerator. There was a workbench to his left with a selection of tools laid out alongside it. Milton reached down and took a hammer.

There was a door next to the fridge; he gripped the hammer and approached it, listening intently. He heard nothing.

Milton reached out for the handle and turned it. The door was unlocked. He pushed, opening it all the way, and then stepped inside.

He was inside the kitchen. The blind was pulled down and the room was dark. The oven had an LED display that cast enough dim light for him to be able to see. There was a sink, dark countertops, a washing machine and a dishwasher. There was another door in the opposite wall.

Milton stepped deeper into the room. He opened the opposite door and went through into the living room. The blinds were drawn in here, too. The room was empty and lit by the luminous green glow of a digital clock that sat on a sideboard. Milton opened the doors to each bedroom and checked those, too. The beds were made. There were no signs that anyone had been inside the rooms recently.

He took out his phone and called Hicks.

"It's empty," he reported.

"What do you want to do?"

"Have you heard from Ziggy?"

"He just called. He hasn't seen anything."

"We stay here, then. I'll wait here. Watch the road for me."

"Copy that."

Milton ended the call, put the phone back into his pocket and settled down to wait.

Chapter Sixty-Eight

HICKS MOVED the car farther up the road so that it was well away from the sentry post and much less suspicious. He settled back in his seat, watching the gentle flow of traffic that passed alongside.

"What's your son's name?" he asked Josie.

"Angelo."

"Is he with your partner?"

"With my mother."

"You're not married?"

"I was. Not anymore. He was killed."

"I'm sorry—"

She waved his apology away. "We were separated."

"How did he die?"

"One of the president's bounty hunters. You know about him? The president? What's happening here?"

"Just what I've read."

"The war on drugs," she intoned. "Duterte promised that the fish in Manila Bay would grow fat on the bodies of criminals. My husband's name was on a list. Someone killed him because of it."

"He was involved in drugs?"

She shrugged. "I don't know. Maybe. Maybe not. His name was on the list. That's reason enough."

Hicks shifted a little uncomfortably.

Josie must have sensed it. "How about you?" she said, filling the sudden silence. "You said you had two."

"I do. Caleb and Lucas. They're with my wife."

"She doesn't mind you coming here?"

"We owe Milton a big favour. She doesn't mind."

"What did Milton do?"

He found it easier to talk about it with her than he had with Ziggy. "My wife had cancer. She needed treatment in the

States, but we couldn't afford it. Milton found the money for us."

A car passed them and slowed for the turn into the compound.

"What do you think?" he said to her.

"Mendoza has a Porsche," she said.

"That's not a Porsche."

"No."

She frowned. "You think he's coming?"

"Maybe. We haven't got anything else to go on."

"Where is he?"

#

MILTON SEARCHED the property.

It was of a reasonable size, and he took his time working his way through it. For the most part, he found what he would expect to find: summer clothes in the closet, utility bills filed neatly in a bureau in the space that was used as an office, neatly stacked laundry on a shelf above the washing machine. There was a laptop computer in the office, and Milton disconnected it and put it to one side, confident that if there was anything of interest stored on it, then Ziggy would be able to recover it.

He moved into the master bedroom and, as he dropped down to his stomach to look under the bed, he found a black aluminium case. He pulled it out. It was locked, with two padlocks threaded through metal-reinforced grommets.

Milton put the case on the bed, went back to the study and collected two paperclips from a bowl that he had noticed earlier. He opened the clips and bent each of them into an L shape. He used one of the clips as his pick and the other as his wrench, and, as he applied slight pressure, he was able to pop the lock. He repeated the trick for the second padlock, slid them both out of the grommets and opened the case. Nestled inside a foam inset were two Taurus PT111 Pro G2 handguns. The model was lightweight and had a thin profile, perfect for concealed carry. The guns were chambered in 9mm, and the case also contained two magazines with twelve-round capacities. Milton took one of the pistols, pushed a magazine into the butt and put it in his pocket. He would give the other one to Hicks.

He had noticed something else under the bed. One of the floorboards extruded above the others and, when he investigated further, he saw that there were scraping marks around the bed's metal feet. He pushed the bed aside so that he could take a closer look. The floorboard was loose and, using the claw of the hammer, he was able to prise it open.

There was a void beneath the floor and, stuffed within it, Milton found a leather satchel. He took it out, unzipped it and counted ten thick bundles of banknotes. He riffled through one of the bundles and saw denominations for two and five hundred pesos. It was difficult to guess with precision, but he suspected from the number of notes that there was perhaps two million pesos in the bag. One hundred thousand dollars.

He put the banknotes back in the satchel and went through into the lounge. It was approaching five in the afternoon.

Where was Mendoza? They had no other leads to go on. There would come a point where he would look at another way to find a route back to de Lacey, but, until then, he figured that patience was the best policy.

There was nothing to do but wait.

#

THEY WAITED in the car for five hours. It was ten minutes after nine and darkness had fallen when Hicks saw the glow of headlights at the end of the road.

"You see it?" Josie asked him.

He nodded.

"That's a Porsche," she said.

Hicks watched as the car slowed and drew to a halt at the gate. It was a white Boxster with the roof down.

"What do you think?" Hicks asked Josie.

She squinted through the darkness. "I think it's him."

He took out his phone and dialled.

"*I'm here*," Milton said as soon as the call connected.

"There's a car at the gate. We think it might be him."

"*Copy that. Leave the line open.*"

They watched as the guard came out of his hut and spoke with the driver. It was too gloomy to identify him save that he was male. The guard concluded the conversation and went back to the hut. A moment later, the gate rolled back and the car drove into the compound.

Hicks put the phone to his ear once again. "The car's coming inside."

"*How many people?*"

"One," he reported. "Male. It's too dark to ID him."

"*Copy that. Stay outside. If he comes back out again, follow him.*"

"Affirmative," Hicks said.

The line was quiet.

"What's he going to do?" Josie asked.

"He'll get answers."

"You've done this before," she said. It was almost an accusation.

"A few times," he replied, watching the bright red glare of the taillights as the car headed into the compound.

"I want to do this properly," she said. "Mendoza—I want him to be brought in."

"He will be."

"I'm serious. I'm going to arrest him."

Hicks didn't answer.

Josie reached across and grabbed the phone from him. "This is Hernandez," she said. "This gets done properly, Milton, you understand? I want to bring him in."

Hicks couldn't hear Milton's response.

"That's how we do it," she continued. "Otherwise I'm

going to go up to the gate now and tell them to let me in. Your choice."

Hicks looked at her: she was animated, her cheeks flushed and her eyes flashing with anger.

"He wants to speak to you," Josie said to Hicks, handing the phone back to him.

"Hicks here."

"Get ready to come through," Milton said. "If it's Mendoza, I'll tell you. I'll need you both in here with me."

#

MILTON WAS in the living room. He heard the motor of the garage door as it slid up and back and then the sound of a car's engine as it was driven inside. The engine was switched off and the motor buzzed again as the garage door closed. He heard a car door opening and then slamming shut.

Milton crossed the room to stand behind the door to the kitchen.

A light was switched on in the kitchen; he saw the illumination beneath the door. He heard the sound of the microwave as it was programmed and then started, and, after a minute, he heard the ping as the program completed. He heard the hiss as a ring pull was opened.

Milton held the gun in his hand, his back pressed up against the wall. He was calm. He knew what he had to do.

The door opened, the light from the kitchen streaming into the room.

A man came inside.

Milton let him walk ahead and then stepped out from his hiding place.

He raised his hand and, with a hard and firm downward strike, he crashed the butt of the pistol against the top of the man's head.

Chapter Sixty-Nine

BRUNO MENDOZA felt as though his head was split down the middle. It was the pain that brought him around; it throbbed and pulsed and, as he opened his eyes, he was rewarded with such a pounding that, for a moment, he felt as if he was going to be sick.

He tried to bring his hands to his face but found that he could not.

He glanced down.

He was sitting on one of the wooden chairs from the dining room. A length of cord had been fastened around both wrists and looped beneath the seat of the chair. Another length of cord had been bound around his torso, securing him to the seat back.

A man was sitting opposite him. He had positioned the standard lamp so that it made a silhouette of him, obscuring his face and shining into Mendoza's eyes. The glare made his headache worse. He blinked the brightness away. When he opened his eyes again, he saw that the man had a pistol pointed at his head.

"Wake up, Bruno."

He grunted woozily.

"Speak English, please."

He swooned. "You—"

"Your head's a bit sore, is it?"

"You hit me."

"That's right."

"Who are you?"

The man reached up for the lamp and twisted it so that the brightness fell down onto his own face.

Mendoza recoiled. The man's face was bruised and disfigured, his skin a mess of purples and blacks and reds, but he recognised him.

Smith.

"You're supposed to be—"

"Locked up?"

Mendoza struggled, trying to free his hands.

"I *was* locked up. That's right. Because of you, wasn't it?"

The man reached for the shade and angled it so that it shone directly into Mendoza's face again.

He blinked. "No," he gulped out. "I didn't—it wasn't—" He stopped.

"Don't worry," Smith said. "I'd rather not have to hurt you. If you answer my questions, there's no reason why anything bad should happen."

The threat was implicit and unmistakable. "What do you want?"

"Let's get back to me being locked up. You were involved, weren't you?"

"I don't know—"

Smith leaned forward and pressed the muzzle of the pistol against his forehead.

"I think honesty is going to be your best policy here, don't you? Let's try again. What did you do?"

Mendoza gulped for air. "They told me to have you transferred to Bilibid."

"And you did that?"

"I didn't have a choice."

"What?" Smith asked. "They threatened you?" He gestured around the room. "Look at all this. You're on the take. They *paid* you."

"They would have killed me if I said no. I didn't have a choice, I swear."

Smith brought the chair a few inches closer. The angle of the light changed, and now Mendoza could see his face more clearly. He could see his eyes. They were icy cold, glacially blue, and without any hint of compassion or empathy.

"We're going to have a discussion," Smith said. "You

and me. I'm going to ask you a few questions about what happened and you're going to answer them. If you don't, I'll have to persuade you why it's better to cooperate. That won't be a pleasant experience for you."

"I'm a police officer," he managed to protest.

"And I'm a fugitive on the run from a prison break. I've got nothing to lose. If you can't help me show that I didn't murder my friend, what use do I have for you?"

"What do you want to know?"

"Who have you been working with?"

"He's English."

"Are you sure?"

"He had an accent like yours."

"What did he look like?"

"Your height. Black hair. Well dressed. Like a peacock. He always wore a suit, even in this heat."

"Name?"

"I don't know."

"Is it Logan?"

"He never told me."

"How did he find you?"

"I was working for someone else."

"Fitzroy de Lacey?"

"Not for him, for his company. Tactical Aviation. They wanted me to find evidence that they could use to get him out."

"How long had that been going on?"

"Two years? Three? I can't remember exactly."

"But they paid for all this?"

Mendoza nodded.

"Go on."

"They said I would be working with someone else on a new project."

"When?"

"A week ago. They told me to go to the docks in Tondo and this man met me there. He said there had been a murder that day. I said 'Which one?' We have murders every day.

He said it was in a cheap hotel. An Englishman had killed a girl. We had you in custody by then—I knew it had to be you."

"And what did he want?"

"He said to make sure that the investigation was wrapped up quickly. We weren't to dig into it too far. I was okay with that. We're too busy, and I didn't think we'd find anything even if we did. And then he said you were to be transferred to New Bilibid."

"But suspects waiting their trials stay in Quezon City."

"I told him that, but he said it was important that you were moved."

"He say why?"

"No."

"What else?"

"I met him again the next day. He said that one of my officers was causing trouble. He said she was stirring things up. That wasn't what we'd agreed, and he said that I wouldn't get paid unless she backed off. So I told her. I said the case was closed, you were guilty, she needed to move on. But she wouldn't let it drop. I found her at the bar where you and the girl went the night she was killed. She was trying to get the tape from the security camera."

"And?"

"And I told the man."

"And then the barman was killed. Did you know?"

"I saw the report."

"Was it you?"

"No," he said. "I didn't—"

"You might not have pulled the trigger, but he'd still be alive if it wasn't for you, wouldn't he?"

Mendoza swallowed.

"Keep going," Smith said.

"He called again. He said that my officer had gone to visit you in Bilibid. He told me to deal with her."

"Meaning?"

He didn't answer. "I had to get her to stop."

"What did you do?"

"I tried to frighten her."

"Did you put something under her door?"

"A picture of her son."

"And?"

"A bullet." Mendoza swallowed and looked away.

"Okay," Smith said. "You're doing very well, Inspector. A few more questions. This man—how do you get in contact with him?"

"I can't—"

"When you told him about the video at the bar, how did you reach him?"

"A phone number."

"Can you remember it?"

"I have it written down."

"Good," he said. "You're going to call him for me and set up a meeting."

He squirmed; the cord cut into the soft flesh of his wrists. "Please. I don't—"

"You're going to call him and set up a meeting and then you're going to the police station and you're going to sign a confession admitting to everything you just told me."

"That's not—"

Milton stopped him mid-sentence. "Josie?"

Mendoza was suddenly aware that there was someone else in the room with him. He heard the sound of footsteps and, as he turned his head to the left, he saw Josie Hernandez.

"Did you get it?"

She was holding a smartphone.

"Josie?" he said.

"Hold on."

Josie played with the phone.

"*He came back the next day. He said that one of my officers was causing trouble. He said she was stirring things up—*"

Mendoza's eyes widened a little as he listened to his own voice.

"*Josie—*"

"You piece of shit," she spat at him.

"It's not what it—"

Smith reached ahead and backhanded him. "Pay attention, Inspector. The recording is one thing. The other thing, and you want to remember this very carefully, is this: I know where you live. Here and your place in the city. And even if you run and you go somewhere else, I'll find you. You might think that the man you were dealing with is dangerous, but you don't know me. The reason you're still drawing breath is because Officer Hernandez wants to do this the right way. But, and I swear to God, if you deviate a fraction from what I've told you to do, I'll hunt you down and I'll make whatever you think he might have done to you look like a gentle stroll in the park."

Josie had a pair of cuffs dangling from her hand.

"Officer!" Mendoza barked. "What are you doing? Remember who I am!"

Josie stared at him with undisguised disgust. "You have the right to remain silent," she said coldly as Smith unknotted the restraints, stood the inspector up and prompted him to put his hands behind his back. "Anything you say will be used against you in a court of law."

Mendoza's appeal to authority was abandoned pitifully quickly. "Josie, please."

She fastened the cuffs around his wrists and dragged back on the chain until he stood.

"Please. Think of your family. Your son."

She struck him across the face and then, barely pausing, she continued. "You have the right to an attorney during interrogation. If you cannot afford an attorney, one will be appointed for you."

"It's not what it looks—"

"I've heard enough. You're under arrest."

Chapter Seventy

MILTON HAD frisked Mendoza after he had knocked him out. He had found his Glock and his smartphone. He held up the gun now so that Mendoza could see it.

"Just so you don't get any stupid ideas," he said.

He laid the smartphone on the table. Mendoza was sitting at one end of the table. Milton had pulled a second chair around so that he could sit next to him. He rested his arm on the table, the pistol held loosely in his hand.

"Call him," Milton told him.

Mendoza did as he was told, his finger navigating the display with a series of deliberate presses.

"Put it on speaker."

Mendoza pressed a button on the screen and they could hear the buzzing of the repeated chirps as the call tried to connect.

"Hello?"

The accent was unmistakably English. Milton recognised the voice. It was Logan.

Mendoza swallowed. "It's me," he said, his voice straining a little.

"Who?"

"Mendoza."

There was a pause for a moment. *"What do you want?"*

"You've got a problem. With our friend."

"I shouldn't have, Inspector."

"Have you been watching the news?"

"What problem? I paid you to make sure I don't have problems."

"This isn't something I could have done anything about."

"Go on."

"There was a riot at Bilibid. Very serious. The doors were opened and the inmates got out. The place is overcrowded. The guards were outnumbered. The rival gangs got to each other and then the army stormed it—one way or another, a lot of inmates got killed."

There was a new focus to Logan's voice. *"And our friend?"*

"That's the problem."

"He got out?"

"Dozens did. I just checked. He wasn't one of the bodies and he's not where he's supposed to be. So, yes—he got out."

There was another, longer pause. Mendoza looked as if he was going to vomit. Milton gestured to him, circling his finger in a suggestion that he should continue.

His voice cracked when he spoke again. "It might not be as bad as you think."

"Really? You don't know our friend like I do."

"You don't understand. I'm saying I know where he is. I can help you fix it."

"That's very generous of you," Logan said sarcastically. *"And this is out of the goodness of your heart?"*

"No," he said. "I've already done what I said I would. You wanted him moved. I did that. You wanted the investigation wound up. I did that, too. Everything just like you asked. But this is extra."

"You're going to need to give me a little more than that, Inspector."

"He's been getting help. My officer, Hernandez, she went to see him again. She knows he didn't do it. That's where he is. With her."

Mendoza couldn't help looking up at Josie as he said it; she glared at him, and he looked away again.

"I thought you'd handled that?"

Mendoza stared at the phone. "So did I."

"And now you want payment because something you *didn't handle is causing* me *a problem?"*

Mendoza looked as if he was about to speak, but Milton held up a finger and he held his tongue.

"All right," Logan said. *"You'll tell me where she is?"*

"I'll do better than that. I'll take you there."

"How much?"

"Twenty."

Milton found that he was holding his breath.

"Meet me the same place as before. I'll have your money. I'll pay you and then we can sort this out."

"When?"

"Midnight."

The line went dead. Milton took the phone and double-checked that the line was closed.

"Where do you meet him?" Milton said.

Mendoza looked like a beaten man. "Tondo," he said. "I told you."

"It's in Manila," Josie added. "It's a slum down by the docks."

Milton looked at the clock on the wall. It was twenty to ten. "How long to get there?"

"Depends on the traffic. Ninety minutes?"

"Logan will get there earlier than midnight," Milton said. "We need to get there first."

Chapter Seventy-One

MILTON AND MENDOZA had driven north into the teeth of a ferocious storm. Hicks and Josie followed behind in the rental. The rain had started to fall as they passed Santa Rosa. It had been a light drizzle at first, but, as they continued into San Pedro and Muntinlupa, the conditions worsened until Mendoza had to slow down just to be able to navigate the road. The sky had been lit by regular veins of lightning, and thunder boomed loud enough to be audible over the growl of the Boxster's engine.

Milton told Mendoza to take the expressway into the city. The policeman had a prepaid E-Pass that raised the barrier as they pulled up to it. There was a camera attached to the side of the booth and Milton made sure that he was looking into it as they passed through.

Tondo was in the north of Manila. It was famous for Smokey Mountain, a vast pile of garbage that was picked over by impoverished locals who somehow scavenged a meagre living from it. There were clutches of kids in shorts and T-shirts, congregating on the corners despite the late hour and the apocalyptic conditions. One young child, surely no older than five, was hauling a cart behind her that had been loaded with plastic bottles. Another child stared at them as they went by, a wall of plastic sacks stacked up behind him. The child was barefoot, his face covered with grime that was streaked by the rain. The area earned its name thanks to the fires that burned around its edges. The locals burned tyres and wood, and now, despite the rain, the acrid tang of the smoke seeped into the car with a cloying sensation that settled on the tongue and in the back of the throat.

The inspector drove carefully. Milton was next to him, covering him with the pistol that he had stolen from the bedroom.

"I can't see a thing," Mendoza complained, gesturing to wipers that were struggling to keep the windshield clear.

"Keep going."

Milton glanced up into the rear-view mirror. The second car was close behind them. Hicks was driving, with Josie next to him. Milton had given careful thought to the best way to proceed. His preference would have been to bring the inspector to the rendezvous alone. He would have waited until the meet took place, secured both participants, got the information he needed and then shot both of them. He would have no further use for either and he had no interest in being merciful. But Josie had insisted that she take Mendoza into custody, and Milton had reluctantly agreed. She had put herself at risk to break him out, and he owed her for that. And, he found to his surprise, he liked her. For as long as it was possible, he preferred that she not see him the way he saw himself. Milton was a killer, and, even though he suppressed that with the strategies that he had learned in the rooms, he always would be.

He would give her Mendoza.

He couldn't promise her the same for Logan. The same mercy would not be extended to him. Hicks and Josie could take Mendoza away when Milton had Logan. Milton wanted to be alone with him.

They passed through a rusty arch that read "BRGY 105 TEMP HSG." The area beyond was a temporary housing site that had outlived the notion that it might be transient and had taken on a permanence that would now be shifted only by fleets of municipal bulldozers. There were more people here, slathered in mud from streets inundated with water from the ongoing downpour. The smell changed: now it was a mix of urine, sweat, smoke, and rot.

Mendoza drove them northwest to the docks. A sign read NAVOTAS FISH PORT COMPLEX. He turned off the main road before they could reach the complex and picked a route through a warren of narrow streets until they reached the water's edge. A series of rickety huts had cropped up on the waterfront, some of them projecting over the water and supported by struts that were buckled and bent. The water was slicked with grime, pocked with cakes of yellow crust that rose and fell on the gentle swell.

Mendoza parked. The Boxster was a seventy-thousand-dollar car and it was hopelessly out of place here. Hicks pulled up behind them.

Rain hammered down on the soft top and slicked across the windshield.

"This is it," Mendoza said.

Milton checked the time. They had made good progress and were early. Logan was a professional. He would likely be early, too. Milton had to hope that they had beaten him.

He looked left and right, assessing the location, and then he called Hicks.

"What do you want me to do?" Hicks asked.

"Get out of sight and scout the area. See if you can get around onto the other side of the dock."

"Copy that."

The cabin of Mendoza's car was lit up by the headlights of the rental as Hicks navigated around them and turned into a side street that led away from the water.

Mendoza left his hands on the wheel. "What do you want me to do?"

"What happened the last time you met him here? Where did you meet?"

"Here."

"He came to the car?"

Mendoza nodded.

"And then?"

"He got in, we spoke, he gave me my money. Then he left."

"He was alone?"

"I didn't see anyone else."

Milton gripped the pistol a little tighter. "This is what we're going to do. You stay here. I'm going to wait where he won't be able to see me. You're going to act as if this is just like the last time. Understand?"

Mendoza nodded.

Milton pressed the muzzle against the side of the inspector's head. "I would very happily shoot you and throw you in the harbour, but Officer Hernandez doesn't want that to happen. She wants you to be charged and tried. I owe her, so I've agreed." He pushed with the gun until he could see the cords stand out on Mendoza's neck. "But if you run, or if anything happens to spook Logan, the deal is off. And I'll come for you."

Milton pulled the gun away. He opened the door and stepped out into the deluge. The smell was overpowering: the odour of rotting fish mixed with the stench from the nearby dump. Milton felt the urge to gag. He swallowed it down and hurried across the road to a line of ancient freight containers. They must have been on the dock for months; they were corroded, patches of rust spreading across the metal like lichen, the doors jimmied open and whatever they might have been holding long since looted and carried off. He walked to the nearest container. He looked inside and saw an inky blackness. Milton went in, his boots ringing off the metal floor. The storm hammered against the metal, a constant drumming that rang in Milton's ears. He turned and looked back. The container offered an excellent vantage point and he knew that he would be invisible for as long as he stayed inside it.

He closed his fist around the butt of the pistol, lowering it so that it rested against his thigh.

He had no idea whether Logan would make the meet. He was obviously a careful man; he and Mendoza could have met anywhere, yet a place like this offered discretion and the multiple exit points that would make it very difficult to follow him should he decide he needed to leave.

Milton had to hope that the news of his escape from Bilibid would be sufficiently important to flush Logan out of the shadows.

He looked out through the curtain of rain that ran off the roof of the container. He looked onto the dock and at

the car, the interior light casting a faint glow on Mendoza
as he lit a cigarette and blew smoke out the window.

Milton had no choice but to wait.

Chapter Seventy-Two

JOSIE WAS soaked to the skin, her hair plastered against her face and her waterlogged uniform cold and heavy against her skin. She followed Hicks as they moved around the rear of the dockside area. There was a road that ran parallel to the dock, and it allowed them to change position without revealing themselves to Mendoza or anyone else who might be waiting near the water's edge. The storm was unpleasant to be out in, but it would make it even more difficult for Logan to see them.

Hicks stopped suddenly and reached back with his right arm, then shepherded her roughly into the doorway of a warehouse building.

"What is it?" she hissed at him.

"Car," he said, pointing ahead.

She followed his gesture and saw it. The car was running without lights, driving slowly on the other side of the junction with the road that led down to the dock. They both pressed themselves into the doorway as the car turned into the road and then disappeared from view.

"Milton," Hicks said into the telephone, "car coming."

Josie couldn't hear Milton's reply.

"The lights are off," Hicks continued. "It looked like a rental. Could be him."

Josie took the opportunity to glance around. She didn't really know Tondo all that well. The slums seemed to grow larger every year, gradually spreading out to cover more and more of the capital, like fungus spreading across abandoned trash. This area was less populous than the districts around Smokey Mountain, but there were still people here. She saw a group of kids fifty feet away, sheltering beneath a tarpaulin tent and watching them.

"Come on," Hicks said to her.

He stepped away from the building into the rain and set off, jogging in the direction of the junction.

Josie followed. She reached across her body and felt for the reassuring bulge of the pistol in her jacket pocket. She had conducted her own quick search of Mendoza's property while Milton's attention was on the inspector and had found the pistol in a drawer in the bedroom. It was a Springfield XD-S. She was fortunate; it was one of the best carry guns on the market. It had a single stack magazine that could hold five rounds of .45ACP ammunition and another in the chamber. The gun squirmed a little in the hand, but you could get around it with a firm grip. There was a spare magazine in the drawer, too, and she pocketed it with the pistol.

She was determined that this was going to be done properly. She was going to arrest Mendoza and whoever it was he had come out here to meet. Milton could ask his questions, but the men would be arrested and given the benefit of due process.

There was enough death in Manila. The police indulged in it, encouraged by the government. She would not. Her parents had taught her to do things the right way. Her training at the academy had been the same. And, most important of all, she wanted to set Angelo the right example. She knew that she wouldn't be able to look her son in the eye if she turned her back and allowed Milton to do whatever it was he was planning to do.

It needed to be done right.

She would make sure that it was.

#

"CAR COMING."

Milton pressed the phone closer to his ear.

"What can you see?"

"The lights are off. It looked like a rental. Could be him."

"Stand by."

He saw the car. It turned out of the road that led to Smokey Mountain and crawled along the dock toward him. Its lights were still off. Milton could see the shape of the driver, but it was too far away and too dark for him to make out any detail.

The car stopped.

Mendoza's Porsche was between Milton and the new arrival.

The second car lit its headlights, tunnels of brightness that burrowed through the slanting rain. Milton could see the vague outline of the driver, but nothing else. He looked away and blinked. The short wait had given his eyes the chance to adjust to the gloom, and if he looked into the lights, it would take time for them to correct themselves again.

The headlights flicked off.

Milton heard the click of the door and watched as it opened.

He looked to Mendoza. He was still in the Boxster.

"Where are you?" Milton whispered into the phone.

"Behind the new car."

"Can you see anything?"

"Not much."

"Is it him?"

"Can't say."

"Whoever it is, we've got him penned in."

"Copy that."

"Where's Josie?"

"With me."

Milton fought the urge to groan. "She wouldn't stay in the car?"

"Afraid not."

"Fine," he said, exasperated. "Just try to keep her out of the way."

"Copy that. Milton—"

The driver of the second car stepped out and raised an umbrella.

Milton crouched down as low as he could manage without compromising his vantage point.

The man set off. There was fifteen feet between the two vehicles. He moved calmly, confidently, sheltering beneath the umbrella. There was a crack of lightning and the dock was flooded with a snap of bright white light.

It was enough: Milton recognised Logan.

Logan reached the Porsche. He opened the passenger door, folded the umbrella, and got in.

Milton gripped the pistol.

#

JOSIE WATCHED the man get out of the car and walk over to Mendoza.

"What are they doing?" she hissed, more to herself than to Hicks.

"We need to wait," he said, his pistol clasped in both hands.

"And then?"

"Leave it to Milton."

"I want to take them in," she said. "I—"

There were two flashes.

Josie thought it was more lightning, but then realised that it wasn't.

The flashes had come from the interior of Mendoza's car.

Josie gasped.

The noise of the gunshots was muffled by the rain, but still audible.

"Shit," Hicks said.

Josie pulled the gun and stepped around Hicks.

"Josie," he said, but she ignored him.

The Boxster's door opened and the man stepped out.

Hicks reached for her arm, but she shook him off.

The shooter's back was facing her. He hadn't seen her yet.

"Police!" she called. "Get your hands up!"

The man turned.

He had a gun in his right hand.

He aimed.

Josie fired.

She knew she had missed as soon as she pulled the trigger. She was too far away for the little Springfield to be truly accurate, and the shot passed harmlessly over the head of her target.

He fired back.

Josie felt the sharp sting as the bullet struck her in the top of her right thigh. It was as if she had been punched on the muscle; there was no pain, though, just a feeling of numbness. She staggered back, the Springfield slipping from her fingers, and then, unbalanced, she keeled over. She felt strong hands reaching beneath her arms before she could fall and felt her heels scraping against the ground as she was hauled backwards. The numbness was curious, but it didn't last for long. She looked down and saw the blood on her trousers as it seeped out of the hole that had appeared on the side of her leg.

A second shot came; it crashed into the wall just behind her.

The pain rolled over her in waves.

The idea suddenly seemed preposterous. "I've been shot!"

"Hang on," Hicks grunted. "I'm going to get you out of here."

Chapter Seventy-Three

"POLICE! Get your hands up!"

Milton saw Josie step forward, falling into a shaft of brightness cast by one of the only working lamps on the dock.

She had a pistol in her hands. Milton had no idea that she was armed.

Logan turned and aimed his own weapon.

Josie fired.

Milton saw the flash from her pistol and heard the bright *ching* as her bullet ricocheted off one of the metallic containers farther along the dock.

A bad miss.

Logan fired back.

Milton saw Josie stagger and fall.

Logan fired again, then ducked behind the open car door, covering himself from the position that Josie and Hicks had taken up.

Milton stepped out of the container and aimed.

"Logan," he called out.

The man spun around.

Milton fired. He aimed low, into Logan's gut.

It was an easy shot. The shot found its mark. Logan fell back against the open door and, reaching down for his stomach, he dropped onto his backside.

Milton squinted his eyes against the rain and aimed down as he approached Logan. Logan had his left hand pressed over the wound in his belly, and he clutched his pistol in his right.

"Drop it."

Logan did as he was told, extending his arm to the side and releasing the pistol. It splashed into a filthy puddle of water.

Milton moved quickly, closing the distance until he was

alongside. He swept his foot and sent the pistol splashing away. He glanced into the car. Mendoza was leaning forward, his body held in the seat by the belt. The impact of the gunshots had turned his head to the side, enough so that Milton could see the exit wounds. His blood and brain matter had been sprayed haphazardly across the ceiling and smeared over the inside of the windshield and the door.

Milton covered Logan with the pistol in his right hand and held the phone in his left. He put it to his ear.

"Hicks?"

"She's been shot."

"How bad?"

"In the leg. Can't say how bad, but she's losing blood."

"Get her to a doctor."

"What about—"

"Now, Hicks. Take her. Mendoza is dead. I've got Logan."

Milton put the phone away and crouched down. He grabbed Logan by the collar and hauled him away from the support of the car door. He dragged him forward until he toppled over, his face in the muck and the grime and the rivulets of water that hurried down the slope to the dock. Milton put his knee in the centre of Logan's back and frisked him quickly and expertly. He found a wallet, a phone, a set of car keys, a lighter, a pack of cigarettes, a magazine of ammunition, and a small butterfly knife.

He tossed Logan's belongings onto the hood of the car, yanked him up and dumped him back against the door.

Milton looked at him: the man was handling the situation with about as much composure as could be expected. He stayed still, facing ahead, his fear betrayed only by a tic that jumped in his cheek. He had both hands pressed to his abdomen now. Blood pumped out regardless; his shirt was thick with it, and it seeped out beneath his palms and between his fingers.

Milton had been accurate. It was a gut shot. Logan would die without treatment, but it would take him thirty minutes to bleed out. Long enough for him to know that his cause wasn't lost, but not so long that he might think he had any chance of surviving without help.

Logan spoke first. "I'm sorry."

"Too late for that."

"I know," he said. His voice was weak, and Milton had to listen for it in the rain. "They gave me my orders. I carried them out. You would've done the same."

"Yes, once. But not anymore."

"I need a doctor."

"You do," Milton said. "You're losing a lot of blood."

"You going to help me?"

"Tell me what I need to know."

"Can I trust you?"

"Got any other options?"

A trickle of blood ran down from the corner of Logan's smile. "Don't suppose I do."

"No," Milton said. "You don't. But if you help me, I'll help you. I'll drop you outside a hospital."

Logan nodded. "Go on, then. Ask."

"Who are you working for?"

"You know," he said. "De Lacey."

"And before? SAS?"

He shook his head. "SBS. I was a marine; then I was selected to C Squadron. Did that for five years before I went freelance."

"Doing what?"

"I'm a handyman. Like you were. Client gets a job that needs doing, they send for me."

"And *this* job?"

"I was recommended."

"By who?"

"MI6. They told me to come to Manila." He coughed. "I corresponded with someone in de Lacey's organisation. Told me what they wanted me to do. I don't know any more than that. You know how it works."

"Who are your contacts at MI6? Names, Logan. Give me their names."

He coughed again, more blood bubbling over his lip. "I don't know their names. Male or female—I don't know. The operation was codenamed Corazon. That's all I have."

"What did they tell you?"

"They said de Lacey was going to be working for us. The FO was negotiating with the locals to get him out. Don't ask me why—I couldn't say. But they said he wouldn't play ball unless we delivered you to Bilibid. He's not your biggest fan, Milton. He's been stewing on whatever you did to him for years, but he couldn't find you."

"But you could."

"The spooks could. It took them ten minutes. You were hardly hiding."

Thunder boomed overhead. Milton gripped the pistol a little more tightly. "Go on."

"They said you had a thing with a girl you met when you were working on de Lacey's file when you were out here before. Someone who was working for him. De Lacey's people had already come up with the story: she had your kid and she wanted you to know about it. I just had to get you to believe it."

"How did they get to her?"

"They already had her on board."

"In exchange for what?"

He coughed again. "What do you think? She had a son. That's easy leverage. They threatened her. They said they'd take him away from her. Does it matter?"

Milton bit his lip and looked up. His anger was stirring. He needed to tamp it down for a few minutes more. He took a breath and looked back down at Logan. He coughed yet again, leaned to the side and spat out a mouthful of blood.

"I'm fucked," Logan said, managing a humourless chuckle.

Milton grabbed him by the shirt front and shoved him back against the car door. "So you killed her?"

He nodded. "She was out of it, Milton. She wouldn't have—"

Milton interrupted him. "You drugged us?"

Logan spat out another mouthful of blood.

Milton looked down at him; his eyes were swimming. He slapped him across the cheek. "Logan?"

"Sorry," he said. "What did you say?"

"You drugged us?"

"Roofies. Something to knock you out."

"The hotel manager and his wife?"

"Mendoza killed them."

"The owner of the bar."

Logan nodded. "Mendoza."

He was losing too much blood to carry on for much longer.

"A couple more questions, then I'll get you to a hospital. How do you make contact with de Lacey?"

His voice was weaker when he spoke again and Milton had to lean closer. "Gmail. A dead drop"

"Is he expecting anything else from you?"

Logan shook his head. "No. I told them the job was done. As far as they know, you're still in Bilibid. I'm headed home."

Milton had the beginnings of an idea. "Think carefully. De Lacey has no idea what you look like?"

"No. Never met him."

"And you've never met anyone else who works for him?"

Logan shook his head.

Milton believed him. There was no reason for him to lie.

"Doctor," Logan said faintly. "Please."

Milton stood.

Fingers of lightning spread out across the darkness, heralding another detonation of thunder.

Logan looked up at him.

Milton aimed downward and fired.

Once.

Twice.

Logan jerked and then lay still.

Milton took no pleasure in what he had done. He just

felt deadened. There was no elation, no satisfaction, not even any relief that he had expunged the need for revenge that would otherwise have eaten away at his insides. He felt hollowed out and blank, an absence of emotion that took him back to the first time he had killed a man and the discovery that his lack of empathy made him perfectly suited for the profession that would later come to define him.

He remembered the feeling, and it frightened him.

This was how he had come to feel during his career with the government. Guilt and remorse would flood the vacuum and he would drown those feelings out by drinking himself into a stupor.

The thought of a drink was attractive now.

Milton shoved the pistol into the waistband of his trousers so that he had both hands free and then grabbed Logan's limp body beneath the shoulders. He dragged him backwards, opened the door of the Porsche, and dumped him in the passenger seat. He popped the trunk and took out the jerry can of gasoline that he had noticed when he had searched the car before they had left the compound. Mendoza was a conscientious driver, prepared for being caught out by a thirsty car; that was fortunate. Milton poured the gasoline over the bodies and then throughout the interior of the cabin, front and back. The car quickly stank of it.

He went back and found Logan's pistol. He wiped the weapon clean of fingerprints, then grasped it firmly to ensure that only his would be found on the trigger and grip. He placed the gun on the ground a few feet away from the open passenger-side door; close enough that it might look as if it had been tossed out of the window at the order of someone else.

Milton collected the rest of the things that he had confiscated from Logan. He put the wallet, phone, butterfly knife and car keys into his pocket. He put his own fingerprints on the spare magazine and tossed it into the

Porsche. He tapped a cigarette from the sodden pack, put it between his lips, and tried to fire it up with the lighter. The cigarette wasn't quite as damp as the pack, and it caught. He took two long drags, letting the smoke fill his lungs, and then, holding the cigarette between thumb and forefinger, he flicked it through the open window.

A ripple of blue passed over the seats as the gasoline ignited, and then blooms of flame burst out in bright oranges and yellows and reds. The heat quickly climbed as the fire settled in, consuming the upholstery and the clothes of the two dead men. Milton heard the crack as the windshield fractured down the middle, a jagged line that ran from the top of the frame to the bottom, the glass swiftly blackening from the belching smoke. The windshield popped and then shattered. The smoke issued out, pouring up into the rain.

Milton took out Logan's keys and went and sat in the car that he had arrived in.

He took another cigarette, lit it and, clamping it between his lips, he started the engine and slowly drove away.

Chapter Seventy-Four

MILTON DROVE.

He took out his phone and dialled.

"Ziggy?" he said.

"What's up?"

"Where are you?"

"Still at the airport."

"I need you to come back to the city."

"Where?"

Milton held up the key card that he had taken from Logan's pocket. The plastic oblong was stamped on the reverse with the logo of a hotel chain. "Logan had a room at the Conrad Manila. We need to take a look."

"Where's Logan?"

"Out of the picture."

"And Mendoza?"

"The same. Get in a cab, Ziggy. I'll tell you when you get here."

Milton heard the sound of Ziggy's footsteps. "I'm on my way."

"I need you to do something on the way. I don't have Logan's room number."

"That'll be easy," Ziggy said, before Milton heard him call out to hail a taxi.

"I'll meet you outside."

Milton put the phone away and drove. The hotel was on the waterfront, five miles to the south of the Fort. The city grew more prosperous the farther he travelled. The slums of Tondo became set in stark relief against the well-kept lawns of Rizal Park, the Embassy of the United States and the Zoological and Botanical Gardens. The road curved around the Manila Yacht Club, with million dollar vessels rising on gentle swells illuminated by overhead lights, then passed Star City and the Philippine International Convention Center before he finally arrived at the Conrad. The hotel was fabulous. It resembled the prow of a vast ship, each ascending floor jutting out a little beyond the floors beneath it so the building appeared to lean out toward the beach. There was a large Ferris wheel on the promenade and the sea beyond was rough and angry.

Milton pulled up just as Ziggy was stepping out of a cab. "Did you get it?"

He smirked. "I hacked housekeeping. Took five minutes."

"Just tell me where it is," Milton said; he had no patience right now for Ziggy's showboating.

"Room 432."

"Thank you."

"Are we going in?"

"Yes," Milton said. "Just follow behind me. No talking. Don't even look at anyone. Nice and casual."

It was just after one in the morning when they approached the large glass doors to the hotel. Milton ignored the staff behind the reception desk and crossed the lobby to the elevators. Ziggy was alongside him; Milton knew that he was the vulnerability, and feared that he would say or do something that would give them away, but he did not.

"Easy," Ziggy said as they were out of sight of the staff.

"We're not there yet," Milton said.

Each elevator car was activated by a room key; Milton pushed Logan's into the slot, waited for the door to slide shut, and then pressed the button for the fourth floor.

"Where's de Lacey?" Ziggy said as the lift started its ascent.

"I don't know."

"But you spoke to Logan?"

"He was a mercenary. The government recommended him to de Lacey. He was working for him to get back at me."

"The British government?"

"Yes."

"Why would the government help de Lacey?"

"I don't know, Ziggy."

The lift slowed.

"You think Logan might be able to lead us to him?"

"That's what you're here for."

The lift opened. Milton followed the quiet corridor to the correct door and slid the key into the reader. The red light turned green, the lock disengaged and the door fell open.

Milton pushed it ajar and went inside.

The room was tidy. There was a closed laptop on the bureau, a suitcase on the bed, a pair of running shoes pressed together next to the wardrobe and a suit hanging inside it. Milton opened the case: a suit, spare underwear, shorts and a T-shirt, a bag of toiletries, everything neatly folded. Logan's time in the military was obvious; Milton shared the same fastidiousness and preference for neatness and order.

"Looks like he was ready to leave," Ziggy said.

"He was. As far as he was concerned, his work was done."

Ziggy went over to the laptop and opened it.

Milton took out the items from the suitcase and started to search through them. He went to the wardrobe and looked inside: there was a holstered Sig Sauer hanging from the clothes rail. He took it out and placed it on the bed next to the rest of the things.

"What do you want me to do?" Ziggy said.

"Get everything you can about Logan. Email, phone calls. Anything you can find that might tell us where de Lacey is."

Ziggy powered up the laptop. "Shouldn't be a problem."

Milton noticed the lock screen. "You need a password?"

Ziggy shook his head and rapped his knuckles against the top of the screen. "I have physical access," he said. "That means game over. It'll take me ten minutes."

Chapter Seventy-Five

MILTON PACED the room. Ziggy was busy. He was sitting cross-legged on the king-size bed with two laptops open in front of him: his machine, the lid decorated with stickers and decals, and the one that had belonged to Logan. The cellphone that Milton had taken from Logan was next to the laptops, connected to Ziggy's machine by a USB cable.

"Come on," Milton said impatiently.

"I'm going as fast as I can."

"You said it would take ten minutes."

"It's a little more complicated than I thought it would be."

"You've had an hour."

"And I'm going to need more than that." He waved his hand to forestall any more complaints. "Can't you go for a walk or something? I'll be quicker without you looking over my shoulder."

Milton was about to retort, but he bit his tongue. Finding de Lacey was dependent on Ziggy being able to work his magic, and upsetting his prickly disposition would just lead to an argument and a longer delay.

"Fine," Milton said. "I'll go and find supplies. What do you want"

"Strong coffee."

#

THERE WAS a twenty-four-hour 7-Eleven on Harbor Drive, a ten-minute walk from the hotel. Milton set off, taking out his phone and calling Hicks as he walked.

"It's me," he said.

"What happened?"

"It's done."

"Logan?"

"Won't be a problem."

"And de Lacey?"

"Ziggy is working on that now."

"But we're not done."

"No. Not even close."

Milton walked by the huge Ferris wheel, the spokes looking ghostly in the light thrown up by the streetlamps on the promenade.

"How's Josie?" Milton asked.

"Lucky. The bullet hit clipped on the thigh. Flesh wound. They're stitching her up now. I doubt they'll be able to keep her in. She's already told them she wants out."

"Have you spoken to her?"

"Yes. She said she wanted to see you. She's stubborn as a mule. Says she wants this to be done properly. By the book."

Milton stared out into the darkness.

"Milton?" Hicks said. "What do you want me to do?"

"Stay with her. Call me when she's been fixed up. I don't need any more surprises from her."

He went into the store and got supplies: a pack of Fortune menthol cigarettes, two bottles of Coke, a handful of chocolate bars and pre-made sandwiches and two cups of black coffee.

He paid the clerk, thanked him, and set off back to the hotel.

Chapter Seventy-Six

ZIGGY WAS still working when Milton returned to the room. He was wearing a pair of headphones and Milton could just hear the muffled sound of music.

"Hey."

He didn't hear him.

"Ziggy!"

He looked up, nodded, and took off the headphones. "What?"

Milton handed him one of the cups of coffee. "Well?"

"It was a little more difficult than I expected." Milton could hear the sound of something loud and aggressive until Ziggy thumbed it off. "Sorry," he said. "Helps me concentrate."

"How much longer do you need?"

"Nothing. I'm done."

"What did you get?"

"So I used the Offline NT Password and Registry Editor to change the admin password on the laptop. You use that if you forget—run it off the USB, boot the machine in Linux, mount the Windows partitions, then make the filesystem and registry changes you need so you can change the admin password. Easy. And when I've done that…" He clicked his fingers. "Open sesame." He held up the phone. "Between the phone and the laptop, I was able to get into all his email. I reset his passwords, gathered data and accessed everything else: email, social, financial."

"I don't care how you did it. I just want a link between him and de Lacey."

"Fine," he said, bridling a little at Milton's impatience. "So we know they used a Gmail dead drop. Standard email is clear-text. The NSA can sniff that easily. Data transmitted to and from Gmail's servers within a browser is encrypted, so those transmissions don't usually get intercepted. *Usually.* Whoever set this up with Logan probably thought they were being clever, but they don't know that Logan is dead. Here. They sent this last night."

Ziggy navigated to an open browser window that showed an open Gmail account. Ziggy moused over to the drafts folder and clicked to open it. There was an unsent email inside. Milton read it.

FINAL PAYMENT MADE. YOU HAVE MY THANKS.

"Can you find the payment?"

"Of course." Ziggy opened another window and Milton saw a statement from an account at Scotiabank in the British Virgin Isles. "This is Logan's account," Ziggy said. "He received a large payment yesterday." He moused up and highlighted a figure in the deposit column. "Half a million."

"From Polemos?" Milton said, noticing the details of the depositor. "Who's that?"

"It's a front company. Registered in Vanuatu. I've just started looking into it. It's the second payment he's had from them." He scrolled back and highlighted another payment for the same amount.

"Half up front, half on completion," Milton said. "A million dollars to bring me here and put me in jail."

"Maybe I should drop them a line and tell them where they can find you," Ziggy suggested with a grin, but, as he looked up at Milton and saw him solemnly looking back down at him, he replaced the smirk with a straight face.

"You said the dead drops can't usually be intercepted. But sometimes they can?"

"It doesn't get sniffed, but Google still has the metadata. Including the IP address where the draft was composed."

"You hacked Google?"

He shrugged. "Not exactly. I have a friend who works there. Tells me things that he probably shouldn't. That's why it took a little longer than ten minutes."

"So where is he, Ziggy?"

"How about I show you?"

He went to the wide window that faced out to sea and pointed.

Milton followed his instruction and looked to the south. A channel separated the land on which the hotel stood from a collection of condominiums. "What am I looking at?"

"I found the IP address. It's over there."

"The condos?"

"No," Ziggy said. "That's Alphaland Marina. It's a very exclusive yacht club. And Tactical Aviation owns a yacht. A big one. It docked three days ago. That's how he's going to leave. In style."

Chapter Seventy-Seven

MILTON TOOK the cigarettes out to the balcony, shook one out of the pack and lit it. He looked to the marina, a mile away to the south. Dawn was two hours away and it was still too dark to see anything in detail, but he could make out the shape of the yachts from the lights on the jetties. There was one yacht in particular that arrested his eye. It was anchored in the bay and much larger than the others, its sleek lines picked out by the bright white running lights that were set around the perimeter of the superstructure.

Ziggy had found a report in CharterWorld saying that Tactical Aviation had purchased a ninety-foot superyacht six months ago. She was called the M/Y *Topaz*, and, when Ziggy had checked the records at the Manila customs house, he had found papers for a yacht of the same name.

Was de Lacey on board now?

It seemed likely.

Milton finished the cigarette and went back inside.

Ziggy was busy on his computers, sitting amid empty sandwich packets and discarded chocolate wrappers. "I've got something else for you," he said. "The captain of the *Topaz* applied for departure clearance yesterday. Everyone on board who wants to leave needs to be noted on the application. Look."

Milton watched over Ziggy's shoulder as he scrolled down through a series of scanned pages from the passports of the passengers aboard the yacht. He stopped scrolling when he reached the page from the passport of a Mr. Fitzroy de Lacey.

Milton peered at the photograph. De Lacey was staring straight at the camera.

"When are they leaving?"

"Eight tonight. In sixteen hours."

"So we need to send the email."

Ziggy nodded. He grabbed Logan's laptop and navigated to the Gmail client that he had been using.

Milton looked at the email that they had decided upon. It was simple; just five words.

WE NEED TO SPEAK. URGENT.

"Save it."

#

THEY WAITED.

Ziggy refreshed the browser every minute, and then every five minutes. There was nothing.

"The payments to Logan," Milton said. "From the shell company."

"Polemos," Ziggy added. "What about them?"

"Can you prove that de Lacey made them?"

Ziggy rubbed his eyes. He'd been up all night, too. "I can try," he said.

Milton went back out to the balcony and called Hicks.

"Good timing," he said. "She's just discharging herself."

"Can you get over here? I think I'm going to need you."

"Sure," Hicks said. "She'll want to come, too."

"You can't just leave—"

"No. She'd probably arrest me if I tried."

Milton sighed. "Fine."

"Where are you?"

Milton told him that he was at the Conrad. Hicks said he would be there as soon as he could. Milton hung up.

He took out another cigarette, aware that he had already smoked half of the pack and hardly caring. He lit up and inhaled, then stared at the distant yacht through the wisps of blue smoke. Dawn was breaking, a slow lightening at the horizon that seeped up into the darkness, gradually revealing more and more of the marina and the yachts that were berthed there.

Milton looked out into the bay and to the *Topaz*.

De Lacey was there.

Was he asleep in one of the luxurious cabins that Milton remembered from his time aboard the yacht's predecessor?

He found himself wondering what he would do if there was no response to his message. A direct approach would be impossible. The boat was anchored in the bay, for a start, and that alone would make an assault impossible. He could take a boat, but it was difficult to imagine how he could get aboard that way. He could swim out to the yacht, but then he would be limited in the equipment that he could take with him. He remembered from before that there would be a well-armed security detail in place to protect de Lacey. Milton would be outnumbered. He would need more gear than he could transport underwater.

He closed his eyes, aware that he hadn't slept. He thought of Jessica, and the shape of Logan's fingers in the bruises around her throat. Logan had paid the price for what he had done, but that was only half of the revenge that Milton was minded to exact.

He needed this to work.

He went back inside.

"Have they responded?"

"Not yet."

"What about Polemos?"

"It's not easy."

"That doesn't help me."

"I told you—Polemos is registered in Vanuatu. You know how secretive it is over there? It makes Switzerland look wide open."

"I know that. But you said—"

"I'm *trying*, Milton. You know how it works? The directors of Polemos appoint nominees in Vanuatu. The nominees sign powers of attorney to hand control back to the directors. But no one knows who the directors are. There's nothing recorded online. And if there isn't, there's nothing for me to hack."

"I need to prove that de Lacey made the payments. I

need it in black and white."

"I'd have to get into the bank in a big way. Not possible in thirty minutes."

"How long?"

"A few days."

"De Lacey's going tonight."

Ziggy shrugged. "I don't know what to say."

Milton closed his eyes and tried to remember back to the time before, when he had been closer to the centre of de Lacey's circle.

A thought occurred to him.

"How much of the Polemos paperwork is publicly available?"

Ziggy looked at his screen. "The nominee declaration. That's there for everyone."

"Show me."

"Hold on." Ziggy worked for a moment and then started to read. "I, Richard Taylor, Director POLEMOS LTD, having agreed to the appointment as Director of a company duly incorporated under the laws of Vanuatu, hereby declare that I shall only act upon instruction from the beneficial owners—"

"Not him. Keep going. The names. Just give me the names."

"There are five," Ziggy said. "Cocks. Sparks. Connors."

"The last one," Milton cut him off. "Is it Olsen?"

Ziggy looked up in surprise. "Yes. Marthe Olsen. How did you know that?"

"I remember it from when I was with de Lacey before. He has companies all over the Caribbean. I remember the name of one of the nominees."

"Why that one?"

"Marthe Olsen is my ex-wife."

"I didn't even know you were married."

"It was a long time ago. The names were a coincidence. It stuck in my—"

"Shit," Ziggy said.

Ziggy had absent-mindedly refreshed the Gmail page. The draft email that they had saved had been deleted and replaced with another.

IT'S DONE. WHY DO YOU NEED TO SPEAK?

"What do you want me to say?" Ziggy asked.

"Give them the website."

Ziggy switched windows and navigated to the home page of the Manila Bulletin. The lead story was headlined BILIBID JAILBREAK SPARKS MANHUNT. Ziggy copied the URL and pasted it into the email. He looked up at Milton for approval.

"Do it."

Ziggy pressed save.

He waited, and then refreshed.

INCLUDING OUR FRIEND?

"Say yes. And say that you have news, and that you need to meet."

Ziggy typed in the message and saved it.

Milton found that his stomach was clenched tight with nerves.

Ziggy refreshed the browser.

Nothing.

He tried again.

Still nothing.

"They're thinking about it," Milton said, more to himself than to Ziggy. "Come on. Come *on*."

Ziggy refreshed for a third time, and a new message had replaced the old one.

WHERE ARE YOU?

"Tell them we're at the Conrad."

Milton clenched his fists and tapped them against his thighs.

Ziggy refreshed.

BE OUTSIDE AT 1200. WE WILL SEND A CAR.

Chapter Seventy-Eight

HICKS AND JOSIE arrived shortly afterwards. She was walking with the aid of a stick, her face bearing witness to the pain that each fresh step was causing her.

"Josie," Milton said. "How do you feel?"

"Like I've been shot through the leg."

She sat down, wincing.

"You should—"

"Don't bother telling me I should be in hospital," she interrupted testily. "This needs to be finished. And I want it to be done properly."

"That's fine. Me, too."

"Hicks wouldn't tell me what happened. He told me to ask you."

"Mendoza's dead."

She groaned. "Logan?"

"The same. They both are."

She closed her eyes. "Damn it, Milton."

"They got what they deserved."

"That's not the point. What happened?"

"You saw," Milton replied. "Logan shot Mendoza."

"Why? To clean up?"

Milton nodded. "Things were starting to look messy. Too many variables. He didn't want anything to lead back to him."

I would have done the same, Milton thought.

"And then?"

"And then you did what I told you not to do and you got shot because of it."

"I know that," she said, laying her fingers on the spot on her thigh where the bullet had winged her. "After that?"

"I shot him."

"Did you get what you wanted?"

"Some of it."

Milton kept the content of his conversation with Logan—and especially its conclusion—to himself.

"What about the bodies?"

"I put them in Mendoza's car and torched it."

She sighed and shook her head. "Of course you did."

"It's important that Logan isn't identified today."

"Why?"

"Because I don't want de Lacey to know that he's dead."

"Because this isn't finished?"

Milton shook his head. "No," he said. "Nowhere near."

"What are you going to do?"

"Do you want to be involved?"

She didn't answer at once.

"Josie? Hicks said that—"

"I think I'm done with the police."

"Why? You're a good—"

"Don't patronise me, Milton," she said. "I know I am. I know I'm good. But it's not that. Things have never been as bad as they are now. I thought, when I enrolled, that I'd be able to make a difference. But that's naïve. Men like Mendoza are everywhere now. They think they can do whatever they want. Maybe they can. Maybe. And you know what? I'm not just naïve. I'm selfish. I have Angelo to think about. He's already lost his father and then *I* got shot last night. I was lucky. It could've been worse. So I swore to myself that I'm never going to put myself in a position where he might end up losing his mother, too."

"So you don't—"

"*After* this," she added. "That's when I'll stop. But I want to do one more thing the right way before I do. If de Lacey did what you say he did, then he should be in prison. I swore an oath to uphold the law. And so that's what is going to happen. If you want him, it has to be by the book. We bring him in and charge him and then we let the prosecutor take him to trial."

Milton had given his next move careful thought, and the

conclusion that he had reached was inescapable: he couldn't easily get to de Lacey on his own. It would be too difficult even though he knew that Hicks and Ziggy would volunteer their help. And, more than the practical difficulties, he knew that he owed Josie. Logan had killed Jessica, and now Logan was dead. He would have preferred to kill de Lacey, too, but there was a poetry to the idea of sending him back to rot in the prison that he had tried so hard to leave.

"All right," Milton said. "I'll give him to you."

"That's not enough."

"What do you mean?"

"All I've got is you telling me that he was behind all this." Milton started to protest, but she waved away his objections. "I believe you, Milton. But that's not enough. I need to make a case against him. I can't bring him in just because I believe what you've told me. I need evidence."

"Ziggy?" Milton prompted.

"Evidence," he said. "Yes. I can help with that."

Ziggy told Josie about the two payments into Logan's account, and that Polemos—the company that had made them—was likely connected to de Lacey.

She listened with an expression that grew more and more incredulous. "So, let me just make sure I'm understanding this. You're making the connection based on the fact that a woman with the same name as Milton's ex-wife was involved in the formation of Polemos and another one from years before? That's it? Seriously?"

"I know it's circumstantial," Milton said.

"Are you out of your minds? And this evidence about the payments," she went on with increasing agitation, "not that I'd call it evidence—how exactly did you get it?"

"I…" Ziggy started to speak, but the words trailed away.

"He hacked it," Milton finished for him.

She put her hand to her forehead. "So you've broken the law to get it?"

Ziggy shrugged.

"It's *completely* inadmissible. It's useless."

Milton took a breath. She was right, of course. It *was* useless. Milton didn't need to deal in absolutes. He knew, of course, what had happened and who was responsible. His standard of proof was low. But Josie wanted to do things the right way and, if she was to do that, she would need evidence that would stand up in court.

"All right," he said. "We can do better."

"I really hope so."

"What about if we could get a confession?"

She nodded. "Of course. But how are you going to do that?"

Milton turned to Hicks.

"I'm going to need some help," he said.

Chapter Seventy-Nine

MILTON TOLD Ziggy to find out everything he could about Logan, and then he went out to the balcony.

Hicks followed. He pointed to the pack of cigarettes in Milton's hand. "Give me one of those."

"You don't smoke."

"I used to. And it doesn't seem like such a bad idea right now."

Milton shook out another cigarette.

"You want me to be him, don't you?" Hicks said. "You want me to be Logan."

Milton nodded. "I can't think of another way."

"And they never met?"

"He never met de Lacey or anyone who works for him. I asked. They don't know what he looks like."

"And you're sure about that?"

"Logan knew he was dying. Being helpful was the only way he was going to save his life. There was no reason for him to lie."

Hicks lit the cigarette and put it to his mouth.

"You don't have to do it," Milton said. "It's dangerous. I'd understand if you didn't want to."

"I'm not saying that."

"I can't ask Ziggy."

"I know," Hicks said with a wry laugh. "He wouldn't last five minutes. Has to be me."

"What do you say?"

Hicks nodded. "Yes."

Milton put his hand on his shoulder.

"You sure?"

He nodded.

"I appreciate it."

Hicks waved it off. "I still owe you."

They stood together for a moment. The sun was halfway through its climb now, and the big yacht was easily visible in the bay. As they watched, a tender cast off from the dock and bounced across the gentle waves toward it.

"So we lay a trap for him," Hicks said. "And you're the bait?"

Milton gazed out. "I'm the only reason he'll come ashore."

"And if he does?"

"Then we get him to implicate himself."

The tender slowed down as it approached the yacht. There was a boarding platform at the stern, with the bright blue square of the yacht's swimming pool behind it. A mooring line was tossed out and the tender was tied up.

Milton finished his cigarette and ground it underfoot. Hicks dropped his unfinished cigarette over the balcony and followed Milton back into the hotel room.

#

ZIGGY HAD moved his laptops to the table. They left him alone to work. His eyes were rimmed with red and patchy five o'clock shadow had developed on his cheeks and chin. He looked tired. Josie was sitting in one of the room's armchairs with her leg up. Her hand was pressed against the spot where the bullet had gone in.

"Okay," Ziggy said after an hour had elapsed.

Milton crossed the room to Ziggy. "How are you getting on?"

"Making progress."

"His service records?"

"That was easy. They're limited, as you'd expect, but I'm in."

"How much can you change?"

"As much as you like. But it's one thing to know that I can change them and another thing to know how much it's *safe* to change. We need to be careful. It's safer to tweak the stuff that conflicts obviously with what they'll see when they meet you. If we leave the rest, it'll be less likely that anyone notices. Better if you can remember everything else."

"That's fine," Hicks said. "What do I need to know?"

"Your name is William Logan. Let's start there. We're lucky that he was around the same age as you. Similar build, too."

"Married?"

"Unmarried."

"So you'll have to take that off," Josie offered, pointing at Hicks's ring finger.

Hicks reached for his wedding band and worked it off. He dropped it into Milton's palm. "If you lose that, I'll be a dead man."

Milton put it into his pocket and motioned for Ziggy to continue.

"No sign of any relationship. You have an interest in slightly deviant porn—but we can brush over that. No siblings. Parents are dead. You have a flat in Shad Thames owned outright, no mortgage. You have social media accounts, but you haven't posted into them for years."

Milton and Hicks crossed the room to stand behind Ziggy. They looked over his shoulder as he flicked through the various open windows on his screen.

"You joined the Royal Marines at the age of eighteen. One year later, you attended selection for the Special Boat Service in Poole. You were successful."

"No commando unit first?" Hicks said.

"You got an exception. Apparently you were quite the soldier. You served most of your time with the SBS, but had secondments to the SAS and 14 Intelligence Detachment, both times serving in Northern Ireland. You left the Detachment and had a sabbatical for a year before you went back to the SBS, where you were posted to Maritime Anti-Terrorism operations for a year. One year after the posting to MAT you were transferred to MI6. Details are a little more sketchy from this point on. It looks like you left two years ago and went mercenary. There's no reference to individual jobs, although I've found references to you in Africa, South America and the Middle East."

"Is that all?"

"This is all off unencrypted servers," Ziggy protested. "That's the low-hanging fruit. I might be able to get more, but the Secret Service is more difficult. It'll take a lot longer to get through it. And you're meeting them this morning."

"But?"

"I'll keep working. We just have to hope they don't have a way to get the material I can't reach in time, or, if they do, that there are no photographs or anything else that would contradict your story."

"Well done, Ziggy," Milton said.

Ziggy nodded, evidently satisfied with Milton's praise. "Look at this." He moused over and pulled up a new document. Milton looked: it was an internal personnel record from the navy's human resources department. There was a face-on picture of Logan and a list of details including his address and next of kin. Ziggy had unlocked the document and, as Milton watched, he removed the picture and replaced it with one of Hicks that he had taken on his smartphone earlier.

"Very good."

Ziggy's fingers flashed over the keys again. "I'll change the pictures on his social media accounts. When I'm finished, it'll stand up to basic scrutiny. We'll just have to hope it's enough."

"Very reassuring," Hicks said drolly.

"This is crazy," Josie said. She stood, wincing again as she put weight on her bad leg. "Are you sure this is the best we can do?"

"I'm open to alternatives," Milton said. "But he's leaving tonight, so you'd better make it quick."

She shook her head. "I don't know. It's just—"

"What's the one thing he wants?" Milton cut in. "Me.

He made that a condition before he agreed to work with whoever it was who got him out of jail. He's obsessed. Hicks tells him that I'm still alive, and that he knows where to find me, and I'm betting de Lacey's judgment is affected. He'll buy it. He'll come after me."

"And when he does?"

"We're going to need backup. Is there anyone you can trust?"

"In the department?" Milton nodded. She paused as she gave the question thought. "My partner," she said eventually.

"What's his name?"

"Dalisay."

"See if you can get him to help. We'll need some firepower, too."

"He has a shotgun."

"Tell him to bring it."

"Bring it where?"

"I was hoping you might be able to help me with that. We need somewhere out of the city where we won't be disturbed."

"I know the place," she said.

Chapter Eighty

HICKS PREPARED himself, dressing in the suit that Logan had left in the wardrobe. He grabbed the shoulder rig, together with the Sig Sauer P226 nestled inside the holster. He spent ten minutes obsessively checking the weapon to ensure that it was properly functional. He had expected that it would be. He looked up as he reassembled it and saw that Milton was watching him. The two men shared an understanding: it was a routine that both used to distract themselves from the uncertainty of an impending operation.

#

HICKS WAITED in the lobby. It was midday now, and the sun was burning bright. A Mercedes GLE pulled off the road and glided up to the entrance. The doorman bent down to speak to the driver, and then came inside.

"Mr. Logan?"

"That's right."

"Your car has arrived."

Hicks followed the doorman outside and allowed him to open the rear door for him. Hicks stepped down and slipped into the car.

There were three men waiting inside for him: the driver, big and with a blond ponytail that was trapped against the seat behind his broad shoulders; a passenger next to him, shaven-headed and with broad shoulders; and a third man, sitting in the back, next to him. He looked to be in his late fifties, although he appeared fit and strong. He had a full head of hair, although it was greying a little at the temples, and his face was broad and flat. His eyes were dead, and, when he looked at Hicks, the feeling was disconcerting.

"Mr. Logan," he said. "I'm Major Albert Lane-Fox. I work for Tactical."

Hicks felt a flutter of nervousness. That could be a bluff. What if Logan had been lying, and he had met this man before? What if that wasn't his name?

He nodded to the men in the front. "Tango and Cash?"

"They work for us, too. Shall we go for a drive?"

Hicks nodded. The driver touched the gas and the Mercedes pulled away.

"Where are we going?" Hicks asked.

"Just for a drive, Mr. Logan. I'd like the chance to talk to you about what you said."

#

ZIGGY PULLED AWAY. Milton was lying across the seats in the back.

"They're going south," Ziggy reported.

"Stay well back."

"I know what to do," he said indignantly.

Milton knew that he did *not* know, that his experience in surveillance was most likely derived from Hollywood, but there was nothing else for it. He couldn't drive the car without being seen, and they needed two vehicles so that they could swap in and out of the pursuit and minimise the possibility that they might be made by whoever was in the other car. It was far from ideal. Hicks was in a car driven by men who were most likely skilled in counter-surveillance, and the only team he could assemble to follow them comprised a one-legged police officer and a middle-aged computer hacker who had delusions of being Popeye Doyle.

Needs must, he thought. He had no other choice.

He took out his phone and called Josie.

"I'm on the move," she said over the phone's speaker. "Where are you?"

He poked his head around so that he could see the satnav.

"On the expressway headed south. Just coming up to the bridge over the Paranaque river."

"I'm on Quirino Avenue."

That was east of them. It ran parallel to the road that they were on.

"Get ahead," Milton said into the phone. "Can you get onto the expressway at Victor Medina?"

"No," she said. "Not there. The Longos Flyover."

"Good," Milton said. "Let me know when you're there. We'll stay on them until then."

#

LANE-FOX WAS quiet for the first ten minutes as they started to head south. Hicks knew what he was doing: he wanted him to know that he was in control, that the conversation would begin when he wanted it to. Even though he could predict the behaviour, it didn't make the silence—and the two big men in the front of the car—any less disconcerting.

"Thank you for your message," Lane-Fox said at last. "It was unexpected."

"I didn't expect to have to deliver it."

"Well, as I say, we were grateful for the warning. It seems that quite a few men escaped. Are you sure that Mr. Milton was among them?"

"Yes," Hicks said. "I'm quite sure."

"How's that?"

"Because he's tied up in a trailer north of Manila."

Lane-Fox cocked an eyebrow. "Really?"

"Yes. Really."

"You found him?"

"I did. Yesterday evening."

"And yet he only escaped yesterday morning."

"He was working with a female police officer. I was watching her. She led me to him."

"And the officer?"

"Not a problem any longer."

"You continue to surprise me, Mr. Logan. Your resourcefulness is impressive."

"That's very kind of you. But I'd like to discuss it with Mr. de Lacey if I might."

"It doesn't work like that," Lane-Fox said. "He's a busy man, especially so soon after his release. You see me first. If I think what you have to say would be of interest to him, maybe you get to see him. If not, you don't."

#

JOSIE MERGED onto the expressway and picked up speed. It was a three-lane road, and she indicated and made her way over to the fast lane. She put her foot down and saw the rental that Ziggy had hired from the airport just a few hundred feet ahead. She closed up until she saw the black Mercedes GLE that had arrived to collect Hicks from the hotel.

Her phone was on the seat next to her. It was on speaker. "I'll take over," she said.

Milton acknowledged her, and Ziggy touched the brakes to slow down.

Josie went by, and, as she passed them, she exchanged a quick glance with Ziggy. Milton was in the back; she couldn't see him.

#

THE CAR picked up speed. Hicks realised that he had no idea where they were going.

Lane-Fox spread his hands. "So what would you like to discuss with him?"

"I thought that he'd be interested to hear that I can deliver Milton to him."

"For the second time."

"That's right."

"And were you to do that, am I right in thinking that it wouldn't be free?"

"Like you say, I've already discharged my obligations under our previous agreement."

"Indeed you have. So this is new work?"

"I don't do this for charity."

"Can you prove that you have Mr. Milton?"

Hicks took out the phone that Milton had collected from Logan. He opened the photo album and tapped the one that they had taken in the hotel parking lot that morning. Milton was in the trunk of Hicks's rental. His hands looked to be secured behind his back. The marks on his face were visible.

Lane-Fox examined the photograph and then made an affirmative noise. He leaned forward and told the driver to pull over. There was a gas station ahead, and the man indicated and turned into the forecourt.

"Would you mind stepping out of the car for a moment?" Lane-Fox asked. "I'd like to make a quick phone call."

"Not at all," said Hicks. He opened the door and stepped out into the boiling midday sun.

#

THE MERCEDES indicated that it was about to exit the expressway. Josie dabbed the brakes and watched as it slowed down and turned onto a ramp that led to a gas station.

"They've turned off," she reported. "There's a Petron gas station. I can't follow."

She looked over at the station as she drove by. The car had pulled over and, as she watched, she saw Hicks get out.

"Hicks is out of the car."

"Copy that," Milton said. "We'll take over."

"What do you want me to do?"

"Head north. I'll see you up there."

#

HICKS CROSSED the forecourt to the gas station shop and bought himself a can of Coke. He popped the top and waited in the shade for Lane-Fox to finish his conversation. He guessed that he was speaking to de Lacey. He knew, if that was correct, that the success or failure of Milton's plan depended on what was being said right now. He had no idea whether he had been convincing. He had been on edge the entire time, fighting down the paranoia that every comment and every question was a test designed to trip him up. Everything was predicated on Logan having told Milton the truth. Maybe he had been lying. For all they knew, Logan might have been operating from a cabin aboard the *Topaz*. And if the paranoia was justified, if they knew that Hicks was lying… well, whatever might come next would not be pleasant.

The car horn sounded. Hicks looked over; the man with the shaven head had lowered his window and was beckoning him over.

Lane-Fox opened the door as he approached.

"Get in, Mr. Logan."

Hicks did as he was told.

"Mr. de Lacey will see me?"

"He will. Now, actually. How would you like to see the yacht?"

He closed the door.

The car pulled away.

Chapter Eighty-One

THEY TURNED around and retraced their route back to the north. Lane-Fox didn't speak again until they reached the signs for the Alphaland Marina Club.

"The yacht is at anchor," he said as the driver turned off the road. "We'll transfer across to it."

The driver edged between rows of hundred-thousand-dollar sports cars until he reached a disembarkation point near the water. Hicks had seen the marina's clubhouse from the windows of Logan's hotel room. It was built on pilings in the middle of the water and accessed by a covered bridge. The man with the shaven head got out and then came around to open the door for Hicks.

"Sir," he said, indicating that Hicks should get out, too.

"Are you armed?"

Hicks nodded.

"Please."

He unbuttoned his jacket, reached in for Logan's Sig Sauer and handed it to the man.

"Thank you," Lane-Fox said. "You'll get it back afterwards."

The four of them made their way through the marina to the water's edge. There was a tender waiting for them. It was a beautiful vessel crafted from mahogany and metal, its chrome fixtures glinting in the early afternoon sun. The rear of the craft was taken up by a U-shaped leather banquette, and Hicks sat down with the driver on one side of him and the passenger on the other. He had noticed the subtle bulges under the jackets of both men that indicated that they were armed. That was no surprise, but it was a reminder to him that he was vulnerable.

\#

ZIGGY BROUGHT the car to a halt at the entrance to the yacht club.

"It's clear," he said.

Milton raised his head. They had a view down to the water and, as he watched, he saw a brown and white tender with five people aboard skim across the water toward the big yacht anchored in the bay.

"Not much we can do now," Ziggy opined redundantly.

He was right.

Hicks was on his own now.

#

HICKS STARED at the yacht as they bounced across the gentle waves toward it. The vessel was large and, despite that, still managed to look sleek and graceful. It had sugar-scoop windows and a glass lounge that seemed to blend the yacht more seamlessly into the water. Crew in white shirts and khaki shorts busied themselves on the decks, making their final preparations. Deckhands cleaned the outside of the boat. Sun-loungers were set out on the teak deck, the towels placed out on them rolled in tight, neat cylinders.

The tender approached the stern of the yacht. A deckhand threw out a line and the pilot caught it, looped it through a tow-eye and knotted it tight. The tender was brought up close and secured, and the passengers were encouraged to disembark.

"Welcome aboard, Mr. Logan," Lane-Fox said. "This way, please."

Not all the men he saw were deckhands. Hicks saw four other men, big and with close-cropped hair, who could only have been de Lacey's private security detail. They were dressed in dark suits, they wore dark glasses and headsets and had noticeable bulges beneath their arms indicating shoulder holsters and handguns. One of the men hovered pointedly as Hicks clambered aboard, fixing him with an even, professional regard.

Lane-Fox led the way through a wide aperture at the stern of the boat and into the interior beyond.

Female stewardesses busied themselves, tidying and cleaning in anticipation of their departure.

Hicks thought it all a little vulgar. It was all about status. A yacht like this was hardly practical, and the costs of running it must have been exorbitant, but it served other purposes. More so than a multi-million-dollar residence, or an Italian sports car, this was the ultimate projection of wealth. It was also the perfect location for business meetings where illicit transactions might be discussed.

Lane-Fox led the way to an open area where another man was speaking on a telephone. He had his back to Hicks, but, as he turned, he recognised him at once. He was tall, with a pot belly that signified good living, a sun-beaten face, and greying hair that was swept back from a wide forehead. He was wearing a pale blue suit with a crisp white shirt and cravat. His eyes glittered, matching the sunbeams that sparkled off the water.

Hicks recognised him at once: Fitzroy de Lacey.

De Lacey finished the call and put his phone into his pocket.

"Bertie?" he said to Lane-Fox.

"This is Logan."

De Lacey's face broke into a broad smile. "Mr. Logan," he said. "A pleasure to finally meet you."

"Likewise, Mr. de Lacey."

"Although in less than ideal circumstances. We're leaving tonight, as you might be able to tell. But we certainly can't leave until we've sorted out the unpleasant surprise you dropped on us. I'd like to talk to you about it, if I may."

"Of course," Hicks said.

"Come," he said. "I'll show you the boat."

Chapter Eighty-Two

THE MERCEDES had been handed over to a valet who had driven it around the back of the buildings that lined the boardwalk. Ziggy found it easily enough: there was a private car park where an array of expensive cars were kept while their owners went about their business in the club. The lot was open, and inadequately guarded by a single man in a booth. His attention was facing outward, away from the cars in his charge, and it was a simple thing for Ziggy to walk between a Hummer and the Mercedes, shielding him from the unlikely possibility that the guard might turn and look into the lot. He reached into his pocket for the small device, flicked out the antennae with his finger, switched it on and slapped it inside the wheel arch. The magnet attached with a satisfying *clunk* and, without waiting any longer than necessary, Ziggy turned and made his way back to the car.

#

"CAN I offer you a drink? Tea? Coffee?"

"Coffee, please."

De Lacey spoke to one of the crew members, then turned back to Hicks. "They'll find us. Let's take a walk."

They climbed a curved stairway that was surrounded by scalloped silver leaf and equipped with an ostentatiously expensive hand-carved banister. The deck above was dedicated to the dining room, with Baccarat crystal chandeliers, a vast table and alligator hides and kudu horns on the walls.

"Do you like my little boat?"

"I'm not sure I'd describe it like that."

De Lacey smiled, evidently pleased to be able to show

off the benefits of his riches. "I bought it from a Russian," he said. "I would have commissioned one myself, but I didn't want to wait. We can accommodate eighteen guests. Perfect discretion. Unmatched privacy, obviously. It's difficult to think of a better place to conduct a business meeting than in the middle of the ocean, away from prying eyes. The security is world-class, too." He rapped his knuckles against a broad, tinted window that wrapped around the superstructure. "Bulletproof. Ultrasonic guns and an anti-missile system, too. Practically impregnable."

"It's very impressive."

They walked on, climbing to the bridge deck. The yacht had been equipped with a stunning infinity pool, and, as de Lacey stopped and turned back, Hicks was able to look out between two vast sun canopies across the water to the sea and, beyond that, to the verdant hills of the coast.

De Lacey sat down at one of the shaded tables and indicated that Logan should do the same. He did, and, as he settled back in the comfortable chair and shaded his eyes against the glare of the sun, a uniformed waiter arrived with a silver platter that bore two cups of coffee, a sugar bowl and a plate of biscuits. He placed the cups and saucers on the table, left the sugar and the biscuits in the middle, and, with a barely noticeable dip of his head, he left them and made his way back down to the lower deck.

"So—Milton. Tell me what happened."

"There was a jail break. He was one of the ones to get away."

"A jail break? Really?"

"There was a fire alarm. The doors opened automatically."

"They do that? I would've left them locked in to take their chances. The men in there are scum, Logan. It would have done the world a favour."

Hicks ignored that. "There was a riot. The guards were overwhelmed. They had to send the army in eventually, but it was too late by then. They lost several hundred, including Milton."

"But you have him?"

"Yes."

"Might I ask where?"

"There's an old shabu factory north of the city. I did some business out here a few months ago. It's still there."

"That's where he is?"

"Taped hand and foot and shackled to the wall. He's not going anywhere."

"Can I ask how you managed that? Milton is a very resourceful man."

"Yes, he is. But not everyone is as careful as he is. The police officer who arrested him evidently changed her mind about his guilt. She visited him in Bilibid on three occasions. I was told about it."

"What's her name?"

"Hernandez."

"Who told you?"

"Mendoza."

"Ah, yes. The tame policeman. What happened to him?"

"Milton killed him."

If de Lacey was surprised, he masked it. "Is that so?"

"Mendoza was sloppy. Milton found out that he arranged his transfer from Quezon to Bilibid. And there was a situation with the owner of the hotel where we staged the murder. Mendoza very clumsily tried to clear things up. So, yes, Milton knew he was involved. Hernandez set up a meeting with Mendoza and Milton ambushed him."

"And you were there, too?"

"I followed Hernandez. Milton was there and Mendoza came last of all. Frankly, Milton saved me a bullet. I'd already decided that Mendoza was a liability."

"And then you recaptured him."

Hicks nodded.

De Lacey used the silver tongs in the bowl to remove a cube of sugar and dropped it into his coffee. "Where's the factory again?"

"North of the city."

Hicks picked up his cup and sipped his coffee. It was deliciously bitter. The caffeine would be useful. He had managed only a few hours' sleep over the course of his time in Manila.

"Would you take me there?"

"Of course. But—"

"Yes, you'll want to be paid. That's fine. I don't expect favours." De Lacey stood up. "The same again?"

Hicks knew that Logan had already been paid a million dollars. He stood, too. "A million is too much. Half is reasonable."

"To include disposal of the body?"

"Of course."

De Lacey extended his hand and Hicks shook it.

"Shall we?"

"When?"

"No time like the present."

Chapter Eighty-Three

ZIGGY SLOUCHED against the rail and looked out at the yacht as the tender was untied. The boat turned around and sped back to the marina.

He went back to the car. Milton was down low in the driver's seat.

The window was open. "They're coming back," he reported.

"Hicks?"

"He's on it."

"And de Lacey?"

"Yes. I think so."

"How many others?"

"I saw three including the pilot."

"Four total?"

"If you include de Lacey."

Milton started the engine.

"The tracker is working as it should."

"Update me if they go somewhere they shouldn't."

"Anything else?"

"Walk back to the hotel and clean up. No prints. No sign we've been there. Keep your phone on. I'll call if I need you."

#

THE SPOT that Josie had suggested was remote and deserted. It was two hours north of the capital, down a road that led off the main Route 8 in the rolling foothills that surrounded Mount Arayat. The road was paved for the first half mile and then became little more than a track. It descended into a depression, a shallow bowl in the landscape that was fringed with large trees. It provided natural cover for the structures that he saw at the bottom of the bowl. There were rickety-looking shacks and two old trailers.

There were also two cars. Milton recognised Josie's and parked behind it. The second car was nearby. He didn't recognise it.

Josie came around a bend in the track and raised her hand in greeting.

Milton got out of the car. It was sweltering hot.

"Is this it?" he asked.

She nodded.

Milton looked at the collection of buildings. None of them were permanent: one of the trailers was no more than a burned-out shell, and three small corrugated iron huts slouched nearby. A chain had been strung up between two trees on either side of the road, blocking the way ahead.

"Will it be okay?" she asked.

"What was it?"

"They made shabu here," she said.

"Meth?"

She nodded. "The trailer caught fire. My partner busted them last week."

"No one comes down here?"

"I've just had a look. It doesn't look like it."

"It looks good."

Milton started to work out the best way to proceed.

"Are they coming?" she asked him.

"They're on the way. So we need to move."

"Manuel's over there."

They set off toward the trailers. Josie limped heavily on her cane, each step eliciting a wince of pain.

"Are you all right?"

"Hurts like hell."

"You don't have to be here."

"Yes," she said firmly. "I do."

They reached the two trailers. The one that had caught fire had been completely destroyed. The windows were gone and the roof had been consumed. The second was intact, and someone had propped a shotgun against the side. The door opened as they approached and a man stepped out.

"Manuel Dalisay," Josie said. "He's my partner. Manuel—this is Milton."

Milton pursed his lips. "Just him?"

"You told me to ask someone I trusted."

"I was hoping for—"

"I trust him," she said. "I don't trust anyone else."

The man looked nervous and Milton's negative reaction was making it worse. Milton put out his hand. "I'm John," he said as they shook. "Thank you for coming."

"She said it would be dangerous," Dalisay said as he collected the shotgun. "You think we need more police?"

"More would've been better," he said, and then, when Dalisay grimaced and Josie frowned, he added, "but the man coming here thinks that he's going to find something else. There are four of them. If we're careful, we'll be able to surprise them. We've got enough."

"Okay," Dalisay said uncertainly.

Milton glanced down at the shotgun. "You know how to use that?"

"Sure I do."

"You got another one?"

"In the trunk."

"So we'll be just fine."

"Did you bring the other things I asked for?" Josie said to him.

Dalisay nodded back to the second car. "In back with the shotgun," he said.

Milton knew that Josie didn't trust many people in the department, but he was not impressed with Dalisay. But no matter how querulous he looked, the man was here and willing to help and that stood for something. Ziggy had said that de Lacey was bringing three other men with him. De Lacey had four guns and Milton had three, with Hicks as a wildcard. He knew that de Lacey's men would be professionals, and they were likely to be better armed. Josie was hurt and Dalisay didn't fill him with confidence. On the other hand, Milton had surprise on his side.

He would have to hope that that would be enough.

He looked at his watch. It had taken him two hours to drive up here. Ziggy had called en route to tell him that the tracker was reporting that the Mercedes was also headed north, on Route 8, and that he had a fifteen-minute head start on them.

"When will they get here?" Josie asked.

"Fifteen minutes," he said. "Twenty minutes maximum."

"Then we need to set up. Where do you want us?"

#

DE LACEY was in the front with the driver, the man with the ponytail. Hicks was in one of the back seats, with the shaven-headed man on one side of him and another similar specimen from the security detail on the other.

The driver turned around. "Where now?"

They had been driving for nearly two hours. Mount Arayat had started as a rumple on the horizon, but now it dominated the way ahead. Hicks had told them to take Route 8 and head for San Fernando. He had never been to the site that Josie had chosen, but she had described it in detail and then Ziggy had 'driven' him there with the benefit of Google Street View.

"You're going to come up to a road on the right," he said. "Goes to Magalang. Take it."

The driver grunted his understanding and returned his attention to the road.

Hicks heard the sound of a phone's chimes.

De Lacey reached into his pocket and took out his phone. He looked at the display, his expression inscrutable.

"Everything all right?" Hicks asked.

"Just business," he said. "I have rather a lot going on, as you might imagine."

The men on either side of Hicks reached down and collected metal carrying cases. They each took out a Heckler & Koch MP5 and set about checking them.

De Lacey noticed in the mirror that Hicks was watching them. "Milton is dangerous," he said.

"He is. But he's chained to a wall."

"Nevertheless. No chances."

Chapter Eighty-Four

IT WAS dark in the undergrowth between the trees. Milton stayed low, trying to ignore the cramping from muscles that had taken a beating over the past few days. He shifted his position a little, stretching out his legs. He was painfully aware that if his muscles locked up now then he would be seriously reducing the odds of him—and everyone else—walking out of here alive. Dalisay had brought a second shotgun and Milton had it. It was old and battered, but he was confident that it would fire when he needed it to.

There was only one way that de Lacey could approach them and, with that in mind, he had arranged the three of them very carefully. First, he had instructed them to drive the cars between the trailers and then farther down the track until they were well out of sight. He was in the vegetation to the right of the road, with a clear view along the track as it climbed out of the depression. Josie was on the same side, thirty paces to the north of him. Dalisay was opposite her position.

Milton's instructions were clear: they were to let de Lacey, Hicks and anyone else that came with them get out of their vehicle and make their way to the clearing where the trailers were. Then, on his mark, they would declare themselves and call for them to surrender. If the plan proceeded as Milton hoped it might, they would catch them within a crossfire. Provided Josie and Dalisay followed his plan, Milton was hopeful that the confrontation could be brought to an end without violence.

Twenty minutes passed. He listened. He could hear the steady chirruping of nearby cicadas and then the sound of a larger animal as it crept through the deeper vegetation behind him.

He froze. He thought that he heard the sound of an engine.

He watched as a Mercedes crested the hill and started to descend toward them.

It slowed and stopped, and, after a moment, the doors opened.

Two large men armed with submachine guns stepped out from either side of the passenger compartment.

Hicks came next.

Then the driver.

And then, finally, Fitzroy de Lacey.

Milton stayed low. He clutched the shotgun and waited.

De Lacey called over to Hicks. "Here?"

"Yes. The trailer."

One of the other men spoke. "I don't like it, sir."

"It's fine," Hicks said. "Nothing's changed. It's as I left it."

There was a pause.

"He's tied up?" de Lacey said.

"Wrists and ankles, shackled to the wall with a bag taped over his head."

"Thank you. Now—get on your knees, please"

Milton tensed. He parted the fronds before his face so that he had a slightly better view. Hicks had turned back to de Lacey and Milton couldn't see his face.

"What?" he said.

"Knees. Now."

Milton squinted between the branches. One of the men, a broad-shouldered thug with a shaven head, had stepped up to Hicks, his MP5 aimed squarely at his chest. He jabbed his finger toward the ground.

"What are you doing?" Hicks said, doing a good job of maintaining his composure.

The shaven-headed man closed quickly and struck Hicks with the butt of the pistol. He stumbled back and dropped down to one knee. The other man, a heavy with a long blond ponytail, trained his MP5 on Hicks.

"Milton," de Lacey called out. "Where are you?"

Milton held his breath.

De Lacey pointed to the trailer.

"Shoot it," he said to the man with the shaved head.

He aimed the MP5 and pulled the trigger. The submachine gun fired on full-auto, a barrage of rounds striking the thin metal walls of the old trailer. The glass blew apart and fell with loud crashes, and the metal popped as the rounds passed through it.

The man stopped firing.

#

JOSIE WAS well placed. Both she and Dalisay were adjacent to the Mercedes but, most importantly, behind the five men who had emerged from it. They all had their backs turned to her: de Lacey was in the middle; the driver of the car and a man with a ponytail were on either side of him; the man with the shaven head who had just fired into the trailer was several paces beyond them, standing next to Hicks and, although he couldn't know it, nearer to Milton. Hicks was facing in her direction. He was on his knees and covered by the weapons of the two men next to de Lacey.

"Milton!" de Lacey called.

Josie glanced into the tree line, trying to see where Milton had hidden himself; she was pleased to note that she couldn't, that it was too gloomy, and assumed that de Lacey and his men wouldn't be able to see him, either.

She heard a noise from the other side of the track. She looked across and saw movement: Dalisay was making his way slowly through the bushes toward the men.

Stop.

She wanted to call out to him, but she knew that she couldn't.

Stop!

They were to wait for Milton's signal. That was what they had agreed.

Dalisay was low down, trying to minimise the noise that he was making.

She could hear him, though. Surely that meant that they would be able to hear him, too.

She had to do something.

There was a narrow path through the bushes just inside the cover that shielded her from the road. She parted the overhanging fronds and branches and started along it, trying to stay level with Dalisay.

Chapter Eighty-Five

HICKS LACED his fingers together and put his hands against the back of his head. The man who had shot up the trailer was a step away from him. Hicks could have reached out and touched him. He ached with the urge to do something—*anything*—and fought to control his breath. He had to wait. There were three men just a handful of steps away from him who would turn him into Swiss cheese if he made a move. He had to trust Milton. He couldn't be far away.

De Lacey walked over to him.

"What's your real name?" de Lacey said.

"Logan. You know what my name is."

"No," he said. "I don't know what your name is, but it certainly isn't that."

De Lacey knelt down and took his phone out of his pocket. He tapped on the screen and then turned it around so that Hicks could see it. There was a picture of a man there: late twenties, glasses, his hair already thinning a little.

"Who's that?" Hicks asked.

"That's William Logan. What happened to him?"

"What are you talking about—"

"Did he tell you that he never met his clients face to face? He told us that, too. It was one of the reasons I thought your offer was a little strange. Bit of a radical change of policy. It made me think, so I had a word with the lads I've been working with at MI6. Good lads, they are. Helpful. When I started working with them, one of the things they did for me was to vet Mr. Logan. It was hard to find anything much about him, but they went back into the archives and dug out what they could. They found this. It was taken when he joined the SBS. And you don't look very much like him at all."

De Lacey's jacket fell open and Hicks saw the pistol in

its holster. De Lacey noticed that he was looking at it, smiled, and took it out. He held it up so that Hicks could see it better.

"Nice, isn't it?"

It was a Browning Hi-Power, but, rather than the usual matte black, this one was finished in titanium gold.

"I love guns. They made me what I am. This one is special. It belonged to Gaddafi. They found it after he was captured. I expect you saw the pictures. They found it when they dragged his body out of that filthy sewer he was hiding in. It went underground, but I had a man find it for me. It cost a quarter of a million. I had Bertie buy it for me while I was locked up. This'll be the first time I get to use it."

"You're making a mistake."

"Am I? I don't think so."

He stood and pressed the muzzle of the gun against the top of Hicks's head.

"Last chance. Where's Milton?"

"I don't know."

De Lacey pushed down; the muzzle of the gun pressed hard against Hicks's scalp.

"Milton!" de Lacey called out. "You've got until I count to five to come out or I'm going to shoot whoever the fuck this is. And then, when I've done that, I'm going to find everyone who helped you escape and kill them, too. Starting with the policewoman. What was her name? Hernandez?"

"One."

Hicks closed his eyes.

"Two."

He started to doubt himself. Was this the right location?

"Three."

Had he made a mistake? Had he taken a wrong turn?

"Four."

Where was Milton?

Hicks heard someone crash through the undergrowth between the trees. Hicks didn't recognise him; he was a Filipino, and he was toting a shotgun.

The man yelled out. "Get your hands up!"

One of the men still near the Mercedes spun around and brought his weapon up in a smooth and practiced motion.

Hicks watched in dumb horror: the newcomer stumbled out from between the trees, his feet tangled in a stray vine. The shotgun suddenly jerked down to the ground as he fought to maintain his balance.

The MP5 chattered and jumped in the first man's hands as he pulled the trigger.

It was too close to miss. The spray caught the man in the stomach. He fell to his knees and then over onto his side, the shotgun tumbling out of his grasp.

"No!"

Josie burst out of the greenery from the other side of the track, the despairing cry still on her lips. Her Glock was raised and aimed.

She fired.

The shooter was facing to the side, away from Josie, and she shot him.

Hicks felt the muzzle of the pistol pull away from his head.

De Lacey had left his side. He had started to run.

The shaven-headed man who had shot up the trailer started to turn.

Now.

Hicks seized the moment. He surged to his feet and tackled the man, wrapping his arms around his body and forcing him down to the ground. The MP5 was caught between their bodies, and Hicks held it with his left hand and punched with his right, driving down with his fist and then striking even harder with his elbow.

#

MILTON POUNCED.

De Lacey was running at full speed in his direction. Milton came out of cover and clotheslined him. The older man's attention was distracted, and he saw Milton much too late. Milton's forearm landed across de Lacey's windpipe and turned him inside out. His legs flew out from beneath him; he corkscrewed in the air and slammed down on his stomach. Milton lunged onto him, grabbing his right wrist and forcing it behind his back and then sharply up, ensuring that the Hi-Power was pointed away from his body. He yanked up and twisted at the same time, forcing de Lacey's face down into the mulch on the ground.

Hicks had rolled atop the second man, pummelling him with rights and lefts until he stopped struggling.

Milton saw the garish pistol. He scooped it up and pressed it against the back of de Lacey's head.

"End of the road, Fitz."

"Milton!" Josie called out.

"Don't," de Lacey said. "It's over. You got me."

Milton gritted his teeth. He pressed down, his finger sliding through the trigger guard. He could end it here. All of de Lacey's money and influence and power could cause trouble later, just like they had before, but they were impotent now.

It was just the two of them and the Browning.

Milton felt the familiar old feelings surging back again, the power he had once revelled in, the ability to snuff out life at a whim, all of it amplified this time by the unquestionable certainty that this was the right thing to do.

"Milton! I'll shoot!"

Milton's moment of disinhibition would pass, and, if Milton let it, he knew that there was a chance that de Lacey would be able to rescue himself.

If he gave him the chance.

"John."

It was Hicks.

"She means it. You have to trust her now."

Milton looked up. Josie was edging around toward him. Her gun was on the third man, and Milton could see that he had noticed her distraction. The longer she had her attention split between the two of them, the more likely it would be that he would take his chances. They had the advantage now. It was theirs to lose. It was time to cash in his chips.

Milton reached to the side and handed the gun to Hicks.

He stood and turned to Josie. "He's all yours."

He thought that he heard the sound of laughter.

He turned back. De Lacey was on his elbows, looking up at him. His face was a mess from where Milton had struck him: he grimaced through a mask of blood and mucus and spit. But there was the barest hint of a smirk on his face.

"What was that?" Milton said. "You think this is funny?"

"Do as you're told, John, like a good boy. You should've shot me. You won't get another chance."

De Lacey's head was at the same height as Milton's shin. That was convenient. Milton drew back his foot and booted him in the jaw.

"He's all yours," he said to Josie again as he crossed the clearing to secure the man she was covering.

Chapter Eighty-Six

JOSIE SAT across the table from de Lacey. The digital recorder was between them, and the camera in the corner of the room focused its little black eye down upon them. She had arranged for a trolley with a TV and PC to be wheeled into the interrogation room, too.

The interview had not gone very well. She had taken de Lacey back through the events of the previous day and then asked him a series of questions. He had refused to answer any of them, responding with a mixture of nonchalance and ease that she quickly found infuriating. She concentrated on maintaining her professionalism.

"Milton was sitting where you were last week," she said. "He was there and I was here. And now look."

"Lawyer," de Lacey said.

"You know you're going to be charged with attempted homicide, don't you?"

"Lawyer."

"Your friend shot my colleague. A police officer. He's in intensive care. They don't know whether he'll make it. Fifty-fifty, they said. If he doesn't, you're looking at murder."

"Lawyer."

"Are you sure, Mr. de Lacey?"

"I am."

"It won't matter," she said. "There are three witnesses to what you did. There's nothing a lawyer will be able to say that will make any difference."

"Milton's going to testify against me? Really? I doubt it."

"He doesn't have to. Let me show you something."

She went over to the PC and woke the screen. It was the native video player, and she set it to play.

The frame filled with the video that they had shot from

inside the wrecked trailer. Dalisay had brought the old camcorder that Josie remembered him using at the tenth birthday party of his daughter a month or two ago. It was a small palm-held unit, and they had been able to install it in the back of the burned-out space so that it could record through the broken window without being too obvious from the outside. She scrubbed through the footage until she saw the Mercedes making its way down the slope to the clearing. She pressed the play button so that it ran at normal speed, presenting a nice clear shot of the men who got out of the car and the weapons that they were carrying. Hicks and de Lacey were clear, too, and, as she let the footage run, they watched as the other trailer was shot to pieces, as Hicks was ordered to the ground, and as de Lacey came forward to press the barrel of his pistol against Hicks's head.

Josie saw de Lacey's reflection in the screen: he looked almost bored.

She stopped the playback before Dalisay was shot. She had watched it once to make sure that it had been recorded, and she had no interest in watching it again.

The picture froze with de Lacey snarling down at Hicks, the gun at his head.

"You see?" Josie said. "I don't need Milton. I don't need anyone. I've got all I need."

"Lawyer."

She clenched her fists and fought the urge to bang them against the table. "You're going back to Bilibid, Mr. de Lacey. And you won't be getting out this time."

He smiled at her. "Lawyer."

"Fine. You had your chance. We're done."

She reached over and switched off the recorder.

"It's going to give me a lot of pleasure to put you away," she said.

She stood and went to the door.

"Officer," he said.

Josie stopped and turned back.

De Lacey was staring at her. "Do you really think your

government is going to want to put me on trial? Be honest—do you *really* think that's likely?"

"I think they'll relish it after what you've done."

"Then you're even more naïve and out of your depth than I thought."

"Am I?"

"You know how long I've been in business? Years. Even when I was locked up, I still had people working for me. Nothing stops. The wheels keep turning. There are always deals to be done. People always want the goods I can find for them."

"Do you want me to remind you? You shot a police officer."

De Lacey ignored her. "I've worked for all kinds of people. I've worked for individuals. I've worked for companies and organisations. And I've worked for governments. Another question?"

"Shoot."

"How do you think I got out of Bilibid?"

"I don't care."

"You should. There is a deal to be done between two governments. It needs me before it can be completed. Pressure was exerted. A phone call was made and favours were offered. The deal still needs to be completed and I'm still needed. All you've done is slowed things down by a day or two. How long do you think you'll be able to keep me here before you're told to let me go?"

"That's not going to happen."

"We'll have to agree to disagree, then, won't we?"

"I suppose we will."

He looked up at the clock on the wall. "I'll give you my prediction. I'll be out of here by the end of the day."

"Good luck with that."

"I mean it. I'll be out of here before you finish your shift and go back to your mother and your child. How are they? It's Angelo, isn't it? Your boy?"

Josie fought against the sudden pulse of rage. She had

to bite down on her lip so hard that her tooth sliced into the flesh and she tasted blood. He was threatening her. He was threatening her son. She felt almost light-headed: a mixture of fury, fear and outrage that he had so little regard for her that he was prepared to make threats despite the certain knowledge that the camera overhead was recording everything that he said and did. He thought his money could buy him impunity.

She was afraid because she knew, deep down, that it was true. He was confident for good reason.

He smiled at her and leaned back in his chair. "Now," he said. "I'd like to speak to my lawyer, please."

#

JOSIE ARRANGED for de Lacey to make a phone call and, before the hour was out, she heard the clamour as two men and a woman were shown through the station and down into the basement where the holding cells were found.

Josie went to the door to the stairs. Gloria joined her from the lobby.

"Lawyers?" Josie asked.

"Wearing suits that cost more than I make in a month."

#

"OFFICER HERNANDEZ?"

It was Station Commander Ocampo. He was responsible for the Sampaloc district and was an ornery, irascible veteran of thirty years. Josie had never spoken to him before, and he had only ever made fleeting visits to the station.

She had been writing up the events of that afternoon. She stood, grimacing at the throb of pain from her leg. "Yes, sir?"

"Were you responsible for arresting the man in the basement? Mr. de Lacey?"

"Yes, sir. I was."

"You've got to let him go."

"What?"

"You heard me. Let him out."

"One of his men shot Manuel Dalisay. I've got it all on tape."

"Let him out, officer. That's an order. And, if I were you, I'd lose the tape."

"No," she said. "I won't."

The commander took her by the elbow and led her into the corridor where they were less likely to be overhead. "I'm serious, officer," he said sternly. "You think I want to do this? I know what he did. But this comes from the top."

"What does that mean?"

"It means the District Director called me twenty minutes ago and told me that he's been leaned on by someone senior in the Justice Department. *Very* senior. Do you want me to spell it out for you?"

He paused.

"It's Josie, isn't it?"

"Yes, sir."

"*Think*, Josie. This is being discussed way above us. Someone very important wants de Lacey to be out. We can't just put him back inside again, despite what he's done. If even half the things that I've heard about de Lacey are true, if he's connected to even a *fraction* of the people he claims, can you imagine for one second what would happen next? That the president won't get a phone call from Langley telling him that he has to make the problem go away? Or Beijing? Or Moscow?" He shrugged. "I'm not blaming you. You didn't know where the case was going to go. You did a good job. But when it turns out this way, sometimes you just need to be pragmatic. This is one of those times."

"No," she said. "That's bullshit. He shot Manuel. He might die. And we know he's already directly responsible for at least four deaths."

"What? The girl?"

"The owners of the bar and the hotel, too. At least. He threatened me and my son."

"How is any of that going to count when you set it against the trouble that this could unleash?"

"He killed someone. That counts. He can't be above the law. I'm sorry, sir, I can't close my eyes."

"It doesn't matter what you can or can't do," he said. "You will process him and then let him out. That is a direct order."

"If I let that go, I—"

"This is the big leagues, Josie. You don't count for shit. I've been here for thirty years. I don't count for shit. Decisions get made at pay grades way above us and, if we want to stay employed, we do exactly what we're told to do. That's the way this works. If you can't deal with that, you might as well just hand in your badge and go back to whatever it was you were doing before."

Josie took a breath. There was no point in arguing. "Fine," she said. "I understand, sir."

"There's one other thing. I need you to take him to the marina. You are to see that he gets onto his yacht tonight. That's from me. He's not welcome in the Philippines any longer. You are to stay there and watch until he sets sail."

"Yes, sir."

"You've done good work. It'll stand in your favour when the time comes."

"Thank you, sir," she said.

He nodded down at her leg. "And go home, please. You shouldn't even be here."

He went back to the front of the station.

Josie limped to the bathroom. She took out her phone and stared at the blank screen.

She was shaking with anger.

Let him go?

How could she do that?

De Lacey had to pay for the things that he had done.

She thought of Manuel in the hospital. There was a good chance that he would die. She thought of his wife and child. She wasn't sure how she would be able to reconcile herself with that. She thought of the owner of the bar. Dead. The husband and wife who had been shot in their office and then burned. Dead. She thought of Mendoza's corruption. She thought of what Milton had been put through.

De Lacey cloaked himself in death. It followed him everywhere.

She thought of her mother and her son.

She knew that they wouldn't be safe.

No.

She woke the phone and dialled.

Chapter Eighty-Seven

JOSIE STRAPPED on her weapon, grabbed her cane, and hobbled through the office to the stairs that led down to the basement. She paused for a moment at the top to gather her composure and, her nerves settled, she started down.

De Lacey was lying on the bench at the side of the cell. There were only four other detainees, and they had arranged themselves so that they each had space to stretch out. De Lacey looked reasonably comfortable; he was flat out on the bench, his legs straight and his arms folded across his chest.

She went to the clipboard where the paperwork was kept, took it down and signed that she was taking custody of prisoner 1535, de Lacey, Fitzroy.

De Lacey saw her and swung his legs around so that they were on the floor. "Ah, Officer Hernandez. Nice to see you again."

"Get up," she said.

"I told you," he grinned. "I'd be out before you finished your shift."

"You did," she said. "Turn around. Hands through the slot."

"What for?"

"I'm going to cuff you."

"No, you're going to *release* me. Why do I need to be cuffed?"

"My station commander has ordered me to transport you to the marina and put you on your yacht. He wants to make sure that you leave the country."

"I can get my own driver to collect me. This isn't necessary—"

"Turn around and put your hands through the slot, please, sir. The sooner you do that, the sooner I can put you on your yacht and watch you fuck off over the horizon."

"Where are my lawyers?"

"We told them that you're being released," she said. "They'll meet you at the yacht."

He looked as if he was going to protest before he shrugged his shoulders, turned and put his hands through the slot. "Fine," he said. "Get on with it."

She took her cuffs and slapped them on.

"Careful," de Lacey said with a grimace of pain. "You caught my skin."

"Sorry about that."

She called for the door to be unlocked and, when it was, she led him out.

#

SHE COULD have taken de Lacey in the back of a squad car, but that didn't suit her. One of the station meat wagons was being hosed out after, she guessed, it had transported an addict into custody. The trucks grew hot and the druggies often threw up in the back. The smell always seemed to linger no matter how many times they were washed out. The thought of de Lacey baking in the back of the truck with the acrid tang of someone else's vomit in his nostrils gave her a small measure of pleasure. It was something.

An officer that Josie knew was playing solitaire in the office. His name was Carlos. The rumour was that he was part of Mendoza's crew, and he was certainly someone with whom she would not normally have chosen to speak. But he was here, she needed a driver and, she thought, he was well suited.

"Give me a ride?" she called out.

"I'm off duty," he said.

"Just to the marina. It'll take twenty minutes. Station commander wants it done."

"So take a squad car."

"He shot Dalisay," Josie explained.

That got through to him. "This is him?"

She nodded. "I want him to get a ride in the truck."

He tossed his cards down on the table and got up.

Josie led de Lacey around to the back and waited for Carlos to grab his keys and unlock the door.

"Get in," she said.

"It stinks," de Lacey complained.

"You want me to put you back in the cell again? Your choice, sir. You either get in and I get you on your way, or you can go back and wait for someone else to take you. What's it going to be?"

Carlos was a meathead, and Josie had plenty of reasons to doubt his morals, but she knew how he would react to attitude from a man who had shot a fellow officer, no matter how important he was reputed to be. He didn't give de Lacey a chance to answer. Instead, he grabbed him by the lapels, marched him up to the back of the truck and then bundled him inside. De Lacey's shins clashed against the lip of the entrance and he cursed in pain; Carlos slammed the interior door and then the exterior one before he could complain.

"Let's get him out of here," he said.

#

IT WAS a journey of around five miles from Police Station 4 to the marina. There were two ways that Carlos could have chosen: the fastest would have been to take the Skyway to Abenida Epifanio de los Santos, continue west to the Globe Rotunda and then go south on the J.W. Diokno Boulevard. The alternative was more direct but along slower roads: east on Edison Avenue, then Buenida Avenue and finally south on the Boulevard. Carlos paused at the top of the station ramp and indicated that he was going to turn right, toward the Skyway.

"Go the other way," Josie said.

"Why? It's slower."

"Traffic. There was a crash earlier. It was backed up then and it's the rush hour. It'll take forever."

"All right," he said, flicking the stalk to indicate left instead and pulling out onto Edison.

The streets were named after famous inventors: Edison, Morse, Faraday, Bell, Marconi. Edison was a narrow street for most of its length, with cars parked on either side and a series of stalls set up on the pavements. They passed traders selling knock-off T-shirts, containers of fresh water, and trays of withered vegetables. Trash had been dumped at the side of the road and the buildings were beaten up, many of them sporting tarpaulins where roofs and walls should have been.

"It's true, then?" Carlos asked.

"What's that?"

"He shot Dalisay?"

She nodded.

"And we're letting him out?"

"Tell me about it."

"What do you say we pull over? I could have a word with him about it in the back."

"I wouldn't mind that," she said, "but I don't think it's worth the aggravation. I'd rather just have him off my hands."

Carlos grunted his dissatisfaction. "I don't know what's happening right now. First Bruno, now Dalisay. If people think they can take shots at us and get away with it, then—"

A car raced out of Faraday Avenue and blindsided them, slamming hard into the wing on Josie's side of the truck. It had been travelling quickly, and the impact sent them skidding across the road and into the back of a car parked next to a repair shop. Carlos jerked forward, his forehead cracking against the wheel. Josie had braced herself, but the shock of the first and then second impacts had crashed her injured leg against the gear shift and sent a buzz of pain up and down her body.

Carlos groaned and spat out a mouthful of blood

Josie looked outside. The car that had hit them was an old Toyota Camry. It had wedged itself beneath the truck; their off-side wheel was up on the crumpled hood of the car. The driver of the Toyota opened his door and stepped out as a second vehicle—a white delivery truck—skidded to a halt alongside them.

The driver of the Camry was masked. He went around to the trunk of the car and took out a shotgun.

"What the fuck are they doing?" Josie said.

The man aimed his shotgun at them. "Get out."

Josie turned to Carlos. "What do we do?" she said.

The second man banged on the window. "Out."

"Call for help?" she said, pointing at the radio.

"Won't get to us in time," Carlos mumbled. "We're fucked."

"So, what—we get out?"

"No choice. That window's not bulletproof. If he shoots, we're dead."

"They're bluffing."

"Are they? They just rammed us. I'm not taking the chance."

Carlos opened his door and, after a moment, Josie did the same. The two men had circled around so that one man was on one side of the truck and the other man was on the opposite side. They had both doors covered.

"Out," the man facing Josie barked. "Hit the deck. Face down. If you move, you're dead."

"Relax," Josie said loudly so that Carlos could hear her. "We'll do whatever you want."

She lowered herself to the ground. The asphalt was hot, the grit abrasive against her cheek as she turned her head to watch.

The second man was behind Carlos, leading him at gunpoint around to the back of the truck. Josie could see their feet and ankles beneath the chassis, and heard the man tell Carlos that he needed to unlock the door.

"Stay down," the man above her ordered.

The rear door was unlocked. She heard the heavy thwack of something solid striking flesh and then saw Carlos fall to the ground and lie still. His head was turned toward her and she saw blood leaking out of a fresh gash on his forehead.

The doors—exterior and interior—were opened, and then she heard a single barked command: "Out."

She saw the feet and lower legs of de Lacey as he stepped down and watched as he stumbled around to where she was lying. The other man was behind him, his shotgun jabbing de Lacey in the back as he was shepherded to the delivery truck.

"Open the door."

Josie turned her head so that she could see. De Lacey said something and was rewarded with the butt of the shotgun jabbed against his ribs.

"Open it."

He did as he was told, and, before he could complain again, he was bundled inside. The door was slammed shut and the man hurried around to the front of the vehicle.

"Stay there," the man behind Josie said before running across to get into the truck.

The engine whined, the tyres squealed, and the truck left tracks of hot rubber as it raced away.

Chapter Eighty-Eight

THE BACK of the van was uncomfortable. De Lacey was sprawled on the floor, his hands still shackled behind him. He felt every bump as the van set off. The interior was divided into two compartments. The first was for the driver and co-driver. A tinted glass screen partitioned that area from the rear. It was dark in the back, with just a little dim light filtering through the tinted glass screen. De Lacey could see the shapes of the two men in the front compartment. He saw them remove the balaclavas that they had been wearing, but their features were hidden by the opacity of the glass.

He managed to turn himself around so that his feet were facing the door. He started to kick out at them, putting all his weight behind each blow, but the doors were solid and didn't budge.

"Help!" he called out as loudly as he could manage. "Help!"

The van got going.

#

IT WAS difficult to judge the passage of time. They seemed to have been travelling for an hour, but it might have been longer. De Lacey managed to arrange himself so that he could get up onto his knees and looked forward, trying to see the detail of the road ahead, but the glass in the dividing screen was too opaque and he couldn't make out much of anything at all.

"Let me out!" he shouted.

Nothing.

"Do you have any idea who I am?"

The co-driver turned; he was little more than a silhouette.

"What do you want? Money? I'll pay you."

The man glanced back at him, said something to the driver, and then turned to face the road again.

"Come on!"

De Lacey lost his balance and toppled onto his back. He kicked out, both feet thudding against the partition, but neither man turned around. They faced ahead and the van kept moving along.

#

DE LACEY tried to guess. They must have been on the move for two hours now. The vague outlines of buildings that had been visible through the screen were no longer there. The light was fading as night drew in. They had left the city and must have been somewhere in the countryside that enclosed it. De Lacey was about to kick the partition again when the van slowed. He settled down, bracing his back against the wall and wedging his feet to keep him there as they bounced off the asphalt onto rough ground. The axle vibrated and the back of the van bounced up and down, each small impact jarring him.

They slowed.

"Hey!" he shouted. "Hey! Let me out!"

The bouncing subsided and then the van drew to a halt.

The driver and then the co-driver opened their doors and stepped outside.

The rear door opened. The sun was setting and de Lacey was unable to make out the man who was standing outside.

"Get out."

De Lacey squinted into the fading light.

"Oh fuck."

It was Milton.

He was wearing jeans and a T-shirt. His face was still marked by the beating that he had taken in Bilibid, dried cuts and bruises that were only now starting to heal.

The second man joined Milton. De Lacey recognised

him: it was the man who had tried to fool him as Logan. Milton had a pistol. The other man had a shotgun.

"Get down, Fitz," Milton said.

De Lacey backed away, but the compartment was small and there was only so much space he could retreat into.

Milton clambered up, grabbed him by the lapels and hauled him toward the door.

"Come on," de Lacey protested, unable to resist with his wrists still cuffed. "Come on, Milton, this isn't necessary."

Milton didn't reply. Instead, he gave a final yank and propelled de Lacey out of the door. He managed to land on his feet but he stumbled, his boot catching against a patch of scrub. He fell heavily, his face grinding into the small stones and gravel on the surface of the road.

Milton jumped down from the back of the van.

"Get him up."

The other man reached down with one hand, grabbed the back of de Lacey's shirt and hauled him up.

"You want me to come?" the second man said.

"No. Just me and him."

De Lacey got his feet back under him and took the opportunity to look around. The road here was little more than an off-road track, scattered over with stones and littered with scrub. The van had left the track and driven for three hundred yards; he could hear the sound of traffic passing on a busier road to the west. They were surrounded by stands of bamboo on both sides, with taller palm, pili and durian trees stretching out overhead. There were splashes of colour from sampaguita flowers, and bright orchids littered the way ahead. It would have been beautiful in other circumstances.

"Where are we?" de Lacey asked.

"Walk."

"Take the cuffs off."

"Walk."

Milton pushed de Lacey between the shoulder blades hard enough to make him stumble forward. He turned. The second man stayed by the truck.

"Where are we going?"

Milton pushed him again. "Walk."

There was a pit of fear in his stomach.

"Hernandez was in on this?"

Milton said nothing.

"You set me up. You're working together."

He said nothing.

"She wants to think carefully about that."

"Do you think it was a good idea to threaten her family, Fitz? She's a good officer. Honest. She wanted to do this by the book. But you couldn't help yourself, could you? And this is what happens."

"You think I was bluffing?"

"No, I don't. And neither did she. But look where it's got you. It's just you and me now. You can't make threats anymore."

"Come on. This hasn't gone too far. Take me back."

"I don't think so."

"They'll lock me up again. You don't need to do this."

"You were locked up before and you still murdered someone who was important to me. You like to remind everyone that you're a rich and powerful man. The money. The yacht. Friends in high places. You would've been better to forget all that."

He felt sick. "What does that mean?" he said, even though he knew exactly what it meant.

"Walk."

They continued. Radiant waves rose from the sun-baked forest, and mirages shimmered at the edges of his vision. It was hot and humid. The fear, though, was worse. It leeched the strength from his legs, hollowing them out, churned his stomach and loosened his bowels.

They descended a gentle slope to a burbling brook and de Lacey couldn't stand it any longer.

He ran.

It was awkward, with his hands behind his back, but he ran.

Three paces.

Four.

He aimed for a thicket of bamboo on the other side of the water. Maybe if he could get there before Milton did...

Ten paces.

Fifteen.

He felt the blast of pain a moment before he heard the crack of the pistol.

He lost his balance and fell, splashing down into the water.

The gunshot echoed back from the foothills.

His leg was on fire. He was lying face down, water in his eyes and mouth and nostrils. He felt the hot blood, each fresh heartbeat sending another pulse to flow out around his helpless fingers.

He turned his head to look back.

He hadn't managed to get very far.

Milton was walking toward him. His right arm was extended and angled down. He had his pistol in his hand.

De Lacey tried to scramble to his feet, but his leg wouldn't move and his arms were still shackled behind his back

Milton reached him. The setting sun was behind him, casting a long shadow and blackening him in silhouette. The shadow fell over de Lacey's body.

Milton crouched down and flipped him over onto his back.

De Lacey tried to speak, but his throat was dry and choked with water and the words wouldn't come. He closed his eyes.

"Who put the pressure on to the Filipinos to get you out?"

He felt something press against his forehead. It was cold and hard. He knew what it was.

"Answer me, Fitz."

"The Circus. Who do you think?"

"Why do they want you out?"

"They want me to front a deal with the Iranians. Missiles. Artillery. Ammunition. They don't care about the equipment. They want intelligence and they know I can get it for them. And the Iranians trust me."

"And you said yes."

"With one condition. They got you for me."

"How'd that turn out, Fitz?"

De Lacey didn't answer.

"Who were you dealing with in MI6? Names."

"Latimer and Fox. I never met them."

"Who did?"

"Bertie. He handled the negotiations. You'd have to speak to him."

"I will. "

Milton put his gun down and placed his hands around de Lacey's throat. He started to squeeze. De Lacey felt the coolness of the water as it ran around his head, and then the increased pressure around his throat as Milton leaned forward and pressed down with all his weight. He tried to breathe, but his breath wouldn't come.

"Goodbye, Fitz."

His eyes bulged as he stared up into Milton's eyes—cold, impassive, emotionless—and then his face, the jungle, the sky, and everything else above him all faded into black.

Chapter Eighty-Nine

MILTON AND HICKS drove back to the city after they had finished burying the body. They torched the stolen van, changed their clothes, and took a taxi the rest of the way to the airport. Ziggy was waiting for them in the landside Starbucks.

"Everything okay?" he asked.

"It's done."

"What happened?"

"It doesn't matter. What about the police?"

"I monitored the radio. Josie gave you five minutes and called it in. She said she didn't get a good look at the van. They put out a bulletin but there was no way they would've been able to find you in time."

"The other thing?"

Ziggy sipped his coffee and nodded. "They've identified the bodies at Tondo. Bruno Mendoza was easy—the car was registered to him, and they matched his teeth to his dental records. The second body has been reported as John Smith, recently escaped from Bilibid. They found the gun, pulled the prints from it and when they searched against them they had a match with the prints you gave them when you were arrested. They can't confirm it for sure, but it's strong circumstantial evidence. As far as they're concerned, John Smith is dead. They're looking for someone who shot him and Mendoza."

"Good," he said.

"You think it'll stand up?"

"I doubt they've got anything that would help them to identify the body as Logan. Even if they can take his fingerprints, I'd be surprised if he's on record anywhere. And I've got an idea to make it even tighter."

Hicks scrubbed his eyes; none of them had had much sleep.

Milton reached into his pocket and took out Hicks's wedding ring. "Here," he said. "Better not forget this."

Hicks took the ring and screwed it onto his finger. "Thanks."

Ziggy looked up at the departures board. "We'd better check in," he said. "The flight goes in an hour."

"Thank you," Milton said. "Both of you. I'd still be locked up if it wasn't for what you did."

"You'd be dead," Hicks corrected.

Milton nodded. "More likely," he agreed. "But I mean it. I'm grateful. Really."

"Forget it."

Milton put out his hand and shook with Ziggy and then Hicks.

"What are you going to do?" Hicks said.

"Some people I need to see," he said.

"And then?"

"I don't know yet."

#

MILTON ARRANGED to meet Josie in a café near the Napindan Castle hotel where she was staying. He arrived first. He put the leather satchel that he had taken from Mendoza's villa on the floor beneath a vacant table and then went to get his food. The place offered a breakfast buffet, and he doled out a generous portion of *tocilog*. He hadn't eaten since the sandwiches he and Ziggy had shared the previous night, and the trays of sweetened pork, egg and fried rice were impossible to resist. He finished his plate quickly, and, as he took it up to the counter for another portion, he saw Josie looking for him in the doorway.

He waved her over.

She had a bag in her left hand and her walking stick in her right. She hobbled over, rested the bag on the floor next to the table and sat down. "Well?"

"It's finished," he said.

"Where?"

"We buried him. He won't be found."

She turned away from him, biting her lip.

He felt the need to justify himself. "There wasn't any other choice."

When she turned back to him, her eyes were cold. "I'm not sorry," she said. "He got what he deserved."

Milton knew: she had striven so long to do the right thing and now his news—and the sure knowledge that she had facilitated de Lacey's murder—was her repudiation of it. She was angry with herself, not with him. The curtain had been pulled back and now she saw how the world worked.

"It's my own fault," she said, as if she could read his mind. "De Lacey called me naïve. Turns out he was right."

She reached down and placed her hand on her injured leg.

"What about you?" Milton asked. "What happened afterwards?"

"After you took him? They took us to the station. We were questioned. But Carlos backed me up. The crash, the two of you taking him and driving away. Our stories tallied. They said they believed it. What else were they going to say?"

"And then?"

"They had the whole district out searching for you. I told them I didn't get a good look at the truck, but there were witnesses on the street who did. Where is it now?"

"We torched it."

Milton noticed that she was looking around him to the door. He turned and looked. An older woman who bore a striking resemblance to Josie was standing there. She was holding the hand of a young boy.

"Mama!" Josie called out, waving at her.

The old woman turned. The boy turned, too, and, on seeing Josie, he tugged his hand free and ran full pelt toward the table.

Josie hugged him, grimacing as he bumped up against her leg, and then delicately disentangled him.

The old woman reached the table and looked down at Josie's stretched out leg and the walking stick. She put her hand to her face. Josie struggled to her feet and embraced her, then spoke earnestly to her again. Milton could tell that she was trying to reassure her. The boy saw the stick and Josie spoke calmly to him, too.

They finished their conversation. "They haven't seen me since I was shot," she explained. "I haven't been home. And I thought it best not to tell them on the phone. They'd only worry."

"Do they know who I am?"

"No." She gestured to where Milton was sitting and spoke in Filipino again. Milton caught his name at the end of the sentence.

He turned to Josie's mother. "Hello," he said.

The woman regarded him with unmasked suspicion.

Josie spoke to her again. "Mama is very protective of me. She doesn't mean to be rude."

"It's fine," Milton said. "I'd be suspicious, too." He turned to the boy. "And this is your son?"

The boy looked up at him shyly.

The boy looked at his mother and then at Milton. He showed the same suspicion as his grandmother.

"Angelo," Josie chided, "say hello."

"Hello."

Milton had never been good with children. "Hello," he said. "How are you?"

The boy shrugged.

"He's shy," Josie apologised. "But he speaks very good English."

"Do you?" Milton asked.

"Mama says so," Angelo said quietly. "Are you her friend?"

"I am," Milton said.

"She's been *shot*."

He said it with wide eyes, as if the information, when shared with his friends at school, would mean an elevation in his status.

Milton smiled at him.

"Mama," Josie said, before continuing in Filipino.

The older woman nodded and took the boy's hand and led him away from the table.

"I asked her to give us a moment," Josie explained.

Milton stood. "It's okay. I'll go. You should be with them. I don't want to intrude."

She ignored that. "You asked what I did last night. I didn't get to finish. I went to see Dalisay in the hospital. He's going to make it. Another centimetre either side and he'd be dead now, just like I could've been dead. We were both lucky. I spoke to him and he helped me make up my mind. So I went back to my desk, wrote up my resignation letter and mailed it. I'm done."

Milton listened to her and, when she was finished, he reached out and laid his hand over hers.

"I don't blame you. I would've done the same thing."

She took her hand away. "Principles are great, but now I have to put food on the table. Got any ideas?"

"Maybe," he said.

"I'm listening."

"There's one more thing you can do for me first."

She nodded that he should go on.

"They've identified Logan's body," he said. "They think it's me."

"And you want them to think that?"

"Yes. I left my prints on the gun I left there. They've matched it with the prints you took when you arrested me."

"So you want me to say that I saw you being shot? An unidentified man shot you and Mendoza, and then the same guy shot me in the leg."

"Could you do that?"

"Sure. What's one more lie going to mean? I'm already up to my neck in them."

"When I was in the car with Mendoza on the way to Tondo, I made him take the expressway. Do the cameras on the toll booths work?"

"Usually," she said.

"If you check the video, you'll be able to find his car. I made sure I was looking at the camera. We used the second lane from the right. You'll be able to match it with my photos and prove I was in his car. I doubt you'll need anything else."

She nodded. "Okay," she said. "I'll do it."

"Thank you."

Milton took the leather satchel and gave it to her. "You asked if I could help. I can. Here."

She unzipped the satchel, opened the mouth and looked inside. Milton could see the thick wedges of bank notes.

"What is this?"

"I thought you—"

"Where did you get it?"

"From Mendoza. I found it under the floor in his villa."

She zipped the bag up again and put it on the table. "No."

"You said it yourself—you're going to need money."

"Not if it's dirty."

"It's just money. It doesn't matter where it came from."

"Of course it does."

"Keep it. Donate it. Do whatever you want with it. It's up to you."

She stared at the bag for a moment. Milton could see that she was considering it. He could guess at her competing thoughts: she was weighing the integrity that was so obviously important to her against the exigencies of providing for her son without a regular wage.

"Thank you," she said at last.

"It's the least I could do."

He offered her his hand and she took it.

"Be careful, John."

"You too."

He was about to leave when she put her hand to her forehead. "Wait," she said. "I almost forgot. I brought you something, too."

She reached down awkwardly and collected the bag from the floor. She put it on the table and pushed it over to Milton. He opened it and reached inside. It contained the things that she had taken from him when he had been arrested.

He took out his copy of the Big Book and flipped through the pages.

"I went and got it from evidence," she said. "I thought you'd want it."

"I do. Thank you."

He saw the flashes of yellow where he had highlighted the passages that meant the most to him. They reminded him that he needed to get to a meeting.

"Where are you going to go?" she asked.

"Haven't decided yet. I need some time to think."

"I'll see you around then, Milton."

"Good luck."

The old woman and the boy were waiting in the road outside the café. Milton paused and knelt down before the boy. "Your mother is very brave," he said. "Look after her."

Milton didn't know whether Angelo would understand him, but the boy stood a bit straighter and gave a solemn little nod. "I will," he said.

Milton smiled at him and shook his little hand.

He stood, said goodbye to Josie's mother, and made his way back to his car.

Chapter Ninety

MILTON DROVE for four hours. The city of Lucena was a hundred and twenty miles southeast of Manila, and he followed the main north–south route to Calamba and then turned to the east. He passed the wide inland waterway of Laguna de Bay and then the holy mountain of Mount Banahaw. He stopped to refuel and looked out at the volcano, its huge bulk wreathed with clouds and dominating the landscape for miles around.

His thoughts ran away with him again. He had spent the drive thinking about Josie and Angelo, and that, in turn, had prompted him to think about Jessica and her son. The suggestion that he might have been a father had stirred up a maelstrom of feelings that he hadn't even started to unpack; in truth, he didn't know where to start. That vague possibility, raised by a woman that he hadn't seen for ten years, had caused him to leave his cloistered life and fly halfway around the world. It had defused his natural caution and had very nearly led to his death. His impulsive reaction was out of character and it raised questions and possibilities that he had never considered before.

He had never thought himself capable of paternal feelings. Children made him feel awkward. He didn't know what to say to them. He didn't know how to deal with them. More than all of that, he didn't think he deserved the happiness that children might bring. He had shunned conventional relationships for the same reason. He had always believed he had too much to atone for to allow himself the luxury of happiness.

What had changed?

He didn't know.

He didn't really know why he was driving south, either, only that it was something that he felt he had to do.

Milton went inside the gas station to pay and bought a bundle of twelve *cigarillos*, unfiltered cigarettes that were wrapped in colourful printed paper. He went outside and lit up. The stick was longer than the brands that he bought at home, and the tobacco had a sweet kick during the drag. They were probably unhealthy, but Milton didn't care. He needed a vice, and this was better than the alternative. They were more intense, too, than the cigarettes that he usually smoked, and that was something he could use to take his mind off his confusion and what he was intending to do.

He got back into the car, wound down the windows, and set off to the east once more.

#

THE ADDRESS that Ziggy had found was on Evangelista Street.

It ran through a low-rent commercial district, and, as Milton cruised along it, he passed a pharmacy, a car wash and a women's fashion shop. The satnav bleeped that he had reached his destination; he pulled over into a space at the side of the road, checked the address once again, and got out.

He walked back along the street until he got to Papay, a fast-food bakery that was advertised by a cartoon character designed to look like Popeye in a chef's hat. There was a faded hoarding above the shop, and suspended from two chains attached to a rickety L-shaped pole was a sign that creaked as it oscillated back and forth in the light breeze that blew in off the sea. The café was housed on the ground floor of a two-storey building. The paint was peeling away, the windows were barred, and washing had been hung out to dry on the first-floor balcony.

Milton approached. Access to the interior of the bakery was blocked by a metal cage, with transactions carried out through an open slot. Milton idled there, pretending to look at the simple menu that had been painted onto a wooden board and propped against the wall. The café specialised in *pandesal*, sweetened dough that was rolled into long loaves that were then rolled in fine bread crumbs. The bakery also sold hot coffee, and Milton watched through the bars as an old woman ripped off a hunk of a loaf, dipped it in her mug and then ate it.

There was a woman being served ahead of him, and he watched as she chatted with the man serving her. She put a dozen of the loaves into a white plastic carrier bag, gave the man a handful of pesos, and went on her way.

Milton stepped forward.

"Hello," he said. "Do you speak English?"

The man shrugged, his top lip curling a little. "What do you want?"

"I was looking for Jessica."

"Who are you?"

"A friend."

"She dead," the man said.

"What?"

"Last week."

Milton feigned shock. "How?"

"*Manila*," the man said, as if the suggestion that someone should go to the capital was the height of foolishness. "Someone kill her."

"That's awful. I'm sorry."

The man shrugged. "Not so unusual there. Should have stayed here."

"Are you family?"

He shook his head. "I just work here." He pointed behind Milton at a woman who was waiting to be served. "What you want?"

"Did Jessica have any family?"

"Her father. He owns the bakery."

"And children?"

The man frowned his annoyance at the continued questions. "She got a boy. You want any bread, mister?"

"Yes," Milton said. There was a tray of prepared snacks

just inside the bars. Milton pointed to one. "What's that?"

"Peanut butter and jelly sandwich. You want?"

"Please."

The man picked up the sandwich with his fingers and folded it inside a piece of grease paper. He handed the parcel through the bars. "Seven pesos."

The menu said that the sandwiches should have cost three pesos. The man was taking advantage of what he must have concluded was a naïve foreigner, but Milton didn't mind. He gave him a ten-peso coin and held up his hand to say that he didn't expect the change.

Milton stepped aside. The woman behind him came forward, regarding him with a distasteful expression and then saying something in Filipino that drew a derisive chuckle from the server.

Milton took his sandwich and crossed the road. He got back into the car and settled in to wait.

#

TWO HOURS had passed when Milton saw a boy on a bicycle pull up outside the bakery. He put the half-finished sandwich on the passenger seat and looked out at him: he was young, perhaps ten years old, and slender. He was wearing a gold and black New Orleans Saints cap beneath which Milton could see an unruly mop of black hair.

Milton put his hand on the handle of the door, and then paused.

He realised he still had no idea what he had come here to do.

The boy took a key from his pocket and unlocked a door to the side of the metal cage. He opened it and wheeled his bicycle inside.

Milton stayed where he was.

The boy emerged again, closed and locked the door, and crossed the road to the car wash on the other side.

Milton clenched his fists in frustration.

He grabbed the plastic bag from the passenger seat, opened the door and got out.

"Hello."

The boy looked at him anxiously. "Who are you?" he replied in excellent English.

"My name is John. I was a friend of your mother. What's your name?"

"Danilo."

The boy had dark skin and dark hair and his eyes were dark and soulful, just like his mother's had been. He wasn't the same as the boy whose pictures Milton had seen. That boy had borne a resemblance to him, but Danilo could never have been mistaken for his kin. There was no similarity at all.

"I just wanted…" Milton was floundering. "I just wanted to say that I'm sorry about what happened to her."

The boy looked at him in confusion.

Milton heard an angry shout from the bakery. He turned to see that the cage door had been opened and a man was coming out. It wasn't the server to whom he had spoken before, but an older man with white streaks in his hair and a grizzled grey beard.

He called out in Filipino.

Milton waited for him to make his way across.

"I'm a friend of Jessica," he said.

"I never seen you before."

"It was a long time ago."

The old man took the boy by the elbow and impelled him back to the building.

"She's dead," he said gruffly once the boy was inside and out of earshot.

"I know," he said. "Are you her father?"

"That's right."

"I'm sorry. I have something for you. For the boy, really."

He handed the man the plastic bag. He opened it and looked inside.

"What is this?"

The man reached in and took out one of the bundles of banknotes. Milton had split Mendoza's money: half for Josie and half for Jessica's son.

"What is this?"

"It's yours," Milton insisted.

"Where you get it?"

"I hope it helps."

Milton didn't wait for the man's response. He got back into the car and looked out of the windshield as the man stared dumbly from the bundle of notes to the car and then back again.

He started the engine and drove off, leaving the bakery behind him.

He tried to work out how he was feeling.

Was it relief?

Disappointment?

He sat quietly and realised that he knew what it was.

It was that same sense of loneliness that he had come to consider as his closest friend. It had been his companion for all the months he had been travelling, all the thousands of miles that he had covered. It had been there as he had tried to make a modest life for himself in London. It was always there, an ache in his gut that he could always find whenever he closed his eyes and searched for it.

He had kept a tiny fraction of the money for himself. It was in the glovebox. There was enough for a ticket on the long-distance ferry from Manila to Ho Chi Minh City and then enough to keep him going for a month or two after that.

He hadn't been to Southeast Asia for years. He thought he might start in Vietnam, then head into Thailand, Myanmar and India. He liked the idea of Nepal. He hadn't seen Everest before. Maybe he'd go to Base Camp. That would be something to aim for.

It would be just him and the road. That was fine. He enjoyed his own company. He welcomed solitude. He decided to cherish it for a little while.

He turned north, back to the city and to whatever might come next.

GET EXCLUSIVE JOHN MILTON MATERIAL

Building a relationship with my readers is the very best thing about writing. I occasionally send newsletters with details on new releases, special offers and other bits of news relating to the John Milton, Beatrix and Isabella Rose and Soho Noir series.

And if you sign up to the mailing list I'll send you this free Milton content:

1. A free copy of the John Milton novella, Tarantula.

2. A copy of the highly classified background check on John Milton before he was admitted to Group 15. Exclusive to my mailing list – you can't get this anywhere else.

You can get the novella and the background check **for free**, by signing up at http://eepurl.com/b1T_NT

IF YOU ENJOYED THIS BOOK...

Reviews are the most powerful tools in my arsenal when it comes getting attention for my books. Much as I'd like to, I don't have the financial muscle of a New York publisher. I can't take out full page ads in the newspaper or put posters on the subway.

(Not yet, anyway).

But I do have something much more powerful and effective than that, and it's something that those publishers would kill to get their hands on.

A committed and loyal bunch of readers.

Honest reviews of my books help bring them to the attention of other readers.

If you've enjoyed this book I would be very grateful if you could spend just five minutes leaving a review (it can be as short as you like) on the book's page.

Thank you very much.

ACKNOWLEDGEMENTS

Thanks to the members of Team Milton for technical advice and support. Thanks to Pauline Nolet and Jennifer McIntyre for editorial assistance. And thanks to you for investing your time in reading this story. I hope you enjoyed it as much as I enjoyed writing it.

John Milton will be back.

ABOUT THE AUTHOR

Mark Dawson is the author of the breakout John Milton, Beatrix Rose and Soho Noir series. He makes his online home at www.markjdawson.com. You can connect with Mark on Twitter at @pbackwriter, on Facebook at www.facebook.com/markdawsonauthor and you should send him an email at mark@markjdawson.com if the mood strikes you.

ALSO BY MARK DAWSON

Have you read them all?

In the Soho Noir Series

Gaslight

When Harry and his brother Frank are blackmailed into paying off a local hood they decide to take care of the problem themselves. But when all of London's underworld is in thrall to the man's boss, was their plan audacious or the most foolish thing that they could possibly have done?

The Black Mile

London, 1940: the Luftwaffe blitzes London every night for fifty-seven nights. Houses, shops and entire streets are wiped from the map. The underworld is in flux: the Italian criminals who dominated the West End have been interned and now their rivals are fighting to replace them. Meanwhile, hidden in the shadows, the Black-Out Ripper sharpens his knife and sets to his grisly work.

The Imposter

War hero Edward Fabian finds himself drawn into a criminal family's web of vice and soon he is an accomplice to their scheming. But he's not the man they think he is - he's far more dangerous than they could possibly imagine.

In the John Milton Series

One Thousand Yards

In this dip into his case files, John Milton is sent into North
Korea. With nothing but a sniper rifle, bad intentions and a
very particular target, will Milton be able to take on the
secret police of the most dangerous failed state on the
planet?

Tarantula

In this further dip into his files, Milton is sent to Italy. A
colleague who was investigating a particularly violent
Mafiosi has disappeared. Will Milton be able to get to the
bottom of the mystery, or will he be the next to fall victim
to Tarantula?

The Cleaner

Sharon Warriner is a single mother in the East End of
London, fearful that she's lost her young son to a life in the
gangs. After John Milton saves her life, he promises to help.
But the gang, and the charismatic rapper who leads it, is not
about to cooperate with him.

Saint Death

John Milton has been off the grid for six months. He
surfaces in Ciudad Juárez, Mexico, and immediately finds
himself drawn into a vicious battle with the narco-gangs
that control the borderlands.

The Driver

When a girl he drives to a party goes missing, John Milton
is worried. Especially when two dead bodies are discovered
and the police start treating him as their prime suspect.

Ghosts

John Milton is blackmailed into finding his predecessor as Number One. But she's a ghost, too, and just as dangerous as him. He finds himself in de ep trouble, playing the Russians against the British in a desperate attempt to save the life of his oldest friend.

The Sword of God

On the run from his own demons, John Milton treks through the Michigan wilderness into the town of Truth. He's not looking for trouble, but trouble's looking for him. He finds himself up against a small-town cop who has no idea with whom he is dealing, and no idea how dangerous he is.

Salvation Row

Milton finds himself in New Orleans, returning a favour that saved his life during Katrina. When a lethal adversary from his past takes an interest in his business, there's going to be hell to pay.

Headhunters

Milton barely escaped from Avi Bachman with his life. But when the Mossad's most dangerous renegade agent breaks out of a maximum security prison, their second fight will be to the finish.

The Ninth Step

Milton's attempted good deed becomes a quest to unveil corruption at the highest levels of government and murder at the dark heart of the criminal underworld. Milton is pulled back into the game, and that's going to have serious consequences for everyone who crosses his path.

In the Beatrix Rose Series

In Cold Blood

Beatrix Rose was the most dangerous assassin in an off-the-books government kill squad until her former boss betrayed her. A decade later, she emerges from the Hong Kong underworld with payback on her mind. They gunned down her husband and kidnapped her daughter, and now the debt needs to be repaid. It's a blood feud she didn't start but she is going to finish.

Blood Moon Rising

There were six names on Beatrix's Death List and now there are four. She's going to account for the others, one by one, even if it kills her. She has returned from Somalia with another target in her sights. Bryan Duffy is in Iraq, surrounded by mercenaries, with no easy way to get to him and no easy way to get out. And Beatrix has other issues that need to be addressed. Will Duffy prove to be one kill too far?

Blood and Roses

Beatrix Rose has worked her way through her Kill List. Four are dead, just two are left. But now her foes know she has them in her sights and the hunter has become the hunted.

Hong Kong Stories, Vol. 1

Beatrix Rose flees to Hong Kong after the murder of her husband and the kidnapping of her child. She needs money. The local triads have it. What could possibly go wrong?

In the Isabella Rose Series

The Angel

Isabella Rose is recruited by British intelligence after a terrorist attack on Westminster.

Standalone Novels

The Art of Falling Apart

A story of greed, duplicity and death in the flamboyant, super-ego world of rock and roll. Dystopia have rocketed up the charts in Europe, so now it's time to crack America. The opening concert in Las Vegas is a sell-out success, but secret envy and open animosity have begun to tear the group apart.

Subpoena Colada

Daniel Tate looks like he has it all. A lucrative job as a lawyer and a host of famous names who want him to work for them. But his girlfriend has deserted him for an American film star and his main client has just been implicated in a sensational murder. Can he hold it all together?

Printed in Great Britain
by Amazon

23964025R00225